SPELLS & DEMONS

DEMON HUNTER IN HIDING SERIES
BOOK FIVE

TRUDI JAYE

With thanks to all my readers, I'm beyond grateful for every single one of you!

CHAPTER

ONE

THREE DAYS AFTER MEI'S KIDNAPPING...

"Hazel, I'm asking you," says Damien, his voice hoarse. "No, I'm *begging* you. Please use the last wish to release Mei. Mr. Fookes will understand. He'd want you to save Mei if you could. It's important, and not just because she's my daughter, and your friend. We can't leave the spell web in the hands of the director." Damien looks feral, his hair standing on end, and his dark eyes wild. Next to him at the kitchen table, Seth looks even worse. Both of them are intently focused on me. We're still in Newport News, in Seth's brother Mike's kitchen, for what has turned out to be the worst meeting of my life.

I take a breath, shifting anxiously in my seat, my heart breaking. The silence in the room is painful. I understand their desperation; I want Mei back as much as they do. And I don't want the director to have control of the spell web, either.

But should I do it at the expense of Mr. Fookes? A life for a life? Is that fair?

My skin is hot and itchy, and I don't know what to say. This is a decision that I won't win, whichever way I choose.

Everyone else in the crowded kitchen is staring, too. Carrick is standing just behind Damien, his craggy features set like stone. Zane is leaning against the doorframe, looking dark and dangerous as usual. Mike and his wife Tracey are leaning against the counter side by side, arms crossed. Tracey's eagle eyes are sharp, taking everything in.

The weight of expectation is lying so heavily across my body, it's like a physical blanket. And it's not just covering me—it's choking me. Next to me, Blade shifts, and his thigh touches mine. He's the only one who understands how hard this is. I take another breath, trying to figure out what the hell I'm going to do.

Can I really leave Mr. Fookes inside the toaster? *I gave him my word.*

But I can't leave Mei at the mercy of the director, and I definitely can't leave the spell web in his hands either. She's been missing for three long days, and we have no clue where she is. They've searched everywhere. The only way we know she's still alive is because the spell web is still in place.

Fingers shaking, I pick up the tiny toaster that's mostly been hanging around my neck on a gold chain for the last few weeks. It feels heavy and solid in my fingers, almost like it's the weight of a real toaster, instead of a pendant.

Damien clears his throat, and I glance up. He's watching me with an intensity he seldom shares with the world. Usually he's suave and a bit blasé—to the point of being rude. Right now, he's staring at the toaster hungrily, like it's going to answer all his problems. I glance away, not looking at anyone else. I can't. I'm definitely not going to look at Seth. I can feel his heat burning into me, and that's enough.

In the last three days, Seth has become increasingly desperate. He's on the edge, his phoenix self close to the surface at all times. Flames flash constantly in his eyes, and there's a light around him that has nothing to do with whether it's night or day.

I scrunch up my eyes, wishing I was anywhere but here. For a crazy moment, I wonder if I could use my final wish on a request like that. I'd wish to be somewhere safe, and fun, where I could have chocolate chip cookies, and maybe a game or two to play. I'd take Blade with me, and we'd curl up on the sofa, ignoring the world.

Except that's worse. I'd be letting even more people down.

I put my hand to my chest. It's almost like I have the favor bond back again. My heart is being ripped in two. The pressure is too much. Blade shifts again, and he puts one hand on my thigh, trying to calm me down. He understands. I've been keeping this wish, saving it for Mr. Fookes. The idea that I have to betray him, to use the last wish for someone else...

It's breaking my heart.

It's going to break *his* heart.

But I have no choice.

Mei is missing. It's a desperate situation.

Everyone is here, watching.

Waiting.

My hand hesitates over the metal toaster. Maybe I should tell them I need more time? Just to make sure? I think of Damien's face, and know he's not going to wait patiently. No one in this room is going to wait patiently.

My hand lowers to the toaster, and I cup it gently between my palms. Taking a deep breath, I rub the tiny toaster that holds Mr. Fookes, my genie. My brain is still whirring frantically.

What am I going to wish for? My stomach churns and my little demon buzzes inside me. I think I'm going to throw up.

Thick smoke fills the room, swirling majestically around everyone crowded into Mike's kitchen. I blink a few times, trying to stop my eyes watering. But it doesn't smell like normal smoke. I take a sniff, and notice for the first time that it smells like waffles.

Mr. Fookes's favorite.

To one side of me, Tracey, who has clearly never seen anything like this before, is staring wide eyed. All eyes are focused on the toaster and the swirling smoke. Without thinking, I glance at Seth. He's staring at the smoke and the toaster like it's going to answer all his dreams, which I guess it is. He desperately wants Mei back. My stomach churns again. I want her back, too.

Mr. Fookes appears in a perfect swoosh of air, his genie charisma almost painful to experience. Perfect hair, perfect teeth, eyes that sparkle like he's got a million diamonds hiding inside them.

"Yes, master? You have a last wish for me?" he says, his soothing voice filling the room.

I wince. I've never gotten used to him calling me that. It's almost like he's poking me with a sharp stick, reminding me of the balance of power in this relationship. He's the all-powerful genie with the ability to grant me anything I want—but I'm the one who controls him. I push my glasses up my nose, and let the tiny toaster drop back against my skin.

I stare at him closely, but there's no hint of emotion on his face, nothing to say that he's angry I might be about to betray him. He's hiding behind a smooth surface version of himself. I don't know if it's real, if this is all the emotion that a genie can have. Or if he's burning, boiling, seething inside.

I really miss my old friend Mr. Fookes, who was always a little bit disheveled, had stains down his front and a pot belly. He also had kind eyes and a sense of humor and protected everyone in our building no matter what. This strange genie version just isn't him.

"Yes." My voice squeaks as I say the word, and I clear my throat. I put one hand down onto Blade's, where it's still lying on my thigh. My whole body is shaking.

Mr. Fookes bows his head regally. "I am yours to command," he says.

I take a breath. "My final wish is...." I clear my throat on the words. It's like my throat has closed over, and it won't let me speak the words. "My final wish is..." I clear my throat again.

"Yes?" says Mr. Fookes impassively.

"My final wish is... to free you, Mr. Fookes, from being a genie," I say the words in a rush, unable to stop them coming out. I don't look anywhere else except into Mr. Fookes's eyes. In that moment, I see on his face that he knew exactly what was going on. That he expected me to betray him. And he can't quite believe I didn't.

For a second, there's silence. Mr. Fookes is hanging in the air, his dark eyes still focused on me. A shimmering light appears around him, getting brighter and brighter, making it difficult to look directly at him. I blink, and suddenly everything erupts around me.

Seth leaps out of his chair, snarling, flames lapping at

his body. Damien is holding him back, but he's also staring at me with an incredulous expression, like he can't believe what I just did. The others are all moving closer, looming over me and Mr. Fookes. My throat closes up, and I'm struggling to breathe.

"Take it back!" shouts Seth, flames licking his body.

I jerk away from him, leaning into Blade. I can't quite believe what I just did.

"It's not too late. You can take it back. You can still find Mei," says Damien, even as he struggles to hold Seth in place.

But it *is* too late.

Mr. Fookes is changing. He's losing his perfect sheen, and starting to seem more like the hairy, portly, tomato-sauce-splattered super I've known all this time. His eyes have gone from being emotionless to being filled with tears. He's looking at me with an expression I can only describe as devotion.

Blade stands up, dragging me with him. Only a couple of yards away, Seth is changing, his expression full of a raging wildness I've never seen before.

"I don't think he's in control," says Blade in a low voice. "He wasn't expecting that."

"I wasn't expecting it," I say. I purse my lips for a second. "But I'm not sorry. I made a promise."

Seth is transforming into his phoenix shape, and I realize for the first time that he's actually going to be a problem. He's out of control, and if he's going to attack anyone, it'll be me.

I hold up my hands in an attempt to be placating. "I'm sorry. I couldn't break my promise to Mr. Fookes. I'll help find Mei. I won't leave any rock unturned—"

"We don't need your help," snarls Damien, his expression hard. "You've shown us which side you're on." His eyes are darker than I've ever seen them, and he has scales up one arm. Not for the first time, I wonder what his supernatural side is.

"I didn't—" I don't get more than a couple of words out before Seth screeches and lunges for me.

It's only because Carrick and Damien are holding him securely, Damien barking orders into his ear, that Seth is prevented from leaping over the table and ripping me apart with his phoenix talons.

I glance between Damien, Carrick, and Seth, but none of them are sympathetic to what I just did. Are they right? Did I make the wrong decision? I'm still struggling to breathe properly. Mr. Fookes steps closer to us, angling his body in between me and Seth. I'm not sure what he could do against a phoenix, but I appreciate the thought.

"We need to get out of here, fast," says Blade. He grabs my arm and pulls me around the other side of the table to Seth, toward the door. Mr. Fookes follows. Seth screeches again, and the flames on his body burn higher. Damien swears and steps away, but Carrick keeps hold of Seth's arm. The large mountain super's eyes—normally so gentle —are like granite when he stares at me across the kitchen.

I swallow hard. No one in this room is taking my decision well.

"I can't believe you did that," mutters Mike from just behind me, his eyes wide as he watches us go by. "I'm not a fan of Mei's, but she's being held by *the Man in Black*." He glances uncertainly at Mr. Fookes, clearly wondering why I chose him over Mei.

I blink yet again and shake my head, trying to get Mike's words out of my head. The idea of what Lakas might do to Mei is something that will haunt me. Did I make the right decision? Will we really be able to find Mei without the help of a genie?

I swallow down the bile that's rising in my throat. I did what I had to do. What I promised I would do. Blade puts his arm around me as Seth screeches again behind me. This time, chairs are knocked over and the table scrapes along the floor as if it's being pushed to one side.

Zane is at the entrance to the kitchen, his whole body tensed. He gives Blade a long look, and then follows us outside.

"We need a ride out of here," says Blade to Zane, his voice tense.

Zane glances back toward the house, nodding in agreement. "I've never seen him like that before," he says. "He's not in a control."

Seth screeches from the kitchen as if in agreement. The sound is painful, heartbroken, and angry all at once. I shudder from my position in Blade's arms. Everything is starting to look a little blurry; I'm only just realizing the full implications of what I've done. They were all so angry at me. I cost them a chance to find Mei. If she's hurt, tortured, anything like that from now on, it'll be my fault.

Because of *my* decision.

Zane throws off his clothes and transforms into his dragon shape, holding out one leg to help us climb. I keep checking behind me, to see if they're following us outside. Surely Damien isn't really that angry at me? Surely Seth will see that I had to let Mr. Fookes out? But all I hear is the sound of Seth's tormented screeches and furniture being knocked around the room.

Blade grabs Zane's clothes and then pushes me up onto Zane's back, climbing on behind me. He leans down and helps Mr. Fookes scramble up behind him.

I see movement at the back door, and Seth emerges out into the garden, his body a flaming half-transformed phoenix shape. He lifts his head and screeches at us as Zane takes off, directly into the sunset. My heart is pounding in my chest. He's going to chase us down and burn us all to a crisp because I didn't save Mei with the final wish.

Except... he's only half transformed into his phoenix shape. He can't fly. It's like he can't focus quite enough to make the full transition. Maybe he's just too upset? I let out a rush of breath. At least he can't chase us through the clouds, his burning flames licking at our skin.

I close my eyes and lean back into Blade, my thoughts whirring inside my head. I don't know why I chose to set Mr. Fookes free and make everyone in that room hate me. I wish I hadn't hurt Seth like that.

All I know is, I can't take it back now.

CHAPTER
TWO

Zane lands with a thump onto the roof of Mr. Fookes's building, the Sanctus Apartments.

Dust rises around us, and I sneeze. It feels painful, all the way inside my chest. My little demon fizzes inside me. Mr. Fookes climbs down first, his movements stiff and awkward.

It's been almost twenty-four hours since we escaped from Seth's anger at his brother's Newport News home. We stopped for a rest on the way, but mostly we've been flying straight for hours. It's been a long trip back to Stanford, and for almost every moment along the way, I've been thinking about what I did. The expressions on all their faces. The shock. The despair. The anger.

How much pain I've caused them.

And now, after everything that's happened, my head hurts like someone's been using it as a practice rock for their pick axe. Added to that, my vision is blurred and I'm cold all over. I can barely think.

I half fall off the side of the dragon, and my legs wobble as they hit the ground. It's only because Mr. Fookes is there to grab me from Blade that I stay standing. I grasp onto his strong forearms, and look up into Mr. Fookes's eyes. There's pain and grief and relief and joy inside those eyes. For a brief moment all I feel is a wave of thankfulness that I freed him. He's a real person, my friend, and I promised him. I couldn't break my promise. He would have been lost to us, lost to Daphne. He would have been a slave again, forced to do the bidding of one master after another.

Behind us, Blade climbs down from the dragon, then picks me up in his arms, despite my weak protests. "I'm too heavy. You're just as tired," I say.

"Quiet," he growls in my ear, and I subside against his neck. I'm so tired, I don't think I could even have made it to the roof's door, let alone down the stairs.

Mr. Fookes hovers to one side as Blade strides across the roof, and through the door. There's no elevator in the apartment building, and now that I know Mr. Fookes better, I realize it's on purpose—I'm sure he could actually fix it if he wanted to.

My head lolls to one side as Blade takes the stairs downward. I let out a little sigh as he stops in front of my apartment on the second floor. I haven't been here in so long, and I've missed my home. My furniture. *My bed.*

Mr. Fookes has the master key on his key chain, and he opens the door wide, so Blade can take me straight through the living room and down the hall into my bedroom. Neither of them are talking, but I can imagine the looks they're giving each other. I think I might look like death warmed up. I certainly feel like it.

Blade lays me gently onto the bed and pulls off my shoes, then tucks me carefully under a blanket. Mr. Fookes is still hovering to the side of the room, watching silently.

"We need to plan," I say weakly, flapping one hand at

Blade as he pulls the blanket up under my chin. "We need..." *We need to find Mei.* I can't find the words, I'm so tired.

"You need to rest," says Blade firmly. He's fussing with the pillow under my head, making sure it's comfortable.

"We have to save... her," I say. My eyelids half close and I fight to keep them open. I don't have time to rest. I'm to blame if something happens to Mei.

"You've had a difficult experience. You need to give yourself time to rest," says Blade. "Then we'll save her."

"They were so angry with me," I whisper, opening my eyes suddenly, and looking up at Blade as tears start to leak down my cheeks.

His expression hardens. "They were desperate, Hazel. They shouldn't have asked it of you. You did what you thought was the right thing."

My attention snags on his phrasing. Does *he* think it was the right thing? Or is Blade just trying to make me feel better? The thought churns inside me, as I try for the thousandth time to figure out what I should have done. I feel like I've lost my moral compass, my ability to see what's right and wrong. I keep making bad decisions that hurt people. Is it because of my chalice powers? Or because I've got a demon inside me?

"I thought I was supposed to be good at fixing things?" I say. "I'm just making it worse."

"You *are* good at fixing things," says Blade fiercely. "This doesn't change that."

"But—"

"This isn't about you making bad decisions," growls Blade. "This is because you *care* about people. You lead with your heart, Hazel. You have a big heart, and you're always willing to put yourself on the line for the people you love. That's not a problem. That's a miracle."

Tears leak out the corner of my eyes as I try to take in what he's saying. "I keep seeing the expression on Seth's face as he realized what I'd done," I say brokenly. The loss of hope, the reemergence of fear. "How are we going to find Mei now? What are the director and Lakas going to do to her?"

I shouldn't have chosen Mr. Fookes over Mei.

It was the wrong decision. Fear and grief threaten to overwhelm me as I imagine what Mei is going through right now. Unable to help myself, I glance over at Mr. Fookes. He's looking at me with an anguished expression, like he knows exactly what I'm thinking. I blink, trying to think what to say to him.

"I will be forever grateful you set me free," he says, before I can even open my mouth. His words are fervent, like a prayer. "I know you could have chosen to ignore your promise to me. I know that maybe you *should* have ignored it, and I know it leaves us all in a difficult position. But I am forever in your debt. You have a life bond from me, and I will always be there to help you." He closes his eyes and takes a deep breath, like he's composing himself. "I won't let you bear this burden by yourself. I'll help you find Mei."

"As will I," says Blade. His dark eyes bore into me, and I feel like he can see into my soul at that moment. He sits down beside me, and strokes one hand down the side of my head, brushing back the loose ends of hair.

I flick my gaze back and forth between the two men. I give a watery nod, accepting their help.

"But first, before anything else, you need to rest," says Blade sternly.

This time, when I lean back into the pillow, there's

more ease. My thoughts are less frantic. They'll help me find Mei. This doesn't have to be a disaster. My eyes start to close, and my breathing evens out.

"I'll talk to Freddie, make sure he's able to get back here from Newport News," says Mr. Fookes softly. "Then we'll have a meeting. Figure out what we're going to do." He's not talking to me.

"Sounds good," Blade replies. "We'll need his help. Maybe he'll know a way to sort out the spell web."

I nod softly into my pillow. We need to find Mei, then find a way to get the spell web out of her.

And then we need to sort out the demon problem that's still gaping open around us.

But right now, the forces pulling me into sleep are much stronger than the need to stay awake.

CHAPTER
THREE

I wake slowly, a sharp pain in my eyes the first thing I notice. There's a bright light on the other side of my closed lids, like someone is pointing a flashlight at my face. For a moment, my fuzzy brain has me back at the mountain prison, and it's Lakas with some new torture planned for me. My whole body feels wrecked, and I can't hold in the tiny sob of breath.

Except it can't be the prison. There's a warm blanket under my hands and a soft mattress keeping me cozy. I'm home, in my own bed. *I'm safe.*

Then what the hell's going on?

Holding one hand in front of my face, I open my eyes the tiniest of bits, trying to keep the worst of the glare away. Except there isn't a light shining at me. There's no one else in the room. The light is coming from my *own body*. I'm covered in a demon-blue glow that's so strong, the room is lit up, bright as day. Outside my window, it's clearly night, but inside my room, there's not a spare inch not lit up like a demon-colored Christmas tree.

I sit bolt upright and look at myself, pushing aside the

covers to check. I'm in a t-shirt and panties, my bare legs glowing like they're a beacon for lost ships in the night. The tiny glow that used to be just on my hand has spread to... well, everywhere. I hold up my arm. It's exactly the same blue as a demon—anyone looking at me would think I was one of them, minus the weird metal scrapings. What does it mean?

My breath catches. Is it the demon side of my powers finally taking over?

Immediately I close my eyes and try to connect to the deep well of energy that sits inside me, but it's lying dormant, not reacting to anything that might be happening. I can still sense my little demon—despite the fact it's not bouncing around—but again, it doesn't feel like it's powering this glow. Clearly it's not an ominous attempt by the demon to take over my body and turn me into a killing machine. So why *the hell* am I glowing?

For another second or three, my response remains fearful. What if this is some new demon power I haven't come across before? Or maybe a demon somehow affecting me without even possessing me? My heart thuds heavily in my chest and I clench my hands into my blanket. I whip my gaze around the room like a demon is about to leap out of the wardrobe or crawl out from under the bed.

But eventually common sense seeps over my irrational responses and I remember: this has happened before. When I was doing the spell web tests with Mei in the basement lab at Blade's cliff-side house, I turned blue just like this. It frightened Mei at the time, even if she was half out of it with her reaction to the spell web. But it didn't mean I was about to turn into a demon. I let out a breath and attempt to calm down.

I'm just over-tired, I've had an anxious few days—

weeks—and it's all finally catching up to me. What with being at SIG headquarters, being arrested and sent to the mountain prison, escaping, and then the demon infestation... I just need to take it easy, remember how to relax. I lean back against the headboard on my bed, and close my eyes.

And that's when the very specific events of yesterday come flooding back to me.

Freeing Mr. Fookes.

Leaving Mei with Director Holden and Lakas.

Seth almost attacking me when he realized what I'd done.

A sharp pain hits my chest, and this time I know it's nothing to do with the demons. I sit up again, suddenly unable to relax. Seth's expression—distraught, unbelieving —is burned into my brain and I can't stop thinking how he must be feeling right now. I've been sleeping like a little princess, and he's probably so worried about Mei, he can't do anything. The knowledge I could have saved him from that is the pain I feel in my chest. This isn't just about Mei, and whatever she's experiencing at the hands of the director, although that's bad enough by itself. It's also about the people who love her, and are desperately worried about her.

I have a feeling I won't be able to get rid of the pain in my chest any time soon. Not until we rescue Mei, and make sure she's okay.

Not until I know that keeping my promise to Mr. Fookes wasn't the worst decision I've ever made.

I push my legs out of the bed, suddenly needing to move, to get going. To do something to help find Mei. Sitting around is no longer an option.

Where's Blade? My next impulse is to find him, to make sure he's okay.

I grab an old, comfortable pair of jeans from my drawers. Pulling them on feels more like I'm fighting with a live snake than the usually easy process of dressing. I don't know why everything is so difficult, maybe it's the blue glow that's putting me off, or maybe I'm just more tired than I realized. But I'm not going back to sleep. That's not an option.

Eventually I open the door and peer out into the hallway.

There's light down the hallway, coming from the living room. Do I want to go out there and show Blade that I'm glowing all over? What if it means something bad? What if it means that I'm being taken over by the demons? There's so much I still don't know about being a chalice.

What if it's the beginning of the end?

I used to be afraid that Blade would kill me because I was possessed by a demon. It was basically his job, to kill supernaturals who'd been possessed before they could harm anyone else. A demon inside a supernatural is a recipe for disaster; death and destruction always follow, usually on a large scale. The only way to avoid it is to "eradicate" them—Blade's words, not mine.

Luckily I never behaved like a supernatural who'd been possessed, and I managed to scrape through that situation without a knife to the heart. *Just.*

But now... I hold my hand up, and the glow lights up the hallway.

Would Blade still...?

I swallow hard over my suddenly dry throat. I don't even want to ask myself the question in my head. Blade is all about duty and honor, protecting people who need to be protected. Except... I'm sure he wouldn't. We've been through too much. He cares about me too much. He would never hurt me on purpose.

I think. Probably.

I hesitate in the hallway, my brain buzzing as I try to solve this new puzzle, while the blue glow from my visible skin lights up the white painted walls next to me. I let out a loud breath and give myself a little shake. I'm being ridiculous. It's like my brain has gone back to my old fearful, untrusting way of thinking, just because I'm back in my cozy little apartment.

Blade isn't going to hurt me. He doesn't need to. I'm a chalice. I don't need to be afraid of Blade and what he might do. I can control demons, not the other way around. I'm obviously way more worn-out than I realized. I shake my head, trying to ease some of the fuzziness. There's way too much going on for me to take time out right now. I hold my breath for a moment, and the glow dims.

I keep creeping forward, planning to see what Blade is doing. I just want a glimpse of his familiar face, maybe hold his warmth tight against me. I don't want to interrupt him. Maybe he's sleeping on the sofa? I can't hear anything from the room, so he's not watching television. Maybe he's reading a book? On the computer? I quietly push open the door into the living room, and look expectantly at the sofa.

He's not there.

I walk further into the room, and check the kitchen, but he's not in there either. I walk over and pick up the television remote from the side table. I flick it on, meaning to check the time. I have no idea how long I've slept. The screen is immediately filled with images of Randy Crowe, the front man for Sunday Lies, my father's favorite band.

"...Crowe has been released after being jailed for two

months on drugs charges..." the television reporter is saying. The view flicks to a blurry video of Randy Crowe walking out of a building flanked by lawyers. Flashing bulbs and journalists are pushing in at him on all sides. Dark circles hang under Randy Crowe's eyes, he looks thinner and somehow more rugged than usual. He also looks about ten years older than he did the last time I saw him.

"He wasn't arrested on drugs charges," I mutter to myself, unaccountably annoyed at this new evidence of the spell web working its magic. "He was arrested for demanding equal rights for supernaturals." My stomach churns as I continue to watch the screen. It flicks back to the main reporter, who tells the anchor that authorities would be closely monitoring the rockstar from now on, and had said he would return to jail if he even considered breaking his parole restrictions.

"...Authorities are now focused on a no-tolerance for illegal drugs stance for all celebrity singers such as Crowe..."

"It certainly doesn't appear to be doing Crowe any good. He looks terrible," says the anchor with a laugh.

"He probably doesn't even do drugs," I mutter, pressing the button on the remote to turn off the television. "They probably just tortured him." My stomach grumbles, and I head into the kitchen to see if there's anything to fill the gap. The fridge is fully stocked with vegetables and meat and there's fruit on the bench top. I grab an apple and bite into the juicy flesh.

Then I look around me, trying to decide what to do. Where's Blade? Where's everyone else?

They must be down at Mr. Fookes's place.

I grab the key from the shell on the kitchen bench and

head out the door. Just as I'm in the hallway locking it, my twelve-year-old neighbor Nelson pokes his head out from the door on the other side of the hallway. His silver eyes flash, standing out as usual against his brown skin. He's wearing jeans and a t-shirt, and he looks so wonderfully familiar I give him a huge watery smile. He comes out to give me a hug.

"I missed you," he says against my stomach.

Tears threaten to fall, and I have to blink quickly to stop them. I hug him tighter. "Me too, buddy."

"Blade said you were tired, and I had to leave you alone. But you're up now, so it's okay, right?"

"Absolutely," I say, one arm around his shoulders. I hadn't realized until this moment how much I've missed being in my apartment building, seeing familiar faces like Nelson and Mr. Fookes. They're the family that I've been missing for the last five years.

"You wanna play a game of FastRacer?" he says wistfully.

I glance at the stairwell, and then down at Nelson's upturned face. He looks so eager and hopeful, I can't say no.

"Just give me a few minutes to go downstairs and see the others, okay? You go in and set it all up on the PlayStation." Surely it won't hurt to spend half an hour with Nelson? I can multi-task. I'll come up with plans to get Mei back while I'm racing my favorite neighbor.

Creeping down the stairs of the building, I hear voices coming from the apartment where Mr. Fookes lives. The voices are talking, chatting, laughing. I hear Daphne and Poppy, as well as Blade and Mr. Fookes.

The door to the apartment is open, and I peer inside. Daphne is pottering about next to Mr. Fookes, her face happy, although she looks tired and thinner than when I last saw her. Poppy is talking to Blade, both of them sitting at the dining table, pouring over a map.

Everyone looks so happy that for a moment, I just watch them, my heart contracting. This is what I was thinking about the whole time I was at SIG Headquarters and the mountain prison. Every time Lakas tried to interrogate me, or any time the director seemed more threatening than usual, I just had to think about this place, and these people, to calm myself down. To keep going. To survive.

Mr. Fookes looks up like he's sensed I'm here. He probably did, or at least his apartment building did. He's so connected to it, I wouldn't be surprised to learn it worked like that. He whispers something to Daphne, and she glances over at me, then heads in my direction. She comes to the door, letting herself out, and closing it behind her.

Her eyes are fierce as she looks at me. For a second, I wonder if she's mad at me. Then she walks straight up to me and hugs me so tight, I'm struggling to breathe. But I hold onto her, too. We've been through a lot, me, Daphne and Poppy.

"Thank you," she whispers. "Thank you for keeping your promise."

I nod, but don't say anything. I can't help the sharp pain, and the feeling I made the wrong decision. *The thought that maybe I should have rescued Mei.*

"He thought you wouldn't do it," says Daphne, pulling back to look me in the eyes. "Even before he went back into the toaster, he knew there was a chance you would leave him in there. It's happened to him before."

My chest tightens at the thought. "And he did it anyway? Even thinking that?"

"He knew it was important. He's an honorable man." Tears form in Daphne's eyes, and fall silently down her cheeks. Her grey-blonde hair is sitting in layers around her face. She looks more comfortable in herself than I've ever seen her, despite everything.

"I almost didn't save him, Daphne. It was the hardest decision I've ever had to make," I admit, trying to be honest. "Seth was so..." I can't say the words.

"Robert told me. He told me what happened," says Daphne, pulling me into a hug again. "Hazel, we're going to find Mei. We're going to make sure this works out." Daphne's voice is fervent, and she means every word she's saying.

I nod again and again, wanting to believe her, trying to push away the crumbs of doubt burning inside my chest.

CHAPTER
FOUR

"Come on everyone, grab your plates and get some food." Mr. Fookes's voice carries easily over the noise in the living room at Anna Blade's luxurious mansion in Palo Alto.

"Yum," yells Ben, Suzanna Blade's youngest boy, as he immediately scrambles up from where he was playing cards on the floor next to his older brother, Finn. There's a ripple of laughter across the room as the gathered guests watch him line up at the front of the queue for dinner.

We're here because Blade's grandmother invited everyone to a massive Operation Rescue Mei meal. She wanted to have a celebration for me coming home, but since none of us felt like we could celebrate until we rescue Mei, she had to settle for what she could get.

I'm seated on a plush leather sofa, watching as the guests move about the room. Everyone here has knowledge or information that might be helpful in some way in our mission to rescue Mei and solve the problem of the spell web. It's like a convention of all the people I've met since I first found out about the supernatural.

Poppy and Daphne are chatting to Fleet, who looks completely different from the dangerous ex-special ops soldier who joined us on the rescue mission to Ravenwood. He almost looks... relaxed. He winks at me, and I give a small laugh. Fleet is a chameleon, always changing to suit the situation.

Nearby, Professor Hasselblatt is talking earnestly to Anna Blade on the other three-person sofa. She nods serenely like she's listening to every word, but I have an idea it's just a front, and inside her head she's actually composing a stern email to the board of directors, or trying to figure out some complicated business problem. She's elegant as usual, her long gray hair curled in a chignon, and her matching pale cream shirt and pants combo probably worth more than my yearly rent. Across the room, Suzanna is trying to wrangle Ben and Finn, and talking to Nelson's mother, Cassie. Nelson has been outside helping Mr. Fookes cook on the grill, along with Detective Capello.

Freddie's standing in one corner talking to Walter, my old work friend from Larry's Pawn Shop, and his sister Iris. He arrived back from Newport News yesterday on one of the Raven Technologies helicopters. Freddie's just as elegant and suave as he's always been, in an expensive suit —the shirt open at the neck—and a Rolex watch; except now he's wearing the family heirloom I found for him at the SIG Headquarters around his neck. It doesn't look like much, just a small piece of bone covered in runes, but I can feel the power emanating off him from across the room. His eyes seem even darker and more mysterious than they did before. Iris stands next to him, her dark eyes and dark skin contrasting to the pale lilac pantsuit she's wearing like she's just jumped off a runway in Milan.

Mr. Fookes however—standing by the large double

doors that lead out to the veranda, still waving his tongs at us—looks the complete opposite to the suave genie I had to deal with when he was in the toaster. He's wearing jeans and a blue T-shirt, with a red apron over top that says "Mr. Goodlooking Is Cooking". There are a ridiculous amount of stains on the front of the apron, almost like he made himself messy on purpose. He's been cooking on a complicated-looking barbecue that seems to have more cooking options than the oven in my apartment.

"Come along, that means everyone, not just Ben," says Mr. Fookes with another grin.

Everyone starts murmuring to each other, getting to their feet, and moving outside. Based on the delicious smells that have been wafting in from outside, Mr. Fookes has outdone himself this time.

Blade, who's been sitting quietly next to me, stands up and grabs my hand, pulling me up next to him. "Mr. Fookes will think we don't like him if we don't eat his food," he says, his mouth quirked in his particular half smile. His black hair flicks down messily over his forehead, and somehow accentuates the intensity of his emerald-green eyes. He's watching me carefully, like he has for the last three days since we've been back from Newport News. I don't know what he thinks I might do, but he's clearly worried.

"No, he won't," I say. I saved Mr. Fookes's butt from the toaster, after all. He knows how I feel about him. I smile, trying to show Blade that I'm fine, even if I'm starting to wonder. We still haven't heard anything from Damien or Seth. Not that I really expected them to get over it so quickly, but I guess part of me was hoping they'd relent. Maybe realize that I had to keep my promise to Mr. Fookes?

Instead, they're still mad at me, and everyone associated with me. Freddie said they barely spoke to him after I left. So now we all have to work separately, possibly even at cross purposes. It will be even harder to find Mei if we're not working together. It makes her seem further away, more out of reach. I swallow hard against the tendril of panic that's attempting to worm its way up into my chest.

I need to move on from the tornado of fears that have been plaguing me. What's done is done. I can't take it back. All I can do right now is focus on rescuing Mei, and finding a solution to the spell web problem. Everyone here has said they'll help all they can, and I'm going to use every resource I can to make it happen.

As I turn to head outside, a small book tucked into one corner of Anna's bookshelf catches my eye. "Is that an SIG Manual?" I say, pulling Blade over to look. I pick it up, and flick through the pages. It's much nicer and cleaner than the old battered copy Blade gave me, but it's definitely one of the manuals. "Who did this one belong to?" I ask Blade curiously.

"It's Blade's father's," says Anna, coming up beside us, like she knows it's going to be a difficult conversation and she wants to be there to help us through it. I've discovered that she's extremely protective of her grandchildren.

There's a flicker across Blade's expression at her words, but that's all the indication he gives that the topic of his father is a difficult one.

"It looks like he barely used it," I say, flicking through the pages. I stop at my least favorite page—the one describing demons, and how you should deal with them. It's all so wrong, wrong, *wrong*. "Who writes this baloney anyway?" I ask. I flick to the front, looking for a name to attribute to the writing.

"Dorothy Adler used to do it in my day," says Anna helpfully. "I assume she's retired now."

What? "Dorothy Adler? The SIG librarian?" I stare at Anna incredulously.

"She's still there?" says Anna.

"She never even leaves the library," I say, understanding dawning. It becomes very clear why the manual is so ridiculous. "Does she even talk to agents? Ask them if this stuff is useful?"

Anna shakes her head, glancing from me to Blade. "I don't know, my dear." I think this conversation has taken a turn she wasn't expecting, but I can't help it. The idea that Dorothy Adler, the librarian who hates me, is the one writing the SIG Manual has blown my mind.

I look back down at the book, the reason for the misinformation inside it now abundantly clear. "She's literally making this stuff up. Does she even consult the books in the library? Does the director know about this?" I'm outraged.

"It probably doesn't matter too much any more," says Blade, amusement in his voice. "You're an escaped prisoner of the Supernatural Intelligence Group. I'm pretty sure you're not getting any Agent of the Month awards any time soon."

I humph in Blade's general direction, but he's right. As much as this little manual annoys me, it's not my problem any more. What does it matter to me if SIG agents are being given a whole book's worth of incorrect information?

"Would you like to keep the book, my dear? I have no particular use for it. I was just keeping it out of habit more than anything," says Anna.

I frown down at the manual. "I don't know," I say, hesitating. Do I really want it? I run one hand over the cover, and find that part of me still feels connected to the manual somehow. I lost my other one when Lakas dragged me away from the SIG. "Actually, yes, I'd like that."

"That's settled then. Come, let's go wrangle this mob, and solve all our dragon-related issues," she says. She links arms with me, and then I'm walking beside Anna as she leads us toward the veranda, Blade following behind us.

There's a mild breeze outside, but the late afternoon spring sun is keeping things warm enough for us to eat at a large wooden picnic table. We're all dressed warmly—Anna warned us she wanted to sit outside if the spring weather played nice—and everyone looks relaxed as they gather food onto their plates. Surely we'll be able to use our collective hive-mind to find Mei? Surely someone here will know something useful, something that will help us create an ingenious plan for finding and rescuing Mei? I put the manual under my arm, pick up a plate from the side table, and join the small queue for the sausages and steaks fresh off the grill, hoping I'm right.

Detective Capello is standing next to Mr. Fookes at the barbecue and putting sausages on everyone's plates using a large pair of tongs. He grins at me as he puts one on my plate, then grabs another one off the grill for Blade.

"Thanks Detective," I say.

"Hazel..." he says warningly. "I've told you already."

"Okay...uh, thanks, Marco." I feel weird calling him by his first name, even though he's asked me a couple of times already. He saved me from the police station, and he's more than just a police detective to us now. But old habits...

"I might need your investigative skills for a side project," I say mysteriously.

His eyebrows rise up. "Don't you have Poppy for that?"

"I thought maybe you could work with her. It's important and I think it might need both of you." I've been thinking about how Connor was searching for the previous lives of the demons. If we could find the previous life of the little demon that's possessed me, then maybe we could find out why it came back. If the little demon is a lost soul, I want to help it, just like the translated book says I can.

"Sure. Just let me know." His kind crinkled eyes are smiling down at me, and I can't believe I'm standing here with the police detective who arrested me all those months ago. It feels like a different lifetime.

I move down the line and Mr. Fookes hands me a piece of steak using another oversized pair of tongs and I grin at him before heading to the table, already looking at the delicious array of salads that Anna—or more probably Fleet—has put together.

I sit down in the middle of the long table, next to Poppy. Blade sits on my other side, and reaches out to fill his plate with the large lettuce salad in front of him. The clatter of cutlery fills the air as everyone focuses on getting food on their plates.

I reach for a spoon and dip it into the rice salad next to me, watching as Poppy grabs some garlic bread and dips it into the beetroot dip she's placed on her plate.

"Wow, that's a big call," I say, half laughing. "Beetroot and garlic bread."

Poppy makes a face at me. "Keep your eyes on your own plate if you're going to judge me," she says, before biting into the garlic bread.

"I just talked to Detective Capello—Marco—about the special project. He said he's happy to help."

Poppy nods. "You really think we'll be able to find out what you want us to?"

"I need you to try. If my little demon really is just a lost soul wanting to right a wrong like the translated books said, I want to know what happened. I want to find a way to help my demon move on."

"What if it's something you can't help with?" she asks softly.

"We'll cross that bridge when we come to it. For now, I just want to see if we can figure out who it was before it died and became a demon."

"I'll do my best, Hazel."

"That's all I ask," I say, dipping a piece of sausage in tomato ketchup and putting it in my mouth.

CHAPTER
FIVE

We've been eating from the delicious spread in front of us for a few minutes before I clear my throat and bring up the reason we're here. "We need to make a co-ordinated effort," I say loudly. "To find Mei."

There's a rumble of agreement from everyone at the table.

"It's not just about finding Mei, either," says Freddie thoughtfully. "There are a few projects that need to be looked at to keep us ahead of everyone else."

I open my mouth to ask who he's talking about, but I already know. Dr. Green, Connor, Gavan, Lakas and Director Holden are the five big assholes in my life—in all our lives—and they're all pretty much out to destroy the world.

"Like what?" I ask instead.

"The increasing number of demons, for one," says Blade.

Freddie nods. "That's probably the most urgent."

"Finding out more about your chalice powers, for another," adds Blade.

I shake my head, immediately rejecting what he's suggesting. "We need to start with Mei and the spell web. Then move onto the other projects from there."

"We don't need everyone working on finding Mei. After tonight at least," says Freddie. "It's not a good idea to ignore the demons."

"Or finding out more about your powers," repeats Blade like a broken record.

I wave my fork—still with a piece of sausage skewered on it—at Freddie. "The most important projects are Mei and the spell web. No arguments."

Freddie holds up his hands in supplication. "Of course. I'm not arguing that point." Blade nods in agreement, but the two men glance across the table at each other in some kind of silent agreement. I know I'll hear more from Blade about this later, but for now, I let it lie.

"So what do we do first? What's been done to find Mei so far?" asks Anna crisply from the head of the table. I imagine it's her boardroom voice, for when she's bossing around her minions.

"They looked in all the obvious places first and couldn't find her in any of the SIG's prisons, or the headquarters in New York, or with the Earthbound. That much we know," says Freddie. "All the magical connections they have to her need to be at close range. They couldn't find her through them."

I think back to Seth and the wild desperation in his eyes. I know Mei and Seth had a connection, a way to talk in each other's heads. But even that wasn't enough. I can't imagine what he'd be like now, after another three days of not being able to connect to Mei.

"I'm sure the ravens have tried everything as well," I say. "They have Damien and Seth hounding them."

"I'm sure they haven't tried everything," says Blade. "Or they would have found her."

Freddie shrugs. "They're using all their resources."

"We should be working together," says Blade, his frustration suddenly crystal clear in his voice.

"Damien still not taking your calls?" Freddie asks sympathetically.

"No," he says shortly. It's hard on him. He's known Damien a long time. And it's not over something he did. I was the one who had control over the last wish, and I was the one who chose to set Mr. Fookes free. I squeeze his hand, trying to show him that I appreciate that he's on my side.

"Just let him calm down," says Freddie with a shrug. "He'll come around. He'll see that it was the only thing Hazel could have done."

I smile at Freddie, appreciating his words more than I can say.

"In the meantime, we need to start our own investigations," says Anna.

"We're a group of almost twenty people, and we've all got different networks. We need to start by checking our contacts, seeing what people are saying. We'll find out all sorts of information, I know it," says Blade, looking around the table at everyone. There's a general nodding in agreement. "The murkier the connection the better. Someone must know something. There's always a leak, especially with someone like Mei, who's so well known."

Walter leans forward. "I'll talk to Larry. He's got some dodgy customers." He glances at Detective Capello. "Allegedly."

Poppy takes a breath beside me. "I don't want to be a downer, but I've already been checking around to see if anyone knows anything. They've been keeping it real quiet. There's no chatter anywhere about Mei. It's like she's disappeared."

"Except we know she hasn't," says Blade sternly. "They'll make a mistake somewhere. Director Holden might be smart, but he's not infallible. We just have to stay focused, and take our opportunities when they come."

"What else can we do to find Mei?" asks Anna. She's peering around the table, looking for ideas.

"We could have someone tail Director Holden?" says Poppy.

"He's a professional spy. He'd spot a tail in two minutes flat," says Blade.

"Does anyone know where a minokawa might have a lair?" I ask. "Lakas might have taken Mei there."

There's a murmuring up and down the table, but no one has any concrete ideas.

"Are there any secure SIG facilities that you know of Blade? Somewhere else they could have hidden her?" asks Detective Capello.

"It'd be like searching for a needle in a haystack. We don't know where he's taken her. They could be anywhere in the US by now. Maybe even overseas," says Fleet.

"I don't think he'd take her overseas," says Freddie. "He's got plans for her. He's going to get rid of her as soon as they make their new spell web."

I can't help my wince after he says the words. Blade shifts next to me, moving closer like he's trying to shield me from the truth of the situation. But we've already talked about it, and we both know exactly what the plans are for Mei once they've figured out how to recreate the spell web. Connor and my father were very clear about that.

"It just means we have to act fast. I think for now, we just need to all talk to our connections," says Anna. "Who knows, one of us might know the one person who's going to crack this wide open for us."

"We need one person to report back to who can be the center of the operation to find Mei," says Blade.

Poppy puts her hand up. "I can do that. Everyone can report back to me. I can use my fox senses to assess what information is relevant."

"What else can we do?" says Freddie. "There must be more."

"This is an ongoing project, and this is just step one. We gather intel first. We all have twenty-four hours to check through our contacts, then we see what we find. Then we'll decide what we do based on that information."

"What about magic options?" asks Freddie.

"What magic do we have?" says Blade, looking between Freddie and his sister Iris, who's sitting just down from him.

The siblings glance at each other, then back at Blade. "We can look through some of the older spells. There's nothing I have that would be useful, I don't think," says Freddie. He looks at Mr. Fookes. "What about you?"

Mr. Fookes shakes his head. "I don't have the ability to find people. If you want to make something seem bigger inside, I'm your man. But this isn't something I can help with. But I do have some contacts who might know something."

"What happens if we find out something?" says Fleet suddenly. "Who's going to go rescue her?"

"We put together a team, based on her location," says

Blade. "The fewer people the better. Ideally, we want to get in, and get out with Mei, wherever she is."

We keep talking and eating, discussing the plans. In the end, everyone agrees that we have to start by checking our connections, and going from there.

"Now, what are we going to do about the spell web?" asks Anna, again shepherding the conversation.

"I guess that has to be me," I say awkwardly. "I know Connor and Gavan are working on it, and that it's got something to do with my birth father's powers. So I guess that's my powers too. I just have to figure out what it is." Part of me is frustrated that I can't just go back to the SIG Records and Relics room and look it up. There must be any number of books on the topic. The fact that I was able to find a book about chalices and demons already just proves that. "I have more information about being a chalice than I did before. Blade was able to translate a book from the SIG library. It helped me create the heli-copters."

Walter raises his eyebrows at me from the other end of the table. "Helicopters?" he says.

I shake my head, understanding his misconception. "I didn't make the helicopters, I turned them into relics that could be used to kill and absorb demons."

"I don't know why you think that's less impressive than making a helicopter," says Walter wryly, shaking his head.

"Does anyone else have any other ideas on how to find information on the spell web?" asks Anna. "Who can we talk to? Where would more information be stored?"

Walter makes a noise and leans forward. "I could check in my networks for that as well. There are some strange creatures that like to come in and purchase the cursed objects Larry sells."

Detective Capello's ears perk up. "Cursed objects?" he says.

"Allegedly cursed," says Walter swiftly.

"The mountain clans have lots of spell-web information," says Blade. "Maybe we could talk to Carrick about looking at the documents at the Compound."

"Carrick hates me now," I remind him. "He was just as angry as Damien and Seth."

"But surely if it was to save Mei...?" says Poppy, her face concerned.

"They won't answer my calls," I say. "Told me they didn't want my help."

Blade lets out a frustrated breath. "We just have to give them time. At the moment, they're still angry."

"Is there anyone else we could ask?" says Poppy. "Other supernaturals that we haven't pissed off to the point of hating us?"

I give her a look, but her words actually spark a memory. "There's the mountain super guard at Pismo Beach. He liked me."

"The Pismo Beach mountain clan are very old," says Mr. Fookes. "They're probably older than the Earthbound Compound itself."

"So they might have information?" I ask. Suddenly it seems like there might be a lead, and it's a huge relief.

"We can only ask." Mr. Fookes shrugs, his hairy shoulders a little more muscled than they used to be.

CHAPTER
SIX

"So what do we do now?" I ask, the irritation in my voice clear to me, even if it's not to anyone else. I'm sitting in one of the big sofas at Mr. Fookes's place, my dad's old baseball cap pulled low over my face, and my frustration at our lack of progress boiling to the surface.

It's been four long days since we had dinner at Anna Blade's house. I left her house buoyed up by how eager everyone was to help, and all the ideas we came up with. But In the time since then, I've found out nothing about the spell web, nothing about how to stop it from killing Mei, and nothing about where Mei is. Added to that, I've come up with a grand total of zero ideas for what to do about my father and Connor and their plans to use demons for a new spell web.

No clues. No ideas. No nothing.

All I've got instead is a constant nagging worry, and the vision of Mei sitting in some prison cell somewhere, being tortured by Lakas. I haven't glowed blue since the first day I arrived back at Sanctus Apartments, but I feel like I'm

39

glowing red on the inside from the frustration of getting nowhere with our enquiries.

Mr. Fookes and Poppy are sitting on the other sofa watching me carefully, like they're expecting me to explode at any second, and Daphne is in the kitchen brewing tea and coffee for everyone. Freddie is across from me, leaning casually against the mantlepiece of a large fireplace that wasn't here last time I was at Mr. Fookes's house. It's like it appeared because the apartment knew Freddie would need it to lean against for the meeting.

Blade is next to me, my hand in one of his big, warm ones. I've been getting increasingly grumpy and irrational as the days go by, and he's trying to use his Jedi mind tricks on me to get me to calm down.

But only one thing will calm me down right now. We need to find Mei, and soon. Otherwise I'm never going to forgive myself.

"I've talked to as many of my contacts as I can think of," says Blade, not quite answering my question. "But no one has any idea where they're keeping Mei. It's like they've disappeared to another dimension."

I look up at him quickly. "Is that possible?"

He shakes his head, and I slouch back down into the sofa. He's always mocking me for how I don't believe in things that seem far-fetched when I believe in demons. Now I'm not always sure what's possible, and what's not.

"I've checked with many of my... associates... too," says Freddie. "The answers so far are vague. Whoever has her is being clever. Maybe some kind of magical protection?"

"We have magic too," says Mr. Fookes firmly. "If that's what it takes." He's looking much more stern than usual; I think he's finding it stressful as well.

Daphne walks back into the room just then, carrying a

tray with cups of tea and coffee on it. She's wearing a new knitted sweater, this one with a large smiley face on it. She starts handing out the hot drinks, remembering what everyone ordered perfectly.

"Have we heard back from any of the others?" I take my cup of lemon and ginger herbal tea from Daphne with a smile. "Do we know anything more?"

Poppy shakes her head. "I've been getting answers back from everyone who was at Anna's place, but they're all saying the same thing. Whoever has her, it's being kept really quiet. I've never seen anything like it."

"It's starting to seem more and more like the only way this will get sorted is if we use magic," says Mr. Fookes. He takes his coffee from Daphne, the last on the tray, and pats the sofa next to him for her to sit down. Daphne sits, leans into him, and his puts his free arm around her. They both look so happy and contented.

"What magic do we have?" says Poppy. "My fox senses are useful if I'm sniffing out information, or being able to spot a lie when I'm interviewing someone. It's not going to help find Mei if she's this well hidden."

Mr. Fookes takes a sip of his coffee and nods slowly in agreement. "There might be some useful objects in my treasure room. I can have a look in there once we're done."

Daphne frowns and flicks a worried look at Mr. Fookes. "I thought you said that room was dangerous and you didn't want to ever go back in there again?" she says.

Mr. Fookes makes a wry face. "That was because I was annoyed the Diamond Necklace of Dajiboodi tried to curse me with my own magic. I didn't really mean it."

"So that leaves me," says Freddie. "Iris and I searched for a way to find someone, but the only locator spell we could find requires a personal item from the person."

"How does it work?" I ask.

"It's a voodoo spell that can find someone who can't be found." Freddie leans the tiniest bit toward me, his whole body tense. "But we need something of Mei's. Damien's not answering my calls, and I can't get through to Carrick either. They've completely blocked us out. I have no way to get anything of hers. I don't suppose you have an item of clothing of hers or maybe some jewellery? Some hair or skin?"

I shake my head. "I don't think so. I could check at the lab, to see if I have any of her hair lying around, maybe." My frustration rises again. We should be working together with Damien and Seth and the others, not hobbling ourselves like this. Mei's life is at stake.

Freddie leans back with a huff of breath. "We need something of hers, something close to her, something inhabiting the very essence of who she is."

I go through the inventory of my lab, trying to think what I have that belongs to Mei that would be helpful. "What about blood?" I say. I took samples from Mei when I was testing her abilities.

Freddie raises his eyebrows, his expression amused. "Blood is the best of all. It's just that people don't usually have blood samples lying around, so I didn't ask for it. I should know better than to underestimate you, Hazel."

I lift one shoulder as if it's no big deal, but I'm secretly pleased with his remark. "I was doing tests on Mei at Blade's place before it was compromised by Connor's men. I had to leave the samples there, but they were properly stored, so they should still be okay."

"The place that was compromised?" says Freddie. "Where you were attacked by Connor's men?"

"Yep," I say.

"Is it still compromised?" asks Freddie, turning to Blade. "Can we get into the lab for the blood?"

"Probably, if I go," says Blade. "There are a couple of secret entrances. It's also fully protected with security cameras, so I know exactly who's been there."

"Have they ever come back?" I ask curiously.

Blade shakes his head. "No. But then, they probably have it monitored in some way, and we've never been back either."

"That's great. So we can get Mei's blood and do the spell," says Freddie. "That should give us a direction."

Hope sparks in my chest. This feels like genuine progress. Now I just need to figure out how to get the spell web out of Mei, and we'll be golden. My heart sinks again.

"Where are you at with your research into a new spell web, Hazel?" Poppy asks, almost like she can read my mind. "That's our other big problem. No point getting Mei back, only to have her die on us because we can't solve the spell web problem."

I take an aggravated breath, trying to push away my fear of failing Mei. "Basically I'm nowhere. I know it's *possible* to create another spell web, because Gavan and Connor are working on it. But I don't have much to go on with regard to the actual *how* of doing it."

"So we need to find more information on that as well. Did you manage to contact the Pismo Beach guard?" she asks briskly. I have to remind myself that she's not having a dig at me, she's just moving the investigation along like a good investigator would.

I shake my head. "I rang the record store, asked to speak to the guard underground, and he just asked me how many drugs I'd taken, and could he have some."

"You might have to go in person to get what we need,"

says Poppy. "That's how it worked when I went last time. People are always more willing to talk in person."

"So which problem do we focus on first?" asks Daphne. Her gaze flicks to Mr. Fookes, like she needs to keep checking that he's really back.

"Finding Mei," I say firmly just as Blade says, "Working on the spell web."

Everyone laughs, although it doesn't feel funny. We have too much to do, and too much is riding on us being able to figure out something that seems impossible right now.

"We have to find Mei," I say again. It doesn't matter if I know how to fix the spell web if we can't find Mei.

"Even though they don't want you to have anything to do with finding her?" Poppy asks me carefully.

Blade's hand tightens around mine, and I realize I'm trembling. "Even then," I say firmly. "Mei is my friend. We need to help her."

"And it's important to *everyone* that we find her," says Blade. "We can't let the spell web die again. The humans didn't mix well with supers when they knew about us."

Freddie shifts position, drawing attention to himself. "We need to split up. Work on both problems from different angles," he says. "It's the only way."

"What do you mean?" says Blade slowly.

I tighten my hands around Blade's. I can guess what Freddie means, and I don't like it.

"You and I get the blood from your place and do a locator spell for Mei. Hazel goes to Pismo Beach and talks to the mountain clan about the spell web," says Freddie.

Blade shakes his head but doesn't say anything. The idea of being separated from him at the moment makes me feel like I've got lead in my stomach. We're only just back together after months apart. Except... It feels like Freddie might be right.

"I'll go with Hazel," says Mr. Fookes, clearly agreeing with Freddie. He stands up and steps into the middle of the room like he's a superhero accepting an important mission. I know why he's volunteering to be my bodyguard—he feels responsible for me. He thinks I saved him, and now he has to repay me.

"If you're going, I'm going with you," says Daphne firmly. Her eyes change color, and I see her wolf in her expression for the first time in a while. Mr. Fookes smiles down at her as if she's the most amazing thing in the world.

I get a little rush in my stomach as I watch them. Daphne was a shell of herself when she was locked up at Ravenwood, it's like she's a completely different person now. Mr. Fookes has helped her with that.

Blade shifts on the sofa next to me so our bodies are even more closely aligned, and he pulls my hand over onto his thigh. His whole body is tense, and he looks just as reluctant to separate as I am. It warms my heart and perversely, makes me able to think more clearly about the situation.

"It makes sense to separate," I say slowly, despite every part of me wanting to deny it. Blade's hand clenches on mine, fighting against my words. "I'm the one who'll have to figure out the spell web. And Freddie needs Blade to help him at his place. We'll get more done. It'll only be for a couple of days." The last bit I say directly to Blade. It's annoying when what I *have* to do isn't the same as what I *want* to do.

Freddie is watching both me and Blade from his position next to the fireplace. He looks like he's in a casual position, all understated ease. But Freddie's finger is tapping on the edge of the mantle, and his eyes are like a hawk's focused on us.

"You really think we should separate the group like this?" asks Blade carefully, looking between me and Freddie. "We worked pretty well as a team at Ravenwood."

"Teams sometimes have to split up," says Freddie softly. "For the greater good."

Blade tightens his grip on my hand. "I'm not sure it's a good idea."

I clear my throat, trying to ease the tightness. "We haven't managed to get anywhere since we got back from Newport News. We have to shake it up a little, try new things, that's all." I can't believe I'm arguing for this plan. I feel hot and cold at the same time. My fear for Mei is at war with my desire to stay glued to Blade's side.

Blade looks down at me, and his jaguar wildness is shining out of his eyes. He doesn't want to agree. He growls, sending a shiver along my skin.

"I know how you feel," I say quietly to him. "I don't want to do it either. But it's a good plan."

Blade glares over at Freddie, like he's blaming him for the situation. "Fine," he growls out.

Freddie nods briskly. "Okay, good. Blade and I go to his house, Hazel goes with Mr. Fookes and Daphne to Pismo Beach, and Poppy stays here to look after the Sanctus Apartments, and keep coordinating everyone else."

"It'll give me a chance to work with Detective Capello on Hazel's other project," says Poppy. "I might even bring Walter in on it, see what information he can get from his contacts." Poppy and Walter hit it off at Anna's party, both of them interested in mysteries and unsolved crimes.

Blade looks at me with raised eyebrows. "What other project?"

"I want to find out more about demons, especially the lost souls, the ones I can help. I thought I could start with my little demon, find out why it stayed behind."

"Have you got any information on the demon?" he asks curiously. "I didn't know you had any kind of a connection to the demon inside you."

I guess I haven't really ever told him much about the little demon, or how it helps me when I need it. I was always worried he'd think it would mean the demon was taking over if I told him too much. "It helps me sometimes..." I say with a shrug. "And I've seen... images... that it throws up at me sometimes. I have a feeling it was a man, but that's not definite."

"How are they going to find anything out?"

I shake my head. "I don't know. But they're going to try. I've given them everything I have, all the images the demon has ever given me. Professor Hassleblatt gave us an approximate timeframe for how long the demon would have been at Stanford. Poppy thinks it might be enough to go on."

"It'll give us a place to start. See what we can find," says Poppy, as she leans back in her seat. "Makes it more interesting if I'm going to be stuck here."

"You better take care of my apartment building as well," says Mr. Fookes with a mock scowl. He doesn't look entirely happy with our plans either. I guess he's been locked in a toaster for the last few months, maybe he just wants to stay home. We all have things we'd rather be doing than trying to save the world, I suppose.

Freddie glances at Mr. Fookes. "Poppy could also search the treasure room if you don't find anything today—she's already been in there and survived."

"Well, now you're making me feel less safe," says Poppy jokingly. The last time she went in there she came out covered in scratches and bruises. Except there's a light in her eyes, and I don't actually think she minds the danger.

Blade stands abruptly, pulling me with him. "We'll leave first thing in the morning, then. Everyone, get a good night's rest tonight. We need to be in top form."

He stalks out of the room without looking back, my hand still tightly attached to his, dragging me behind him.

My alarm goes off, and I roll over in my bed, groaning as I slam down the button. Surely that's not right? It can't already be morning?

The bed moves and Blade's arm snakes around my waist, pulling me close against his muscled chest. A warm shiver runs along my body, and I smile.

"Morning," he rumbles into my ear. His legs tangle with mine.

I breathe in, and his scent fills my nostrils, wilderness and pine, mixed with a sweet, tart citrus. We were up far too late, Blade trying to make up for lost time by giving me the best orgasms I've ever had in my life. "Morning," I whisper back.

"We have to get up. Freddie's meeting me downstairs in ten minutes," he says, not moving an inch. He kisses the side of my neck, lingering on the sensitive point just under my ear. "You sure you want to go in different directions?" he asks again, his breath sending shivers across my skin.

I sigh, keeping my eyes closed. "Not really."

"Should I—"

"No, you need to go with Freddie." I run my fingers over his forearm, smoothing along the ridges of his muscles. "He can't do this on his own. And I need help with the spell web. Mr. Fookes is smart. He knows his way around. We'll be fine." I'm not sure who I'm trying to convince, me or Blade.

"Just keep your head down. Remember you're still technically a fugitive. Keep your identity hidden, especially from other supers."

"I'll do my best." While I'm resigned to the idea of leaving him again, nervous butterflies are back in my stomach. What if something happens in Pismo Beach? What if Lakas finds us? How would I fight him if I haven't absorbed any demons? I need Blade to help me—

Blade tightens his arms around me as if he can tell I'm scared. I guess he probably can.

I force out a long breath. My fear of the minokawa isn't rational. And Blade makes me feel safer than I've felt in years. "We need to do it," I say, as much for myself as for Blade. "It's vital we find Mei and save her from the spell web. For her sake, but for ours as well. We need the spell web. Both goals are equally as important."

Blade kisses the side of my neck again. "It's the right thing to do. I just don't want to do it," he says, echoing my sentiment exactly.

I close my eyes and give in to the sensation of him against my skin. It feels right, as if this is where I'm supposed to stay. "You won't take any stupid risks?" I whisper.

"Of course not. You're the one who takes risks, not me," replies Blade, his voice a low rumble.

He shifts one leg, and I shiver as it rubs against my skin.

I lean back into him, wanting to hold him close, and not worry about the outside world.

Except I can't. "What about my father and Connor? The demons?" I whisper. It's been gnawing at me this whole time, the thought that I need to find a way to stop my father as well. Their plans to create a new spell web from demon energy seemed ludicrous, and yet...

"We'll deal with them next. We can't do everything at once."

I nod, hoping it won't be too late. What if they really do manage to make another spell web? Getting the spell web out of Mei won't save us if that happens.

Blade turns me over, so I'm lying on my back, and he's looming over me. "We're going to be fine," he says. "We can figure this out. You're a freaking genius at figuring things out." He leans in and touches his lips to mine, starting softly, and then moving more urgently against my mouth. I wrap my arms around his shoulders, holding him close, trying to tell him with my actions everything he means to me.

He growls and then pulls away. "I have to go. Freddie will come up here and find me if I don't meet him." He gives me one last quick peck on the lips and then pulls himself out of the bed. I watch his muscled body appreciatively. I'm not sure he'd like me saying this, but he's so graceful. It must be the shifter genes. He's got the instincts of a jaguar in him at all times, and it makes him so easy in his body. He disappears out the door, and seconds later I hear the shower start up.

I lie back in the bed, letting my mind wander. Are we doing the right thing? It's so hard to know. I remember back to the time Damien and Blade were here with me in this very room. Damien had just made me sign the SIG agreement, and he was telling Blade that the only way to save me was to stab me in the leg. How did he know that was the right thing to do?

I shake my head. He was so sure. I wish I were more like Damien, who never seems to have a problem with knowing what's right and wrong. I feel a pang of regret. Will Damien ever forgive me for not saving Mei with the last wish?

The door to the bedroom opens abruptly, and Blade walks in, a towel slung low over his hips. He's still a little wet, and looks so good, I can't stop devouring him with my eyes.

"Keep looking at me like that, and we'll never get anywhere," he says, his eyes dark.

I swallow and nod, looking away. Our time is up. The real world has intruded.

He grabs his clothes from the chair and dresses quickly in black jeans and a shirt, strapping on his knife in the same casual way he puts on his socks. Despite what he said, I can't help watching him hungrily from my bed. My heart is aching, and I wish we lived a different life. One where the fate of the world wasn't dependent on us getting up and going out into the world.

Finally finished, Blade glances at me, still lying naked in bed, and his eyes darken. He stalks back to the bed, leans down, and kisses me. This time it's not soft, or gentle. It's intense and dark and filled with emotion. I lean into him, trying to get closer, trying to feel every part of him.

He pulls back, gasping for breath, and leans his forehead gently against mine. "I love you, Hazel. Stay safe. I don't think I could live without you." The words are whispered, raw. He kisses me on the lips one last time and strides from the room.

I gaze after him, my whole body dazed from the feelings

he so easily produces in me. He's everything I didn't know I needed. I feel warm and easy in a way that I never have before. There's a lightness in knowing that whatever happens, Blade will be there for me. It's been so long since I felt that with another person, I almost don't know how to act. I don't know when I started to fall in love with him—maybe from the very first time we met—but the feeling is so integral to me now, I can't remember what it was like to not have Blade in my life. He's everything to me.

I love him, too.

Oh shit.

I didn't say '*I love you*' too. He doesn't know that he has to take care of himself so he can come back to me too.

He doesn't know I feel the same way.

I leap out of bed, pull on the first things I see—sweat-pants and a T-shirt—and race after him. I slam my way out the door of the apartment and race down the stairs. I almost trip and fall halfway down, I'm concentrating so hard on Blade and not on where I'm going. I have to force myself to go a little slower and watch my steps.

I get to the bottom of the stairs—a little out of breath, I'm going to have to work on that—just in time to see Blade and Freddie drive out of the parking lot and onto the road. I race to the double doors at the entrance to the building, but it's too late.

They're gone.

And Blade doesn't know how I feel.

"They'll be fine," says a voice behind me.

I turn to face Mr. Fookes. Mostly he looks the same as he always used to: hairy with a pot belly, even down to the jelly stain on his shirt. He's wearing a knitted cardigan that looks suspiciously like something Daphne might have made for him. But there's something steely about his eyes.

Something that makes me look twice at him. He's not the same after all. A little bit of the genie from the toaster is still with him, giving him an edge that never used to be there.

I can't decide if it's a good or bad thing.

"I hope so," I say, glancing back out the doors to where Blade and Freddie just disappeared. A nervous feeling flitters about in my stomach.

"We leave in half an hour," says Mr. Fookes, looking at my T-shirt. "You might want to have a shower, clean yourself a up a bit."

I look down. I'm wearing my green and black Teenage Mutant Ninja Turtle T-shirt, still covered in stains from the last time I wore it. I glare at him and look pointedly at his jam stain before turning to stomp my way back up the stairs.

EIGHT

"Pismo Beach is such an adorable town," says Daphne, peering out the window from the front passenger seat of Mr. Fookes's Jeep Cherokee.

I jerk awake, startled out of my daydream. I'm in the backseat, squished down against the leather seats, half dozing. A faint, blue light glows against the leather, and despite my brain being sleep-blurred, I immediately know what it is.

There's a demon in the car. My heart leaps into my throat.

"I haven't been down here in years," Mr. Fookes is saying, looking over at the sea, then back at the road. He's not looking at the back seat.

I frantically search around me, looking for the demon, but as soon as I raise my hand, I realize it's not a demon.

It's me.

My hand is glowing again.

Which is almost as annoying as a demon appearing in the car. I check on Mr. Fookes and Daphne again, but they don't seem to have noticed. I focus on my hand and the demon energy, pushing it back into the well of power inside me until the glow disappears again. I let out a breath. At least I wasn't glowing over my whole body this time.

My little demon skitters around inside me, sending feelings of calm and reassurance, like it knows I'm worried and it's telling me it's okay. I'm not sure I can believe it, but for now, I just have to keep ignoring the glow. I'll have to fix my glowing problem once I've fixed everything else.

It's been a long drive, and I'm tired. Instead of the cool van with the ability to time travel, Mr. Fookes insisted on driving in his usual SUV. Apparently the van takes up too much of his genie powers, and Mr. Fookes wants to keep as much as possible to help protect me and Daphne while we're in Pismo Beach. I couldn't argue with that logic, so here we are. And although the SUV is way more comfortable to drive in... it's taken us the normal amount of time to drive from Stanford to Pismo Beach.

I check my phone, trying to distract myself, and there's a message from Blade.

We're at the house. I miss you.

I stare down at my phone, trying to decide what to text back. I wish I were better at relationships. I've had this weird gap in my life where I've been hiding from people, cutting myself at a distance from people in case I got caught again. My fingers hover over the buttons. He said he loved me. That's big. I've never had a guy say that to me before. I've never said it to anyone other than my parents, and that was a long time ago now. Can I text it back to him? Say I love you for the first time via technology?

I don't think I can.

I should have said it back to him at the time, but I didn't even think about it. I just lay there like an idiot, feeling the warmth of being loved by Blade.

I've pulled my phone out and almost sent an "I love you" text at least twenty times this morning. But I don't want the first time I say it to him to be via text. I want to be able to look him in the eyes and say it and show him I mean it. I want it to be special. Texting it isn't special.

We just arrived at Pismo Beach. I miss you too.

Five years of being a loner means I really don't know how to act around men. Or anyone really. I wish I knew if my message was enough. I can only hope Blade understands the subtext to my words.

I aggressively punch the silent mode on my phone and shove it back in my pocket, like it's the phone's fault I didn't say "I love you" back to Blade like I should have done this morning.

"Maybe once we're done, we could check out the beach," Daphne adds wistfully from the front seat. I don't answer her. I'm not sure what to say, other than it seems like an inappropriate time to spend a day at the beach. But then, I also just want to get back to Blade as soon as possible so I can say *I love you* to him in person, which isn't exactly part of saving the world either.

"I think we need to focus on our mission, Daphne," says Mr. Fookes gently. "I'll bring you back here another time just the two of us, and we can do all the sights." He's still wearing the knitted cardigan, and I'm now certain it's something Daphne made for him.

She smiles over at him, a dopey look on her face. "That would be wonderful," she says.

I frown, watching how she's interacting with Mr. Fookes. Do I smile like that at Blade? Part of me hopes not —it's a little icky. But then, if I don't smile all gooey-faced at Blade, how is he going to know how I feel about him? Is he even now wondering if I love him, like he loves me?

"We all need to keep an eye out," Mr. Fookes is saying. "We don't want to be noticed by anyone who will tell the director we're here. He's got spies everywhere." He glances at me through the rear vision mirror. "Especially seeing as Hazel is a fugitive again."

I nod, agreeing in principle with what he's saying. But now that we're here, I'm having a hard time imagining something leaping out at us, or bad guys hanging out in a place like this. It's an ordinary beach town. The sun is shining, the waves are playing on the beach, and there are people wandering around in shorts, despite it still only being cool spring weather. Ice cream shops are selling their wares, and cafes are filled with people sitting out and drinking coffee in the sun. It all looks so ordinary. So peaceful and normal.

I put one hand up to touch the tiny pin that I attached to the lapel of my jacket. It's my mother's chalice pin that was in the locked box. Last time I was here I took it with me, and for some reason I decided to wear it today, to remind me of her. She used to live in this town, walk along these sidewalks, drink in these cafes. Sing in the local bar. I still can't quite imagine it, even though I've listened to the CD of her singing a million times now.

"So, where to, Hazel?" asks Mr. Fookes. He's looking back at me in the rearview mirror, his pale blue eyes almost violet in this light.

"We need to stop off at a cafe first," I say, sitting up properly and looking along the street.

"We only just ate," says Mr. Fookes. "Surely you could last a little longer...?"

I shake my head impatiently. "Not for me. For the guard. And we need a sudoku puzzle book."

Mr. Fookes parks along the main street, and he and

Daphne go in search of a coffee and blueberry muffin, while I try the bookstore for the puzzle book. I make sure I get a magazine style one that comes out every month, so it's not one he's likely to have already. When we meet back at the car, Mr. Fookes holds up his offerings. "What now?"

I point to the side street where the record store is located. "We head down there."

Before long, we're pushing through the door of Everyday is Sunday Records, the buzzer going off overhead like an angry mechanical bee.

It's the same dingy store as last time. Boxes and boxes of records line every surface, posters of bands line the walls. This time Sunday Lies is even playing on the stereo speakers overhead. My gaze flicks to the wall that has the photos lining the wall, and I easily spot the one with my father and Randy Crowe. I feel a pang in my chest, and all of a sudden, I really miss my dad. My adopted one, not my horrible birth father. I can almost imagine him in the store, roaming the aisles, searching the boxes of records.

The same greasy-looking guy with the medieval beard is at the counter, this time wearing a *Star Wars* T-shirt, and he gives us the same annoyed glare I got last time I came in here with Blade.

I can't help myself, I'm drawn to the wall of photographs, and I walk slowly along the row, trying to spot my father in all the pictures. Last time I thought he was only in about three or four of them, but I see him in the background of at least another three of the photos. There's a dark haired woman in the background who seems vaguely familiar. My heart jumps in my chest as I realize it's my birth mother. She must have hung out at the store too, been part of the music scene. It makes sense, given that she was clearly a singer. I feel silly for only just putting that information together in my head.

"Who's in the photos?" asks Daphne, coming up behind me and making me jump. I'd forgotten she was even here. I was gazing at my dad and Randy Crowe, laughing like they've just told each other the best possible joke. There's the edge of someone else in the photo, just a hand and the side of the body visible, but I think it might be my birth mother. *She was there too.*

"It's..." I hesitate, and swallow over the lump in my throat. "It's my adoptive dad. He... He must have worked here or owned the store or something at some point."

Daphne puts one arm around my shoulders. "He looks like a lovely man," she says softly.

I nod jerkily. "Come on, we better get this over with." I lead Daphne and Mr. Fookes down to the back of the store, emotions churning in my stomach—a mix of grief, shock and sadness. What happened to break up their life? They looked so happy in that photo. How did it all go wrong? How did my father end up living at an out of the way survivalist compound, after having everything he'd ever wanted in a dingy music store in Pismo Beach?

The 1998 Sunday Lies concert poster looks just the same, pinned to the wall at the back wall of the store. It's such a familiar sight, the logo of the band scratched into the top corner, I stop suddenly. I can almost imagine my father putting this poster on the wall, his hands touching the paper, working with whoever spelled it to open the door to the locked area behind it.

And suddenly, I miss my adoptive father—and my adoptive mother—so much, it's a physical pain. They were always so supportive, they loved me so much, I always knew they had my back, no matter what. Even now, when

I've discovered all the secrets my father was keeping from me, I know he loved me.

What would they think of the world we're living in now? What would dad say about Mei and the spell web, and the director? How we're trying to save the world? Would he prefer me to still be hiding at the Elm Creek Compound, living a quiet life, sheltered from all the danger and drama that I've been living through? Maybe. Part of me wishes I could deny my magic, deny everything I've learned since meeting Blade and finding out who I am, and go back to that life.

Except I've never been someone who hides from the truth. Everything I've been doing for the last five years has been about *finding* the truth. I take a breath, desperately hoping the guard will be able to tell us what we need to know.

I quote the snatch of lyrics from the Sunday Lies song that unlocks the poster. Everything goes hazy, and then a door appears in the wall next to us, just like last time. I let out my breath, relieved it worked.

Daphne's eyes are wide as the secret doorway opens and I lead them inside.

It's dark, and we don't have the light from Blade's knife to guide us, so I pull out my phone and use the flashlight app, pointing it around the room. It's the same dark foyer made of stone with a set of stone steps leading downward into even deeper darkness. Behind me, I hear Mr. Fookes pull out his phone as well.

"What is this place?" whispers Daphne unevenly as she looks around.

"It's a secret storage lockup for supers," I say. I force myself to use my normal voice, even though I want to whisper just like Daphne. This place is so creepy, you can't help wanting to make as little noise as possible.

"I didn't even know places like this existed," she says.

"You didn't even know you were a super five years ago," I say drily.

"True."

I lead the way down the stone steps, the light from my phone giving us patchy illumination, until we get to the next foyer. This time there's only an old wooden door with no markings and nothing to indicate where we are. A dim lamp in one corner casts more shadows than light. The door that leads to the guard is right in front of us. I hope he's in there. When does he work? It suddenly occurs to me that maybe he doesn't work every day. Maybe his meaner and grumpier fellow worker is the one on duty today, and he won't help us at all. This is a terrible idea. I don't know why I thought that he'd be able to tell us anything.

I glance back at Mr. Fookes. "Maybe..."

He steps forward, past me, and opens the door. He stands next to it and gestures for me to head down first again. "After you," he says grimly.

"That's not exactly protecting me, making me go first," I grumble.

"Don't worry, I have your protection foremost in my mind," he says.

He says it like he's making a vow, and I glance at him with a frown. "I was joking."

"And I'm not. And this isn't the kind of place that would allow people to be kidnapped or hurt. I can feel the magic surrounding us, the protection spells that are in place to ensure no one is harmed."

I raise my eyebrows at him. I can't feel anything. "How much of your genie magic did you keep this time?"

He grins at me, and the seriousness floats away like it was never there. "I'm full of juice right now. But as the years pass, the longer I'm out of the bottle—or toaster—it will get less and less." He gestures for me to first. "Come on. We don't have all day."

I head into the room, not as afraid as I was when Blade and I came down here. I know what's in here—I hope—and he's a perfectly nice mountain super. Mr. Fookes and Daphne follow me in.

The stone walls are the same as everywhere else down here, and dim light comes from multiple Victorian-style lamps strewn about on small antique tables. The enormous wooden cabinet that holds row upon row of locked drawers looms at the back of the room, and I try not to concentrate on what I learned here. Nothing has turned out as I thought it would when I stood here last time. I thought it would be amazing to meet my biological father—not that he would turn out to be the dictionary definition of asshole.

I switch my attention to the large, wooden desk that still dominates the middle of the room. Seated behind the old-fashioned desk is a large man with craggy features... except I can't see if it's the same guard, because there's a bright lamp beside him, and my eyes aren't adjusted to the light. He doesn't seem to recognize me, whoever it is.

I blink quickly, trying to acclimate my eyes. At first, all I can see is the shape of him.

Then I see the familiar craggy face. "Hi there," I say nervously. I notice the tiny horse and soldier figurine on his desk that I fixed for him last time. I grin.

"Hello, Hazel," he says carefully, his expression wary. He doesn't move. His large bushy eyebrows look like they're trying to escape his face. "Are you back to look at your locked box again?"

I shake my head. "No." I gesture beside me. "These are my friends, Mr. Fookes and Daphne."

"Hello," says the guard cautiously, as they nod back at him. The air is thick with tension, as the guard sizes them up. "You're not casing the joint this time, are you?" he asks me.

"Nope," I say. "Not at all."

"Then why are you here?"

"We brought gifts." I hold up the sudoku puzzle book and the bag with a blueberry muffin.

He doesn't reach out to take them.

I try again. "I'm hoping you might be able to help us."

"I'm not allowed to help people," he says. "My contract is very clear."

I put the sudoku book and muffin on his desk. Daphne moves forward and puts the coffee next to them.

"It's nothing bad, I promise. I just need to know what you know about the spell web. How it's—"

He shakes his head. "I can't help with that."

My heart jumps. "So you know something, but you're not allowed to help?" I say carefully. I can work with that.

"I'm not allowed to help anyone," he says.

"Do you know enough to maybe help us get the spell web out of someone?" I ask, ignoring his words. "Do mountain supers know that kind of thing?"

"Hazel, I can't tell you anything. You're risking my job by being down here asking me these questions." He's starting to look agitated, and I realize that my questions are upsetting him.

I hesitate, trying to think. "Do you know anyone else who *can* talk to us?"

"I can't tell you that either, Hazel. It's very specifically something I can't discuss."

Mr. Fookes clears his throat. "Perhaps if you can't help, you could introduce us to the mountain super clan from this region," he says.

I watch the guard's face, but he's got himself back under control and he's staring impassively at me.

"It's important," I add. "Life and death."

"I could get fired if they find out I'm talking to you, let alone giving you introductions to the clan."

"But—"

"I'm sorry, Hazel. The answer is no."

CHAPTER
NINE

T he one thing I've definitely learned in my life is that the final answer is never the first no.

"You know, I still don't even know your name," I say, picking up the small horse.

He doesn't answer but reaches out and takes the coffee. He sniffs and then takes a sip.

I'm guessing he's not allowed to tell me. No matter. I'll figure it out.

"May I?" I ask, gesturing to the switch that turns it on.

He nods cautiously. "Go ahead."

"I thought it was for your son?"

"I took it home for him, let him play with it, but he almost broke it again." He clears his throat. "He's a little too young yet. I decided to bring it back here with me for a while longer."

I smile. I can hear a certain note in his voice. He couldn't bear the thought of his young son wrecking his beloved toy. I'd take a bet that he won't ever give this to his son, not while he's young enough to enjoy it, but also break it.

"Makes sense," I say. I turn to Daphne. "Watch this. It's

amazing." I flick the switch, and the tiny horse rears up on its back legs, the tiny rider holding on closely. I hear Daphne's gasp, and she moves forward to stand next to me to watch. The horse runs around the desktop, for all the world like it's a real tiny horse. It's beautiful, and I allow myself the joy of watching it for a few moments before I focus back in on the guard.

He's watching me warily. He has a good idea of what I'm capable of. I convinced him to give me the password question last time after all.

"Have you heard of Mei? The dragon shifter?"

He blinks, clearly not expecting the question. "Sure. Everyone has."

"What do you think of her?" I hold my breath, hoping against hope he's not one of the people who thinks she's ruined the world.

"I don't know what you mean," he says carefully.

"Do you think she's a renegade out to destroy the world?"

He shakes his head cautiously.

"Do you think she's trying to protect supers?"

He doesn't move. Answering this question incorrectly could get you in big trouble with the SIG. I'm asking him to take a side, and he's not going to do it.

"I'll tell you my take on it, then," I say, taking a huge chance. "I think Mei is a good person who's trying to save the world. She's trying to find a way to stop bad things happening to supers, and she's only an enemy of the SIG because they're being run by a corrupt megalomaniac."

Behind me, I hear Daphne's gasp. It's not safe to say things like that about the SIG to people you don't know well, even when you're a fugitive on the run from one of their high security prisons.

But I have a good feeling about this guy. He's kind. And smart. Surely he can't be on the director's side.

"That's treasonous talk," he growls. "The SIG will lock you up for saying things like that."

"Do you disagree with them? Will you tell the SIG?" I put pressure on him. I need him to take a side. To take *our* side.

He hesitates. "You shouldn't say things like that," he says stubbornly.

"Mei's my friend. She's in trouble, and I need your help."

He looks up at me and narrows his eyes. "How do I know you're telling the truth?"

"You know me. You know my greatest secret. You know enough about me to judge whether I'm telling the truth." I stare at him, pushing him.

"What kind of trouble?"

"She's been kidnapped by the director. He's holding her prisoner. I need to find her and help her escape."

"Is it a kidnapping if it's the government who has you?" he asks. "Isn't that just being detained by the authorities?"

"He kidnapped her," I say firmly. "He's a terrible man who needs to be stopped."

"And how are you going to do that?" he asks dubiously.

"With your help."

He shakes his head. "I can't help. I'll get fired."

"Then point me in the direction of someone who can help."

He sighs. "You're like a dog with a bone, you know that, Hazel?"

I lean in closer. "It's important," I say, willing him to believe me. "I wouldn't ask if it wasn't. This isn't just important for me. We need to find her, so we can save the world. Save everyone from what's happening."

He raises his eyebrows, his craggy face looking dubious. "That's a big statement."

"I can back it up. There's a demon plague coming, and we need Mei and the spell web to be in place. We won't be able to control them otherwise." I've never said those precise words aloud, but I know deep in my heart that it's true. Mei is central to us surviving the demon plague that my father and Connor are intent on creating. Energy crackles around me, and I hope he can tell what I'm saying is nothing but fact.

"Do you like bowling?" he asks suddenly.

"What?"

"Ten pin bowling. You know, with lanes."

I frown. Is this really the time...? I blink and remember standing outside the secondhand record store, wondering how it was going to be useful to me. "Yes. Yes, I do."

"There's only one in town. Try it out. Best bowling you'll find all along the coast."

I nod slowly, trying to act like I know exactly what he's saying. I mean, I think I do. He wants us to go to the bowling alley because we'll get a clue as to where to find the rest of the mountain clan. But what if I'm wrong? What if he's just telling me to "get lost"? I mean, *bowling*?

"Are you any good at bowling?" I ask, trying to make sure.

"Sure. Best in my league." He stares at me, his face blank, giving nothing away.

I nod slowly. "Okay, then I guess we'll go bowling." I hesitate. "Are you ever allowed to tell me your name?"

He shakes his head. "I can't tell you anything about myself. It's to protect both of us. But if someone else told

TRUDI JAYE

you"—he shrugs—"that would be fine. It's not against the rules."

I take a deep breath. He feels like a friend now. He's trying to help us, as best he can. And he definitely helped me last time. I wish I knew his name.

"Maybe I'll come down and visit you again?" I say.

There's a tiny tic next to his eye, the only change in his granite-like face. "No, best not to visit. I think this should be the last time you come down here, except if you want to get access to your locked box."

I blink. I can't help the pang I feel. Is he saying he never wants to see me again? I thought we had a connection. I fixed his grandfather's toy. It's not like we're best buddies, but it still hurts. I nod, trying to act casual, as if it's no biggie that he's rejecting me. "Okay then. Well... thanks for your help."

"You're welcome, Hazel." His voice is low and gravelly, and I imagine there's a sadness in it, the same as in mine.

I turn and follow Mr. Fookes and Daphne out the door, closing it firmly behind me.

"Well, that was weird," says Daphne. "You want to go bowling, in the middle of a crisis?"

I lead the way up the stairs, wanting to get out of this place as quickly as possible. "It's a clue. I think. Or he was just trying to get rid of me. I'm not entirely sure."

CHAPTER
TEN

The big neon sign flashes in front of us.

Bowl-o-rama. A bowling good time!

Streams of teenagers are heading in the front door, and the parking lot is full of people in garish bowling shirts. "Are you serious about this?" says Daphne dubiously. Mr. Fookes is standing next to her with a matching expression.

I hesitate. "I think so. It's all we've got." I still don't know if the guard was just trying to get rid of us, but it's our only lead. I pull out my phone, checking for a text from Blade. It's been a while since his last one. Has Freddie done the locator spell yet? Have they found Mei?

My finger hovers over the phone, and I debate whether to call Blade. Should I let him know we have a lead? A way maybe to find Mei? I don't want to interrupt him if he's in the middle of a situation. What if he's hiding from intruders in his house, and it's my call that tells them where he is?

I definitely can't call Blade.

The other person I'd like to call is Damien. Tell him that we're helping. That we're going to find Mei, no matter what. Would he even answer my call?

I don't think he would. He was so angry when I saw him last.

"What if he's making fun of us? Testing if we'll do the ridiculous thing he sent us to do?" Mr. Fookes glances around. "What if he's watching us right now, laughing his ass off?"

I glance up and around, checking the parking lot almost automatically. "He's not like that. He wouldn't send us here if there isn't some kind of point to it." *I hope.* I take a breath. "He said he was the best in his league. So let's go straight to the league photos, you know, the ones where they take photos of people with their trophies? If he's there, we'll know it's real. If he's not, we'll leave."

"It's as good a plan as we have right now," says Mr. Fookes grimly. Despite his knitted cardigan, he looks ominous, like he's preparing for the worst.

I can't help myself, I flick Blade a text. Hopefully he has it on silent. *Guard no help. Checking new lead.*

I hesitate over the phone. Should I add the three extra little words that have been bouncing around inside me, pushing to get out? I shake my head. I need to stop second-guessing myself. I want to be with him in person, to have his skin against mine, and to say it while looking into his eyes, to see if they change color, like I hope they will.

I miss you I text instead.

We head up to the double doors at the entrance and line up behind a group of teenagers chatting and laughing as they wait in line.

"We should have done this on a weekday," mutters Mr. Fookes. "Too many people."

"We don't have time to be worried about a few extra people," I say. "Lives are at stake."

We eventually make it to the front counter. The woman serving customers is a tall redhead who looks suspiciously craggy. I think she's a mountain super.

"How many to bowl?" she says with a bored voice. She's not even really looking at me.

"Uh, do we have to bowl?" I ask.

Her gaze sharpens. "There'd be no point coming in otherwise." She narrows her eyes and stares at Daphne and Mr. Fookes behind me.

I nod, trying to look like I'm someone who loves to bowl. "Oh sure. Of course. I mean, I was just asking. Three to bowl, please."

She presses a few buttons on the register, still looking at me suspiciously.

I pull out some money and pay for the three of us, then go inside before she decides we're *too* suspicious.

"Are we really going to bowl?" asks Daphne as we wander into the darkened bowling alley. Lights are flashing, and people are laughing and talking all around us. "I've always wanted to try."

I exchange a look with Mr. Fookes, but I don't think either of us has the power to resist the wistful expression on Daphne's face. It's like she's never had a holiday.

"We'll look around first, just in case this is some kind of a trap," I say, trying for neutral.

Daphne nods, but she's not really paying attention to me. She's watching the rows of bowlers, all of them launching the bowling balls down the lanes, but with varying degrees of success.

I spot a cabinet full of trophies and rows of photos on the walls to one side of the entrance. I wander over, wanting to check my theory that that guard will be in one of the photos if he's as good as he said he was. I peer through the glass at the trophies, and it reminds me of the cabinets at Freddie's place. His were way more interesting, filled with curios and relics. This cabinet just has trophies with titles like "Best All-Lane Champion, 1988" and "Best Woman's Team, 2007".

The photos are on the wall next to the cabinet, five rows of them, with the older photos higher up, and the photos getting newer and newer as they get lower to the ground.

"They'll need a new spot for the photos soon," says Mr. Fookes behind me. He's peering at them, too.

I nod absently. I'm searching for my guard friend, hoping against hope I'll find him here. I want to be right about trusting him. The rows of faces, either lined up as a team, or individuals holding up huge trophies, seem over-whelming at first. There are so many of them. And then I spot something.

Not the guard.

My dad.

The breath gets knocked out of me, and I freeze. What does this mean? My adoptive father was friends with the people here?

He's in a team photo, his face grinning out at the camera. It's like I'm looking at a ghost. A whole other life that belonged to my father that I didn't even know about. I touch his familiar face in the picture with one finger, wishing I could just see him again, talk to him about what's been happening. I peer more closely at the photo, and I see another face I recognize. *What the hell.* I step back from the wall, feeling like I've just been stung.

My birth mother is in this photo as well.

Gazing around, I can't help trying to picture it. The two

of them, hanging out at the bowling alley, grabbing a lane, competing to win. A bowl of fries and a beer each, laughing and having fun together. Is this what it looked like when they were here? How often did they come by?

"Did you find something?" asks Mr. Fookes, coming to stand beside me, looking concerned.

"It's, uh..." I hesitate, not sure if this is relevant to our search or not. "It's my adoptive father, and my birth mother. There," I say, pointing to the photo with them in it. It's from twenty-three years ago, when their team won the social league. They're all laughing and making faces at the camera.

"They're in this photo?" he repeats, like he can't believe it. He peers at it, searching the faces.

"Yeah. I guess that's our proof we're in the right place. If my birth mother hung out here, they must know about chalices. It can't be a coincidence."

"Did you find the guard anywhere?"

I shake my head slowly. "Maybe he knew I'd see this photo? Maybe it's not him we should have been looking for, maybe it was them?" I pull my phone out of my pocket and take a photo of the picture on the wall. My chest feels hollow. These photos make me think of everything I don't have, everything that's not easy or simple in my life. It's been a rough day, and being reminded of my dad everywhere I go has made it even harder.

"So if we're in the right place, we just need to find the right people," I say, looking around again. I take a deep breath to reset, then walk carefully down the back of the room, looking around and trying to see if I can tell who's a super and who isn't. Even after all this time, I have no idea. They could all be humans for all I know—

Except there's a group of people at the end row. They're all really big. Solid. *Craggy.*

Like a mountain.

Four of them are in the padded seats by the end lane, and others are seated in the dining area just behind them. There are so many of them, I start to think that perhaps the three of us might be in trouble. Is it dangerous to be here? They could easily overpower us.

I glance at Mr. Fookes. He's not a powerful genie anymore. He says he still has powers, but is it enough to overcome that many mountain supers? I don't have any demon energy inside me right now, which means I'm fairly useless in a fight. My little demon buzzes inside me, and I don't know what it's trying to tell me. That it'd protect me if it could? I shake my head, amused by the demon's determination.

"Over there," I whisper to Mr. Fookes.

He looks in the direction I'm pointing, then nods. "That's them." He gestures at Daphne, who's been watching the bowling with rapt attention. She hurries over, her face alight with her enjoyment of the bowling alley. I make a mental note to take her bowling back up at Stanford when we get back.

"We've found them. We need to stick together, and take care of each other," says Mr. Fookes warningly to us both.

I swallow hard. "Will they talk to us?" I ask. Carrick hates me right now. I don't even know the guard's name. What if he's sent us into a trap? What was I thinking? My breath comes a little faster and I peer around, searching for the nearest exits. The one thing we have going for us is that there are so many people around. We look less visible than if we'd walked into an empty alley.

"Mountain supers aren't known for their friendliness," says Mr. Fookes quietly. "So don't expect them to be excited that we're here. But they're not likely to attack unexpectedly either."

I nod. Obviously my worries were visible on my face. And in the way I was just standing there staring at them instead of moving over there. I take a fortifying breath, then stride determinedly toward the large group of mountain supers.

One of the beefed-up mountain men notices us walking toward them and nudges an older man next to him. The old man looks up, big bushy white eyebrows hovering over strangely intense blue eyes. Immediately it feels like I've been hit with a baseball bat. His gaze is so strong it's like he's pushing me away with just a look.

I frown. It must be some kind of magic, something they use to keep the other bowlers away from them. I keep walking, even though all I want to do is turn around and head out the door.

Behind me, Daphne whimpers and then growls, her wolf coming closer to the surface. I falter in my forward motion.

"Just keep going," says Mr. Fookes urgently. "You're taking the brunt of it. We're fine."

I clench my fists and set my muscles into a hard line and keep walking toward the mountain supers. The old guy is frowning at me now, making his craggy features seem scarier. This close, his shaggy white eyebrows look like they could house an entire family of mice, and his hair could rival Einstein's for puffiness. He should look like a crazy old hobbit, but somehow he seems dangerous and sinister.

And I keep walking toward him.

He says something to the man beside him, the one who noticed me first. The man turns back to me. He's younger, but just as craggy. He's bigger than the old guy with the eyes, and when he stands up, he towers over everyone else around him—including the other mountain supers.

He could be a wrestler with that physique. He could join the circus and be the strongman. Or carry really heavy objects around at a factory. His enormous arm muscles stretch against his teal-blue bowling shirt, making it seem like its on the verge of ripping. If he decided he wanted to beat me into a pulp... he could.

Easily.

I swallow hard. If he were a demon, this wouldn't be scary. But there's something overpowering about the size of this man, like he could break me like a twig if he wanted and wouldn't care if that's what he had to do. The only other mountain supers I've met are the guard, who can't help me, Carlos, who works for the SIG so I don't know if he'd be on our side, and Carrick, who I saved, but who hates me now. They're all good honorable men in their own way, but these men all look far more aggressive and untrusting.

I keep moving forward. Part of it is my stubborn streak, the same streak that kept me going when I was alone and on the run, when times were tough, but I was determined to be tougher.

But the other part is the thought of Mei in the hands of Director Holden and Lakas. I know they need her alive for now, but they also need her to do what they want. And Lakas loves that kind of a challenge. He felt constrained by the rules that the director put on him when I was his captive.

But the director hates Mei. I don't think he'd care if Lakas decided to push the boundaries. We need to find her and rescue her. And then we need to get that spell web out of her. It's the only way Mei is ever going to be safe.

So I don't stop. I keep putting one foot in front of the other. I need to talk to these men, I need them to tell me what they know about the spell web. And who knows, maybe they know something about where the director is keeping Mei. I can be strong. I can face down these strangers if it helps Mei.

I'm almost at the group when the large mountain super moves to stand in front of the others. He's got eyes the color of ice at the arctic, and at the moment, they're flinty and hard. He's not amused that we've come this far.

He crosses his arms over his enormous chest, and the closer I get, the more I find myself looking up. I'm not tall. In fact, I've been called short many times in my life. But this dude is taller than anyone I've ever seen, including Carrick, the Mountain King.

It's the memory of Carrick that keeps me going. I was scared of him the first time I saw him too. But he turned out to be an honorable and kind person. He's mad at me at the moment, sure. But it's because he loves Mei like a sister, and I refused to save her.

I clear my throat. "Um, hi." I'm going with awkward geek instead of cool charm.

"Get out. We don't want your sort in here."

My sort? "Uh... what sort do you think I am?"

"The sort that causes trouble. That sort."

I shake my head. "I don't *cause* trouble. I'm trying to *prevent* it."

"I know exactly who you are, and where you've been for the last few months. My cousin Carlos talked about you. You're an SIG puppet, and we don't want your sort here." He glares down at me. "So get out, before I tell them to throw you out." He gestures with his head to the three large men wearing matching teal-blue bowling shirts who've come to stand behind him. They're not as big as he is, but they're close.

"I'm not—" As soon as I start to speak the three goons move forward, looming ominously over me.

ELEVEN

I hold up my hands. "I'm not an SIG flunky," I say quickly. "I was arrested. They put me in prison!"

The goons hesitate, glancing at their boss. *The head bowler.* I feel like I'm in some alternate reality.

"Prove it."

"I can't *prove* it. What, do you think I have snap shots of being held in a prison cell? Written references from my interrogator?"

Mr. Fookes steps up to stand next to me. "I can vouch for her," he says, his knitted cardigan swishing.

Daphne steps up on my other side. Her wolfish eyes flash with defiance. "So can I."

The head goon smirks. "Check these three out. They think I'm gonna take the word of some hairy dude wearing knitwear, and an old lady who looks like she's—"

He doesn't get to finish his sentence. Mr. Fookes expands in all directions, suddenly making himself taller and wider than the three goons standing in front of us. He snarls down at them, his face turning into the handsome genie, this time with sharpened teeth and a glint in his eyes that promises retribution. I stand next to him, trying to look like this is totally normal for me.

"Say what you like about me... But don't you dare disrespect my girlfriend," he growls. His words echo around the walls, and I glance behind me to see how the humans are reacting to Mr. Fookes suddenly blowing up like a balloon. No one has noticed. Bowling is progressing as per usual. I shake my head. Sometimes the spell web makes no sense to me at all.

The head goon is staring up at Mr. Fookes like he's never seen anything like him before. He probably hasn't. His eyes are enormous, and his mouth is wide open like he wants to say something, but his brain isn't connecting to his lips.

"Stand down, Ethan," comes a sharp command.

I peer around our would-be escorts to figure out who's issuing the orders. It's the old dude who was trying to stare me down. He's standing now, looking up at Mr. Fookes. "I haven't seen anyone do that in a long time," he says. "You're a genie?"

"I was," says Mr. Fookes.

"And the woman speaks the truth? You swear you're not here at the behest of the SIG?"

Mr. Fookes nods solemnly. "I do."

"Then welcome. Come, sit with us." The old man waves his arms in a gesture toward the seats next to the bowling lane.

"But, sir—"

"A genie never lies." The old man's voice is sharp, like he's not used to being questioned. "They may bend reality, but they will never lie to a direct question. They are who they say they are."

I glance at Mr. Fookes, who is currently deflating like

some kind of demented human-shaped balloon. I bet telling people he can't lie to them is on the top of his to-do list. *Not.*

Once he's back down to his usual pot-bellied, hair-covered self, I watch him, waiting for his signal that he's okay again before I turn to walk forward. I'm not sure what blowing up like that does to a person, but I can't imagine it feels good.

The teal-bowling-shirt goons reluctantly stand aside to let us pass, and I can't help making a face at the first guy. He glares down at me but doesn't move. It tells me a lot about the power of the old man we're about to sit with.

The old man waves us into a seat beside him, and soon we're all awkwardly perched on the padded seats.

"So, tell me. Why are you here?"

I lean forward. "I need your help. We're—"

"Troublemakers," says the big guy. He's standing just across from us, arms crossed and scowling like a little kid who's not getting his way.

"Quiet, Ethan. Let her have her say. Then we decide."

"My name is Hazel. We're trying to find more information about the spell web and how to make a new one. We need to replace the current spell web with something else." I don't mention that Mei has the spell web inside her and that it's killing her.

The old man shakes his head. "It cannot be done."

"Cannot, or is it just that you don't want to help?" I ask, immediately annoyed at the speed of his answer. "I'm not some crazy person who wants to mess with the spell web. This is important."

"In my time, I've learned that everyone thinks their quest is important," he says with a hint of humor on his craggy face.

"I'm not just imagining this. Ask Mr. Fookes. He can't lie, he'll back me up." I turn to look expectantly at Mr. Fookes, who nods solemnly.

"This is important," he says. "I vow on my genie honor."

The old man shrugs. "I'm sorry. I wish I could be more helpful. The records are all long lost," he says, shaking his head. "It's not possible."

"Do you have verbal histories? Anything that's been passed on through a clan story?" *That's how desperate I am, I'm voluntarily asking for verbal histories.*

He shakes his head. "We've never messed with the spell web, and neither should you."

"You don't understand," I say, a little desperately. "Lives are at stake here." I can see I'm going to have to tell him more. His craggy face would make a poker champion proud.

"I'm sure you think so," he says with perfect calm.

"I *have* to find information," I say, taking a deep breath. "My friend Mei Walker was kidnapped by SIG Director Holden. We can't find either of them. And..." I hesitate.

"And what?"

I glance at Mr. Fookes. He nods, briefly, once.

"And Mei *is* the spell web. She has it inside her. Which means Director Holden has control of the spell web, the complete opposite of what she was trying to achieve when she did it. Even worse, the spell web is killing her. If we don't find her, she'll die, and the spell web will die with her. If the spell web dies, we'll all be back to where we were when the humans could see us." I remember what it was like to have the humans aware of the monsters out there—*carnage*—and I don't want to go back there.

"When did all this happen?"

"About a week ago."

The old man glances at his head goon Ethan, who nods

and turns away. "Ethan will check in with some of our contacts to verify your story."

I nod distractedly, wringing my hands together. "We have to figure out a way to get the spell web out of her, and create a new one that doesn't rely on dragon energy to sustain itself," I say, my words all jumbled and in a rush.

His sharp eyes watch me closely. They're a similar icy blue to Ethan, his big goon, so I'd guess they're related somehow. "You are sure of your facts?" he says.

"I'm sure that Mei is dying. I saw it for myself. And I'm sure that with no host, the spell web will die as well. Unless we can find a way to get it out of her or make a new one." We have to find Mei to do any of this, but I don't mention that right now.

"You think you could do that?"

I try to give off a certainty I don't feel. "I'm good with science. I have magic. I'm good at fixing things. There's a good chance I could do it."

"Better chance than most, I'd say," Mr. Fookes puts in.

The old mountain super keeps staring at me. Up close his skin looks like chiseled rock, and sitting next to him is like being next to a mountain. It's strangely soothing. His solid presence makes everything else seem small and insignificant. Like maybe the problems that I thought were so big aren't that big after all.

"Stop that," says Mr. Fookes sharply.

I blink. The soothing feeling abruptly stops, and my problems appear again. "What did you do?" I ask, annoyed I fell for it so easily.

"You seemed upset. Fraught. I was just trying to let you know that no problem is too big for us to solve. Nothing is too much for us to survive."

"What about a demon plague? Or an arrogant SIG

85

director who thinks it would be fun to create and control demons in order to make money?"

"What?" The old man's craggy features are knotted into a look of confusion.

"Director Holden is working with Connor McKenzie—a billionaire obsessed with demon energy—and Dr. Green—who likes to experiment on supers for kicks—to create more demons. They think they can control them and use them as a power source." I think of what my father and Connor told me at the power plant. "Maybe even as a source for a new spell web."

"How do you know this? What do you know of demons?" he asks suspiciously.

I take a breath, trying to calm myself. I feel like I'm about to admit something that has the potential to harm my cause. "My birth name is Hazel Zoya. My birth parents were Arabella and Gavan Zoya, and I'm a chalice."

The old man's whole body rocks back. His face is more pale than marble. "*You're* the chalice?" He looks at the pin on my jacket pocket. "So that isn't just an accident? You're really the chalice?"

I blink, unprepared for his reaction. "You say that like you've heard of me."

"We heard through our networks there was a new chalice. I didn't connect the dots fast enough."

"People were talking about me?" My voice squeaks a little at the idea that I'm a topic on the rumor mill.

He looks amused. "Only in a vague sense. No specifics."

"What were they saying?"

"That you're Gavan's daughter. And your powers are stronger than his."

I wince. "I bet he'd hate that rumor if he heard it."

"Oh yes. Gavan's not known for playing well with others."

"So do you believe me now?" I ask impatiently. It's the only reason I told him who I am. "You believe there's a threat?"

"Let's just say I'm considering it. I could possibly be more of a help to you with regards to your chalice powers. Your mother used to spend some time here. I was able to watch her first hand using her powers."

I blink, my brain switching from the spell web to my desire to know more about my chalice powers. "I'd like that. I was raised away from anyone who could help me learn about my powers."

"We were deeply saddened by your mother Arabella's death." He bows his head for a moment, and I feel the sadness coming from him, almost like an invisible mist. "She was a wonderful woman."

"Thank you," I say awkwardly. "I didn't know her. I was raised by a friend of hers, Anton Miller."

"Ah yes, Anton. I knew him well. What happened to him? He disappeared after Arabella's death."

My heart surges up inside my chest, making me feel like I'm at the top of a rollercoaster, about to go down the first massive hill. *He knew my dad.* "He took me away. Raised me in secret. He said I had enemies and he needed to keep me safe." It's been a long time since I thought so much about my father. This day has been full of surprises.

"That may well have been true," he says with a nod. "Your mother was kind. She saw the best in people. Didn't like to hurt anyone. But she also had some radical ideas." His tone holds an element of disapproval.

"You sound like you didn't entirely approve of her ideas?"

The old mountain super shrugs one shoulder. "She believed she had an important mission in life."

I lean forward. "Was that why she married Gavan? I've been told it wasn't because she loved him, like Gavan says."

"She did everything for a reason, so I'm sure marrying Gavan had a purpose. It wasn't because she fell in love with him."

I nod absently. This is all information I already know, but it's good to have it confirmed. "Is Gavan in town now?" I glance around like my birth father is going to pop out from one of the bowling lanes.

"Not that I'm aware of. I've been told that he has abandoned his usual post at the Grill for a new top-secret project."

"Yeah, destroying the world," I mutter.

"He's involved in this?"

"Of course he is. He's the one telling them he can create a new spell web if they find him the demons to do it."

"Then we better help you with this project."

"Just like that? I thought you weren't sure."

"Gavan is one of the few people who might just be capable of doing what you're telling me he's going to do."

"Full disclosure," I say, trying not to wince, because I know this might change things. "The Mountain King Carrick is really angry with me right now. He's kinda not speaking to me."

"Why?" asks the old man, his face more curious than horrified.

"I chose to honor a promise I made to Mr. Fookes, instead of finding and saving Mei," I say. I'm half expecting him to change his mind.

"That just makes me like you more, my dear," says the old man, a twinkle in his eyes.

TWELVE

"Do you really—"

Suddenly everything around me goes weird.

I can't take a breath, and I can't move. It's almost like the air around us has crystallized, and instead of a gas, it's hardened into a solid. Except not solid like concrete, more like we've been shoved inside a giant tub of kid's see-through goo. But the consistency doesn't matter, because I can't breathe, and I'm choking from lack of air.

I look for Mr. Fookes, fear stuck like a bone in my chest. He looks just as surprised as I am, and just as stuck. My little demon is bouncing around inside my stomach, like it can tell something is wrong. I reach up with my arm, and it's like I'm pushing through thick slime or mud. I can only just get my arm to move and it's slow, hard going. I'm already feeling dizzy, the lack of air affecting me. I try to hold my breath, to force myself to stop trying to gasp in air that doesn't exist. My eyes are watering with the effort.

Was this meeting an elaborate trap after all? Is this a mountain super power that I didn't know about? I try to see where the mountain supers are. Can they breathe? My brain is on fire, in full panic mode. If I can just get to one of them, maybe I can do something—

Except as I move closer to him, I notice the old super is stuck in one place too, struggling to breathe through the slime that's surrounding us. His goons nearby are gasping just as much as I am. The old man's not even physically strong enough to push through the slime like I can. His face is going red, and if he doesn't get to breathe soon, he's going to keel over.

We all are.

So it's not the mountain supers. Who's doing this? How do we fight them? I look around, trying to find the source of this terrifying new power. I push myself to standing; it's not easy, especially when my body is fighting the lack of oxygen.

I peer through the murkiness, to see if it's affecting anyone else in the bowling alley. I can't see past the people in my immediate vicinity. It's like we're inside an enormous blob of semitransparent glue. I've never felt so vulnerable in my life, and that's saying something. I just hope that it's not going to just go hard and leave us inside it like we're insects in a resin display. Worst thing is that there's nothing I could do about it, if that's what's about to happen.

The little demon is pushing images at me, fast and furious, and I can't quite catch any of them. All except one. A fuzzy interpretation of the director, standing at the SIG, yelling at me.

It this the director? Did he find us already? I want to scream with frustration. Surely this isn't it? Surely this can't be where my journey ends? The little demon is pushing at me, prodding me into action, but darkness is starting to cover the edges of my vision, and my lungs are in agony. I desperately wish I was with Blade, somewhere peaceful and easy, not battling my enemies at every turn.

I never got to tell him "I love you", and it's one of the biggest regrets of my life. What if I die here and now, and he never knows? I should've text it to him. I should've told him this morning in bed. All I want to do is gasp in a breath, but there's nothing to breathe in. Tiny dots of light appear in my vision. If the slime wasn't keeping me standing, I think I would have collapsed to the ground by now.

And that's when I notice something else important about this slime. It's draining away my power, sucking at the deep well of energy inside me. Instinctively I try to grab with my hands—I'm not sure what I think I'm grabbing at —as if I can stop my power leaving my body. I'm an empty shell of my usual self, half blind, unable to breathe, my power almost completely gone.

If this is really the director, then it's stealing my powers like the spell web. Is he using Mei and the spell web? If he is, it's a distorted version where the person stealing our supernatural powers doesn't care how much we're harmed in the process.

Or perhaps Gavan and Connor have already created the new spell web using demons? Maybe this isn't Mei at all, maybe this is the new distorted demon spell web. Is this what we'll be in for from now on? The thought is enough to send me over the edge into hysteria, except I can't actually do anything that energetic. My body has seized up.

I let out a strange strangled noise that would have been a sob if I could've gasped in a breath. This is it. We're done for.

And then just as suddenly as it appeared, the see-through slime disappears. I fall forward onto the floor, crash landing on my hands and knees and gasping for breath. I hear the sound of people around me hitting the ground in the same way. Everything aches, like I've just been battered by angry orangutans with baseball bats. I'm still seeing stars.

I just concentrate on sucking the air into my lungs. I never noticed how good it feels, how much my body needs the air to survive. Despite the pain, it feels amazing to breathe again.

I'm never taking it for granted again.

Eventually I look up. Everyone else is gasping in breaths of sweet, fresh air as well. The old super looks pale, the lines on his face standing out more than they did a few minutes ago.

Mr. Fookes is crouching over Daphne, his hand protectively on her back. She's on her hands and knees like me, gasping for breath. I look further afield, trying to see if there's anyone who could have done that to us. Everything looks normal, the humans happily bowling like they haven't a care in the world.

Where did it come from? The director? Connor and Gavan? It's frustrating to have no answers. The biggest question is, can they do it again? Will they steal all our powers? My heart is thumping in my chest, and I take another gasping breath, trying to calm myself down so I can think clearly.

Panic won't help. Information will. I need to find out what that was, and if there's some way to stop it ever happening again.

I hope there's a way to stop that from ever happening again.

"What just happened?" I manage to croak out. I look at the old super next to me. He's the most likely to know.

But he shakes his head. "I'm not sure. It's nothing I've

ever experienced in my lifetime."

I hesitate, but I need to know if it affected everyone the same way. "It took my power," I say.

He nods. "Mine too. Not permanently. I can feel it coming back even now, as we talk."

He's right. I can feel my power flowing back into me. It's a revelation to me how much the thought of losing my powers permanently scares me. I might be afraid of it, but I definitely don't want to be without it.

"Anyone know what it was?"

"Something that stole all our powers," mutters Mr. Fookes. "Remind anyone of anything?"

"The spell web?" says the old super sharply. His eyes immediately go to Ethan, his favorite goon. Some kind of look passes between them that I can't even begin to interpret.

"It's never felt like that before," I say. "And it never took so much of our powers."

"What else can steal our powers like that? From all of us at once time?" says Mr. Fookes.

"There isn't some other kind of super I don't know about?" I ask him hopefully.

"Nothing I've seen in all my years as a genie. It didn't feel quite the same as the spell web, but it definitely did the same thing. It was someone who was looking for a power surge. Someone who wants to steal our powers for their own benefit."

"Someone like the director," I mutter.

"We need to get out of here," says the old mountain super suddenly. "This is too public a place for this kind of discussion." He stands up, his ancient bones audibly creaking. Ethan immediately leaps to his side, intending to help him, but the old man waves him away. "I can still manage."

Ethan backs away about a step, but he stays beside the old man and looks ready to catch him if he falls. "Follow us," says Ethan begrudgingly. He's not exactly welcoming, but we need the mountain supers for information. We can't give up now.

They lead us to the back of the bowling alley, and for the first time, I notice a small door in a dimly lit corner. It looks like it goes back outside the alley, and there's a sign on the door "Staff only. Do Not Enter." I feel the pressure of a spell, and a really strong desire to head back into the main bowling area. I push past it and follow Ethan and the old man, who opens the door like he doesn't even feel the spell that I'm forcing myself past.

I'm expecting the doorway to lead outside, but there's a narrow corridor that runs to the left that leads us along the front of the building, and around the side. It's a hidden entrance. Outside sounds are muted, and all I hear is our breathing and our footfalls as we tread on the hardwood floors. It's like we're a million miles from the bowling alley, not a few feet.

Everything seems a little blurry, and I'm pretty sure there's another spell on this corridor that's going to make it hard to remember exactly where it is and how we got through it.

It gives the mountain supers a huge amount of control over us. I feel a shiver of fear in my chest. I hope this isn't some kind of elaborate trap.

I hope we can trust them.

Maybe they're friends with my birth father? Maybe he's convinced them to kidnap me, instead of helping me find out what I need to know. I stumble over my own feet, only just keeping myself standing.

Dammit. No one even knows where we are. I should

have told Blade exactly where we were before we came into the bowling alley. Now, if we never return, no one will ever know where to search for us.

But we have no choice. This is the best and only way we have to find out more about the spell web. They didn't say they wouldn't help. They just haven't said they *will*.

I have to keep moving forward. It's the only way to find a way through this mess. I keep walking, my body on automatic as I follow the two mountain supers ahead of me. Mr. Fookes and Daphne are just behind. I resist the urge to turn around and freak out.

Eventually we come to another door. This one painted black, like a warning of what's to come when we pass through it.

The old super turns to me. "This is not somewhere we bring guests lightly. It is only because of the seriousness of this situation—because of what just happened in the bowling alley—that I'm bringing you in here."

I nod, trying to keep the surprise off my face. What does he think is happening here? I guess maybe not the kidnapping I was just imagining.

"I must have a vow of secrecy. You must promise here and now that you will never tell anyone about this entrance and never lead our enemies back to this place."

"I promise," I say, turning back to look at the others.

"I promise too," says Daphne. She sounds awed.

"As do I," says Mr. Fookes, his dark eyes watching the old super with an intensity that he doesn't usually show.

"Then we proceed. Follow me."

I don't have time to think any more about it. He's opening the door, and there's only darkness ahead of me.

Taking a breath, I follow them toward the door.

CHAPTER

THIRTEEN

I hesitate at the threshold.

I can't see anything past the doorway, only more blackness. What if this is a trap? What if we've walked right into my father's arms? Or some other more sinister person? Who has the power to change the very air around us into goo?

Except they were in the see-through slime too. The old supernatural man looked like he'd been hit by a truck. They wouldn't do that to themselves. Surely?

I have no other choice. This is our first and best clue to finding out more information about what just happened, as well as the spell web. I take a step through the door into the darkness.

The coldness hits me first, and I shiver. There's blackness all around, with a twinkling of lights overhead. Glow worms, I think. What is this place? It takes a few moments for my eyes to adjust, and then I start seeing shapes around me. First Ethan and the old super. Then others. Except it's not people. The shapes around us are jagged boulders, rocks, and other natural formations. We're in some kind of natural tunnel, and it leads off down into the earth.

Mr. Fookes and Daphne follow me in, and we stand together, looking around.

"This looks natural," says Mr. Fookes.

"It is. It's the entrance my clan has used into our underground home for centuries. We just moved with the times when it came to the above ground entrance. Plus I like ten pin bowling." The old super is already looking much better than he did before. He has the spring back in his step, and his eyes are bright again. Is it something to do with being underground? Or just that his power is coming back? Whatever the case, he's recovering faster than I am.

He turns and heads along the stone corridor, which slopes gently downward. The only light is from the glow worms over our heads. Strangely it's enough once my eyes have properly adjusted.

We're heading down, but so far it's a gradual slope and nothing too scary. The corridor is massive, intended for the much larger shapes of mountain supers, so we have no difficulty walking along it. The path under our feet is smooth and easy.

The tunnel feels... solid. Muted somehow, like there's something in here that's blocking out the rest of the world. It could be thousands of years in the past, and we'd never know it. It feels out of time, timeless perhaps. It's all special, somehow. Like we're being given some kind of treat that isn't given to just anyone.

I hope my instincts about this place are right. Because if this is a trap, it's going to be difficult to get back out again without help.

We keep walking for what seems like forever, but it's probably only a half hour or so. The trail is getting steeper and steeper, and there's now a rail to one side to help keep us on our feet. I hear the occasional sound of water dripping, but mostly it's just our scuffing feet, and the sound of breathing. The old super doesn't talk and neither does anyone else. It doesn't feel right. This place feels sacred somehow, like we're trespassing somewhere only the gods dare go.

Eventually, the path widens, and there's a light visible at the end. Everything gradually brightens, and the sense of walking too close to something we shouldn't lessens. As we walk toward the light, my eyes adjust, and I can make out people walking around past the edge of the tunnel. In the background... is that windows carved into the walls?

We arrive at the end of the tunnel, pausing on the edge. I stare out into the enormous space in front of me, my eyes wide like I'm a kid at a candy store. It's an underground village, carved into the rocks deep inside the earth. I've never seen anything like it.

Everyone is dressed in normal clothes, as if this is just some street up on the surface. Only difference is they're all mountain supers—if their average size is anything to go by —and they're all smiling and laughing in a way I've never seen mountain supers above ground doing.

"What is this place?" I ask, gazing around in wonder.

"It's Firasus. The First Village."

"Are we allowed down here?" says Mr. Fookes. "Don't we need permission from the First Elder?"

"You already have his permission," says Ethan dryly, nodding his head at the old super who's been leading us this whole way.

Based on Mr. Fookes's shock, I'm guessing this is a huge deal. I don't know about mountain supers and how their world works, but it seems the First Elder is a big deal.

"Is he higher up than the Mountain King?" I whisper to Mr. Fookes. I know that Carrick is the Mountain King, and he was a pretty big deal.

It's Ethan who answers: "He's older than the Mountain King. More powerful. The Mountain King deals with the politics of leading the mountain supers. The First Elder is the power source."

I'm still not one hundred percent sure I understand the difference, but I nod like I do.

I take another quick glance at the old super, and discover he's watching me, his ice-blue eyes amused. "It's a complicated system," he says. "Outsiders often struggle to understand it."

"So where are we taking them, Elder?" asks Ethan. Down here he seems more relaxed. Less on edge and goon-like than he was up in the bowling alley. Perhaps he was just guarding a precious individual from possible threats?

"To the main hall. I want to talk with the chalice and to see what the Elder Council thinks."

He takes off up the street. Everyone stops and says hello to him, moving out of his way when he indicates he's on a mission. It's like there's an invisible line of power around him, drawing people in, making them want to be around him.

I'm standing just watching the elder when Mr. Fookes nudges me from behind. "Come on. We need to follow him, or we'll get left behind."

I start walking, and they both fall in beside me. "What is this place?" I ask. "It seemed like you'd heard of it?"

"It's not well known. Mountain supers are notoriously secretive. But it's their place of origin. Almost every mountain super can trace their family back to this one place. It's the source of their power." He glances around like he's trying to take it all in. "I'm surprised they brought us here. It's usually forbidden to outsiders."

Fear shivers along my skin. "Why did he do it, then?"

"I think something about what happened up in the bowling alley must have scared him. I know it scared me," says Mr. Fookes.

"What scares an ancient, powerful elder?" I ask, eyes wide.

"Someone able to reach in and steal your power?" suggests Daphne quietly. Her eyes are shadowed, and for the first time, I notice the bags under her eyes. She looks like she's about ten years older than she was when she climbed in the SUV this morning.

Mr. Fookes nods, agreeing with her. "I don't think anyone liked that experience very much." He leans in and whisper closer to me, "My power isn't returning in the same strength as it was before. I'm much weakened."

"Mine is coming back, but I don't have any convenient demons to give me anything to work with," I whisper back.

"So we're essentially at their mercy," says Mr. Fookes. "Let's hope they want to help us, not hurt us."

We walk on in silence. It's a big thing to hope for.

All around us, mountain supers stop and stare like we're an outlandish circus act. I guess non-mountain supers must be a rare event, given the way they're checking us out. The further we go along the street, the louder the silence gets, until it seems like everyone is yelling at us inside their heads.

"I feel like we're in one of those old western movies, where outsiders come into town and are terrible pariahs," whispers Daphne.

"Yep. Or some spooky kind of sci-fi horror movie. If we

get chopped up and buried in the basement, I'm going to be so annoyed," I whisper back.

Up ahead, the elder has stopped walking and turned back in our direction, watching us. He glances at his watch, and his foot twitches like he's thinking of starting to tap it.

"I think we're going too slow for him," I say.

"He's got a point. We need to get this sorted before it happens again."

"Did it affect the people down here?" I ask looking around. "They don't seem too bothered."

"I heard rumors that it was too far down into the earth to be affected by the spell web down here. But that's just an old story, I don't know if it's true."

"Why do they ever come up to the surface, if that's the case?" I ask.

"The bowling?" says Daphne with a grin.

CHAPTER

FOURTEEN

We catch up to the First Elder and his men, and he leads us along a rocky path to a large, arched doorway. There's no door, and we walk straight into the foyer of the structure.

Three wooden doors, one on either side and one directly in front of us, lead off to who knows where.

"We need to talk to the other councillors," says the First Elder. "I've sent messengers to bring them all here, but they're all old, so it'll take a while. In the meantime, come with me."

He leads us into the room to the left, and I follow him into a large kitchen space filled with a delicious aroma. There's a large wooden table in the middle, and kitchen appliances along both walls. Everything is just a little too big for me to feel comfortable using it, but it's just the right size for the mountain supers.

There's a tall woman standing next to a stovetop, stirring something in a large pot. The source of the delicious smell, perhaps. I can't decide what it is, something... tangy? Savory but sweet?

"This is Alvera. She'll get you some food and drink while I go locate those we need for this meeting." He nods, first at Alvera and then at me, Mr. Fookes, and Daphne. Then he disappears out another door at the other end of the kitchen, much faster than his hunched frame should be able to move.

I look at Alvera, still trying to decipher what she's cooking. My taste buds are watering. She's wearing a no-nonsense white apron over a flower-covered dress. Her long brown hair is in a ponytail at her nape, and she hasn't stopped stirring whatever's cooking in the pot.

She looks us up and down. "What can I get you?" Her voice is stern.

"What are you cooking?" I blurt out. "It smells amazing."

She smiles at me, clearly more amused than annoyed at my inability to answer politely. "It'll be the mix of the bread in the oven"—she nods in the direction of the large oven—"and the tomato soup I'm making. It's an old family recipe. Passed down mother to daughter."

"I've never smelled anything so..." I flap my arm, trying to think of the right word, "amazing." I finish lamely, repeating myself.

"If you wait about ten minutes, I can give you some of both. I have enough, you're only tiny."

My stomach rumbles, and I put a hand over it. "I'd love that."

"I'd love a coffee if you have some," says Mr. Fookes, stepping forward to stand next to me and smiling at Alvera.

She nods him. "Of course, I'll see to it." She glances over at Daphne, her eyebrows raised. "What would you like?"

"Can I have one as well?" asks Daphne. She's looking around at the kitchen like she's a kid in a candy store. "Do you mind if I take a closer look around your kitchen?" she adds.

Alvera narrows her eyes at Daphne for a moment, but she clearly can't see anything to indicate Daphne is joking or being sarcastic. "Sure. Look all you like," she says. She waves her arm around the room, then starts bustling about, making the coffees.

Daphne wanders forward, eyes darting around the room, like she's trying to memorize it. She peers into the front of the oven, to look at the bread. "Oh, you've twisted it. I always wanted to know how to do that." Her voice is wistful.

"It's not difficult. I can show you, if you're still here when my next batch has risen," says Alvera with a shrug.

"That would be wonderful," says Daphne, her eyes shining like she's been given a massive treat. Daphne keeps reminding me that she missed out on a huge chunk of life, being locked away in Ravenwood for so long. I truly hope we're still here for the twisting of the bread.

I watch as Daphne wanders around the kitchen, poking her nose into the cupboards like she's a judge in a best-kitchen-of-the-year competition. I can't get over the difference between this Daphne here and now—excited by a new kitchen and google-eyed for Mr. Fookes—and the woman I met at Ravenwood.

"I knew your mother, you know," says Alvera. She's watching me from where she's standing next to the stove, stirring the pot. "You look just like her."

I shake my head, embarrassed. "Oh no. I've seen a picture. My mother was beautiful," I say. I'm nothing like the sultry woman in the photo. I push my glasses up my nose as if to prove my point.

"You're just like her," Alvera repeats firmly. "For a long

time, I thought you'd died in the car crash with her. I was pleased when the rumors of your re-emergence started to circulate."

Again, I'm squeamish at the idea that there were rumors in the supernatural community about me. "Thank you," I say. "Did you know her well?"

"We were on the same bowling team," says Alvera with a small smile. "We won a trophy together."

"The one on the wall in the bowling alley?" I say.

Alvera nods. "She was very competitive. Liked to achieve."

"Was she..." I swallow hard. I don't know quite how to ask the question. "Was she a good person?"

"Of course. I wouldn't have been friends with her otherwise."

"Then why did she marry my father?" I blurt out. It's not exactly the most polite question to ask, and I realize belatedly that perhaps Alvera might have been friends with my father.

But instead she says, "You've met your father, then?" with a grimace.

I let out the breath I was holding. "Yes. And he's..."

"Not the nicest person?"

"Yeah." *That's putting it mildly.*

Alvera looks away from me, into the pot she's still stirring. The smell of the soup wafts through the kitchen—rich tomatoes, fresh herbs and something creamy as the base—and despite everything, my mouth starts watering.

"A couple of years before she died, something happened," says Alvera quietly. "I don't know quite what. But your mother, she changed. She became even more... focused. Less able to just relax and live life. She was suddenly interested in other chalices, and flew to Europe to meet with different chalice families. When she returned home, she had Gavan tagging along with her."

"Was he... better... back then?"

"He made more of an effort to be charming with Arabella's friends and family in the beginning," says Alvera, but there's a note in her voice that says she was never one of the people who liked him.

"Can you tell me—"

The door down at the far end of the kitchen opens. Ethan pokes his head through the door. "The elders are all here and ready to see you," he says. His voice is still disapproving.

"Thanks," I say, looking wistfully at Alvera and the pot of tomato soup. I want to ask her more about my mother. And we didn't even get a chance to taste the soup.

"I'll bring some out to you," says Alvera, catching my look. "And the coffees."

Daphne clears her throat. "Do you mind if I stick around here? Maybe help with the food preparation?" She looks at me and Mr. Fookes. "You two know what you're doing. You don't need me there."

Mr. Fookes frowns, but he nods. "If that's what you want to do, it's fine by me."

"Sure," I say. "If that's what you'd prefer." I look at her intently, trying to make sure something's not going on, that she's not staying out of the meeting for some other reason. But she genuinely seems more excited about being in the kitchen with Alvera than talking to the elders.

In some ways, so would I. Especially if it involved getting some of that soup.

Mr. Fookes gives Daphne a quick hug, whispering something in her ear. Then we leave her to follow Ethan through the far door in the kitchen. He leads us down a dark hallway, his hulking shape leading the way. Should we really have left Daphne on her own in the kitchen? Everything seemed bright and nice in the kitchen. Now I'm getting tense, angry vibes from Ethan and being led down another hallway into darkness. But before I can decide to run back the way we came, Ethan comes to an abrupt halt in front of a door.

"We talked to an informant inside the SIG and it was definitely the spell web," says Ethan, glaring at me as if it's my fault. "It seems to have been done at Director Holden's orders. They were warned and told to prepare themselves for it."

"Shit," I say. "That's bad." I can't believe they found a way to force Mei to use the spell web.

"Yeah, it is. But that doesn't mean you get to keep the First Elder up all hours of the night. Don't overstimulate him, don't tire him out. If I think you're pushing him too hard, I'll break every bone in your body."

His stern words reassure me more than gentle ones could have, and I let out a breath. Mr. Fookes and I both nod; I'm not sure we have much control over whether the First Elder is overstimulated or not, but at least I'm more sure that this isn't some elaborate trap.

CHAPTER
FIFTEEN

than opens the door and leads us through into a large meeting room that's been carved out of the rock. Yet again, it feels solid. Connected to something greater than we are, like the mountain supers were somehow able to create a connection to the very earth when they were building their homes.

It feels warm, welcoming. It even makes me smile, despite everything, and when I see the relaxed faces of the people already in the room—four men, two women—I wonder if there's some kind of spell on the room to make it like this.

"Welcome, Hazel," says the First Elder. "Come in." He turns to Mr. Fookes. "And I was never properly introduced to your genie friend." He holds out his hand to Mr. Fookes.

"Mr. Fookes," says the genie.

"That's an awfully formal name to keep calling you," says the First Elder with a friendly twinkle in his eyes. "I'll give you my name, if you give me yours?"

Mr. Fookes gives an amused snort. "I'm fairly certain

you're aware that if I gave you my real first name it would give you power over me."

I look to the ceiling and try not to give away the fact that I know his first name from when we first did the power of three with Freddie. How much power does it actually give me over him? It makes me uncomfortable that I know something that has the capacity to harm Mr. Fookes.

The First Elder shrugs. "I had to try. I don't give out my name for similar reasons." He leans in closer to us, his bright eyes twinkling. "There's also the fact my mother was not blessed with an ability to name children. She gave me the most terrible of first names. It was a relief to make it to First Elder and be rid of it."

I smile, liking this old man almost despite myself. I wonder how much of that feeling of warmth and goodness is a result of whatever spells they've attached to the room. I glance at Mr. Fookes—he's the one who felt the magic back in the bowling alley and told them to stop. He seems relaxed and not bothered by the atmosphere. Maybe I'm just being overly suspicious.

The First Elder glances behind us. "There was a third member of your party?"

"Daphne stayed with Alvera in the kitchen. She's more comfortable there," says Mr. Fookes with a shrug.

"Alvera will take good care of her. Come, sit with us. The others wish to meet you."

We walk forward, and the council members stand up, nodding their heads in our direction. They're all very elderly, more wrinkles than not on their ancient faces.

"These are the elders of the First Village, the oldest mountain supers in existence. We have seen much in our time," says the First Elder, gesturing around the room.

"Too much, I sometimes think," mutters one of the men.

"It's lovely to meet you all," I say politely. I shake hands with the woman closest to me, her skin papery thin against my hand. She smiles and nods at me. She's at least two feet taller than me, but I still get the sense that she's bowed and shrunken from what she was when she was younger.

"I'm Mariam," she says. "I'm not afraid to give my name." She spares a glance at the First Elder. "Unlike some."

"You already *know* my name," says the First Elder. "It's not like I'm hiding something from *you*."

It feels like this is an old argument between friends, so I smile at her and ignore their banter. "Lovely to meet you, Mariam. I'm Hazel."

"We've been hearing about your exploits."

Exploits? "Nothing too bad, I hope." I'm so used to living under the radar that hearing people are talking about me makes me edgy.

"No, nothing bad."

She steps aside and I go around the room, shaking hands with each of the other elders and gathering their names. Jorges is the tallest of the men, and his green eyes seem to burn into me. Ridge is stocky and solid, his face round and the craggiest. Jacken is bent over and walks with a stick, but his handshake is firm.

The last is Hattie. Everything about her is crooked, from her fingers to her spine. She's so bent over, I'm not sure how she's still standing. She's a fraction taller than me, and when she turns blue-white eyes in my direction, and I realize she's also blind. Despite that, somehow she seems to know where to look to see directly into my eyes. Perhaps she's not so blind after all?

"*Lucem in tenebras,*" she says softly.

"Pardon?" I say, trying not to sound as stupid as I feel.

"The words on your pin. The chalice motto. Bring light into the darkness."

I smooth one hand over the pin on my lapel. How did she even know it was there? There are latin words around the edge, and as I peer down, I see she's right. *Lucem in tenebras* is inscribed on the pin. "That's what it means? Bring light into the darkness?"

"Yes. It's an apt phrase to represent those tasked with the burden of chalice powers."

"You think we bring light to the darkness?" I'm hooked by her words. It's the complete opposite of being evil, which was my fear for a long time.

"Certainly. It's your responsibility to bring light into the darkness, and reset the world," she says softly, her words echoing. "You met my great grandson Carlos when you were at the SIG headquarters, I think?"

I blink at the abrupt change of direction. "Carlos is related to you?"

"He speaks very highly of you. Says you're someone we can trust."

"He's your informant?" I say, realization dawning.

"He's a good boy. Lets us know when something is happening that we should know about."

"He's great," I agree. "Carlos was my favorite person while I was at SIG Headquarters."

"He said you didn't have an easy time while you were there."

I make a face at Hattie and then realize she can't see me. Probably. "I ended up being thrown in prison by the director, so no, it wasn't easy."

"You're vital to the outcome of all this. The demon cycle

is nearing its crescendo, but the demons will win if you do not find yourself." She says the words in a monotone, like it's coming from somewhere else, and she's just the conduit.

I stare at her. "Huh?" Her words have my heart jumping, and the hairs on my arms rising up. "What do you mean?" The little demon inside me starts to skitter around unpleasantly.

"You're lost. You do not know. But you need to know in order to win this battle." Again, her voice doesn't sound like it's hers.

"What don't I know?" I hate riddles. I like a problem that I can fix, sure, and mechanics that have a logical way of being put together. Not things that seem foggy and make no sense at all.

"I cannot explain the words. I just speak the truth to all."

I glance back at Mr. Fookes, who just shrugs at me. "I don't understand. I'm not lost. I'm right here. That's not logical." *What the hell does she mean?*

The First Elder pats me on the shoulder and draws me away from Hattie. "Just ignore her," he says softly. "It's a bit hit and miss these days. In her day, she was a powerful seer. Now..." He glances back over his shoulder, his expression sad. "It seems she is less reliable."

I nod, although I felt the power in Hattie's words, even if I couldn't understand them. And I want her to be right about the chalice motto. Could she be telling the truth? If there's something I need to do to beat the demons, then I'll do it. I just don't know what she means by *finding myself.*

"Come, sit here. We have much to discuss. Ethan told you that it was the spell web that attacked us?"

I nod solemnly. I don't know what to say.

The First Elder pulls out a chair at the large, round table in the room, and everyone takes a seat. Mr. Fookes is next to me, and the First Elder is on my other side.

"Now tell us everything," says the First Elder. "We need all the information we can get if we're going to survive this."

CHAPTER
SIXTEEN

" ... **S**o Blade and Freddie are looking for ways to find Mei, and I'm hunting down ways to get the spell web out of Mei for when we find her, so it won't kill her," I say. "Plus how to recreate a new one to replace it if we need to."

My throat is sore from talking and answering the questions they've been shooting at me. For a table of crazy elders, they're all very sharp. Even Hattie seems different; mentally sharper than she seemed earlier.

Right now, their faces are grim. It's a heavy topic, and we're being hit by problems on multiple sides. I've known for a while about the demon plague that Connor is trying to create, but it's scary to hear about it for the first time. Let alone learning that the spell web is dying, and that Director Holden is a dirty, sneaky rat.

They're doing pretty well considering.

"So this man... this Connor... wants to become all powerful?" asks Mariam.

"And he thinks demons are the best way to go about

that?" adds Ridge. He's got a huge nose and is looking down it at me.

I nod. "He's not a full super. I think he's obsessed by gathering more power because he feels inferior to full supernaturals."

Mariam shakes her head. "Men and their egos."

Jacken glares at her. "Stop being so sexist, you old bat."

I blink. Should I defend Miriam's honor or...?

But she just makes a face at him. "I'll stop being sexist when men stop causing problems, you smelly old hobbit."

Jacken does seem to be the shortest of them all, so I guess the hobbit dig is probably valid. He's still at least a couple of feet taller than me.

"Who're you calling smelly?" says Jacken indignantly, ruining the effect by sniffing under his arm. "I had a bath just last week."

"Anyway," I say loudly to stop Mariam from replying. "Any help you could give me would be appreciated."

"Your mother had a theory," says the First Elder slowly. "She talked to me about it once, not long before she died. She thought the chalice line was being wiped out on purpose."

"But who would do that?" I say, indignantly. It's hard to comprehend having an enemy who doesn't even know me. But then I remember Connor's mother, and how she colluded with Dr. Green. That was for my chalice magic and nothing else. Maybe it's not so incomprehensible.

"She didn't know. But her theory had some validity. There are only two known chalices currently in North America—you and your father. At one time, there were more than thirty. I don't know for certain about Asia, Europe or Africa, but I understand from our networks that it's the same. If the number of chalices is down by such a large number, then it's no wonder there are more demons."

I hadn't thought of it like that. "So you think it's not Connor doing it? You think it's just because there are fewer chalices to control the population?"

"Perhaps. Although I doubt your friend Connor is helping the situation."

"I think my father believed my life was in danger, too. That's why he took me away and raised me in secret," I say.

"There are too many coincidences for it to be entirely accidental," agrees the First Elder. "I'm sorry, my dear. There's a chance Arabella was murdered."

I take a deep breath, trying to take in what he's saying, even though this isn't the first time that idea has been mentioned to me. I'm not sure how I'm supposed to react to it. I didn't know my birth mother, so it's more like a vague feeling of having lost out on something that might have been good.

More concerning is what it means for us right now. "Why would someone be killing off chalices?"

"It has to be something to do with the demons, but we don't know what."

Mr. Fookes sits up straighter. "The problem with all of this is that it's just a theory. We have no proof that anyone killed Hazel's birth mother. And quite honestly it's not the more pressing concern on our plate at the moment."

I nod. "He's right. We have too many other problems right now to even be worried about some potential one. I need access to your records to see if there's any mention of how to get the spell web out of someone without breaking it, or how to create a new one."

"Records?" says the First Elder. "We have no records. Simply us," he gestures to the group in front of me.

A long time ago Mei told me that mountain supers only use verbal records. They pass their stories down from one generation to the next, and that's how they knew all the information they needed to know. At the time, I remember thinking how ridiculous that was. Memory is fallible, able to be broken or changed.

To be fair, I still think that, even though I was desperately asking him for access to any verbal stories when we were back at the bowling alley. "What about written records?" I ask, just in case.

The First Elder smiles at me like I'm a child, which I probably am in comparison to him. Still, it's annoying.

"We don't have written records. Our verbal records are sufficient," he says.

I can't help my scientist's reaction. Memories passed down verbally? Not likely. "Brains are fallible," I say, trying to hold in my impatience. "Memories change over time, get embellished. It's not entirely... efficient." *Or accurate.* I let out a huff of breath. Who knows if what these people remember is actually the truth of what happened in the past?

"Mountain memories are different," says the First Elder. He still looks amused.

I feel a shiver of magic pass over my skin, and I look around, trying to figure out who is trying to use their powers on me. The entire roomful of elders are all looking suspiciously innocent.

"How are they different?" I ask, giving in to the obvious question.

"Better to show you, rather than tell you."

Mr. Fookes leans toward the First Elder and clears his throat. "I don't know if that's such a good idea. You don't know how she'll react to the memories."

"She's strong. She has been judged sufficient," says the First Elder. "As have you, Mr. Fookes the genie. You will both receive the memories and use them to help you in this endeavor."

Mr. Fookes looks shocked, like he's just been told he's the winner of the Nobel Peace Prize. Something that completely knocks him out of the park.

"What's the matter," I whisper to him. "What's wrong with listening to their memories? I thought that's what we wanted?"

"Genies aren't usually considered equal status to other supers," says Mr. Fookes. "We're usually seen as tools or weapons. And we're definitely not someone other people trust."

"I trust you."

He manages a small smile. "You're not exactly normal," he says.

I grin, despite myself. "So you weren't expecting him to trust you with the memories?"

"Not like this."

The First Elder stands. "Come. We need to perform the proper ceremony. Follow me."

SEVENTEEN

roper ceremony? Why can't he just tell us their recollections here in this room? How long is this going to take? It better not be like one of those changing of the guard ceremonies at Buckingham Palace, where they prance about for half an hour when it could have been done in two minutes.

Mr. Fookes gives me a look when I stay seated a second too long, and I figure he must know what's going on. So I stand up, and we follow the First Elder to the far corner of the room, toward a door I didn't notice till now.

It's stone, carved with strange symbols and seems to emanate *weight*. I don't even understand how that could be the case.

He opens the door almost reverently, and instead of it scraping against the floor or being really noisy, it opens silently, like it's been oiled within an inch of its life. It just adds to the eerie feeling that's now wedged inside my chest. The First Elder leads the way into the room, and after a moment's hesitation, I follow him.

Inside, it's pitch black. Genuine, one hundred percent,

pitch black. I keep waiting for him to turn on the lights, but he doesn't do it. The only light is the dim glow from the doorway and the other room. I thought they were just going to tell us their stories. How does being inside a pitch-black room help with that? I'm starting to wonder if this is what I thought it would be.

"Come, further into the room," says the First Elder in a low voice. "The other elders must also fit inside."

I shuffle forward, convinced I'm about to fall into a deep pit or stand on a snake. I feel a hand grasp mine, and I let out a squeak.

"It's just me," says the First Elder. "You must seat yourself in the center of the circle."

I let him pull me toward a seat that seems to have been chiseled out of stone. I can feel a deep, dark magic coming from all angles inside the room. It tingles along my skin, making the hairs on my arms rise. My heart is pounding as I try to figure out if we can really trust these people and whatever's about to happen. My expectation of being told a few old stories around an open fire is very quickly disappearing. This is already way more intense than anything I could ever have imagined. I hesitate over the stone chair, not sure what to do.

There's something about this room and the darkness within, that has a weight of expectation on it. It feels heavier than normal darkness, more inclined to come in close, and nestle itself against my skin. It almost feels like there's another presence in here. Some kind of force that's so ancient and all-powerful we must seem like amoebas, tiny and insignificant in comparison.

Part of me recognizes the power, like it's a long lost connection I didn't know I understood until this moment. I feel it inside me, in the deep well of power that's always there. Even my little demon flutters about inside me in response. I get a sense of curiosity and interest, not fear, from the demon, so I take that as a positive.

Whatever my doubts, we need this information. Lives depend on it. And the First Elder seems like a good guy, someone I can trust. Besides, there's no going back now. I take a breath and lower myself into a sitting position on the stone chair. Mr. Fookes sits beside me, shoulder to shoulder.

"Are you sure this is a good idea?" I ask quietly. It feels like I'm shouting inside the pitch-black room and I wince.

"As good an idea as we have at the moment," he replies in an undertone.

The elders file in, creating a circle around us. I can hear their breathing, loud and scratchy more than anything else. Jorges is still by the door, and he pulls it shut, completely enveloping us all in pitch-black darkness. My heart rate kicks up a notch. It feels like the darkness is leaning in on us, a blanket made of the ancient presence that's inhabiting this room. The elders start chanting, nonsensical words that make no sense, but seem to have meaning anyway.

If we're supposed to understand what they're saying, or to take the information we need from their chants, we're screwed. I scrunch up my face, trying to understand what they're saying. Is it in French? Maybe they assumed that I could speak another language?

I glance in the direction of Mr. Fookes, but it does me no good. His leg is next to mine, and his shoulder is against my shoulder, but I can't see him. My demon is jittery inside my stomach, possibly reacting to my fear, and there's a strange smell. Smoke and... rosemary?

Are they trying to drug us? Has this been a big con to trap us? The First Elder said he knew my father—maybe he's working with Gavan and Connor after all. My fear spikes, and I try to stand, but I'm locked in place, my body no longer responding to me. I can't even talk. Or scream for help. My panic spikes, and I try to push against whatever magic is holding me in place.

The words of the chanting flow over me, adding to the layers of magic that surround us, even as I struggle to move. It reminds me of being back at Ravenwood, and I don't like it. Nothing works, my whole body is frozen, I can't even get my fingers to move. My heart is pounding unpleasantly, and I wish I'd asked more questions before blindly following a supposedly innocent old man into a dark room.

The scent of rosemary and smoke overtakes my senses, and I feel myself floating away, no longer paying attention to what's going on.

The chanting changes, and I start seeing images flashing through my head in response to the words they're saying. They're coming so fast, and there are so many of them, I can't see them on a conscious level. My little demon smashes about inside me, reacting to the onslaught. My brain starts feeling heavier and heavier, the more images flash across my mind.

This isn't what I was expecting. I thought it was going to be nice stories told in the light of the other room. I didn't realize they were going to take us on a roller coaster ride inside our own heads.

Information starts flowing into my brain, and even though I'm struggling to keep up with it, I can see that it might be useful. Shadowy people standing around a glowing orb, possibly the spell web. A time in the past with dragons, flaming everything in their path. The mountain people working with dragons to keep the peace. People I don't recognize, doing strange and wonderful things that

I'm not entirely sure I understand. Magic from the past that we've lost the ability to wield seeps into the images, and then lots of death and destruction at the hands of the lawless dragons.

The only problem is that not much of it makes sense to me. I feel like I'm on the verge of understanding, that the answers are hidden just out of reach. The answers are so close... But they may as well be a million miles away. Maybe if I could concentrate harder, focus more, I'd know more. I feel my frustration building as I try to catch hold of the images, try to make some of it make sense. My hands are clenched tight in my lap, and the smell of rosemary is burning my nostrils. Why are they making this so difficult?

I don't know if Mr. Fookes is making more sense of this than I am, but so far I still don't know how to take the spell web out of Mei, and I definitely don't know where to find her.

The images are still coming, so many images, of people I don't know, and places I've never seen. It's starting to feel uncomfortable, unpleasant. My eyes are hurting, even though it's pitch black in here. The chanting is permeating its way through my whole body, making me alternatively twitch and shiver in reaction.

I'm overwhelmed and overloaded; they're giving me too much information and I can't process it all. I need to take a break, to pause the onslaught. I'm still frozen in place, unable to move or talk. I want to scream at them, tell them it's too much, I can't take any more. The blackness seems to be closing in on me, feeling heavier, pushing at me. It feels like I'm going to be crushed under the weight of it, and I don't know how to tell them it's too much.

That it *hurts*.

I need them to *stop*.

CHAPTER
EIGHTEEN

My heart rate is accelerating, and I'm scared. Really scared.

I don't know how I'm going to survive if they keep doing this. There's too much information, too many images and thoughts and ideas.

Inside I'm screaming, and my pool of energy is choppy like there's a storm happening somewhere deep inside. I feel like I'm full to bursting. That it's too much. Maybe I'll explode into a thousand tiny little fragments—

And then it stops.

I let out a gasping breath and drag in another one, trying to suck in enough air to make me feel normal again. It doesn't work. I still can't see anything around me, but the chanting has stopped. There's now a light breeze flowing through the room that cools off my heated skin.

I don't know how long has passed, but I have a feeling it's been a while.

I try to move my arms. They're heavy, but I can lift them a little. I'm no longer trapped. I try to talk, but it comes out as a croak. I clear my throat and try again. "That wasn't... what I was expecting," I say in a low voice.

"No one ever expects it," says a voice out of the darkness. The First Elder. "That's why we have to just do it."

"How..." I clear my throat. "How... is it going to help me... figure this out?" My throat is rough and sore like I haven't spoken for days. "I don't remember any of it."

"Yes, you do. You just have to access the memories. They're in your head now."

"In my head?" My voice ends on a squeak.

"In your head," he confirms. "We've given you the collective memories of the mountain supers. It's all we have. I just hope it's enough."

I gape into the blackness of the room. I wonder what Carrick will think when the First Elder tells him what he's done. I don't think he'll be happy.

Mr. Fookes is moving restlessly beside me, but he doesn't say a word, and I can't see his face. I feel strange, like there's a giant wad of cotton inside my head instead of my brain. "How long till I feel normal again?" I ask.

"It probably won't take long for you to regain your equilibrium."

I attempt to stand, taking note of the "probably" in his sentence. "What normally happens when you put the memories into people who aren't mountain supers?" I ask. I feel wobblier than a newborn giraffe.

"We've never put the memories into someone who wasn't a mountain super," replies the First Elder, his voice careful.

I sit back down again. "What?" The darkness is heavy around me and the scent of rosemary hangs in the air.

"It's against our beliefs to let outsiders see our memories. But Hattie was having such a strong reaction to your presence, and she was convinced this was the only option, so the elders thought it was important enough to break the old laws." The First Elder says the words calmly, as if he's not bothered by breaking centuries-old traditions.

"You told me Hattie was hit and miss these days," I manage to squeak out over my outrage.

The First Elder clears his throat awkwardly and I remember that Hattie is here in the darkness with us. I wince. I didn't mean to insult her to her face.

"I was just trying to make you feel better about what she was saying to you," says the First Elder. "You were clearly upset by it. Not everyone responds well to knowing the future."

"How did you know it would work? What if I'd died? Or what if I disappear and use your memories for evil instead of good?" I feel sick, my stomach churning uncomfortably. "Why didn't you give me a *choice*?"

"Hattie was sure you'd be fine." He clears his throat. "And that you could be trusted with our memories."

I think of the blind, crazy, crooked Elder... and I'm not relieved. "Are you going to get in trouble for putting your memories in our heads?" I ask.

"Not if you don't tell anyone." His voice is as dry as a bone.

I can't help myself. My outrage drains away and I give a snort of laughter, despite the seriousness of the situation. The First Elder is hilarious, in a dark, offbeat kinda way. I just wish he'd told me what he was going to do before he shoved who-knows how many years' worth of memories magically into my head.

A crack of light at the doorway indicates that someone is opening the door. Whoever it is does it slowly, allowing our eyes to adjust to the increasing light. When the door is fully open, I can see Jorges at the door, his face serious.

"Come on, let's eat," says the First Elder. "I'm starving."

I stand up and feel Mr. Fookes doing the same beside me. I'm still not sure he's okay, but I can't tell anything while we're in this room, so I follow him to the door.

As soon as I cross the threshold back into the main room, a delicious smell hits me. The rich scent of tomato soup, the delicious aroma of freshly baked bread, and big gobs of butter. I'm really, really hungry. My stomach rumbles, and my body forgets about what just happened, in favor of getting to the food as fast as I can.

Clearly memories take up a lot of energy.

Daphne and Alvera are putting out cutlery, and there's a place setting at each place around the table, plus two more. Daphne looks up and smiles at us, but her smile falters when she sees Mr. Fookes. I turn to him and gasp. His skin is gray, and he looks much older, like he's aged about thirty years in the time we were in the darkened room. He stumbles over his own foot, and I reach out to steady him.

"What happened?" I ask him, grabbing his arm and leading him to the table to sit down. Daphne rushes to his other side, and I step back to allow her to tend to him.

"I... I... I don't know," he says, stumbling over his words. "I don't... feel so... good."

I glare over at the First Elder. "What did you do to him?"

The First Elder looks concerned. "Nothing. You had the same experience. You look fine. He should be too."

"Is he going to be okay?"

Instead of answering, the First Elder turns to Jorges and whispers in his ear. Jorges takes off—as fast as he can with his ancient legs—presumably to get help.

Mr. Fookes leans into Daphne, who's crouched down beside him. He looks like he's about to pass out.

Hattie, crooked and demented, shuffles over to Mr. Fookes and lays a hand on him. Daphne is glowering at her and looks like she'd like to tell her to get off. It's possibly the fact that Hattie looks like she's two hundred if she's a day that helps Daphne keep her silence.

Hattie's white-blue eyes flutter for a moment or two. Her lined face scrunches up, and it looks like she's trying to fart. Thankfully no sound emerges from anywhere in her body. "The genie will be fine," says Hattie eventually. "He will live to see another day. It's just a bad reaction to our magic. Kind of like when you eat a bad shellfish."

"Our memories aren't bad shellfish," says Mariam sharply.

Hattie cackles. "For a genie they are."

Ethan enters the room, and his gaze sweeps around, landing on the First Elder to make sure he's okay, then finding Mr. Fookes. "Alex will be here soon," he says. "He'll know what to do."

CHAPTER
NINETEEN

"I'm already feeling better," says Mr. Fookes quietly. "The rest of you should eat."

My stomach rumbles loudly, as if to agree. I shouldn't be so concerned about eating, not until Mr. Fookes is okay. But I'm starting to feel faint. It's like I haven't eaten in a week, and my stomach's curving in on itself. And that soup and bread smells *amazing*.

The elders move slowly toward the table, settling themselves into their chairs. They all look a little worse for wear, too. It clearly takes it out of them to transfer memories.

I sit down next to Mr. Fookes, glancing at him to make sure he's really feeling better. He doesn't look quite so grey as he did.

"You sure you're okay?" I say in an undertone. My stomach rumbles again.

He nods wearily. "I think it's just going to take a while to adjust to my system." Daphne is hovering close to him on the other side, and he smiles at her. "I'm going to be fine," he says to her.

I let out a relieved breath, then I break off a piece of

bread, slathering it with butter. It's still warm from the oven and crispy in all the right places. I take a bite, and my senses explode. It's the best bread I've ever eaten.

I put my spoon into the soup as I chew on the bread and then take a sip. Again, it tastes even better than it smelled, which is pretty impressive, given how good it smelled. I'm feeling better already. "You should try some," I say to Mr. Fookes. "It'll help, I think."

Mr Fookes shakes his head but doesn't say anything. He looks like he's concentrating on getting better, like he thinks he can force it to happen. Maybe he can, he's a genie after all.

"I had some in the kitchen," says Daphne absently. "Alvera insisted. It was delicious."

My spoon is half way to my mouth when suddenly hundreds of images start flooding my head. Alvera as a young kid, then as a teenager. Laughing, scolding, cooking. Layer upon layer, building up to a pile of information until I know everything there is to know about Alvera Stone, housekeeper and chef to the elders.

I take a gasping breath, and my spoon clatters back into the bowl. The images felt like an invasion, like someone was shoving them into my head by force. It's as if the images are weighing me down, or maybe filling me up to bursting. I'm feel awkward and stiff, and that's the last thing I need right now. We have so much to get done.

"How long will it be like this?" I ask the First Elder, who's sitting across the table from me.

"Like what?"

"Heavy?"

His expression is inscrutable. "You become used to it after a while."

"I don't have a while. I have things I need to do." I'm

feeling panicky. How am I going to find Mei and get the spell web out of her, or even fight demons, if I feel like I've been covered in an extra-heavy weighted blanket?

Hattie cackles from the other side of the table. "Carlos said you were a hard worker," she says, her eyes looking milkily somewhere over my shoulder. "But he didn't mention how much of a whiner you were."

I blink, and then frown at Hattie. "I'm not *whining*. We're attempting to save the world from a despotic director and his borderline insane associates. By giving me your memories, you've made it *harder* for me, not *easier*."

Hattie leans forward, this time looking directly at me, her gaze pinned on mine. "Life's not supposed to be *easy*," she says, her voice low and fierce. "You're going to need to dig deep to survive this. That's how it works when you've been picked by the gods."

I open my mouth a couple of times, like some kind of deep sea fish, and then close it again. I don't know what to say to her. She doesn't seem to care that she's made it harder for me. "What do you mean, 'picked by the gods'?" I say instead. It should be a nice thing, to be picked by the gods, but coming out of Hattie's mouth, it sounds ominous.

But Hattie has gone back to eating her soup, and is ignoring me again. I'm tempted to say something more to her, ask her how difficult her life is right now. But it doesn't feel like it'd be a win if I had a go at Hattie. And I'm not entirely sure I'd come out of the experience unscathed.

Instead I glance over at the First Elder. "It's an old mountain super saying," he says. "Picked by the gods. Usually applied to people who have a heavy burden that has the potential to make them show up in the history books as a game changer."

"I don't want to be a game changer. I just want to save

Mei and sort out the spell web." And I mean it. I don't want to be someone who changes the fates of millions of people, or does amazing deeds. I just want to help the people I love.

"You're too scared to take action," mutters Hattie into her soup. "You'll need to get over that if you want to find your friend."

I stare over at Hattie. I don't know why she's decided she needs to be mean to me, but it's getting annoying. "I take action," I say, stung. "We're here, aren't we?"

"Don't listen to Hattie," interrupts the First Elder. "She's just trying to goad you into action. She always was impatient, even when she was a kid."

For a moment, I try to get my head around the idea of them both being kids together, and then decide I can't do it. I glance over at Hattie, and notice a certain something in her eyes. The First Elder's right, she *is* just goading me.

Before I can say anything else, my phone buzzes in my pocket, and I look down at it in surprise. For some reason I expected my phone to be out of range down here.

The First Elder shrugs. "We like to stay in contact."

I pull out my phone and look at the screen. *Blade.*

"I have to take this," I say apologetically.

I answer the phone, a tiny buzz of excitement in my stomach. I haven't talked to him in at least twenty-four hours. So much has happened since then, and I want to update him. My little demon fizzes to match my feeling.

"Hey," I say, going for casual. I really just want to shout "I love you" to him.

"Hey," he replies. "Are you okay?"

"Yeah. We're at the First Village with the First Elder."

There's silence on the other end as Blade absorbs that news. "I had no idea the First Village was in Pismo Beach," he says eventually. "Or that it wasn't just a myth."

"I think they like it that way," I murmur, standing up and walking away from the table. I don't want my conversation to be overheard by the whole table. "Are you okay? What's happening? Did you find the blood vials?"

"We found them. Freddie did his thing..." Blade pauses. "And we think we know where Mei is." There's satisfaction in his voice, and I smile, relief flooding my body.

"Where is she?" I say in a rush, my stomach churning.

"She's here, on the west coast. I don't know how or why, but they're keeping her here, at a location a couple of hours away from the house."

Of all the places they could have been keeping Mei, this is the last place I would have thought to look. I guess that's why they did it.

"We'll be home soon," I say, working through possible rescue plans in my head. "When we get back, we can all—"

"We're already on our way," interrupts Blade. "We have to do this fast, Hazel. Get in, get out."

His words hit me like a punch to the stomach. He knew I'd object. That's why he didn't call until they were already on their way. "But—"

"We'll be fine. Freddie's a dirty fighter, and I've been doing this since I was a kid."

"This is different, Blade. This is the director. He's smart. You don't even know what you're getting yourself into or how many people will be there."

"I'm smart, too," says Blade, his voice a growl.

"That's not what I'm saying." An image of Lakas appears in my head, and this time it's layered with other images of the minokawa, not my memories, but the collective memories of the mountain clans. Blood covered images. Screaming, screeching, crying images. Lakas doing things I couldn't have imagined on my own.

Terrible things.

I let out a horrified noise. "Blade. Be careful. Lakas is involved in this, I know it. He's working with the director. He's worse than anyone else. You need to be careful."

"I will, I promise. But we have to strike fast. It's the only way we have a chance to make this happen."

"It's too risky," I blurt out the words without thinking about them, then cover my mouth with one hand. Risky is one of Blade's triggers.

Blade is silent for a beat. "No, it's not. We'll take every precaution possible. We have to be fast on this, Hazel."

I shake my head, even though he can't see it. "There must be another way," I whisper. Now I know how Blade feels whenever he tells me I'm doing something risky, and I ignore him.

"We've got a plan. We'll stick to it. It's going to be fine."

"What if you told Damien and the others? Seth? They could be—"

"No. They made their position clear." Blade's voice is stark, bleak. An edge of anger. He's still pissed at them for blocking him out because of something that wasn't even his fault.

I understand why he's not going to tell them, but a part of me wonders if it's the right decision. They cut us off because I broke their hearts. They expected me to save Mei, and I didn't do it. I get why they're angry at me. Approaching them with this news might mend the breach...

"What if..."

"Hazel, we have to get her out of there as soon as possible. Freddie and I know what we're doing. We'll save her from these assholes. Isn't that what you want?"

I let out a huff of air. "Of course."

"Do you trust me?"

I hesitate. "This isn't—"

"Do you trust me?" he growls a second time.

My heart twists as I try to find a way out of answering him. I can't. "Yes."

"Then let us do this. You find out how to get the spell web out of Mei and be prepared to get it the hell out of her when we get her back. We can save her, Hazel. We can do this. Okay?"

"Okay," I whisper, wishing I didn't feel so much like I was agreeing to his death warrant. "Just take care of yourself."

Images fill my head, of Lakas flying through the air, blood on his black-metal feathered wings, screeching triumphantly. I shake my head, unable to tell if it's a premonition or another unfamiliar mountain clan memory.

TWENTY

I turn back to face the others. There's a mountain super I don't recognize crouching next to Mr. Fookes, checking over his vitals.

Does Mr. Fookes's genie body work the same way as a mountain super's? Will their medic really be able to tell if he's okay? I think of they way he expanded suddenly when Ethan threatened Daphne. Does that kind of thing change how you're treated medically?

The medic stands up. "He seems fine. Just overstimulated by the memories," he says, then glares at the elders. "Which he should never have been given without proper testing and backup."

The First Elder nods like he's agreeing to what the man is saying, but even I know he's a loose unit, unlikely to listen to what anyone is saying, and I've only just met him.

Was he always like that? Or is it just now that he's part of this shadowy coalition of crazy old people? I glance around the room, my eyes resting on Hattie who's sitting crookedly in her chair, and is now eating her soup with a knife. Needless to say, it's not going well.

Next to her, one of the men—Jacken—isn't even bothering with a spoon and is tipping the bowl straight into his mouth.

But the medic is right. Mr. Fookes does seem better. And Blade's call has reminded me of our mission. We need to focus. Our job is to figure out how to get the spell web out of Mei. I walk determinedly over to where the First Elder is sitting and pull out a chair next to him.

"How do I use the memories to find information on the spell web?" I ask him.

He takes a bite of his bread and chews it slowly. I don't know if it's a stalling tactic, but it makes me antsy. I wait, drumming my fingers on the wood of the table. I need answers, and he's the one who can give them to me.

He finishes chewing and swallows. Even then, he doesn't say anything, just looks at me.

"Well?" I say eventually. "What is it?"

"Time," he says. "That's the only way to use the memories. Give them time to acclimate to your body."

"I don't *have* time," I say, my frustration rising to the surface. "I need help *now*. Can't you just search the memories in your head and tell me what I need to know?" I glance over at Mr. Fookes. "It would have saved a lot of hassle."

"Hattie...." He stops and glances over at Hattie, who is now using her fork as a hairbrush. "She was very sure about it."

He's taking his lead from a woman who's a few bricks short of a barbecue. That doesn't bode well.

"What do you personally know about the spell web?" I ask, trying not to look at Hattie anymore.

"It was created around three hundred years ago by the Earthbound to control the dragons. They were destroying our world. The Earthbound were considered heroes at the time."

"*How* did they create it?" I ask impatiently. Images are crowding my head, but I can't make sense of them.

"There was an energy source in the middle. Something powerful. Some*one* powerful. A sacrifice, if you will."

"Was it a dragon, like Mei?" She told me that the Earthbound's old leader Vincent had said that a dragon could be used to create a new spell web. That's how she ended up with it inside her.

"I don't know. All I know is they used some kind of magic to bind the power source to the spell, and then they created a web that covered every supernatural in the whole world, pulling a small amount of power from every single one of us. And we all gave it gladly, to end the reign of the dragons."

Wait. *What?* "You were there? Three hundred years ago?"

He shrugs. "It's not so very old for a mountain super. And I'm the First Elder, so I'm older than most." His expression turns gravelly. "I don't tell just anyone my age, mind. Keep that under your hat."

"Did you see them do it?"

"No, I was too young, not old enough to be trusted with important work like that. But I've gathered a few memories in my time that may prove useful. You have them now."

I take a big breath, still not entirely sure about this memories concept. "So we need some kind of power source, and we need to know the spells to create the actual web?"

He nods.

"I need to know how to pull it out of Mei."

The First Elder shakes his head. "I don't think you can do that."

My stomach clenches with fear. "I *have* to do it. For Mei and for the rest of us."

"You might not be—" A loud rumbling off in the distance makes me hesitate and look around. The floor under us starts to move, just a little, and a few pebbles fall from the roof over our heads.

Then suddenly everything around us is shaking. It's an earthquake—and we're *inside* the earth.

I grab hold of the table, and my eyes catch hold of the First Elder's. At the far end of the room, a crack appears in the rock ceiling, and dust and stones start falling, filling the other end of the room.

"Everyone, down this end," shouts the First Elder over the noise.

Standing, I rush and pull Hattie to standing, half dragging her to a position next to the First Elder. Mr. Fookes and Daphne have Jorges and Jacken with them. Everyone else crowds in with us. The whole room is shaking. I can't help being aware that we're standing deep underground, with layer upon layer of rocks and earth above our heads. What if it all comes crashing down? We'd be flatter than pancakes within seconds.

A loud crack sounds, and an enormous piece of rock separates from one side of the crack in the ceiling, and lands with a mighty thud on the floor. Someone screams. Dust and debris push up into the air around us, and it becomes impossible to see. If anyone had been on that side of the room, they'd be dead.

I start coughing as the dust makes it impossible to breathe, and I'm not the only one. There are whimpers and other noises, but I can't see who's making them. The very rock around us seems to creak, as if maybe the rest of the ceiling might come down on us any second.

I look at Mr. Fookes—could he do anything to save us if that happened? He's looking looking around as if he'd trying to figure out what he could do... Except he said that his powers were already depleted from when the slime sucked our energy. What if he doesn't have enough to save us all? I'm still holding onto Hattie, her crooked body tucked against mine as we try to stay steady while the floor rocks under us. The dust is hurting my throat, and I can barely keep my eyes open. The rumbling is a vibration through my whole body, and it feels like it's never going to end. What happens if we all die here? Who will save Mei? Who will find a way to create a new spell web?

Through the tiny gap on my eyelids, I see a familiar blue glow in the air. I freak out. Demons, here? That's the last thing I need. But then I look down and see that it's just my hands glowing blue. *It's me.*

Hattie is looking down at them too, her blue and white eyes glowing in the reflection. I don't understand how she could possibly be blind, she always seems to know exactly where to look and what's happening.

There's too much noise for her to say anything, but she definitely seems to be asking me something. Maybe just, *What the hell?*

I shake my head, and then hold my breath and concentrate. It immediately makes the glow dim and then disappear. Even now, when we're about to die, I don't want people to see my blue glow. I don't want them to be afraid of me.

The shaking hasn't slowed down. It's the longest earthquake I've ever been in. Normally they're much shorter than this, and they're fairly common along the California coast.

Usually, the best thing to do in an earthquake is hunker

down and stay in the same place, but it feels really unsafe down here. The slab of rock that fell from the ceiling is still shuddering, dust circulating like it's a desert sandstorm. We have to find a way to get out of here. I turn to the First Elder to see if there's a safe way out, when—just as suddenly as it started—the rumbling stops.

For a moment there's silence, except for our heavy breathing. Dust is still swirling around the room.

"That was the longest earthquake I've ever been in," I say. Hattie's still tucked against me and she's trembling. I'm pretty sure I can hear her clucking like a chicken under her breath.

The First Elder shakes his head. "Earthquakes don't affect us. We are at one with the earth. That was something else."

"Then what the hell was it?" I ask.

"That was an attack of some kind," he replies grimly. He shares a look with Mariam, and I shake my head.

"How could anyone attack using the earth? Is it some kind of mountain super power?"

The First Elder shakes his head. "No, we would never use the earth like that. Sometimes the most obvious choice is the correct answer, Hazel. It must have been the spell web. They've figured out how to force Mei to use the spell web as a weapon."

"She would never—" Surely it couldn't be the director? Mei would never help him. At least not willingly.

"She *is*."

"Then Blade will save her. He and Freddie are on their way to save her right now." I force myself to believe that they'll rescue her, and this will all stop. I rub my hands over my arms, suddenly cold.

Mr. Fookes stands. "We have to get back to the Sanctus

Apartments." He looks grim, and the gray has returned to his face. Or perhaps that's just the dust. He pulls Daphne to her feet, and they stand next to each other, hand in hand, covered in dust.

I sneeze. I guess we're all covered in dust. "We don't know enough yet," I say, looking to the First Elder. "I don't know how to get the spell web out of Mei. I can't use the memories."

Hattie is clucking louder now. I try to ignore her.

"You know as much as I know," says the First Elder. "We don't know how to remove the spell web from Mei. It's never been done before. But we do know how to create a new one." His face looks grim, and I get the feeling that knowing how to create one isn't the same thing as being able to do it. "You've got the memories now. You can see it for yourself."

My stomach curls up as if it's curdling inside me. "How am I supposed to see the memories? They're too fast for me."

"Same way you always do things," says Daphne firmly. She's got a militant look in her eye. "You always figure out how things work, Hazel. It's your thing."

The First Elder nods. "You have the memories. You can access them. Hattie says you can do it." We both look at Hattie, who's using her arms like wings. She starts to crow like a rooster.

The door to the meeting room bursts open, and Ethan runs into the room. "You need to see this," he says, holding out his phone.

On the screen is a newsfeed, with the red line of information flowing across the bottom.

The screen shows the earth being torn apart above

ground. Huge cracks appearing in the roads. People falling into the enormous cracks, to their deaths.

"They're saying it's an earthquake," he says.

The First Elder shakes his head. "It's not an earthquake, we all know that." He glances at me. "It's the director. They're using the spell web against us."

I clench my hands into fists, fear squeezing my stomach like it's a wet sponge. I want to disagree with the First Elder, but deep down inside, I know he's right.

CHAPTER
TWENTY-ONE

Mr. Fookes speeds the whole way back to Stanford and the Sanctus Apartments.

There are enormous, gaping cracks in the road in lots of places, but somehow, we stay out of the worst of it. Emergency services are everywhere, and from the news it seems like hundreds of people have been killed up and down the coast.

I check my phone again, desperate for a message from Blade.

Was it because they found her? Was the "earthquake" something to do with their rescue mission? Did something happen?

Or is it simply something to do with the director?

There's a chaotic, bubbling feeling in my stomach. If this is the director using Mei, then these deaths are my fault. I had it within my power to save Mei, and I didn't take it. I look at Mr. Fookes in the driver's seat. He would have survived. He would have ended up who knows where, serving a master who might have forced him to do terrible things... but he would have been alive.

All these people who died today would be alive as well. I clutch my hands tightly in my lap, staring out the window at the destruction around us. This is all the direct result of my decision. No wonder Damien and Seth hate me. *I did this.*

And if it's really the spell web, and the director's in charge of doing this, then Mei's in real trouble as well. Something has happened to her, and they're forcing her to use the spell web somehow.

Are they torturing her?

The thought makes me feel even more sick. If she's doing this, something really bad is happening to her. She's being forced to do it somehow. I honestly can't imagine Mei giving in to pressure from the director. She's so brave and strong. And she's too focused on saving other people. She'd never purposely hurt so many people.

A shaft of fear goes through me.

We have to find her. Fast.

I have to find her.

We screech into the parking lot outside the building, and thankfully everything is still intact. I'm guessing that Mr. Fookes has some genie protection over it, as well as the demon-infused protection blanket I put over it a while back.

Around us, though, things are looking less awesome. Down the street, there's an enormous crack in the road, and one of the buildings seems to have collapsed inside itself. There are emergency services outside, and people are calling out for lost loved ones.

I hesitate for a moment, looking down the road at the crumpled buildings. Then I climb out of the car, and without conscious decision, I start walking down the street.

"Hazel, what are you doing?" asks Daphne.

I don't answer. I feel like I'm a moth fluttering toward a flame. I'm being drawn to the destruction. It's my fault, after all.

"Stay back, ma'am," says a tall fireman wearing protective gear, holding out one hand to stop me. "There's nothing you can do to help."

"What's happening?"

"Several people fell into the crack. We're waiting on climbing equipment so we can get down to them." But his face is grim, and I can tell he doesn't think they're still alive.

"I can climb down," I say. "I'm a good climber."

"I'm sorry, ma'am. It's too dangerous. Please leave it to the professionals."

Arms go around my shoulders, and then suddenly I'm being enveloped in a tight hug. I press my face against Mr. Fookes's knitted cardigan and lean into the comfort he's offering me.

"It's not your fault," says Mr. Fookes in a low voice. "This is Director Holden's doing. He's the one who's killed these people. Not you." He knows exactly what I'm thinking, because he's thinking it too. He knows I could have chosen Mei, and none of these people would have died.

"He would have killed people in another way," says Mr. Fookes. "He's an evil man. This is not your fault."

I shake my head, but I can't say anything just yet. There's a lump in my throat, and I'm on the verge of sobbing against his chest. Another hand touches my back. Daphne.

"Hazel, we can't do anything about what's already happened," she says quietly, just for our ears. "But we *can* change what hasn't happened yet. We have to find a way to stop this man. Come on. That's our responsibility."

Daphne's words hit home. My job is to figure out how

to get the spell web out of Mei when Blade and Freddie bring her back home. That's what I can do to make amends. My stomach clenches. Is she really still alive? Or is that how the director is doing this? Maybe he figured out how to take the spell web out of her and then he killed her?

I pull away from Mr. Fookes and lean to one side and vomit onto the sidewalk. My brain feels dizzy and for a moment, I think I'm going to black out.

"Come on, let's get you back to the apartment," says Mr. Fookes. He grabs one arm, and Daphne grabs my other, and between them, they support me back in the direction we came from, up the stairs of the apartment building, and into the foyer. All I can see of the apartment are the black and white tiles of the entrance way, and then Mr. Fookes opens his apartment door, and ushers us in.

Poppy leaps to her feet from where she was sitting at the table, her face white, and her eyes scared. "Are you all okay? What's happening? That was the scariest earthquake I've ever been in."

"It wasn't an earthquake," says Daphne. They urge me toward the largest leather sofa, and force me to sit down. Daphne rushes away.

"What?" says Poppy.

"We think it's the director," adds Mr. Fookes. He's standing over me, looking down at my face like he's trying to figure out how to fix me.

I'm not sure I can be fixed. I feel hollow inside. I can't stop thinking how if I'd only rescued Mei, those people down the street wouldn't be dead.

Poppy looks between us, her eyes wide, trying to spot the joke. "Why's he creating earthquakes?"

"We don't know," says Mr. Fookes with a sigh. He sits down next to me on the sofa. "But it makes it even more important to figure out how to get the spell web out of Mei once we find her."

Daphne returns and she's holding a wet face cloth. She wipes my face, clearing away the last of the vomit, and it feels warm and cozy. I close my eyes and lean into the comfort of having someone look after me.

"What happened to Hazel?" asks Poppy.

"She's just a little upset. She'll be fine soon. But we could all do with a hot drink? Maybe a hot chocolate seeing it's so late?" says Mr. Fookes.

Poppy nods and heads to the kitchen to make coffee. Daphne disappears again with the cloth.

He sounds tired, and I turn my head toward him, remembering how ill he was after the memories were given to us.

"You okay?" I manage to croak out.

"We're going to find her, Hazel. I know we are," he says. It's like a vow. I guess he feels it too, the pressure to make this situation right.

I nod. Not because I'm sure of it, but because I hope it makes him feel better.

"What are we going to do?" Poppy asks in a loud voice from the kitchen. She pops her head around the corner of the door.

"Blade and Freddie have gone to get Mei. They think they know where she is," says Daphne, coming back into the room.

Poppy's eyes widen. "When?"

She glances at me. "This morning. Before the earthquake."

I look out the window. It's now almost dark outside. They should be back by now. Why aren't they back?

Mr. Fookes shifts on the sofa next to me. "We need to work with the memories they gave us."

I reluctantly look in his direction, wondering what he's got planned.

"I can use some of my remaining genie magic to delve into the memories inside my head. To find what's useful. But I'm not sure that's the best way to use them."

I nod, letting out a breath. I have to focus on finding Mei. "The First Elder said we'd be able to just access them," I say softly.

Mr. Fookes shakes his head. "I don't know why, but they're just sitting in my mind, like a locked box I don't have the keys for."

"I can't even get to the memories in my head." I close my eyes and dip down into the deep well of power inside me. I feel the memories swirling around inside my power, dipping and diving, twirling and tripping. They're not locked away, but I can't seem to catch any of them. They're like slippery eels, swimming down a river.

There must be some way to access them. I dip down into the flow of demon energy inside me. The memories skip away, dancing across my power.

I go more softly. If they're wild and need me to charm them, then that's what I'll do. I hold out my consciousness. Let it float softly toward them, easy and graceful. Let them know I won't harm them.

And then suddenly the strands of memory are converging on me all at once. They're all over me, and I'm experiencing everything from all of them at once. All the flickering images attacking me, too fast to understand, too fast to even see properly. And the emotions are all on top of me as well, piled high, too much to take in, nothing except the worst of it, the pain.

I'm shuddering all over, and the memories are attacking me, and I can't do anything about it. I try to push them away, to make them stop, but they won't. I'm almost out of energy, almost finished, when a glowing blue light appears from nowhere inside my head. The little demon. It's here for me, as always. It pushes away the memories, forces them back into the waters of the well of power.

It lets me breathe.

I open my eyes. I'm on the ground in front of the sofa I was just in. Mr. Fookes and Poppy are looming over me, their expressions concerned.

"I guess... it didn't work?" I say, my voice croaky.

"You fell off the chair," says Poppy, unnecessarily. "You were shaking so hard."

"We were afraid to move you," says Mr. Fookes. "I wasn't sure what was happening."

"The memories attacked me. All at once."

Poppy moves forward and grabs my elbow, helping me back into a chair.

"Safe to say that I'm not in control of the memories either."

"What's the point of having them if they're not going to be useful?" says Poppy.

She has a point.

"The First Elder said it would get easier with time," I say.

"We don't have time," says Daphne from the doorway. She's holding a tray with steaming mugs. The smell of hot chocolate fills the air.

"She's right. We have to figure this out as fast as possible."

I nod. "Which means I need to get into the lab and try to find a way to get the spell web out of Mei."

"Hot chocolate first, saving the world, second," says Daphne.

I reach gratefully for the mug on the tray, hoping the Daphne can't see the fear that's spiking inside me. I've always been able to figure out how to fix things, to understand their inner workings when I wanted to.

Except this time, it feels impossible.

This time, it feels like I might fail.

CHAPTER
TWENTY-TWO

I take another sip of my hot chocolate. It's already making me feel a little more steady after my shaking fit. There's silence in the room as everyone watches me nervously, like they're waiting for it to happen again.

Desperate for conversation, I look over at the table, and see the scattered papers and notes that Poppy was working on when we came in. She's sitting back up at the table, with her hot chocolate.

"How's your research going, Poppy?" I say, nodding to her notes. She was working on my little demon's original life, so we can try to find a way to help it right whatever it felt was wrong when it died. It reminds me that there's more going on here than just finding Mei.

Poppy leaps on the question like it's a huge relief.

"I've been working with Walter and Marco. We took the information you were able to give us—the possible time frame for when your demon might have died, what the "wrong" might have been, and that it probably happened in the Stanford region—and Marco searched the databases for crimes around here."

"And...?" prompts Mr. Fookes. He's sitting next to Daphne now, his arm around her shoulders. She's snuggled up against him, her eyes half closed. It's been a long day for all of us.

Poppy lets out a huff of breath. "There were a lot of them. But we've started going through the crimes, trying to find ones that involve some kind of unfair element as well as a murder of a man. Or maybe even just the death of a man that's somehow associated with it. Especially the cold cases that were never solved. We figure it's going to be a major crime, like murder or rape. No point getting worked up over something small."

I hesitate, thinking it through. "The translated book specifically mentioned that it could be as silly as stolen sausages. It just needs to be something a person would feel passionate about." The little demon suddenly squirms inside me, and somehow I know it's not just over sausages.

Poppy nods, and takes a couple of notes. "We have to narrow it down somehow. This gives us some concrete data to work with initially. Then we're going to start door knocking." She gives an excited grin, like this is a treat for her.

"Do you think you'll find something?" I ask. I'm genuinely not sure how they'll be able to make this work. Surely it's like a needle in a haystack? The little demon starts buzzing around inside me, like it's excited by what's happening.

Poppy shrugs one shoulder, but her eyes are bright with enthusiasm. "We can only try," she says. "Any more help you can give us, anything your demon has said or shown you, would be helpful."

Are they on the right track? I think the words clearly inside my head, trying to communicate properly with my demon. It's the first time I've thought to do it on purpose like this. Usually it's just when the little demon is saving me from something, like the memories attacking my senses.

The demon speeds up, going faster and faster. A few images flash through my head—as always, they're too fast to catch—but the feeling is clear. We're going in the right direction. "I think it all sounds great," I say to Poppy.

Poppy's phone rings, and she pulls it out, checking the screen. "It's Walter," she says. "I should answer it." She presses the button, and says, "Hey Walt, how's it going?"

I can't help my smile. I've known Walter for almost three years, and I've never called him Walt. Poppy has a way of ingratiating herself with people that's both charming and amusing. When I think back to the angry goth girl I knew at Ravenwood, it's like she's a different person.

"Okay, sure. Come on by," she's saying into the phone. Then she hangs up. "He's coming around. Says he has something important for us."

"What?" It's late, I was planning to go to bed. My eyes feel like they're the size of saucers, and I can hear Daphne's gentle snores from the sofa.

"He said it was important. And he's not far away."

"I think you two can handle Walter," says Mr. Fookes. He stands up, and pulls Daphne to her feet. "I'm gonna get Daphne to bed." They stumble out of the room together, Mr. Fookes helping a half asleep Daphne to walk.

"Goodnight," I say.

"Night," says Poppy.

Mr. Fookes just waves with one hand as they stumble down the hallway toward the bedrooms.

I look at Poppy. "I can't believe the difference a few

years can make," I say. "Could you have imagined this would be your life when we were at Ravenwood?"

"Never. I couldn't imagine anything when I was at Ravenwood," she says, the brightness dimming in her eyes.

I nod, knowing exactly what she means. When we were there, all we could focus on was avoiding the notice of Dr. Green, and escaping. Now that we're out, there's so much more in the world to think about.

There's a knock at the door, and I jump in my chair, spilling a little hot chocolate over the side of the mug.

Blade.

Putting the mug on the coffee table, I stand up and run to the door, opening it in a rush, before Poppy can even blink.

Except it's not Blade standing there, it's Walter, his white hair stuffed under a beanie, and his clothes muted and dark. "Oh," I say, disappointment raging through my body like an overflowing river after a storm. "Hi Walter," I add, trying to sound more enthusiastic.

"You used to be happy to see me in the old days," he says, with a mock frown. His handlebar mustache twitches in amusement.

"I thought you were Blade. We haven't heard from them since they left."

"Ah, okay. That makes sense, then." He leans over and pats my arm. "I'm sure they'll be fine. They're both experienced hunters."

"Thanks, Walter. I appreciate it. Come in," I say, standing back to let him in.

He wanders into the apartment, his sharp eyes taking everything in. "It always amazes me how his house works. Genies have unique magic," he says. "I can't get over how large it is in here."

"Hey Walter," says Poppy, as she stands up to give him a hug. "What's so important that you had to come over right away?"

"Two things," he says. He hands me a small device that seems to be an old fashioned tape player. "It's called a walkman," he says. "Used for playing music tapes, before they were overtaken by other technology. It was donated to the store. Listen to the song on it." He puts the headphones around my ears, and presses down on the big play button.

Immediately the sounds of a bar flows into my ears, with some smooth background music. And then my mother's voice, thanking the crowd. I glance up at Walter. "It's another recording of my birth mother," I say. She's singing now, a sweet song about true love and never giving it up. I listen all the way through, listening to her thank the audience, before I press stop.

I lean in and give Walter a hug. "Thank you," I say. "That's just what I needed to hear."

"I figured you'd want it. But that's not the main reason I came round. I didn't want to tell you over the phone, but there's mutterings on the rumor mill that Damien Walker has disappeared. Some are saying he's been killed, others that he's been taken hostage."

At first, I'm just upset because it's Damien. He's my friend, even if he's angry with me right now. But then the implications begin to set in. "Is it possible the director has him? Could that be how the director is getting Mei to use the spell web against us? By threatening her father?"

Walter nods. "You said she was tough, and it doesn't make sense that she would do something as destructive as the fake earthquakes if she didn't have good reason. I think threatening to kill her father is good reason, right?"

I sit down on the edge of the sofa, trying to think

through what this means. Without Damien, I don't think the others will be organized enough to be a threat. Seth was too on the edge to organize anything, and Carrick would have his hands full just keeping Seth contained. "Have you heard anything about Seth? Where he is? What he's doing?"

Walter shakes his head. "Nothing confirmed, anyway. There were a few reports of burning buildings near Newport News that could have been him, based on what you told me."

"What does this mean for us?" asks Poppy.

"It's a pity we can't ask Seth or Carrick where Damien was last seen, or get some kind of an idea about where he might have been taken. That might help lead us to Mei," says Walter.

"Blade and Freddie already found Mei," I say, trying not to let my worry seep into my voice. "At least they thought they did. They were going to scope out the location, possibly attempt a rescue."

"When will you know if they've been successful?" says Poppy.

I shake my head, and make a face. "I don't know. Any minute now. I'm sure he'll ring as soon as he can."

Walter and Poppy exchange a look, and I try to ignore it. I don't need to know that they think we should have heard back from Blade and Freddie before now. I don't need to know that my fears are founded, and there's a problem.

"I think it's time for bed, I'm beat," I say. "We'll talk to the others tomorrow, and try to figure out what Damien's disappearance might mean for us. See if there's a way to use the information to our advantage."

Walter nods. "I'll see myself out," he says. He nods, and turns to go.

He's almost out the door when I hold up the walkman. "Thanks Walter. I appreciate this."

He nods, then disappears out the door.

TWENTY-THREE

I t's the next morning, and Blade still hasn't called.

I'm trying not to make it mean anything. Maybe they had to hunker down and wait for the right opportunity. Maybe they're asleep at a motel. Maybe they're somewhere that has no cell service. Maybe they've realized they have to save Damien as well, and they're just regrouping.

Maybe it's not a problem that it's been twenty-four hours and Blade hasn't even sent a text to tell me they're okay. I'm too scared to text him in case he's in the middle of something and it either gives his position away or distracts him.

It's early and no one else is up yet, so instead of lying awake in my bed, I'm in my lab in Mr. Fookes's apartment, sitting at one of the long stainless steel bench tops, and staring down at the translation of the book I photographed at the SIG Records and Relics room. I can't stop the feeling that there's something in this book I need to know. My little demon is fizzing around inside me, like it's encouraging me to look again. I'm trying to find some kind of information that I missed the first time, or that might help us now. I just hope it stands out easily.

I know I should be trying to access the mountain supernatural memories for information about the spell web, but ever since they tried to attack me in the living room yesterday, I've been keeping them pushed down inside me. I don't want to look at them again until I've got someone else with me to help, just in case.

In my ears are the ear buds from the old walkman Walter dropped off last night. My mother is softly singing a lullaby that's more suited for a baby than a packed bar, except somehow she makes it work. It's a different recording to the one I have on the CD I found in the Pismo Beach lockup, and she's talking a little more between songs than she did on the last one. It makes me feel a little closer to her to hear how she talked, what she laughed at, how she thought.

I'm doing everything I can think of to distract myself from the fact that Blade is still missing. I have an important job to do—I need to find a way to save Mei when they bring her back. I need to figure out how to make a new spell web with demon energy. It's the only way I'll be able to live with myself.

Except right now, all I can think of is how afraid I am.

I'm basically full to the brim with fear.

Fear for Blade.

Fear of a demon plague.

Fear of not saving Mei.

Fear of not finding a way to recreate a spell web.

Fear of ending up like my birth father, Gavan.

Fear of losing Blade.

The last thought makes my chest clench, and I take a

ragged breath. What would I do if something has happened to Blade? What would happen to my heart?

I don't think I could take it. Not another person I love dying because of me.

It's all my fault. I decided to free Mr. Fookes instead of freeing Mei. I set this whole thing in motion. If I'd agreed to use the last wish to find Mei, the director wouldn't have been able to hurt any of the people he's hurting right now. Hundreds of people died when he used the spell web to create that fake earthquake. Who knows what he's going to do next time.

If I'd found Mei when they asked me to, Mei wouldn't still be at his mercy, almost two weeks after she disappeared.

If I'd found Mei, *Blade would be here with me now*. A sob forces its way up my throat, and I smash the side of my fist into the stainless steel bench top. Pain, bright and fresh, rises up my hand and into my arm.

The pain clears my head, and allows me to think about the other side of my decision. If I'd used the last wish on Mei, where would Mr. Fookes be? He'd be inside his magical toaster. Lost somewhere, vulnerable to the whims of whichever new master found the toaster next. Lost forever to Daphne, his love.

But he'd be okay, even if he was heartbroken and lost to us. *He'd be alive*.

Bile rises up my throat. Whenever I try to make the right decision, to do what's best, I choose badly. At the time, saving Mr. Fookes felt like the only decision I could make. I promised him, I gave him my word that I'd save him, and I couldn't break that promise. I felt it strongly enough that I braved the displeasure of Damien, Seth and Carrick, causing them all heartache and despair.

But every day since then I've wondered if it was the wrong choice to make. Every day I've imagined Mei at the mercy of Director Holden and Lakas. When they used the spell web, all I could imagine is the terrible things they'd done to her to make her use the spell web in that way. Mei's brave and strong. She's not someone to give in easily.

A tiny knock sounds at the door to the lab, making me jerk around in surprise. I'm on edge, unable to relax. "Come in," I yell, then flush when Daphne comes in with a tray holding a hot cup of tea and a plate with toast and peanut butter. Her sunny yellow knitted cardigan immediately brightens up the lab. I look at her guiltily, like she might know what I was just thinking. What would she say about my doubts?

She smiles and brings the tray over, setting it carefully down on the bench next to me. "How's the research going?" she asks, glancing at the notes.

I shake my head. "I'm looking over some translations of chalice books. My little demon seems to think there's something in there that'll be useful. I'm not so sure. I'm too distracted by Blade not calling to really concentrate."

"Don't worry about Blade. He's a big cat, he's got nine lives."

"I hope so. It's just not like him to not update me."

She perches next to me on a second stool, ignoring my worries. "What does it say about chalices? I'd love to know more about what you can do."

"According to the translation, chalices aren't evil. *We're soul gatherers.*"

"You say that like you think you're evil," says Daphne, a frown on her freckled face.

I shrug. "Sometimes I wonder. I'm connected to demons—"

"Who told you that? Dr. Green?" interrupts Daphne indignantly. "You're not *evil*."

I shrug self-consciously. "For a while after I found out what I could do, how I was connected to the demons, I was worried that I was evil, because I was a chalice. Because of my dad and how he is..." I trail off, feeling silly as I say it out loud.

She shakes her head firmly. "What nonsense," she says, like an indignant school teacher. "You're just like anyone else. Better than most people, because you care so much. You do everything you can to help people. That's the opposite of evil, Hazel."

I take a breath, and push down the tears that are trying to force their way up my chest in response to her words. I clear my throat. "Thanks," I say, my voice little more than a croak. I think some part of me still secretly believes that I could be evil just because I'm a chalice, and my fear for Blade is making me doubt myself again. I give Daphne a grateful look, and she reaches out to grasp my hand in hers, holding it tightly.

"What else does it say?" she asks in a calmer voice.

Just having her here with me is soothing and I take another deep breath, trying to ease my overwrought emotions. I look down at the photocopied pages. "It says that chalices help the supers who've come back from the dead—the demons—so they can right a wrong. They're called 'lost souls' when they first come back. Chalices look for the lost souls and help them fix whatever they're so desperate to fix, so they can return to where they're supposed to be."

"That sounds lovely. I can see you doing that kind of thing. Helping people." Daphne smiles at me, and it's a contented smile that I know she wouldn't be giving me if I hadn't saved Mr. Fookes. "What else does it say?"

My heart does an anxious flip-flop. If Daphne knew that I was wishing I'd saved Mei instead of Mr. Fookes, she'd be so upset with me. The thought is almost enough to make me cry again. Whichever way I look, there's someone I'd disappoint.

I clear my throat, and attempt to focus on the words again. "Chalices also control and destroy the severed souls —the demons who've already killed someone or who've taken power from other supernaturals by possessing them. Once they've done that, there's no going back, they're obsessed with gathering energy and magic. I can't help them, even if I right the wrong. They've become energy-hungry monsters, and can never go to the other side."

"There seem to be more of that second sort," says Daphne, making a face. "I've never met a demon I liked."

"Yeah. It's hard to imagine one that's not out to steal your energy. They're mostly all the severed souls, the ones who're past the point of redemption." When I think of all the crazy demons I've faced, with all sorts of strange metallic spare parts attached to them, it's hard to imagine a demon that's just lost.

"What are the lost souls like?" asks Daphne.

"I've never even seen a lost soul, let alone tried to help one," I say, shrugging. "I don't know." I wonder how I'd find a lost soul. It seems impossible right this minute.

The little demon inside me bounces around indignantly. "Unless the demon that possessed me still counts as a lost soul," I say, putting one hand over my stomach. "It seems to think it does."

Daphne looks down at my hand curiously, as if that's

where the demon is hiding. "Does it hurt? Having a demon possessing you?"

"No," I say, glancing down at my hand over my stomach. "I just feel it moving around sometimes. And it helps me when I'm in trouble or it knows something useful."

"Sounds nice. Like an inbuilt sidekick."

The little demon actually *purrs* at Daphne's words. "It likes what you're saying," I say with a small laugh. When I think about it, my little demon has never seemed aggressive or angry. It's always helped me. And it's not scary like some of the demons I've faced. That has to mean something.

"Like a cat," she says. "Except that seems too... tame... for a demon."

I nod, agreeing. "I know what you mean. But I don't think all demons are scary. The one inside me isn't."

"If the book says it's possible, I'm sure it is," says Daphne with complete faith. "Especially if your little demon isn't scary."

"Yeah." I glance down at the photocopied translation. "If this book is correct, demons aren't even demons in the traditional religious sense. Not like they talk about in church. They're not horrible creatures from the depths of hell. They're not the minions of satan. They're just big glowing creatures that are lost." I look up, staring at the wall, my brain whirring. "They need help, not condemnation."

"Do you think there are any demons who might know about the spell web? How to create it, like Gavan and Connor told you they could? Maybe we could just ask them?"

"I'm not sure. I don't know if they have information like that available to them." I think of the demons I've met.

"They're all kind of focused on killing or possessing supers for their energy."

Daphne pats my hand. "I'm sure you'll figure out a way to do it Hazel. If anyone can, it's you." She stands up. "I promised I'd help Poppy with her investigations this morning. But if you need anything else, just yell." She leans forward and enfolds me in a tight hug. "You've got this," she whispers.

"Thanks Daphne," I say, watching as she walks out the door, closing it softly behind her. I realize I can't be sad that I chose Mr. Fookes, not if it means that Daphne was reunited with the love of her life. She would have been devastated if I hadn't brought him back.

But if I'm going to be comfortable with my decision to keep my promise to Mr. Fookes, then I have to figure out a way to get the spell web out of Mei. I have to focus all my efforts on fixing this situation.

And I don't have a lot of time to do it in.

TWENTY-FOUR

I let out a harsh expletive and push myself to standing.

I need to do something active. I need to find a way to learn something new, do something useful. Sitting here reading the same sentences over and over is getting me nowhere. I need some power to work with. *I need a demon.*

Daphne's suggestion that I ask a demon for information seemed crazy at first. But the more I think about it, the more the idea appeals to me. And if they don't know anything, then at least I can absorb some more demon energy to use elsewhere. At the very least, fighting demons will distract me while I wait for Blade to get back in touch.

And I'm not going to find a demon here in the windowless lab that Mr. Fookes made for me. I need to go outside.

The others are all treating me like I'm some sort of treasure to be kept alive. They don't want me going outside on my own, and they definitely wouldn't agree to a demon hunting expedition. I'm supposed to be on "figure out how to save the world" duty.

Like I know how to do that.

But Mr. Fookes's building is sneaky. If you need something, it will sometimes appear for you, separate from Mr. Fookes. It's done it for me before, although not quite in this way. Bowls of candy have turned up nearby, just when I needed an energy boost, and once a bathroom appeared that I would've sworn wasn't there the last time I walked that particular hallway. I'm positive I'm not making it up. The building has a mind of its own.

So I close my eyes and focus on needing a different way out of the house. A side door. A back door. Whatever kind of door that's required, as long as it gets me out into the world, where I can go find some demons to give me power. I allow myself to feel the urgency of it, my desire to get out of here and go find some demons to fight—er, talk to.

I stand up from the table, walk to the door of the lab and open it. Then I peer hopefully up and down the hallway —maybe there's a new door out here?—but everything is exactly the same.

I sigh. It was a bit of a long shot to be honest. Who ever heard of—

I freeze. I've turned around and am now facing the back of the lab. On the far wall is a door that wasn't there just seconds ago, just like I asked for. I walk slowly across the room, until I'm standing in front of the large wooden door.

The hinges are old rusted brass and the handle is shaped like a screwdriver. The wood is ancient, like the building had to find it in the attic—maybe even Mr. Fookes's treasure cave?—and bring it here, just for me. I touch the door handle, still not entirely convinced this isn't a trick of some kind. But when I turn it and push the door open, there in front of me is the side of the Sanctus Apartment building. White stone steps—that definitely weren't there before—lead down to the sidewalk.

I'm getting out of here.

Best of all, I can be out and back before any of the others know I'm gone. No need to worry anyone. It's still fairly early in the day, so not many people are out and about, which is again a huge bonus for me.

Despite being the only person on the sidewalk, I tiptoe along the concrete like I think it's going to keep me from being spotted.

"Hey, Hazel," says a familiar voice, almost like I conjured him with my thoughts.

Nelson.

I stop. I haven't seen Nelson since the dinner at Anna Blade's place, and I don't want to ignore him. He and I are buddies. Plus, I don't want him to know I'm not supposed to be out here. I glance up at the building nervously, wondering how long I have before the others notice I've gone.

"Hey, Nelson," I say, turning back to him and trying for casual. He's even taller than last time I saw him. He's at that stage where kids grow like weeds. I wonder if it's different for wolf shifters than it is for other kids.

"You sneaking out?" he asks, his silver eyes watching me intently.

My eyes widen as I look down at him. I'm going for my innocent, *"who me?"* look. "What makes you say that?" I ask. The person who invented deflection and answering a question with a question was a genius.

"The way you're being sneaky." Nelson doesn't give an inch.

I keep staring down at him, trying to psych him out, but Nelson's glowing silver eyes are impossible to match. I look away, annoyed at my inability to lie to him. "Okay, yes, I'm sneaking out."

"You want company?" he asks hopefully.

I should have known this was more about Nelson's desire for adventure than trying to stop me. I think of the demons I'm planning to summon. It would probably be dangerous for a kid who's only half-shifter to be confronted with demons. Kind of irresponsible of me, if I let him come with.

On the other hand, I'll be in control the whole time. I know how to manage the demons, and I haven't hung out with Nelson in a while. Not since I came back from SIG Headquarters. I miss him. "I'm going to hunt demons at the old train yard," I say warningly. "It could be dangerous. You'll have to follow any instructions I give you to the letter."

Nelson's eyes light up. "I promise," he says.

"Okay, then. You can come with me."

He gives a small victory punch, and then I start walking down the street again, and Nelson follows. It's actually nice to have someone else walk with me.

"Is that why you were sneaking out without telling the others? Because they wouldn't approve?" asks Nelson.

I blink, not sure about the answer. "I need some demons, and I don't want to bother anyone else." I don't want to admit why I'm sneaking out.

We keep walking in silence. There's a huge crack in the footpath up ahead, and it reminds me of Mei and what they're doing with the spell web. My stomach shrivels up with fear and worry. I need to figure out how to find her.

"How's school?" I ask Nelson, trying to get my mind off Mei.

Nelson shakes his head. "I haven't been back since the earthquake. My mom doesn't want to risk it. Says you never know what's going to happen next, these days."

"That's a shame," I say absently.

Nelson gestures to the crack in the road. "My mom says that's something to do with the spell web?" he asks.

I nod. "Yeah. They're using it against us."

"And you're trying to fix it?"

"Yeah."

Nelson nods, like I confirmed his theories. "We're going to find demons in the train yard?"

"There's so much metal there, we'll be bound to find at least one easily."

Nelson nods and keeps walking beside me. It occurs to me that he's always been like that. Not one for lots of conversation, just happy to go with the flow.

"Did I ever say thank you for helping me get Blade up to my apartment that time he was wounded?" I ask curiously.

He shrugs. "I don't think so. But you were kind of jumpy in those days. Less sure of yourself."

"You think I'm more sure of myself now?" I can't help the surprise in my voice.

"Yeah. You seem like you have a plan these days. Before, you didn't."

I look at him. He's just a kid. When did he get to be so observant? "I don't have a plan," I say, just to clarify it for him. "I still have no idea what I'm doing most of the time."

"Maybe it just seems like you do," says Nelson with a shrug. "Or maybe it's more like you've got a *purpose*. Something you're aiming for. Mrs. Grimble in 7A always says you have to have goals to get anywhere in life."

I snort-laugh at the idea that we're taking life advice from Mrs Grimble, but then I nod slowly. She's actually right, and so is Nelson. "I guess I do have more of a purpose in my life these days."

We're almost at the train yard, and I start to worry

about putting Nelson in danger. Getting him to help me drag Blade up to my apartment is one thing. Taking him on a demon hunt is a whole other level. Blade would not approve. I gesture back toward the apartment. "I think it might be better if you went back to the apartment. Just in case."

Nelson just stares at me, a stubborn tilt to his chin. "You said I could come with you. I thought you could control your demon powers?"

"I can," I say indignantly. "But what if something happens?"

"Then you'll deal with it. I trust you."

His simple words feel like a stab through the chest with a particularly splinter-filled stake. It's the one thing I find hard to do. Trust. Blade managed to get an admission out of me, but it felt like I had to bare my soul to do it.

Nelson's giving his trust to me so easily. I peer closely at him, trying to understand how he does it. Except he doesn't look any different than he does all the other times we've hung out. He's just a kid who's trusting me to look after him. Despite the fact that he was kidnapped by Connor because of me. That his life is infinitely more dangerous because of me.

The thought weighs on my mind. Will I be able to keep my word? Will I be able to look after him if we come across a demon?

Of course I will. Nelson's family.

CHAPTER
TWENTY-FIVE

Nelson's grinning at me, like he can already see I've caved, and decided to go through with it. He's clearly ready for adventure. My heart feels squishy when I look at him. He's such a good kid, always has been, even when he was breaking into my apartment and eating my cookies.

"Just do what I tell you, okay?" I say. It's broad daylight. What could possibly go wrong?

"Okay," he says.

"No matter what," I say. "Promise."

"I promise," he says with a grin. I have a feeling he'd agree to whatever I said at this point, just to be allowed to come with me.

"Stay close," I say, as I walk toward the large metal gates at the entrance to the train yard. When I walk right past the main entrance, Nelson starts glancing at me and then at the gates.

"We're going in a side entrance. The front gates are too obvious," I say.

He nods, and then grins, like this makes it better. Maybe it does.

We walk about a hundred yards past the entrance, until we get to the piece of the fence that I cut when I came here the last time. I hold the wire back for Nelson and wave him through, following closely behind him.

Once we're inside, it feels colder and darker. The large, old, decommissioned trains loom over us. Some are here to be fixed, others are her for use as parts, and still others because they don't have anywhere else to put them.

I'm already humming under my breath as we walk along a pathway next to a row of rusted old boxcars. My little demon skitters about inside me, and I can feel the presence of several demons. The deep well of power within me resonates with the reflected energy.

We walk further into the old train yard, and I remember the last time I was here. Blade interrupted me screaming at the demons I'd attracted. Even then, he was trying to protect me, to save me from myself. He didn't know that he didn't need to protect me from demons. Neither did I. It almost feels like it was another life, an alternate reality. Another person. I've changed so much since then. *Everything* has changed.

"How do we find a demon?" whispers Nelson. Just as he says the words, two demons appear at the end of the alleyway we're walking along. They're mostly in their human form, with long muscled legs, thick muscled arms, and big railroad spikes sticking menacingly out of their bodies. I glance uneasily at Nelson. He's watching the demons, his expression curious, but not unduly frightened. His silver eyes are shining with excitement.

Perhaps he should be more scared?

But Nelson's right. I know what I'm doing now.

I take a breath and start singing to the demons, a sweet gentle song aimed at drawing them closer. They come willingly, not realizing what the outcome of this meeting will be. Their eyes are black and soulless, and their enormous bodies tower over me and Nelson. He's so small in comparison. My heart starts beating faster, and the memory of my mother and father being ripped apart by a demon is suddenly foremost in my mind. I can smell the blood and taste the fear even all these years later. I grab Nelson's arm, and drag him behind me. "Stay behind me, and don't catch their attention," I say.

Nelson is looking a little more nervous now, and he stays where I tell him to.

The demons keep moving toward us. They're about ten yards away when I switch to another type of song. This one is designed to keep the demons under my control, so I can try talking to them, and ask about the spell web, and saving Mei.

A random thought occurs to me. Maybe the *demons* know where Mei is?

Once the idea takes hold, I can't get rid of it. Maybe demons talk to each other? Maybe they've got a network of communication? Maybe they have a hive mind, and once one of them knows something, they all know it? *It's possible, right?* I peer at the demons, trying to see if they have a connection between them. Do they seem to be communicating? Maybe it's telepathy, and they talk to each other in their heads? They don't even look at each other, or even seem to notice that there's anyone here but me and Nelson, their next tasty treats.

I move the demons closer to me, still using my song to keep them docile. Maybe they don't communicate with each other after all. But there's still a chance they know something. All I have to do is ask the demons where Mei is. It's so simple.

And that's exactly when I realize I have no idea how to communicate with a demon. I've never done it, except with my little demon. It's always been more on the level of the hunted (me) fighting back against the hunter (the demons). Not so much of the chit-chat.

"Uh, hi," I say hopefully. Surely they still understand spoken communication? They were once supernaturals. But the demons ignore me, even though they're both under my spell. I guess that would have been too easy. I hum some more, pushing them further under my control.

How am I supposed to do this? I ask the little demon inside me.

My little demon pushes images at me, but as usual it's too fast to be helpful. I can't catch enough of it to understand what it's telling me.

I'll just have to make it up as I go along. As usual.

"I need some information. I have some questions for you," I say to the demons. "I might be able to help you in return."

One of the demons snarls, and suddenly it's striding toward me, teeth on show. Because I stopped singing, it managed to break out of the control I had over it. Nelson lets out a small scared noise behind me. Panicking, I sing a note so high and sharp, it's probably enough to break glass. The demon scrunches up its face, holding its hands up to its temples. But it's still looking at me with hunger in its soulless black eyes. Its single focus right now is to take my energy. I don't know how I can tell, but I can. It makes me tremble. If I make one little mistake, this demon will take advantage and kill us both. No second chances.

The demon snarls, fighting to get closer and raging

against the hold I have over it. Frantically, I try to think. They must know something. There has to be a way to communicate with the demons. Only thing is, I have to sing or the demons will attack. How am I supposed to ask them questions? The second demon is standing just back from the first one, and all I can think is that it's waiting for its chance to attack me, as soon as the first one fails.

I feel a small hand on my back, and I glance back at Nelson to make sure he's okay. He grins up at me, still enjoying being here, despite the fact that the demons are so scary. I can't help my smile in return.

As I turn back to face the demons again, the second demon tries to move forward, forcing itself through the song I'm still singing softly. It's snarling and spitting with a burning rage, and it's suddenly obvious to me that I will never be able to communicate with a creature that's as angry as that. It's so lost to its own desire for energy and power that it would never be able to stop and talk to me rationally.

This whole idea that I could ask the demons *anything* is a bust.

I let out a scream so high-pitched that I'm not even sure dogs can hear it. I don't think Nelson hears it, despite his wolf shifter genes. I hold the note, waiting for the demons to feel the effects of my magic. They hold space for a moment or two, and then they explode into blackened ashes, before slowly floating to the ground. The tiny whirring orbs of demon energy emerge out of the ashes, flinging themselves at me. I absorb the two energy orbs almost without effort.

I let out a breath, and put my arm over Nelson's shoulders. "I think I might need to take you home," I say, relieved that we got out of this situation unscathed. "It's actually much scarier to hunt demons when I'm worrying about protecting someone else."

Nelson's eyes are wide, and he's looking at me like he's never really seen me before. "I didn't know that was how it happened," he says. "They went inside you."

"Yeah."

"Does it hurt?"

"It used to, but not so much any more."

"It was awesome," he says, his voice soft.

"Thanks. Now I really think we need to get out of here." I've gone off the idea of hunting demons, and I've now got two demon energy orbs inside me for later use. I'm about to turn and leave when I see another two demons at the end of the row, and another one behind that.

They're watching us. They saw what I did to the other two demons, but they're so hungry for my energy, they're still willing to attack us. I get a sense of their unrelenting hunger and their implacable focus. There's something different and strange about these demons. They're not acting like other demons I've fought before. They're focused on me, like they already know who and what I am.

"Are we still leaving?" asks Nelson.

"Yeah, I think we should go, before they get closer," I say. I can always come back and deal with these demons later, without Nelson.

Except I don't move, I just keep watching the demons. There's some kind of instinct inside me that says not to turn my back on them. The three demons keep moving forward. They're in their human-shaped forms, pale skin and black eyes. These ones have screws and pieces of old trains attached to their bodies. If these are severed souls, and they're just searching for energy, what's the significance of the metal they all seem to attract? I file that thought away to figure out later.

I hold my ground, trying to see what their goal is, but they just keep moving forward. Soon they're so close— about ten yards—I don't feel comfortable. I start to sing, putting some power behind the song I choose. It's an old favorite of my dad's, a Sunday Lies song.

DON'T BE THE ONE,
Don't be the only,
Just be mine.

I NEVER REALLY UNDERSTOOD THE lyrics, but the tune is awesome. Totally badass. I love that I'm using it to draw the demons in and make them sway in time to my words.

The demons float closer, their enormous bodies not quite touching the ground. They're about ten feet away, their faces slack and totally under my control, when the air seems to shudder around us. A bright shimmering light burns into my eyes, and I falter in my song.

The demons stop, their feet touch the ground again and their dark eyes focus back on me.

There's a surge of magic, a flash of pain, and then suddenly my well of power dries up. One minute it's there, and the next it's gone. Nothing but an empty space where the deep well of energy normally resides. The energy from the two demons I just absorbed is gone as well.

The demons are staring at me like they're trying to decide their next move. Fear shoots through my chest as I stand in front of them without my usual power. I have nothing to protect us if they decide to attack. I glance at

Nelson, and he's looking back up at me, confusion large on his face. His silver eyes have gone a dull grey.

"What's happening?" he whispers.

I shake my head. "I don't know. My power is gone." I try not to say the words too loud in case the demons can understand more than I think they do.

"Gone?" Nelson's eyes widen. He glances back at the demons. "Like gone, gone?"

I keep my gaze on the demons, trying to convince them this is all part of my plan. That I'm still in control and know exactly what I'm doing. That I'm still confident I could take them on in a fight.

But I couldn't. I know it. My chalice powers have been sucked out of me, leaving me barren and dry. A terrified shiver runs through my chest. For the barest of seconds, I feel completely out of control, unable to find a safe place to rest, a hummingbird in perpetual panicked motion.

Then I take a breath, and force myself to focus. I don't have time to fall apart. I have Nelson to take care of.

Is it the spell web again? It must be. Except this time it feels like the director is gathering power for a purpose. He's taking all our energy, and he's using it somewhere in the world.

And not for anything good.

One of the demons takes a step forward, and I clench my fists. "When I give the word, you need to run," I say quietly to Nelson.

"You're coming too, right?" says Nelson.

"Just run. Don't worry about me." *I'll be back here fighting off the demons that I don't have the power to fight.*

I don't say the words aloud. I don't want Nelson to worry. "Get back to the building, and tell Mr. Fookes that I'm down here, fighting demons."

"I'm not leaving you," says Nelson stubbornly.

"You have to," I say grimly. "You promised."

The first of the demons takes another threatening step toward us. I growl, using a particular tone that I know is off key and awkward. They all shudder in reaction. I might not have the power to absorb them anymore, but demons still hate discordant sounds.

Fear pounds through my chest, zigzagging around like it's trying to get out. How am I going to deal with three demons? No power, and I don't have any of the old devices I used to use. I don't have *anything*.

This is how it feels to be without your power. I don't know how humans do it. I'm backing away, and I push Nelson—who still hasn't gone anywhere—behind me. He's shaking but determined not to leave me. It should be endearing perhaps, but I just find it frustrating. I don't want us both to die here.

I give another scream, trying to frighten them off, but it doesn't work. My chalice magic isn't skipping along the sound. But the demons don't have their normal glow either, and I notice that one of the railroad pikes on the one in front seems to be sliding out of its skin. Are they affected by the spell web too? Is the spell web sucking away their power?

Hope fills my chest like a bubble rising to the top. Maybe we're not about to die after all. I take a step back toward them. I let out a shriek that would break the most solid of glass.

The demons snarl at me, their dulled eyes glaring down at us. They're not scared of me any more. My hope bubble bursts in my chest.

And then suddenly they turn and speed away.

CHAPTER
TWENTY-SIX

Nelson and I run back to the building, not stopping until we reach the side steps that appeared in my lab. I'm puffing and out of breath when we arrive and I almost throw myself through the door, dragging Nelson with me. I slam the door shut, and pull the bolt across to lock it behind us. I cross the lab and race out into the hallway and down to the main living area, Nelson following closely behind me.

Mr. Fookes and Daphne are already there, talking urgently to Poppy.

"What just happened?" I say as we burst into the room.

"It's the spell web again, it has to be," says Mr. Fookes. The sound of a phone buzzing distracts him, and he pulls his mobile out of his pocket and answers it quickly. "Yes?"

He listens for a moment, and then his eyes widen, and he takes an involuntary step back. "What? When?"

I can only just hear the voice on the other end. It's dark and dangerous and sounds like Zane. He's speaking quickly and urgently, and it doesn't sound like good news.

Is it about Blade?

Everything in the room tilts for a second, and I grab hold of the edge of the sofa to stay upright. The new fear about having lost my powers is overwhelmed by the reminder that Blade is still missing. Could Zane somehow know what's happened to Freddie and Blade? My breath starts coming quickly, and I watch Mr. Fookes like a hawk, looking for clues. Mr. Fookes looks shocked, his whole body tensed as if for action. My stomach churns; the emptiness where my power usually resides makes me even more edgy. What's happening? Nelson leans in close to me like he can feel the stormy emotions in the room. I put one arm around his shoulders and hold onto him.

"What can we do to help?" Mr. Fookes asks. His face is pale, and all I can think is that he looks scared. What could possibly have happened that would scare Mr. Fookes?

"Let me know. Okay. Yes. Talk soon." Mr. Fookes is nodding, even though Zane can't see him. He presses the button on his phone to end the call.

For a moment, he just stands there, looking at us with a grave expression. Daphne moves to his side, and hugs him tight, leaning her head on his chest, giving him comfort, even though we don't actually know what's wrong yet. He looks at me over her head. "The director just used the power from the spell web to attack the old Earthbound Compound," he says. "It didn't last more than a few minutes. They didn't have a chance of defending themselves. The spell web made them too strong."

My first thought is that at least it's not Blade. I'm not proud of that thought, because there were probably innocent people hurt by the director in his attack... *but at least it's not Blade.*

"What's the Earthbound Compound?" asks Poppy, her expression confused.

"It's the old stronghold of the Earthbound, the organization who set up the spell web. Mei took it from them not so long ago and gave it to the mountain supers for safe-keeping. Carrick has been based out of there for the last while."

"Carrick?" Suddenly the attack on the Compound is much more personal. "Is he okay?" Carrick's not happy with me right now, but he doesn't deserve to be attacked.

"They don't know if anyone has been injured. They don't know anything. It's only just happened. Zane says they're putting together a team to go scope it out." He rubs one hand over his face. "He said that Damien has been missing for several days now, and Seth is little more than a wild creature since Mei's kidnapping. Carrick and Zane were trying to keep the search alive at their end. But now...."

"Walter told us last night that Damien was missing," says Poppy, pacing a couple of steps either way in front of the sofa. "It seems like a little too much of a coincidence that he goes missing just as the spell web starts being used again. Director Holden must have Damien, and he's using him to force Mei to use the spell web."

Mr. Fookes nods slowly, thinking it over. "That does seem like a good reason for why she's letting them use the spell web like this."

"So what are we going to do about it?" says Poppy, looking between us. She's all fired up, her eyes sparking.

Instead of giving an answer, Mr. Fookes lets out a sigh. He pats Daphne on the shoulder, and then gently pushes her away so he can walk to the table and sit down. "What *can* we do about it?" he asks sadly, like he's giving up. "We don't have the power to go up against the spell web."

I've never seen him look so tired and withdrawn. He

looks older than I've ever seen him look. Does he feel it too? The responsibility for the decision I made? That if I hadn't kept my word to him, perhaps I might have saved us all this? We could have found Mei, then saved her and the spell web.

Instead we're now dealing with all these disasters. People dying. Homes destroyed. It's almost too much to bear thinking about.

Back in Seth's brother's kitchen, I thought I was making the best decision; that keeping my promise to Mr. Fookes was important. That I couldn't betray him like that.

But right now in this moment, it just feels like I should have picked Mei. And I think Mr. Fookes is thinking the same thing.

Not finding Mei has led to the spell web being used to do terrible things. Blade is missing. Damien too. Carrick might be hurt or worse. Mei is clearly being forced to use the spell web against her will. All of it is adding up to more than I can handle. I thought if we could find Mei and solve the problem of the spell web right after we got Mr. Fookes back, I'd feel okay about it. But now it feels like it's gone too far, and I'll never be able to absolve myself of the guilt of my decision.

Nelson hugs me tighter against my side, and I realize I'm shaking. I glance down at him, and he's looking solemnly up at me, like he's wondering what I'll do next. I think of how he said he trusted me to look after him with the demons. I clench my fists, forcing myself to calm down. I can't fall apart in front of a twelve-year-old kid, even one as strong as Nelson. I tighten my arm over his shoulder and smile reassuringly down at him. "It's gonna be fine," I say to Nelson. "We'll figure this out."

Then I look again at Mr. Fookes. He's looking down at

his hands, skin pale, shoulders slumped. Unpleasant thoughts are very clearly churning in his head. Daphne is hovering nearby, unsure what she can do to help him.

I can't bear that defeated look on Mr. Fookes's face. I won't let him take the blame for my decisions. "This isn't the end. We just have to step things up at our end," I say firmly. "This isn't the time to fall over and give up. This is when we dig in and fight harder." I'm not going to give up; that would mean giving up on Mr. Fookes as well, and I'm not prepared to do that.

"We've tried everything. He's ahead of us at every turn," says Mr. Fookes. "The more we fight, the more people get hurt. Maybe it's time to give up, Hazel. Let him win. Hope that he lets things go back to normal. We can protect ourselves if we stay here at Sanctus."

"Do you even *hear* yourself?" I ask sternly. "You don't get to give up just because this is difficult. We have to fight against the director with every last breath in our bodies." As I say the words, I realize something important. It doesn't matter whether my decision was right or wrong. It's done. It's in the past.

What matters is how we react now.

It's like there's been an explosion in my head and it's blown away all the cobwebs. I can see clearly now for the first time in a while. We have to make our actions now count for something.

"What if that's what it takes? I couldn't bear it if anyone else were to be killed," says Mr. Fookes.

I turn to Poppy and then Daphne. "If it was a choice of living under tyranny, or fighting and dying for your freedom, which would you choose?" All three of us lived under Dr. Green's tyranny for so long, I can't imagine either of them would choose to go back there.

"I refuse to let him win," says Poppy her eyes on me. She knows what I'm asking. "And I don't believe it has to be a choice between death or tyranny. I think we can win this and survive it. We just have to keep fighting."

"We have to *fight*," says Daphne to Mr. Fookes. She places one hand hesitantly on his shoulder, like she's worried he'll reject even that bit of affection. Instead, he leans into it.

"We have to keep resisting him," I say to Mr. Fookes. "There's still a way through this. We just have to find it." I hug Nelson to me, and feel him hug me back. I don't want Nelson to feel like there's no reason to fight any more.

Mr. Fookes sits up a little straighter. He glances up at Daphne, who's hovering beside him. "I'm sorry," he says quietly. "You're right."

"Damn right, we're right," says Daphne with a grin. She puts her arm around his shoulder and gives him a tight hug.

"I'll check in with some of my contacts," says Poppy, pulling out her phone. "See if they know anything more." Seeing as Poppy spent five years with a gang of supernatural freedom fighters, it's likely she'll actually get some useful information for us.

"I'll call Blade again. See if I can get hold of them," says Mr. Fookes. His expression is grim. I know he doesn't think he'll get an answer. Part of me wants to fall to the ground and wail at the injustice of it. But we don't have the luxury of falling apart right now. We have to fight.

Mr. Fookes has his phone to his ear, listening to the ringing as he waits for Blade to answer. Nothing happens, not even turning over to his voice mail. He dials another number. "I'll try Freddie, just in case," he says.

I wait, watching him intently, but he doesn't get an

answer from Freddie either. I'm trying to assume they're okay, that it's not a problem. They're just laying low. But I'm struggling. Blade said he'd call. There must be a reason why he hasn't. I can't lose him this soon after finding him. I didn't even tell him I love him.

Mr. Fookes hangs up.

"What's happened to them? Why aren't they answering?" I ask, my voice cracking. I clear my throat. I don't really want him to answer my question. I don't think I want to know right now.

"They're probably fine," says Mr. Fookes, looking up at me with haunted eyes that seem to say he knows they're not fine. "They're both experienced. They can take care of themselves."

I swallow hard. I know that Blade should have messaged me by now. I know he was expecting to be home by now, with Mei. "What are we going to do?" I ask, trying to keep it together for Nelson's sake.

"Did he tell you where Mei is?" asks Mr. Fookes. "Where they were going?"

I shake my head, feeling stupid that I didn't even ask. "He said it was a couple of hours away from the cliff house." I'd been too distracted by the memories and by his request that I trust him. "Blade was so sure they'd find her and get her out," I say, remembering how growly he got when I was struggling to say I trusted him. I take a deep breath, then another, wishing I didn't feel like a hole had been punched in my stomach.

"Until we hear something, we have to assume they have it under control," says Mr. Fookes.

"Their powers will have been sucked dry as well," I say. "What if they were in a situation where they needed them?"

"If Freddie and Blade can't handle it, no one can," says

Mr. Fookes, his voice holding a finality that I find I can't argue with.

Nelson is nodding in agreement beside me, and for his sake, I manage to keep my cool. He believes in Blade. So can I. I let out a breath and focus on our job. "I still haven't figured out how to get the spell web out of her once they bring her back," I say. The elders said it couldn't be done, but it has to be possible. We need it to be possible.

"Then that's what we focus on. We work on getting information out of those memories," says Mr. Fookes, looking relieved to have something to focus on. "It might help us with the director as well. Maybe give us some intel on the Compound for Zane."

"Okay," I nod. "So what first?"

"Who has their powers back?" Asks Mr. Fookes, looking between us.

Daphne and Poppy shake their heads, looking at me.

I reach inside myself to see if my powers have returned. I shake my head when I realize there's nothing there. It's like the tide has gone out on my deep well of power, leaving only empty memories and tiny broken shells. Even the energy from the demon orbs that I only just absorbed is gone. It's all been taken.

And then I realize I'm wrong. There's one tiny little spark. My little demon. Somehow it survived, hidden inside me. But I'm not sure how that's going to help me right now. "How are we going to access the memories?" I ask.

"The spell web surge messed with my powers," says Mr. Fookes. "I can't access them at the moment. You'll need to be the one who takes point on the memories."

I shake my head. "It's taken all my powers as well. I can't even feel the memories inside me like I could before."

"So what are we going to do?" asks Poppy, who's just

returned from her phone call. Her face says it all: they didn't know anything either.

Daphne clears her throat. "Perhaps we need a more human solution to this problem?" she says.

"What do you mean?" Mr. Fookes literally scratches his head like he can't even comprehend that there's a way a human solution might be superior to anything he can do.

"How about I try a little bit of hypnosis?"

"Hypnosis?" I repeat stupidly. How could that possibly help?

TWENTY-SEVEN

"Yes, hypnosis," says Daphne with an amused smile. "Dr. Green did it with me while I was in Ravenwood, and when we escaped, I learned enough about it to make sure she hadn't messed with me."

"And did she?" I can't even remember if Dr. Green used hypnosis on me, and the thought is horrifying.

"Not that I could discover, thankfully. I was imagining having had a kill word implanted or something equally ridiculous." Daphne pulls her sunset-colored knitted cardigan closer across her body. With her generous smile and cheery clothes, she looks like the opposite of someone who could have a kill word implanted. Still...

"I wouldn't put it past Dr. Green," I say.

"Me either," agrees Poppy.

"How does hypnosis work?" I ask. I don't think it was something Dr. Green ever got around to testing on me.

"Well, we sit—"

There's a loud smashing sound out in the lobby of the building, and Daphne stops. We all stare over at the front door. Is it the director? Has he finally come to get me for deserting the SIG? My heart is pounding, and I can't think clearly with all the adrenaline pumping through my veins.

The sound comes again, like someone or some*thing* is crashing into the doors.

"I think my protection spell should still be in place," I whisper tentatively, not even sure I'm right. "No one who means us harm should be able to get in."

"We don't know if that spell is still in place, given what's happening with the spell web at the moment," says Mr. Fookes. "None of us can tell."

He's right. I didn't even think of that. This whole situation is messing with me, sending my usually sensible and logical brain into a tailspin. But there's one thing I do know.

"We need to check what it is," I say. I stride toward the front door.

Somehow, Mr. Fookes moves and makes it to the door before me. Something slams hard against the wood of the door, and then noisily slides down on the outside.

"I think that's someone who's hurt," says Daphne. "Not someone who's attacking us."

Mr. Fookes hesitates and then pulls the door open. On the ground in front of us is a man, or what's left of him. Bloodied and cut up, the man is gasping for breath like his lungs might be punctured. I take a closer look.

"Oh my God. It's Freddie." The air rushes from my chest. I look out over the foyer, past the front door, trying to find Blade.

Mr. Fookes drags Freddie inside the apartment, leaving a trail of blood behind him. Freddie's groaning like he's in agony, but we have to get him inside.

"We'll have to work together to put him on the couch," says Mr. Fookes. Daphne and Poppy go on either side, and

Mr. Fookes grabs his shoulders. "Come on, Hazel, we need your help."

I grab Freddie's legs, and help them heft him onto the couch. He moans as we do it, and his eyes flicker open. There are gashes all up his legs and torso, plus burn marks all over his body.

"I'll get some towels and water," says Daphne, as she rushes to the kitchen. "Is there a first aid kit somewhere here?" she shouts back at us.

"Under the kitchen sink," replies Mr. Fookes, as he crouches in front of Freddie on the sofa, checking his vitals.

"I'll get it," says Nelson, and rushes to the kitchen.

"Freddie," I say, coming closer. "Where's Blade? And Mei?"

Freddie shakes his head and moans. "It was... a trap... a set up... Mei was there... so were demons... too many demons..." He seems to float off again into unconsciousness.

"No, Freddie. Listen to me. Where is Blade?" I'm shaking his leg, trying to keep him awake long enough to tell me what I need to know.

"Hazel, calm down. You're hurting him," says Poppy. She pulls my hands from Freddie's calf.

I try to breathe through a tear-soaked throat. Where's Blade? Why isn't he here with Freddie?

Freddie wouldn't have left him unless...

"Where's Blade, Freddie?" The words tumble out of me, and I can feel my hysteria rising.

Freddie wouldn't have left Blade unless...

I can't finish the thought in my head. I can't ask him again. I don't want to know what happened to Blade anymore.

"Trap...," says Freddie. His eyes stay closed, and his breathing is shallow. "Waiting..."

Nelson comes back with a small first aid kit, and hands it to Mr. Fookes.

"What happened, Freddie?" says Mr. Fookes gently as he unclips the first aid kit, and pulls out a pack of soft pads. He lifts up Freddie's ripped shirt, looking for the source of the bleeding. There are multiple wounds on his torso.

"Demons," whispers Freddie. "It happened... so quickly. Blade... fought them off... but there were... too many."

"Who was it?" asks Mr. Fookes.

"Connor and Gavan." Freddie's voice sounds raw, like maybe they hurt his throat, as well as everything else.

Daphne reappears, holding several towels and a bowl of water. Mr. Fookes takes them from her, and wets one of the smaller towels. He starts to wipe away the blood around the biggest wound.

"Where's Blade?" asks Mr. Fookes, his voice soft, like he's already guessed the truth.

It feels like there's a jagged spear going right through my heart. I don't think I could hurt more if I were physically attacked.

"They captured us...," Freddie whispers. "...set me free."

I make a garbled noise. Why would they only set Freddie free? *What happened to Blade?*

"What?" Mr. Fookes leans in. "Why?"

"Blade is...."

"What? What's happened to Blade?" I can feel the hysteria rising in my chest. Is this it? Is Blade dead?

Freddie leans back in the pillows, his face wrecked. "They want... Hazel...." He moves restlessly, like he's trying to remember something that's too difficult. "...there's...

some kind of...problem... with their plans. In return... for help... they'll let... Blade free."

He's alive. Thank God he's alive. I sit down heavily on the chair next to Freddie's sofa, filled with relief. For a moment, that's all I can do. *He's alive.*

And then I think about what Freddie's just said.

It's my fault again? They have Blade, but they really want me? All of this was to trap me? I look down at Freddie, at the wounds all over his body, the blood everywhere.

All this to get at *me*?

"When can we leave?" I ask. I'm not leaving Blade there on his own.

Mr. Fookes shakes his head emphatically. "We can't let them have you, too, Hazel. That would give them too much power. Blade wouldn't want you to risk yourself for him."

"They probably won't keep their word, anyway. They'll just kill you both when you're no longer useful," says Poppy.

I give her a look. Of course they're planning to kill us. But if I'm there to help Blade, then we could get him out of there. Connor and Gavan aren't exactly the greatest planners in the world. I'm sure I could find a way to escape with Blade.

"So we just leave Blade there? Don't go help him?" I glare at both Poppy and Mr. Fookes.

Mr. Fookes paces back and forth across the room. His hair is usually a mess, but now it looks like he's channelling his inner Albert Einstein. "We can't leave him there. We have to rescue him." He looks up at me. "But we can't risk Connor or the director getting you in their power, Hazel. They already have Mei."

"So I either help them create a monstrous demon energy project that will likely kill millions of people, or I let

Blade die? Is that it? There's no third option?" I feel like I'm going to throw up.

Freddie moans. "You can't... go back... Blade made me... promise..."

"You promised him, but I didn't promise anything," I say angrily. "I'm not leaving him there." He's not dead. He's alive, and we could save him. It's not a given that they'll capture me.

Poppy sits on an arm of the chair I'm sitting in. "It's a trap, Hazel. You can't do it." She puts one hand on my arm, and it feels heavy, like she's holding me down.

I look up at Mr. Fookes, and he clearly thinks the same thing. "We can't just leave him there," I repeat. *I'll go on my own if I have to.*

"We can't help Connor and Gavan, either." Mr. Fookes looks gray again, the same as he did when he got the memories implanted. "Going there will just play into their hands." He turns his attention back to Freddie. "Was Mei even there? Or was that a trick?"

"She was there. But they... were about... to move her. She's... catatonic. Lying on a hospital bed... tubes everywhere."

"If she's there..."

Freddie shakes his head. He's starting to look a little more lucid. "They were about... to move. They set me free... and then took off." He stops and breathes heavily for a second, as if he's just run a marathon. "Everyone was... leaving. There were... big trucks. They keep moving... that's how they avoided... anyone... finding them."

"I think I might know where they are," says Daphne softly from the doorway of the kitchen. She's holding her phone and watching something playing out on it. She holds the screen in our direction, and I can just see the director standing on a podium, outside a large hacienda-style concrete building.

We crowd around the phone, all trying to figure out what's happening. Behind Director Holden, Connor and Gavan are loitering, both looking smug. There are more figures to one side, but I can't make out who all the people are. In a large cage behind them is a large jaguar with wild, amber eyes and bloodied wounds over his whole body.

Blade.

I let out a whimper. He's in a *cage.* I thought I hated Director Holden before, but it's nothing to the blazing anger I'm feeling right now.

"What's the director doing?" asks Mr. Fookes, his eyes glued to the screen.

"Some kind of press conference. Just for supers," says Daphne. Her eyes are soft with concern, and she's watching me like she thinks I might keel over at any moment.

"Turn it up."

Daphne presses the button on the side of her phone, and the volume increases to match the tiny figure on the screen.

"...it's time to take back control of the supernatural world. The SIG and the Earthbound are working together to return our lives to the way they were. We have had enough of the disruptions, the chaos, the suffering. Enough of being tortured by the humans, of being treated like second-class citizens. Enough of the fear and the terror."

"Why'd they use the spell web, then? If they didn't want to cause fear and terror?" I mutter.

"We have captured the dissidents Mei and Damien Walker, and their fellow terrorist Nico Blade, as well as other members of the so-called resistance."

I put one hand over my mouth to hold in the gasp. He called Blade a terrorist. That's not good.

"That confirms our theory about why Mei was letting them use the spell web," says Poppy. "They have Damien."

"Except Freddie said that Mei is almost completely out of it," says Mr. Fookes. "They probably just drugged her up so much that she didn't know what she was doing."

"Either way, this is serious," I say. "He's making some kind of big move. This is just the start of it."

Mr. Fookes looks carefully down at the screen. "Who else does he have? Could they have Carrick as well...?"

I shake my head, unable to answer. I have no answer to give him. It's starting to feel like the director is holding all the cards. Maybe he's been holding them all along, and we were just too clueless to notice?

"...We have warrants out for the arrest of other dissidents connected to the latest upheaval, including former SIG agents Seth Barnes and Hazel Miller, also known as Hazel Rushton. Both should be considered armed and dangerous and should not be approached by the public."

It takes me a moment to process that he's said my name in the same sentence as *'armed and dangerous'*. "What? I'm not dangerous."

"To him you are," says Daphne.

Director Holden moves to one side and gestures for someone to join him on the stage. I immediately recognize Lakas as he climbs onto the podium, his long lanky legs making him look like a praying mantis. My stomach drops. Nothing good happens when they include Lakas in the conversation.

"I've asked my close colleague Lakas Hagabat to officially head up the Special Operations division of the SIG, while I continue my duties as the SIG Director. We will work together to restore order and ensure the safety of each and every supernatural in the world."

"Safety, my ass," I say indignantly. "That's the last thing Lakas wants or even cares about."

Lakas steps forward and smiles. I can't help the terrified shiver that rocks my body as I see him, but he looks innocently at the camera.

He smiles, and instead of showing his sharp incisors, and his crazy face, he looks calm and in control. His suit is expensive, and his human body doesn't show a whisper of the terrifying creature that he becomes at the drop of a hat.

TWENTY-EIGHT

It's less than an hour later when there's a knock at the door.

Freddie's sister, Iris, is standing in the doorway, looking as elegant and glamorous as ever. She's holding the heirloom that I reclaimed from the SIG for Freddie. She barely looks at any of the rest of us, just rushes over to Freddie, who's still lying prone on the couch. We've managed to clean up some of his wounds and give him some painkiller, but he still seems to be in a lot of pain.

"What happened to him?" she demands, and I wince at the anger in her voice. It still feels like this is all my fault, and I have trouble looking her in the eyes. Luckily Mr. Fookes is there to answer for us.

"He went on a mission with Blade. It was a trap. They still have Blade, and they want to swap Blade for Hazel."

"Who's they?"

I step forward. "Connor and my father."

She gives us all a look of disgust and turns back to Freddie. "You need to take better care of yourself, my stupid brother," she says. Her long black hair ripples down her back as she leans over to get a better look at his wounds.

I move over to where she's now crouched beside him and kneel down. "Can you heal him?" I ask.

"The heirloom can. It's filled with powerful magic from our ancestors."

I remember back to our meeting in Mr. Fookes's living room. "Why didn't he take it with him? Why did he leave it with you?"

She shrugs one elegant shoulder. "He knew there was a risk involved. He did not want the bone to fall into the wrong hands again. They did not know what they had last time. This time they would pay more attention."

Freddie's face is beaded with sweat, and he looks a million miles away from the suave man that I met for the first time at the Palo Alto Country Club. "Anything you need, just ask me," I say quietly.

She nods, but she's already distracted, focusing her attention on Freddie and the heirloom bone. I can feel the magical currents coming off the heirloom, and it feels good to having something powerful in our midst again, even if we can't use it for anything other than saving Freddie right now.

I stand up and move away, allowing her to weave her magic.

I wander over to where Mr. Fookes is consulting quietly with Daphne and Poppy. Nelson went home to check on his mother not long after we watched the director on the podium.

The others stop talking as soon as I get there, and I glare at them, knowing they're discussing how to stop me from going after Blade. "You know we can't just leave him in their hands, right?"

"We were just discussing options," says Mr. Fookes smoothly. "The director is in a powerful position right now. We have to think this through, not do anything too hasty."

"If we wait, they'll hurt him. Maybe kill him." I feel like I'm fighting for Blade's life.

"All I'm saying is that we need to make a plan. If we go rushing in there like maniacs, we'll just get ourselves caught and maybe killed as well. We need to make sure we actually save Blade."

I want to argue with him, but he's making sense. The director has Mei and Damien. He's got the spell web. He's got Lakas. The Compound. Connor. Dr. Green. Gavan. It's like a roll call of all the people who've tried to kill me. He's even got a bunch of demons, if Connor and my father have continued with the dangerous work they were doing.

Which of course they have.

The director has all the power, and what do we have? Currently not much, because we're all without our power.

It's not a great place to be.

My phone starts vibrating in my pocket and I pull it out, just in case it's Blade, and he's miraculously escaped.

It's not Blade.

"It's Connor," I say to the others.

"Answer it," says Daphne. "Tell them not to hurt Blade, or they'll be sorry."

Mr. Fookes gives Daphne a look and then rests one hand on my arm. "Answer it and find out as much as you can about what they want you to do. Information is what's going to help us now."

I let out a breath. Then hit answer.

"Hello?" I say tentatively.

"Hazel," says Connor, all smooth sophistication. I can

almost feel his siren abilities working through the phone. "So lovely to hear the sound of your voice again."

"What have you done with Blade?" I say, unwilling to mess around. I see Mr. Fookes wincing beside me.

"We haven't done anything with him. He was the one who broke into our facility and attempted to sabotage our project."

"You mean Mei? Did you just call Mei a project?"

"I don't know what you're talking about. We're working on a very important government project, and a dissident attacked, intent on destroying it. End of story."

"I saw him on television. He looked terrible."

There's a tiny pause, as if he hadn't expected that answer. "It was an unprovoked attack. We were defending ourselves."

"You better not touch him again," I say, practically growling. I'm so angry, I can barely see straight. I take a breath, and then another, trying to calm myself down.

"That's up to you, now isn't it, Hazel?"

"What do you mean?" I'm trying to listen harder now, to ignore the rage that's inside me and focus on Connor, and what he's telling me. It's the only way I can think of to help Blade.

"If you do what we say, then no one will be harmed. If you don't..."

"What do you want me to do?" I glance at Mr. Fookes, and he gives me an encouraging sign. All I want to do is find a way to reach through the phone line and rip out Connor's throat. Instead I have to play nice.

"You need to come to the compound and work with your father on our project. He needs your help."

My heart thuds uncomfortably in my chest. "What does

he need my help with? He knows far more than I do about being a chalice."

"He needs your power, Hazel. Apparently you're quite the little powerhouse."

"What are you making?"

"You know what we're making. A new spell web. One powered by demons."

"You're really serious about that? You think a demon-powered spell web would be stable?"

"Your father says it will. He says they used demons in the creation of the first spell web, and that one was around a while."

I blink in surprise and look up at Mr. Fookes. "They used demons to create the first spell web?" I wonder if that's what the mountain super memories show. We need to get into those memories, figure out what's truth and what isn't. If only it didn't feel like they were attacking me every time I try.

"Apparently. They didn't tell anyone, because they didn't want anyone else to be able to recreate a spell web. And they thought people would be too afraid of it."

If that's the truth, they were probably right. "And what's my part in all of this?" I know the other aspect of the creation of a spell web is that they need a power source in the middle to sacrifice themselves. "Am I the sacrifice?"

Connor's hesitation on the other end of the line is enough to confirm it. Even when he speaks, it's clear he's covering up. "Of course not, Hazel. We need you because Gavan doesn't have enough power to make this happen. His years of drinking have taken their toll."

"When do you need me there?"

"Now. Yesterday. We have the director breathing down

our necks," says Connor. "He wants it done already. He's says it's too complicated, having to use Mei all the time."

A chill worms its way down my spine. Director Holden wants Mei out of the picture. He wants to be able to control the spell web without an intermediary.

Which means Mei's days are numbered.

"Will Director Holden be there?" I ask, trying not to tremble too hard at the thought. The last time I saw him, he ordered me to be incarcerated in prison—and then let Lakas fly me there.

"He's leaving today for New York with Lakas. He's not interested in the how's. He just wants it done."

I let out a relieved breath of air. They'll both be gone. But maybe not forever, so we need to hurry. We have to get Mei out of there. And Blade. And Damien. And anyone else they're currently holding just because they think they can.

I'm the only chance they have. I'm the only one who can get in there without being killed. I'm sure I can come up with something, some kind of plan to get everyone out.

I can fix this.

I know I can.

Probably.

I look up, and Mr. Fookes, Daphne and Poppy are making big gestures to tell me not to do it. I take a breath. I know it's a trap. I know they'll be doing everything they can think of to keep me there. But...

"Okay, I'll come to the compound. But you have to promise to let Blade free as soon as I get there," I say.

"Of course," says Connor smoothly, and even I can hear the lie in his voice.

TWENTY-NINE

"He's lying," says Mr. Fookes.

"Of course he's lying," I say in exasperation. "I'm not arguing about that."

"Then why are you going?"

"Because if I go and pretend to help them, I can get inside the compound. I can set things up so that we can rescue Blade. We can get Mei free. We can solve this whole situation."

Mr. Fookes is looking at me with sad, knowing eyes. "You feel responsible. This is all because you think you should have saved Mei, instead of me," he says.

I shake my head. "I don't regret saving you," I say calmly. And I mean it. "I'll be honest and say that I've wondered since we got home if saving Mei would have been the better option." I wince when I hear Daphne gasp at my words, and I look at her apologetically. "But I will never regret saving you."

"So I'm right. You *do* feel responsible? You're putting yourself into a dangerous situation just to appease your guilt," he says, quickly, like I've just proven his point.

"Because that's not going to change the fact that you freed me instead of Mei."

I let out a heavy breath. Maybe he might have been right if he'd said that to me a day ago, maybe even this morning. But I've had a realization since then. "This isn't about my decision to save you. I made the best decision I could at the time," I say. "This is about how we react to the situation we're in *right now*. We have to make our actions count for something. This is about rescuing *Blade and Mei*. And not letting the director win. I refuse to sit at home and hope for the best."

Mr. Fookes shakes his head. "If Freddie and Blade couldn't get Mei out...." He looks over to where Freddie's sister is still working with the heirloom to heal Freddie. "They'll have plans in place to keep you locked up." We all follow his gaze, and a grim silence descends.

He's right, except...

"I have a different kind of skill," I say. "It's not an overt skill, like Blade and Freddie's skills. It's not outwardly visible when you look at me. But I can fix things. I can figure out how things work. And I know I can figure this out. I know that if I get in there, I can help them escape." *At least I hope I can.* But I'm not about to say that out loud to Mr. Fookes. He's doubting me enough as it is.

"But if Blade got captured...."

He doesn't need to finish the sentence. Blade is way more experienced than me. He knows how to get out of situations that I haven't even thought about getting *into*.

"We need a different angle," I say, trying to stay calm. I need them to support me going to the compound. *I need their help.* "Blade and Freddie rushing in to save Mei was the expected angle. Me going in, pretending to give up, might confuse them. Make them underestimate me."

"She has a point," says Daphne. "Men have been under-estimating women for centuries. And Connor and Gavan strike me as the kind of men to do exactly that."

"Why do you think the director was so pissed when I helped Damien and Mei escape the SIG?" I say. "Because he thought he had me under his thumb. He didn't think I had it in me to go against him like that."

Poppy makes a disgusted noise, like she's annoyed for women everywhere. I know she's already on board with this idea.

"But that just means the director has a grudge against you now, and he's twice as dangerous," says Mr. Fookes. "Not that he's less dangerous."

"From what Connor said, the director won't be there. And I'm not even sure the director knows they're black-mailing me. He just told them to get the job done, and they're doing it. Connor and Gavan are both loose cannons. They don't follow the rules and they don't play nice."

"Again, you're not making arguments that make me feel better about you going," says Mr. Fookes.

I let out a frustrated huff. "What do you suggest, then?" I say, gesturing with one arm. "We wait here while the director and his cronies destroy the world and make it so we can never get it back? So they can use the spell web whenever they like to suck our powers dry? We know where Mei is now. We have to go there and try to save her and Blade."

"She's right," says Daphne, putting one hand on Mr. Fookes's arm. "We can't just sit here. We're smart, and we're strong. We can make this work, especially because these men all seem to underestimate Hazel. They think she can be manipulated and used. And Hazel is stronger than that. She's smarter than that."

"And it's our only option," adds Poppy with a grin.

I roll my eyes at her. Not the most helpful comment. "I have to go in there. But you guys need to come with me as well. This will still be a team event. I need you as back up."

"You want us to go into the compound with you?" blurts Daphne. Her eyes are wide, and she clutches her cardigan across her chest.

"No, not inside," I say soothingly. "I need you waiting in the next town over. I'll need help as soon as I break everyone free."

Daphne nods with a relieved expression. "We can do that."

Mr. Fookes still looks like he wants to disagree, but he can tell he's outnumbered. "I'll call Zane," he says, his expression grim. He pulls out his phone and starts dialing. "He'll take you."

"What are you planning, Hazel?" Poppy asks in a low voice when Mr. Fookes has moved away to talk to Zane. "I can tell by your expression you've got an idea."

"I think I need to invent a few little surprises for when I'm in there." I'm going through an inventory of the supplies in my lab in my apartment. "I have a few ideas."

"What can we do to help?" Poppy's eyes have lit up. She loves anything that involves trickery and sneakiness.

"Come with me. I'll need you to do some soldering."

Poppy puts her arm through mine and leans in. "How long do we have?"

"I said to Connor I'd get there tomorrow. I don't think there's any need to rush there before then. They won't hurt Mei until they have a new spell web in place, which they apparently can't do without me, and Blade should be safe enough until I get there as well."

We all look over at Freddie. He's still lying on the sofa,

his body twitching occasionally. His sister is hovering over him, her expression grim. It's hard to keep positive when I know that Blade is probably just as badly hurt, except he's in a cage getting no medical attention at all. My determination to rescue Blade hardens as I think about what he's going through.

"The sooner we get started, the sooner we can get this plan underway," says Daphne in her no-nonsense way. She links arms with me on the other side.

Mr. Fookes is still in the corner talking to Zane, but he waves as we head out the door like three little ducks, off to fight in the war.

We traipse up the stairs, one behind the other. It feels good to have a plan, to be moving toward something. I can finally feel my magic seeping back into my central well of power, little rivulets of energy that give me a buzzing feeling over my whole body.

I just hope it's enough.

CHAPTER
THIRTY

We arrive on my floor, and I attempt to fish my keys out of my pocket.

It makes me think of Blade and all the times he's had to help me get in the door, because I couldn't manage it. Today at least, my hands are steady, and I manage to get the door unlocked. We head inside and I can't help the smile on my face as I look over the family room, with my comfy sofa, and favorite chair. I'm even looking at the PlayStation nostalgically, remembering Blade and Nelson playing on it and yelling at the TV screen.

"I love this place," says Poppy. "Every time I come up here, I feel so... cosy."

"It's a great apartment," I agree. Again, I can't help thinking back to a few months ago, when the only people who'd been in my apartment were Mr. Fookes and Nelson —and Nelson wasn't supposed to be there. It feels crowded having Daphne and Poppy in my space, but in a good way.

My life is completely different now. I have my old friends Daphne and Poppy back in my life. I have Blade, who means more to me than I can say. I have Mr. Fookes, who's like a crazy uncle, and Nelson, who's the little brother I never had. Mei had become a good friend before she was captured. I even have new friends like Freddie, Iris, and Zane. Fleet and Suzanna. Damien, Carrick and Seth, too, if they weren't so mad at me.

A dipping feeling in my stomach reminds me that I could lose it all again so easily, just like I lost my parents. It takes so little for everything to tip again, to lose the people I love. Blade and Mei have been captured. Damien and Carrick are angry at me and Seth hates me now, too.

Worst of all, Blade is in the hands of two men who actively dislike me. It's a scary thought.

But I refuse to just lie down and take it. I won't hide away anymore. I'm going to find a way to help Blade and Mei if it's the last thing I do.

"Right. We need some small devices. Things that can go in my pockets, be easily hidden. Things that are going to help me upset whatever they're doing," I say. "We know they're hoarding demons, collecting far too many of them in one place. I think we need to make a device that sets them off. Like a whistle for dogs. No one else will be able to hear it except me, the demons, and my father."

"Won't he try to stop it?" says Daphne.

"He can try."

"What else?" asks Poppy.

"I'd like to have some explosions," I say with relish. "I think I'd enjoy blowing up part of their building."

"Are you sure...?" says Daphne. Her expression is uncertain, like she thinks this is all going to end badly.

"Definitely. Not big ones, more like warning ones, distractions. Lots of smoke. And I want to have something on hand that can deal with the cages that Connor had at his company's smelter. Something that will unlock them. I'm not sure what, but I had the bar for a while, I think I can come up with something." I hope I'm not being overly optimistic, we only have until tomorrow.

"What about a system for communication?" asks Poppy. "We need a way to make sure you're okay, so we can help if we need to."

I hesitate, not sure it's a good idea. What if something happens to me? Would they try to attack, and then get themselves hurt as well? But she's right that we should figure out a way to give updates. "Maybe we can incorporate it into something, like my belt buckle or an earring or something? Do a video feed like we did when we sent Mr. Fookes into Ravenwood?"

"I think that was destroyed when we did the second mission to Ravenwood," says Poppy. "But I have something that might work. A listening bug that I use for when I'm shadowing a mark for a client."

"Okay, that sounds good," I say, a little relieved. I think I prefer that they can only hear what's going on. "So we know what we want to make. We don't have long, maybe a few hours. We have to be fast."

"Perfect." Poppy nods her head decisively. "Let's do this."

I think, like me, she's excited to be doing something more than just waiting and worrying.

FOUR HOURS LATER, we're all tired and sore, but also immensely satisfied.

I stretch my arms up over my head, trying to ease my aching muscles. My deep well of power has come back, which is a huge relief, but with it, the mountain super memories have also returned, and they're pushing at me like they want out. It's like a mosquito buzzing in my ear— annoying, but manageable at the moment. I'm still too nervous of the memories to try looking at them again, in case they overwhelm me like they did last time.

"So do you think you're ready?" asks Poppy, pushing her long hair behind one ear and looking down at me with a serious expression, her dark eyes worried.

"As I'll ever be," I say with a grin. I'm trying not to think too hard about what's going to happen tomorrow when I hand myself over to Connor. I've been having too much fun designing and creating the devices. "I'll just need to go out and absorb some demon energy before I go as well," I say. "Then I might be okay. But thanks to you two, I've got an arsenal fit for a queen."

Poppy puts her arm around my shoulder and gives me a tight sideways hug. "You better use all of it to stay safe," she says.

Daphne comes over and hugs me on the other side, so we're one big pile of friendship. "You have to come back," she whispers. "Promise us that you'll survive this, okay?"

I nod jerkily, but find I can't speak through the hard lump in my throat and the tears that are threatening to fall. We've come through so much, the three of us. It seems impossible that this could be the end, after everything else we've survived. We stay like that for a full minute, before the other two pull away. I catch Poppy wiping the corner of her eyes.

I take a deep breath and look over the devices on the work bench, mentally cataloguing them to make sure I have everything I need.

We've made several of the sound devices, adapting my old demon-calling devices and making them much smaller and easier to hide—about the size of a deck of playing cards.

Poppy's been working on the explosives, which I think she's found extremely satisfying, if the number of explosions coming from my bathroom is anything to go by. She's standing next to the table in my lab, peering down at the devices on the bench, with smudges of black ash over her face and hands, and in her auburn hair. I hope I have a bathroom left.

Daphne and I have been in my lab working on the cages and the communication device. Connor stole my magic stick, which is what I was using to absorb the demons at first, but I used it enough to get a sense of how it worked. I remember the runes on the sides and the feel of the power inside it. Now that I've learned to wield my power better, I feel like I might be able to overcome the locking system on any cages he might still have that are using the same magic.

I've created a universal key, the kind that lock picks use, and I've infused some of my chalice magic into it. I'm hoping that it connects to me and the cage in such a way that I'll be able to control it. It's a long shot... but I'm hopeful.

Daphne managed to attach Poppy's listening bug to the back of my mother's pin, which we tested to make sure it could receive sound over a longer distance. There's a matching receiver for them to use, which means that as long as I'm wearing the pin, they'll be able to hear what's happening inside the compound while they wait outside. We're planning to create some kind of system with words or phrases that I can use to indicate if I need help, or if there's something they can do.

It's all very theoretical, and I have no idea if any of these devices will help... But it's better than going into the lion's den with nothing.

"Let's head back down and see what Mr. Fookes is up to," I say to them both. He's visited us in the lab a couple of times, but he's been working on something of his own. He was acting all mysterious, and wouldn't tell us what it was, so I'm burning with curiosity. "Did he tell you anything more, Daphne?"

She shakes her head with a rueful expression. "He wants it to be a surprise."

I give all my new toys one last glance and then follow Daphne and Poppy out of the apartment and back down the stairs. It feels good to have something to take with me on my mission, as well as to have spent a few hours with Daphne and Poppy.

Despite everything, it's been fun, and we've had a few laughs as we've soldered and exploded things. It's also the first time since I've been back that I feel like I've done something useful.

As soon as we get to the foyer, we hear strange noises coming from Mr. Fookes's apartment.

"What's going on?" asks Daphne, concern on her face. "Is something wrong with Freddie?"

"Only one way to find out," says Poppy, striding ahead of us into the apartment.

CHAPTER
THIRTY-ONE

I can hear Poppy and Daphne's surprised exclamations, but I can't see what's got them gasping.

My heart leaps. What is it? What's he been doing? I peer over Daphne's shoulder, trying to see. She moves forward, and the room becomes visible.

There's a huge white screen set up on the far wall. A projector is sitting at the other end of the room, and Mr. Fookes is fiddling with the buttons on it as if he's trying to get it to work. The delicious smell of popcorn is wafting around the room.

The couches have all been moved to face the screen, and the lights in the room are dimmed like it's a movie theater. A head pops out of the kitchen, and I recognize Zane. A shiver goes down my body. He's here to take us to the compound tomorrow. It's all starting to feel too real. I give Zane a solemn wave, and he gives a tiny nod, never one to get too effusive.

Freddie and his sister are sitting together talking quietly. Freddie doesn't look one hundred percent, but he looks way better than he did earlier. I let out a small, relieved breath. He looks up and smiles, his full-force charming smile. I smile back, glad he's awake and functioning.

"What's happening?" asks Daphne, looking around the strange set up.

"We're going to have a little slide show. I think it would help to have as many of us see this as possible. Get everyone's thoughts."

"What are we watching?" asks Poppy, peering closer at the projector. Her face is puzzled, like she's trying to work it out without being told. "Where's the reel?"

"I've changed this around some. And it's not your usual kind of projector," says Mr. Fookes mysteriously. "Come on everyone, sit down. We made popcorn."

Zane goes back into the kitchen and then comes back out with bowls of popcorn, giving each of us our own supply. Rather than just normal buttery popcorn, this stuff has herbs and spices as well, and it smells absolutely delicious. My mouth starts watering, and I realize I'm really hungry.

Daphne takes a chair, and Poppy and I slouch into one of the couches. Zane takes the other sofa, putting his legs up and relaxing. Mr. Fookes stays by the projector, on a chair from the dining table. His hand is resting on the projector.

"So what are we watching?" I ask, before putting a handful of popcorn in my mouth. It tastes even better than it smelled.

"It might be something you've already seen," says Mr. Fookes. "But it should be new to everyone else."

I scrunch up my face in confusion. That's very specific. What movie have I definitely seen, but no one else has? I could count on one hand the number of movies I've seen in the last few months since meeting Blade, but I used to watch hundreds of them, all recommended by Walter and Beanie from the pawn shop. Could it be some kind of home movie? That doesn't seem right either. I can't even begin to work out what he's hinting at.

But I don't have to wait long for an answer. The lights go out, and pictures start up on the screen.

And he's right.

These are pictures I do recognize, if only vaguely. They're the memories from the mountain supers.

My gaze immediately flicks to Mr. Fookes. How is he doing this? He's watching me instead of the screen, and nods when he sees my reaction. He's doing this for me, somehow. He gestures for me to turn back to the screen.

He's right, I need to take this in.

On the screen, there's no sound, but there's a lot of action.

The first set of images are all mountain supers. It's the beginning of the First Village, people prepping the hidden village, down and away from the rest of the world. The faces are all craggy, rough-hewn, and serious. Grim even. It switches to another time, much later, when the homes look established, and people are walking the streets, and this time they're looking contented. Happy almost.

And then it switches again, to another time. The mountain supers are in the First Village, but these people look like they're in pain. Something is happening. People are falling to the ground, curled up like they're unable to move, they're in so much agony.

"What's happening to them?" Poppy whispers to me, her voice wavering.

"I'm not sure." I turn to Mr. Fookes, who shakes his head. He doesn't know either.

"I think it's the day the first spell web was created," says Zane quietly, his face lit up by the pictures on the screen. "It took so much power from all the supernaturals in the world that some died. Many were in great pain. It never gets talked about, but the creation of the first spell web was an act of aggression on the supernatural population in many ways."

"It *hurt* them?" I hadn't known that. It's never mentioned.

Zane shrugs. "No more than the wild dragons were hurting them, I suppose."

Mr. Fookes clears his throat. "I don't think they knew what they were doing. From what I've seen, it was all very theoretical. And they were desperate. The dragons really were destroying the world." He looks apologetically at Zane.

Zane doesn't say anything, but his expression is grim. I don't know what he's thinking, but it can't be easy to hear that your ancestors—actually for Zane, his peers—were destroying the world.

As if pulled forth by Mr. Fookes's words, the screen is suddenly showing a picture of the surface of the Earth. Dark clouds fill the sky, and through the puffs of air, fire burns. At least twenty dragons fly through the sky on enormous wings, each of them attacking the others in a seemingly random pattern. As if all twenty dragons considered themselves to be fighting all nineteen of the other dragons. Fire bursts lit the sky and showed the devastation on the ground below: fire-damaged houses and bare, ravaged lands. This place looks like somewhere that no one would want to live—or would even be *able* to live.

"It was like that everywhere," says Zane, his voice low. "Even the dragons like my clan who didn't fight all the time, we hid underground, away from all the devastation." His expression is grim, like he's struggling to hide his true feelings.

I look at Zane, really understanding for the first time what it was like in his time. I'd known theoretically that he'd been in a dragon shifter hibernation for more than three hundred years, and had only just been woken recently, but if I'd thought about it, I'd have somehow assumed that his time wasn't so different from ours. But these images are horrifying. I had no idea it was as bad as this when the dragons were at their peak.

The images switch to a darkened bunker where a group of around twenty men and women are working over magic books and a large cauldron. "Is this it? When they made the first spell web?" I ask, leaning forward, trying to take it all in. There's a feeling of resonance inside me, and I know I have these same images inside me somewhere. I don't know how Mr. Fookes has accessed them, but I'm glad he has. The time it would take me to figure out how to get into my memories is time we don't have right now.

"It seems to be. It's a memory they've created from someone else's mind, somehow," Mr. Fookes says quietly. "I haven't seen all these memories properly, either."

"Are they all memories from real mountain supernaturals?" I ask. "Did a mountain super have to somehow witness what happened?"

Mr. Fookes nods quietly. "I think so. They're all from someone's perspective, right? Seen through someone's eyes."

The view swoops in, and suddenly I can see the pages of the books they're working from. There's loads of crossing out and scribbles around the edges, like they've tried things that haven't worked. One man seems to be in charge, and the others are following his instructions like he's a god. Maybe he was, to have discovered something like the spell web through trial and error like this.

He's a tall, thin man, his expression focused, and his face lit with strange shadows from the one source of light in their mostly dark bunker, an open-flame torch attached to a metal sconce in the corner of the room. I see an even larger figure towering over them all to the side of the room—a mountain super helping as well. I peer more closely, trying to see if there were other types of super in the group, but it's hard to tell.

As we watch, the man holds out his hands, and a blue light appears in the middle of his fingers. It's a light I recognize—the exact blue of demon light. This man is a chalice.

I sit back in my seat, stunned.

The person who created the spell web was a chalice? How is it that no one else has ever told me that?

I look over to Mr. Fookes, and he looks equally stunned. He didn't know either.

"Was it a secret? They didn't tell anyone for some reason?" I say croakily.

"Was what a secret?" asks Poppy, her gaze going from me to the screen, where the man is producing more power in the form of a blue glowing ball of demon energy.

"That man is a chalice. It was a chalice who created the spell web three centuries ago."

Zane nods, watching the screen closely. "It makes sense. Who else would have had the power to do something like that? In those times, we were so disparate, so disconnected. Dragons didn't connect with each other and supers didn't congregate the way they do now. There was no chance to get together for the greater good."

"But that's the story they tell," I say. "That it was all the supers working together, making it happen."

"Just goes to show you can't always trust the history you get told," says Daphne, darkly. It occurs to me that she's probably thinking about her family, and what her ex-husband told her kids about her. Or about what she used to think about herself, and what Dr. Green encouraged her to think, despite knowing about supernaturals.

Her alternate history, told to her by outsiders, who had no idea of the real truth. That she's a shifter, a wolf who could break free of her bonds.

Zane shifts on his sofa. "I always wondered about that. When I was told how it happened when I woke up, I always wondered how they managed to gather together and form a coalition."

"There are a few people there," I say. But even I can see they're his assistants, scurrying around at his beck and call. "Maybe the others didn't help with this bit," I say uncertainly.

"Whatever happened, they saved everyone from the destruction of the dragons," Poppy points out. "I mean, it looks like it sucked back then." She glances at Zane. "No offense, Zane. But it does."

Zane shrugs. "I guess it wasn't an easy time. For anyone."

The people on the screen are watching as the blue globe gets bigger and bigger inside the hands of the chalice. There's excitement and expectation on their faces. I lean forward, wondering if this is it, the moment the spell web was created.

Then suddenly the glowing blue orb explodes into the

air, creating a terrifying explosion all around the bunker. The screen becomes nothing more than white light, and it's so bright that it even hurts our eyes as we sit in Mr. Fookes' living room. I hold my hands over my face, trying to ease the pain of the blinding whiteness. I open them again, and the bright light has gone from the screen. It's showing the same bunker as before.

Except now there's only one person in the room still moving. The tall man.

The chalice.

He's pulling himself up again, using the table to pull himself to standing, his expression numb. His hands are shaking as he grasps a pen, and one of the large books, and crosses something out. Everyone around him is lying on the ground, lifeless.

The room starts to get darker, going dimmer and dimmer. I realize it must be the mountain super that I saw in the room. These are his memories. As the screen darkens to nothing, I have a terrible feeling I know what just happened to him.

"Are they...?" Daphne can't quite say the words, but we all know the answer.

How many people died to create the spell web? How many of those crossed out ideas in that book represent people who died helping this man?

I shudder. I think I know the answer to that as well.

THIRTY-TWO

"Are you okay, Hazel?" asks Daphne. She's watching me from her chair. She looks pale, but otherwise composed.

I shake my head. *No, I'm not okay.* We just watched real people dying, even if it happened centuries ago.

The images are still continuing on the screen, silent except for the whirring of the projector. They're showing more dragons destroying each other, but I'm having a harder time processing them. All I can see is that man, the chalice, rising from the pile of bodies, crossing another option off his list.

Like he'd done it before.

Like he almost—maybe?—expected it.

Like he was going to do it again and again, until he was successful.

It reminds me so much of my birth father. He doesn't care about other people, only himself. He's attempting to make a new spell web, not because it's what's best, but because he thinks it will give him power. Is that what my birth mother was really like as well? Did they both have crooked moral compasses... simply because they were chalices?

Maybe I've made up this version of my mother that never existed. I've only ever listened to her talking and singing on a couple of CDs, and read some of her notes in an old book. That doesn't mean I know her. Maybe she wasn't honest and determined and wise. Maybe she was obsessed and compulsive and somehow thought that what she was doing was more important than what anyone else thought or wanted?

The idea is enough to make me feel sick. A shiver of doubt runs through me. I was so convinced that going to the Compound and saving Blade and Mei was the only thing we should be doing. But is it the right thing to do? Or is it just what *I* want to do? Does it just serve *my* interests? Is it just because I can't imagine living without Blade?

"Should we really be attempting to save them?" I ask the room at large. "Are we making a mistake?"

Everyone shuffles where they're sitting, but otherwise there's silence. My heart sinks. I was right. I'm making a decision for selfish reasons, just like my birth father. Taking a ragged breath, I try to prepare myself for the possibility that I might not be able to save Blade. It feels like I'm being torn in two. How can this be wrong?

But then Freddie clears his throat, and everyone looks to him, like we're all relieved someone has something to say. The images on the screen freeze on a picture of a forest scene.

"Leaving him there was the worst thing I've ever had to do," he says slowly, as if he's choosing his words carefully. "He made me promise to stop you from going to rescue him."

I lean forward and open my mouth to reject what he's

saying, but Freddie holds up his hand to say he's not finished. I subside back, reluctantly allowing him to go on.

"But I think this is about more than saving Blade," he continues. "This is about stopping a group of diabolically self-interested individuals from taking over the world. We can't let them do that. We have to stop them creating a new spell web. We need to save Mei, Damien, and Blade, and whoever else they have there. We have to be the ones who do it, because there's no one else. No one else who knows the situation, who has the connections, who has the abilities, that we do."

His voice throbs with sincerity, and I've never felt so grateful for having met him and having him here with us. His grandmother's heirloom is back around his neck, and his eyes are shining with power.

Zane turns from where he was lying on the couch, putting both feet on the ground, and his elbows over his knees. "I agree with Freddie. This is bigger than Blade. Or even Mei. This is us fighting back against a group who are plotting something evil. Some thing wrong. Something where we shouldn't just lie back and wait for it to happen. We have to act."

I glance at Mr. Fookes, where he's sitting next to the projector, his finger tapping gently against the side. He's watching me, like he knows what I'm afraid of. Except I don't think he does.

"It's not about me feeling responsible, not anymore," I say to him, willing him to understand. "I'm glad I used the last wish for you. I kept my promise. But now I want to do what I can to save Mei and Blade. What *we* can. And I need to know that it's not selfish to do that."

Mr. Fookes is still hesitating. My stomach churns uncomfortably. He just watched the same thing as the rest of us. Did he feel it too? This nagging sense that chalices don't have the best moral compass? Has he seen what chalices have done in the past? Was he there three hundred years ago?

Is he worried about what *I'm* going to do, just because I'm a chalice? The thought is like a punch to the gut. I can't seem to get enough air, and I'm taking small panicked breaths. I look around the room, but everyone else is focused on Mr. Fookes, like he's the one who can make or break this whole mission.

But it's not just me making this decision, it's Freddie and Zane, too. And when I look at Poppy and Daphne, they're agreeing as well. Freddie's sister Iris is nodding like she agrees. This is a group decision.

I let out a long breath. Take in another one. "What are you worried about?" I ask him softly. "Is it to do with me?" It hurts to ask, but I need to know.

Mr. Fookes is as still as a statue. It's like he's assessing the situation and wishes there was a way to give himself more time to consider it. Only problem is there isn't more time. This is it. We have to make this happen right now.

"It's my job to protect you, Hazel," he says eventually. "And I can't do that if you're stuck inside the Compound with those two monsters." And that's when I notice the tears in his eyes, and the way he's wringing his hands together. Daphne reaches over from her place in a chair next to him, and touches his arm.

"I made a promise too," says Mr. Fookes. "I don't see how I can fulfill that when this plan involves the rest of us hiding outside."

I let out another long breath. I wasn't expecting... "I know you'll be there, right outside, waiting for my signal," I say, trying to control my own tears. "That means the world to me. I haven't always had that in my life... people who care about me enough to worry. In fact I haven't had it at all since my parents died." I look around the room, at each of them in turn. "And this family we've built up here at Sanctus Apartments means everything to me. But..." My voice trails away.

"We can't stand by and do nothing," Mr. Fookes finishes for me, nodding finally. "That much I'm sure of."

"No, we can't. We have to fight." I echo his head movement, feeling better now that I know it's a group consensus, and not just me.

"Now that we've got that out of the way, let's keep watching these images," says Daphne. "Otherwise we'll be here all night."

"How many more memories are there?" I ask, looking back to the screen.

"Many more," says Mr. Fookes. "We've only scratched the surface."

"Okay," I say determinedly. "Then we better keep watching." I put a handful of popcorn in my mouth, and focus on the images in front of us, even though I don't know how much more death and destruction I can take. But the little knot in my chest has been loosened, and I can breathe again properly.

The next scene is a large cavern filled with cages. I squint a little. "They're exactly like the cages Connor's mother found," I say.

There's another memory of the same place, but this time some of the cages are filled with demons, some moving around restlessly, others completely still, like they've given up. It's almost overwhelming how many there are. I peer at them, wondering if they're all severed souls. Could some of them have been lost souls? Did the chalices even know about that back then? I shake my head. There's so much that I don't know about the chalice history and powers.

"Anyone recognize where that is?" asks Freddie.

No one seems to have any idea. The images flick back to the darkened cavern with the chalice, and again the books are out on the table. They're big, old tomes with gold lettering on red leather bindings. One is opened to a middle page. There are fewer people in the room with the chalice this time, but again, there are one or two other mountain supers who tower over everyone else.

Do they know the last group died? Did they volunteer to do this experiment with the chalice? Or were they somehow forced? I'm looking at their faces, trying to understand their motives, when the chalice starts doing the same thing as last time.

My heart starts beating faster. My vision blurs, and I blink rapidly to get it back. The glowing ball of light gets bigger and bigger, and then suddenly it all explodes again, just like last time. I was ready for it this time, and closed my eyes.

And when I open them again, there's a new image up on the screen. I don't think the mountain supers survived the blast the second time. I put the half eaten popcorn bowl down on the ground. I don't feel like eating any more.

THIRTY-THREE

The next scene on the projector wall is strange. It's craggy mountains, all spiky and sharp and black. There's a shape in the sky, and as it gets bigger, my heart starts beating faster. I recognize the shape. It's Lakas.

Except, as it gets closer and closer, I can somehow tell that it's not Lakas after all. This minokawa is larger, and has a longer beak. This must be a long time ago, because I'm pretty sure Lakas said that his species—his family— were killed by the dragons. Whoever it is that we're watching, they're probably dead now. The lone minokawa flies into a tiny gap between the spiky rock formations, then dives down into a darkened rock cave on a cliff face. I peer at the screen, and see a dozen or more identical landing places behind the spiky rocks. The only way to get to them is by air.

The memories seem to be from someone traveling overhead who swoops around, and then dives closer, then away again. I don't understand what's happening, until I see a line of dragons appear in the sky, all moving directly for the gap in the rocks.

The dragons dive down, and start blasting fire into the cave entrances along the cliffside. We watch as several of the minokawa try to escape the caves, but they're burned to a crisp by the dragon fire before they can even make it into the sky. I see a couple of smaller shapes near one entrance —there are children inside these caves. I let out an anguished noise, but the dragons don't stop their burning rampage, and the children are killed as quickly as the adults. It lasts for several minutes, until suddenly, the dragons all seem to come to a universal decision, and fly away. All that remains are a series of charred and smoking black holes in the cliff.

A few moments later, another figure flies toward the rock formation from the west. When he sees the smoke, he slows for a moment. Then he speeds down toward the burning mess, landing at one of the cavern entrances. I hold my hand over my mouth like I'm trying to hold in the emotion that's bursting to escape. There's something about this particular minokawa that I recognize.

It's Lakas.

Whoever holds this memory, turns and flies away, leaving the solitary minokawa to search through the remains. There's no sound, but I feel like I can hear the screams of the lone minokawa who's just found his family all burned to death.

"What was that?" asks Freddie, his voice anguished. "Who did they kill?"

I swallow hard. "They were minokawa, like the Man in Black. Lakas told me once that the reason he hates dragons so much is that they destroyed his village where he grew up. I think we just saw that happening."

"That was a village?"

"Yeah. I guess they lived inside the cliff caves." I glance at Zane. "They killed women and innocent kids." I think I'd hate dragons too, if that's what they did to my family.

Zane sits up from where he was reclining on the sofa. "I recognized the regalia on a couple of the dragons. They were part of a group called the Militia Wing. I remember them. They were... particularly brutal. One of the only organized groups of dragons, aside from more peaceful groups like mine."

I take a few deep breaths. "I don't know if I want to know more about your time, Zane. I can't deal with it."

Mr. Fookes's face is pale as well, and he nods in agreement. "Let's see if we can fast forward a little. We need to be a bit more selective about what we see. Not all of the memories are going to be useful to us," he says. He closes his eyes and lets out a long breath, as if he's focusing his powers. His hand is still sitting on the back of the projector. The images on the screen start to go faster, too fast for any of us to catch what's happening in any of them. It reminds me of what I see when my little demon tries to tell me something.

When he stops next, it's because it's something he recognizes. The bowling alley in Pismo Beach where we met the First Elder. We've gone ahead almost three hundred years in a matter of minutes.

It's inside the alley, and there's a competition going on. There's a team of people wearing pink and yellow checkered shirts who seem to be winning. Searching the faces, I try to see someone I recognize.

Is that Alvera? My breath stops. *Is my mother there too?*

I lean forward, and it takes another second or two until I find her: my birth mother, smiling and laughing and having a great time at the bowling alley. And if my birth mother was there, who else might I recognize? Is my adoptive dad there too?

"Who's in this one?" asks Zane. "Is a bowling tournament relevant to our mission?"

"It's Hazel's mother," says Mr. Fookes quietly.

"Ah," says Zane and leans back again.

They all wait patiently as I watch what's happening on screen. It's not long before I notice something else. "I can hear sound in this one," I say, surprised. I can't hear what the people are saying, but that seems to be because the person remembering it was watching from a distance.

"Maybe because it's more recent? Those older memories have probably been passed down through several people," says Mr. Fookes.

"Or maybe because it's the First Elder's own memories?" I'm guessing, but it's possible. "The other memories might have been given to him by different mountain supers."

We watch for a little while as the team has a final round and then wins the tournament. We see them take the photo that was on the wall, and then sit and drink and celebrate. At one point my mother looks up, and seems to look straight at the screen.

Then she excuses herself and walks over. She sits down beside whoever has this memory, and smiles. "I need to talk to you," she says. "I need your advice."

"Certainly, Arabella," says a familiar voice. It's the First Elder. "I'll help if I can."

My mother hesitates, glancing around the room, as if trying to make sure she won't be overheard. "I had a vision," she says quickly, as if she doesn't really want to admit it.

"A vision? What kind of vision?"

"Like, a vision that might come true." She looks nervous, as if she's uncomfortable with this conversation.

"A prophecy?"

She shakes her head. "No, nothing like that." She hesitates. "At least I don't think it was. It was more a... dream. A dream that felt really, really real."

"Tell me about it," says the First Elder gently.

"I see a woman, and I know she's my daughter," she says, her eyes softening. "She's beautiful, just like I always imagined she would be. But something terrible is happening. The world is about to end, people are dying. And something has happened to all the other chalices. Like someone has been getting rid of them. On purpose."

"And what happens?"

"She saves them all. Something she does, saves them all."

I can feel everyone else turning to stare at me and a blush creeps up my face. She's talking about *me*. She had a vision, and saw me saving the world.

"How does she save them?"

Tears form in Arabella's eyes. "I didn't see that. I just had this sense that she saves the world, because she's a powerful chalice."

"That's good, isn't it?" says the First Elder. "Saving the world seems a positive kind of vision."

"I also had this really strong sense of time running out. Like I have to get on with having this baby, or it will be too late."

"Ah, I see. Do you not want to have a baby?"

Arabella shakes her head. "No, that's not it. I'd be happy to have a baby. But the vision was very specific. She's a powerful chalice. And if I don't have a baby with another chalice, then it's unlikely any children of mine would be that powerful." She glances back to the team behind her who are still celebrating, and I give a start. There, among the team, is my adoptive father. The man who raised me. He looks happy and relaxed.

"It would mean I couldn't...Not with Elias," she says, confirming that it's my adoptive father she's talking about. *My birth mother was in love with my dad.*

"It's not at all possible...?" asks the First Elder.

"No. He's not a chalice." Arabella's expression is distraught. "I'd have to break up with him."

"And there are no other chalices around?"

"Other than my brother, Tobias," she says wryly. "No."

"Have you thought of going overseas? To one of the chalice enclaves in Europe?"

Arabella looks at the First Elder, her eyes wide. "Do you think I should do that? Do you... Do you think the vision was real?"

"The important question here is, do you?"

She swallows hard. "I do. I really think it was real. And that I have no choice. I need to have that girl. I need to have as many babies as I can, to make sure she's there to save the world."

"Then you have your answer."

I lean back against the sofa, my mind reeling. My birth mother was in love with my adoptive dad. They were *dating* before she left to go overseas. That's why my adoptive dad gave up his old life, everything he had—from the record store, to the bowling alley, to his other friends—take care of me. To take care of her baby. *Because he loved her.*

And she did all of it, because she thought I was going to save the world somehow.

Was that why Gavan hated my dad Elias so much?

Gavan came back with Arabella from overseas and then realized that she didn't really love him.

The images on the screen are still flicking through, and when I hear a familiar voice, I look up again. It's the record store, Every Day is Sunday. And there's my father, standing with Randy Crowe, both laughing uproariously.

"Let's take a photo to mark the occasion," says a voice. I don't recognize it, but it's low and gravelly, so I imagine it's a mountain super behind the camera.

Randy Crowe puts his arm around my dad's shoulders and they grin into the camera like they've just won the lottery.

"How does it feel?" asks my dad. "To finally have a record contract?"

"Best day ever, man. Best day ever." Randy Crowe's voice sounds just like it does on his records. Smooth and rich as butter. "I couldn't have done it without you." He hugs my dad close to him. "And that's the honest truth."

"Your dad knew Randy Crowe?" says Poppy incredulously. "He's a megastar."

"Apparently," I say. I'm still watching them on the screen, and the pain of seeing my dad up and around again, talking like he hasn't a care in the world... well, it's intense. I'm feeling overwhelmed by everything we've learned, and I look at Mr. Fookes. "Is there anything else that you think we need to see before we go to the Compound tomorrow?" I'm hoping like hell he's about to say no.

"I think we've seen the most important memories," he says, looking at me with concern. The images on the screen stop flickering over all of us. No one looks disappointed. It wasn't exactly a lighthearted movie viewing.

I nod gratefully. "We still have to prep everything," I say. "And I think I need to get some sleep."

"Absolutely," says Mr. Fookes, before turning to Zane. "How many of us can you carry to the Compound?"

"It's a five-hour plus flight across country," says Zane, looking around at our group. "I won't be able to take everyone."

"We can take the family jet," says Iris. "We might even land before you." She flashes Zane a sexy grin, and he scowls back at her for suggesting that he might not be the fastest way to get around.

"I'd rather fly with Zane," I say loyally, although it's not entirely true. It gives us more flexibility and the ability to come in under the radar, but it's a terrifying way to travel.

"I can take two more passengers," says Zane, looking around.

"I'm sticking with Hazel," says Mr. Fookes. "It's my job to look after her."

"I'd like to go with Freddie and Iris, if that's okay?" says Poppy. "I'm not a fan of dragon-back. No offense," she says to Zane with a shrug.

"So that's Daphne, me, and Mr Fookes with Zane, and Freddie, Iris, and Poppy in the plane. Is there anyone else we need to come with us?" I look around the room, but there's no one else in our little crew.

"No. Suzanna has the kids, Fleet is looking after Anna, and Nelson is too young," says Mr. Fookes. This is it. We have to make it work with us."

I can only hope it's going to be enough.

CHAPTER

THIRTY-FOUR

Next morning, after a fitful night of sleep, I'm sitting on the steps out back of the Sanctus building waiting for Zane and the others. The skyline is covered in the muted pink glow of sunrise, making every thing seem soft. It's chilly for this time of year, but I don't mind. There's something about the crisp air that calms me, makes my thoughts clearer.

I've spent the night going through everything I learned in the memories, from the work that the chalice did to create the spell web, to the fact that my birth mother believed I was going to save the world. It's a lot to take in, all at once.

My well of chalice power inside me is back to full strength, and I've just gotten back from the train yard, where I absorbed three more demons, so at least I have something to use against Connor and Gavan, should I need it. My little demon is buzzing around inside me, and I feel like it knows that we're preparing for battle.

My bag is packed with the devices that I made together with Daphne and Poppy, and the bugged pin is attached to my jacket. I feel as ready as I can be to make something happen. This is going to work. *It has to.*

I keep thinking of Blade, lying in that cage, his amber eyes wild and filled with pain. I know he heals faster than humans, but he's being held captive by people who know and understand exactly who and what he is. They know how to test his limits.

They better not have hurt him any more before I get there, or I will do more than just destroy their chances of making a spell web. I'll destroy *them*.

And then I give a harsh laugh. Who do I think I am? How am I going to make them pay? They have all the advantages in this situation. All I can hope for is to sabotage their spell web, maybe get rid of a few demons, and to escape again with Blade and Mei and anyone else we can find.

Probably by the skin of our teeth.

"Psst."

My body jerks in surprise and I turn around at the noise, but I can't see anyone.

"Psst." This time it's a little louder, and I finally spot where it's coming from. Walter is hiding in the bushes at the base of the stone steps.

I stand up and walk down to where he's hiding behind a hedge. "Is there a particular reason why you're hiding out here?" He's looking at me through the leaves.

"What are you doing in there?" I ask, confused.

"Poppy told me what you're doing and I wanted to give you something. But I don't want Larry to know where I am," says Walter. "He's annoyed that I went to your barbecue without him."

"Does he have cameras around here?" I ask, searching around me for something that might indicate a spy camera.

"Worse. He has *informants* everywhere. I never know who's going to tell him where I've been."

"I don't want you to risk your job, just to come say goodbye." Even if it's weird that Walter is going to such extreme lengths to placate Larry.

"It's not about losing my job. I think he might have a way to find out more about your demon."

Eyes widening, I stare down at Walter. "How?"

"It's too soon to tell. But I think Larry and one of his cursed objects might have been involved."

Yet again, I feel like I've been hit with a sucker punch to the stomach. There have been so many revelations in the last two days, I almost can't keep track of them all. It feels like my life has been turned upside down. "When will you know?"

"I don't know. Just leave it with me. I also wanted to give you this." He holds out a small object wrapped in a thick cloth. It has the murky glow that means it's a cursed object. "It's a cursed pen," he says. "I thought it might be useful. It gives the bearer bad luck. If you give it to someone where you're going, it might be enough to overturn what they're doing. At least to derail it a little. Just don't take it out of the cloth until you give it to the person. You don't want to end up with the curse attached to you instead of someone else."

I cautiously take the package, making sure I don't touch the pen. I saw firsthand what the cursed watch did to the professor for all those years. "Thanks," I say.

"I gotta go. But take care of yourself, alright?"

"I will," I say quietly. Walter gives a wave, and then he's sneaking off down the line of the hedge, trying to stay out of the line of vision. I don't know how my life got this strange. Talking to someone hiding in a hedge isn't even the strangest part. I shake my head.

"Cold morning, huh?"

I jerk in surprise for a second time this morning. Turning, I see Zane walking around the side of the building toward me. He always looks so dark and dangerous, like he's seen more than I can possibly imagine. I'm sure he has, given everything I saw of his time in the memories last night. Blade told me he was also in the middle of the revolution Damien and Mei attempted when the spell web went down, so he's seen a few things in this time period too.

"It's clear at least. We'd have been in trouble if there were thunderstorms, right?" I attempt a smile, but I'm too nervous, and it's more of a grimace.

"It's going to be fine. We'll get in and out. Get Blade, Mei too, if she's there. We can do this." He sounds maddeningly calm and sure of himself. Surely there's no way he can actually believe it's going to be that easy?

"I hope so," I say, rubbing my hands together anxiously.

"Can I ask a favor?" says Zane as he stops in front of me. He looks serious, even for him.

"Sure." He can ask, but I have no idea if I'll be able to actually do whatever he wants me to do.

"If you see any of those devices that take away a dragon's powers, like the one that was at that prison where we saved you... will you destroy it for me?" Zane's voice is raw, and he's looking at me like this is a big favor to ask.

"Of course," I say, glad it's something I feel like I can do. "I'm happy to do that. That machine was awful."

"Thanks. I appreciate it." He gives me an appreciative smile, a flash of teeth before he returns to his usual solemn expression.

Mr. Fookes and Daphne arrive around the corner just

then, before I can ask him anything more about the machines.

"I guess I better shift, then, eh? I'll put my clothes in this bag. Can you to bring them with you?"

I nod, looking at the small bag he's showing me. He's wearing lightweight sporting type pants and a T-shirt. He's clearly used to having to change on the run. I turn away as he starts to strip, not even worried about who might be watching. I catch a glimpse of some seriously cut muscles before I avert my eyes.

The sound of bones breaking and muscles creaking, accompanied by a strange whooshing noise, is the only indication that something is happening right next to me. Seconds later, Zane's familiar large black dragon shape appears beside me, towering over our heads. Mr. Fookes doesn't look surprised, but Daphne's eyes are wide, and she's staring up at him. She's a wolf shifter, so she understands the concept, but I don't think she's ever seen a dragon do it before.

And to be honest, watching a dragon shift is one of the more impressive things I've ever seen in my life. I grab Zane's little bag of clothes and stuff it inside my bigger bag, then I lead the way onto Zane's back. I feel like a seasoned pro, even though I've only traveled on Zane's back a few times. I don't even remember much about the trip back from Newport News the last time.

Zane says the Compound is much closer than Newport News, and our trip won't take as long, but it'll still be several hours. Daphne climbs up behind me, and Mr. Fookes is last on. He's glowing ever so slightly, and I have a suspicion he's planning to use up some of his latent genie powers to keep us on Zane's back. At least I hope that's what he's going to do.

Before I can get too nervous about flying, Zane leaps into the air, and my thoughts of the ordinary world disappear with the sensation of the wind on my face and the feeling of the weightlessness of flying on the back of a dragon.

CHAPTER

THIRTY-FIVE

My whole body feels like it's been repeatedly hit by a battering ram.

I'm sore in muscles I didn't even know existed. I try to climb down Zane's back elegantly, maybe even a little gracefully. But what actually happens is that I slip down and fall on my butt onto the hard-packed earth. Dust blows up around me and I sneeze.

"Ow," I say peevishly. It's been a long flight. I'm a little concerned about how I'm going to actually be able to do everything I've been planning to do now that I'm here.

Daphne reaches down to pull me to my feet, her expression amused. She managed a much more graceful landing.

We're just outside the Earthbound Compound wall. It's a high eight-foot stucco-covered barrier done in the hacienda-style that blocks out any view of the buildings inside. Everything around us is barren and dry, like we're in the middle of a desert, and I wonder if we're really in the right place. It seems too... deserted. But Zane said he'd been here several times before, and he knew exactly where he was taking us.

"We're only a few minutes away," says Mr. Fookes, for the third time. "Just the next town over. Zane can get us back here right away."

I nod. They're going to wait at the town and try to be inconspicuous. I'm going to walk in the front doors—through that big gate about a hundred feet away. I swallow hard.

I'm at the most difficult part of this plan, forcing myself to actually walk into the lion's den, and suddenly my stomach is jittery in a way that it hasn't been in a while. What would Blade say about the risks involved with this plan? Lucky he's not here to argue with me about it. Although I'm pretty sure he's going to be angry at me when I get inside, rather than grateful that I'm there to rescue him.

"I'll say the safe word when I need you, okay?" I say nervously. I remember to pull Zane's clothes out of my bag and hand them to Daphne, along with the monitor they'll use to listen in to what's happening. This all seemed like a much better idea when we were back at the Sanctus Apartments.

Zane turns his enormous dragon head to me and very clearly nods. Seeing as he's the dude with wings, this makes me feel better.

"You need to keep us updated," says Mr. Fookes, fussing with the monitor that's the other end of the tiny listening device attached to my chalice pin. "Don't forget to talk about what you're doing. Just remember to make it seem like you're just talking to yourself."

They'll be listening in the whole time. It's only a one-way system, which isn't ideal, but we've talked about contingencies, and hopefully we'll be a well-oiled machine when it comes to executing on our plan.

I give Mr. Fookes and Daphne a quick, tight hug each, and then pat Zane on the foreleg. "I'll see you soon. Maybe we'll go get a beer at that place down the road from the Sanctus Apartments when we get home?" I say, trying to be positive.

"Sure," says Mr. Fookes easily, like of course we'll do that. Like there's no fear of none of us getting out of this alive. He helps Daphne back onto Zane's back and follows her up. We've agreed that it will be better for them to leave before I cause a stir by arriving on my own.

"What's the safe word again, Hazel?" Mr. Fookes calls down to me.

"Barbecue chicken," I repeat faithfully.

"Take care," says Daphne, waving with one arm as Zane takes off. Her expression is worried, and I don't know if it's for me, or because she's on the back of a dragon.

Once they're a speck on the horizon, I stride over to the entrance gate, trying to act confident, even if I feel like a shaking leaf on the inside. Mei once told me that it was all about *acting* like you were confident, basically just fake it till you make it. I'd like to think one day I wouldn't have to fake it and could actually feel confident in a situation like this.

Right now, I'm terrified.

At the gate there's only one surly guard inside the guard booth, but there's also an enormous iron gate with barbed wire everywhere and a big camera watching everything that happens. Next to the gate, there's a rock garden with several varieties of cactus adding a bit of green to the overwhelmingly barren brown and grey landscape.

I walk up to the uniformed guard, who's looking down at me like I'm some kind of strange bug through the booth's window. I guess people mostly drive up when they arrive.

"Uh, hi. I'm expected. My name is Hazel Miller. I'm a... guest... of Connor McKenzie?"

The guard frowns but checks a list on the computer next to him. He lifts his eyebrows, clearly surprised. He glances back at me. "You got any ID?"

I shake my head. I didn't think to bring anything like that with me. They're blackmailing me to come here, and I have to prove who I am? "Can you check in with Connor? Get him to confirm it's me?"

The guard lets out an annoyed huff of breath, like I'm interrupting his busy schedule of doing nothing, but he gets on the phone. I watch through the window of the booth, as he argues with whoever is on the other end, presumably Connor. The guard hangs up, and his face is even more sour than it was before.

"You can go through," he says, his tone not exactly happy with the circumstances. Presumably blackmail trumps security when there's world domination involved.

There's a buzzing sound, and small side door next to the main gate opens up. I head in through the door, before the guard changes his mind and decides that I'm the enemy after all. (Which, to be clear, I am.)

Inside the walls, there's a driveway leading up to an enormous hacienda-style building set in lush gardens. It's a complete contrast to the barren-desert landscape on the outside of the big walls. This place is crazy, like nowhere else I've ever seen.

I realize too late that I don't actually know where I'm going, but I doubt the guard will give me any help, so I just follow the stone driveway up toward the main building.

It's a large, stately structure with elaborate gardens around the front and little water gardens that almost seem to mock the barrenness on the other side of the high walls.

Everything inside me is rebelling at the idea of being here. There's something that feels off about it, wrong on a level that I can't explain.

Was it like this when Carrick was in charge? Is this a feeling from the buildings themselves, or is it just because I know the director is in charge here now, and I'm voluntarily walking back into danger? I think of how angry the director was the last time I saw him. He's unlikely to have cooled down since then. Does he know what Connor has promised me? Is he really okay with getting my help, so long as he gets his precious spell web up and running?

I shiver, despite the heat. All I can do is hope that he's not here, like Connor promised, and that I can leave again before he gets back.

I'm about halfway up the drive when I notice a row of guards forming at the top of the house. Three of them, all with their hands on their guns, and their eyes trained on me. They're not moving, but I still feel like I'm about to get gunned down by overzealous guards.

I have no choice, I keep walking toward them.

As I approach the house, I notice charred holes in sections of the building that weren't visible from the gate. It hasn't been that long since Director Holden forcibly took over the Compound. I'd assumed, because he had the spell web under his control, that there was no battle. I was obviously wrong. Maybe Carrick decided he wasn't going to give up that easily. The thought gives me a pang; I hope the big mountain super is okay. He's a force for good in the world, even if he's not talking to me right now.

I look around, but the three guards are the only sign of life. What happened to the people who were here with Carrick? Did they kill everyone?

A figure appears at one of the arches to the side and

waves at me. I recognize Connor, even at this distance. I change course and head toward him, keeping an eye on the guards by the main house. A sick feeling swarms inside my stomach. This is it. I have to somehow plant my devices, get control of all their demons, and get Blade out of here. All in the next couple of days or so. No biggie.

"Hazel," says Connor, and the pleasure in his voice flows over me like a silken sheet. "I wasn't sure you'd actually come."

I have to consciously give my body a shake to force away his siren magic. "I didn't really have a choice, did I?" My little demon buzzes angrily inside me, echoing my feelings toward Connor.

"You could have chosen to let your kitty-cat die." Connor smirks, like he knows that wasn't an option. His eyes glitter with malice.

I tense up, not liking Connor's expression. "Where is Blade? What have you done to him?" I wouldn't put it past Connor to hurt Blade just to make me suffer.

"Come with me, and you'll get to see your precious cat. He's not the great protector you thought he'd be, is he?" Connor starts walking through the archway, and into the a large foyer with tiled floors.

"Remember our deal," I say, doing a run-skip to catch up. "You said you'd let Blade go if I helped you with the spell web." I re-shuffle the position of the bag over my shoulder to make it more comfortable.

Connor keeps talking as if I didn't say a word. "Perhaps you should have sided with me, and had the pleasure of my protection instead, Hazel? You'd have been on the winning side."

His words prick at me like a thousand tiny needles, and

I try not to wince. I keep my face bland and give him nothing. "Who says you've won?" I say, an edge to my voice.

"I don't think you'd be here if we hadn't won, would you, Hazel?" Connor's expression is sly. He's deliberately baiting me.

I hate to admit it, but he's right. If I'd been able to think of literally any other way to get Blade out of here, I would have taken it. So instead of replying, I just ignore him, and follow him along a hallway and further into the building.

The only thing that is keeping me going is the idea that maybe I can pull this back from the brink of disaster. Maybe our plans might work, and I can use my devices to save Blade and maybe even Mei.

Maybe this isn't as bad as it seems right now.

CHAPTER
THIRTY-SIX

Connor leads me through a maze of hallways and then down in an elevator, until eventually we enter a large laboratory space, somewhere near the basement. The walls are made of cut stone, and despite the metal benches and the modern scientific equipment, it's dark and damp and has the feel of a dungeon. Maybe that's what it was, before these two took over.

"Welcome to our little corner of paradise," says Connor with a knowing smile.

In one corner of the room, my father is poring over a series of old books. My heart contracts. With red leather and gold writing on the outside, they're an exact match for the books the chalice in the mountain clan memories was using to record his experiments.

Does he know what they are? How did he find them?

Did the original maker of the spell web write down exactly how he did it in one of those ancient texts? That must be how Gavan knows how to make a new spell web. A buzzing sound fills my head, and I try to stay calm. This is worse than I thought. My father literally has an instruction manual on how to create a spell web. I assumed that maybe he had some kind of vague knowledge, something passed down through the years. That he was testing stuff, giving it the old college try.

Not something this specific.

Not something that could actually succeed.

A door opens at the far end of the room, and a glowing blue light seeps out into the lab. I'm immediately drawn toward it. The energy pulses with a familiar heat that makes me take a deep breath. Demons. My grip tightens on the bag over my shoulder, and my little demon inside me bounces. Even the demon energy I absorbed before I left Stanford reacts to the demon energy beyond that door.

There's a silhouette in the doorway, and I blink a couple of times to try to see who it is. It's only when the door closes, it forms into a real person. Dr. Green. I gasp involuntarily, unable to stop my automatic shudder.

"You didn't tell me she'd be here," I say accusingly to Connor. I struggle against the emotions that always surge inside me around Dr. Green. The remembered feeling of helplessness. The fear of an eighteen-year-old girl who'd just lost her parents, and was left to the mercies of a woman who hates supers with a violent passion. Dr. Green, head of the Ravenwood Mental Health Facility for Violent Offenders. *Professional torturer.*

She looks just the same. A pale gray suit that makes her look like she's about to head into a boardroom meeting, hair scraped back off her face, and a long scar that goes down one side of her face. She's watching me like a cat might watch a mouse.

"I didn't think it would be a good idea," says Connor smoothly. "I thought she might scare you off."

It's like this is a meeting of the people most likely to

hate me. All we need now is Director Holden and Lakas... And if Connor lied to me about them leaving for New York, I think I'm going to have some sort of breakdown. I don't think I'd survive being around so many people who want to hurt me all at one time. It would be a perfect storm of everyone and everything that I've ever come up against, all in one place. It's overwhelming, and for a moment, I ride the wave of my fear, trying to stay afloat.

Dr. Green walks toward us, her eyes roaming up and down my body, like she's assessing if I'm still the same girl I used to be. I swallow hard. I can't let myself give in to the fear. So I scowl at her, determined not to give an inch. I'm *not* the same. My little demon stirs in my belly, agreeing with me and giving me courage.

"You remember Dr. Green, Hazel? You two have such a long history together, I'm sure you do." Connor's voice is a verbal representation of a smirk. He knows exactly what Dr. Green has done to me—it was his mother who had a tracer planted inside me while I was at Ravenwood.

I turn my glare on Connor for a second, and then look back at Dr. Green. Part of me wants to run at her, raging, maybe stab her a few times in the face. But I have a job to do here, and I have to stay calm, or else Blade—and probably a load of other people—will die. That doesn't mean I'm gonna make it easy on them.

"Hello, Hazel. Good to see you again." There's nothing in her voice that says she's annoyed that I knocked her out last time I saw her. I guess she's a good liar.

"It's *not* good to see you again," I say calmly. "The opposite in fact." I don't know where this crazy bravado is coming from, but I like it. Dr. Green tortured me. I don't have to play nice and I don't have to make friends with her while I'm here. They're the ones blackmailing me to help them.

Dr. Green's expression darkens, and she looks like she wants to slap me. Her hands curl into tight fists at her sides, and the scar on her face whitens. But she gives a tight smile and says, "That's not very polite, is it Hazel?"

Connor clears his throat, and then waves in the general direction of Gavan in the corner. "And daddy dearest, down the end. He's excited to have you on the team."

"That'll be a first," I say drily. Again, I can't believe I'm being this rude to their faces, but it feels good.

Gavan doesn't even look up at Connor's words. I can't tell if he's ignoring me, or just absorbed in what he's doing. But I know for a fact that Connor's words are the opposite of what's true. Gavan's been sour on me since I kidnapped him and tied him to a chair. I guess he has a point; it wasn't the nicest thing to do. In my defense, he deserted me as a child, and he's been a complete ass to me since I found him again, so I feel very little remorse.

He's also been attempting to build a demon hoard with Connor, and he's apparently now working with Connor to build a new spell web, with the same world domination objectives in mind. All in all, not the greatest example of a dad.

But is he the perfect example of a chalice?

I hope not.

"Where's Blade?" I ask abruptly. "You promised to let him go."

"We'll show you to him once you've started on some of the work we want you to do," says Connor smoothly.

"Nope. That's not going to happen. You need to show me Blade so I can make sure he's okay." I cross my arms and glare at

Connor. "You promised to let him *go*." I'm pretty certain that's not going to happen, but I want to have it laid out on the table right now, so we all know that Connor has broken his promise to me. Then I won't feel bad for what I'm planning to do to him.

"We could make you do the work, girl," snarls Gavan from across the room, clearly trying for a father-of-the-year award.

Connor smiles and holds his hands wide as if he's playing peacekeeper. "Now, now. Let's not get annoyed with each other so early on in the project."

"I want to see Blade," I say, my voice hard.

"Very well. Who am I to keep the love birds apart?" says Connor. "Follow me."

I narrow my eyes at his easy capitulation. What's he got up his sleeve?

Connor strides to the back of the room and opens the door Dr. Green just came through. The blue glow hits me again, and the demon energy seems to curl over my body like it can't resist and has to get closer. I feel the pull of it, the need to gather the power to me, to control it all inside me, and to wield the power like I know I can.

I glance at Gavan, to see if he feels the pull, just like I do. But he's still focused on the books, not even looking at Connor or the demons through that door.

The thrill of so much demon energy is seeping into every part of me. I feel it down to my bones, across my skin, a feather touch that holds the power of the universe. The last time I was faced with this many demons I was too afraid to really feel what they did to me.

But now I feel it. I feel all of it.

The intense thrumming of the unique demon energy inside me. My deep well of power vibrating in reaction. I hesitate on the threshold, wishing I didn't have to go into this room, feeling like I could get lost in the overwhelming nature of the energy and what it's doing to me... but what choice do I have? If Blade is in there, then I'm going in.

When I step into the room, my first impression is a sense of immenseness. It's a large underground cavern in here. The rock walls haven't been nicely cut like in the laboratory.

Next thing that hits me is demon energy. It's even stronger now that I'm inside the room. There are so many demons. Cages upon cages of them, stacked up on top of each other, and lined up along each side of the room. Everywhere I look I see demons held captive in cages. So many of them.

The third thing that hits me is that I *recognize this cavern*. It's the same cavern from the mountain super memories that we watched last night, the one that was empty, then later filled with demons. I'm guessing that all these cages, this entire cavern, was created by the original chalice when he made the spell web. It has to be. It would also explain how my father found the books. They must have been stored down here and they stumbled upon them. That's the only reason my father has made it this far— because they found the cheatsheets from the original chalice, the guy with the brains.

Who also had a very gray moral compass.

Do they realize what this place is? That this is where the magic happened three hundred years ago? I glance quickly at Connor, to see if he seems to know anything more. But he's just looking around the room with his usual smug grin, like he thinks he's in control of everything.

Just like he was in control when he let all those demons free at the SIG Headquarters and got those agents killed. So, not at all in control.

I gaze around at the cavern, trying to get a sense of the demons inside the cages. Mostly they're in their glowing blue shape, no more than a glowing light with a vague sense of form. There are so many, I can't even count them all. My throat tightens, and I can't breathe for a second. The energy is hitting me like a physical force field, and my well of power is choppy and agitated. This room is like a live electrical wire for me—but Connor doesn't seem worried by it at all. Is Gavan affected like me? Does he feel the pull? Is that why he's sitting on the far side of the laboratory, away from this room?

The other thing about the energy flowing through this room is that it feels part of me, and I have to remind myself that's not real. These demons would kill me before they would let me take their power.

Could I fight all these demons by myself? Could I absorb all their energy? I don't know. There are so many of them. Maybe a hundred or more. The thought frightens me. Connor is standing next to me, enjoying my reaction to the room. I don't think he realizes how close he is to being killed. Does he understand how dangerous this is? If he gave these demons the opportunity, they'd cut him down as soon as look at him.

Maybe he likes it. Maybe the danger makes him feel alive.

Or maybe he's just stupid.

THIRTY-SEVEN

"Impressive, isn't it?" says Connor, like he's showing me his stamp collection. "I thought I had a grand number of them when I had nine demons. This beats that hands down."

"Where did you get them all from?"

"We found an artifact that calls and stores demons. Gavan knew how to use it." Connor shrugs, like it's no big deal. "We've been gathering them as we've travelled around the country with Mei. When Director Holden took over the compound, he suggested we should continue our work here. We've been able to call even more demons, with all these beautiful cages at our disposal."

"What are you going to do with them all?" I ask softly. I have to ask, to make sure.

"You're going to help us use the demons to make a new spell web."

It's no more than I was expecting. At least he doesn't seem to have some even more diabolical plan up his sleeve. "And you're really going to just give it to Director Holden and the SIG?" I ask. That's the part of this plan that I don't get. Connor is far too conceited to think he needs the director.

Connor shrugs. "We may give it to him. We haven't decided. It will cost him dearly if we do."

And there it is. The catch. This is where Connor and his teammates go rogue on the director and try to extort more from him than he's willing to give. Director Holden's going to love that. *Not.*

All in all, this sounds like a recipe for disaster.

"And Director Holden is definitely in New York?" I look around, half expecting him to pop out from behind a cage.

"Like I said on the phone, Director Holden and Lakas have gone back to New York. There was some urgent business to attend to. They left me in charge." Connor smiles, preening over his new increase in rank. I find it hard to imagine those were the director's actual words. I remember how he talked about Connor when the demons he was working with escaped the lab at the SIG Headquarters.

But right this second, I'm more concerned with something else. "Where's Blade?"

Connor gestures to the very end of the room. Peering in the direction he's pointing, I see a cage that's not glowing like the others. It's filled with a semiconscious jaguar.

Blade.

I run down the alley way between the demons to his cage and crouch down beside him. I reach through the bars; aside from a tingle, the spells on the cages don't affect me. His usually glossy coat is matted and bloodied. I touch the soft fur on his flank, and he moves slightly, one eye opening in my direction. He growls.

I don't move my hand away. I'm not afraid. I know why he's growling. He thought I was safe somewhere on the other side of these walls. He thought he'd prevented me from coming by making Freddie promise to keep me away.

"I had to come," I say softly. "I couldn't leave you here on your own."

He tries to lift his head, but it's like it's too heavy for him. He gives another half growl and then closes his eyes again.

"I love you, Blade," I whisper. "I had to come tell you that. I love you, too."

His eyes flick open again, and he stares at me, his amber eyes intense.

I stroke one hand over the only bit of fur near his neck that isn't covered in his blood. I try not to cry at how broken he seems. He lifts his head slightly and licks my wrist. Then he slumps down again.

"What have they done to you?" I ask, the tears starting to fall. He has blood and wounds almost everywhere from what I can see. Have they been testing on him?

And then I see it. A glowing blue band around his back leg. It must be doing something to him, maybe taking away his magic and his ability to heal quickly.

"We kept him alive for you," says Connor coming up behind me. "If it had been anyone else, we would have killed him. Dr. Green was eager to see him in the mix with the demons. To watch how they would have defeated him."

My stomach churns at the thought of them casually killing Blade, but I keep my face averted, trying to keep Connor from seeing how angry I am at him. "You promised to let him go if I came here," I say, even though I know it was a lie. I have to try.

"Hazel, that was very naive of you. Surely you understand that I can't let him go? He's my only insurance that you will do what I say."

I glare up at him, rage boiling inside me. I don't know how, but I'm going to take Connor down, once and for all. He's so casually and easily talking about using me and killing Blade. He doesn't have any morals or sense of right and wrong.

"Then you have to promise not to hurt him anymore...." I growl, letting the words hang in the air, unsure quite how to threaten Connor effectively.

"That's up to you. If you do as we ask, and nothing will happen. You'll be able to leave with Blade when this is all over."

Ha. Likely story.

Beside me Blade growls again, and this time his eyes are on Connor. But I don't need his warning. Even I know that's a big fat lie. We have to find a way to take control in this situation, I know that. I put the backpack I've been carrying this whole time down in front of the cage and lean in closer to Blade. I move my hand along his neck, trying to avoid the wounds, and let him know without words that I know enough not to believe Connor.

Under the cover of leaning in to stroke Blade, I open the zip on my backpack a tiny fraction. He's watching me intently as I pull out the universal cage key, and push it to one side of his cage, out of sight of Connor. Then I grab one of the sound devices that we made and do the same. If I need them, at least I'll have something in here to help me.

I glance over my shoulder, but Connor is still talking blithely about how great it will be once the spell web is back in the hands of the Earthbound, where it's meant to be. He's gazing around at the demons in the cages high above us, apparently oblivious to me and Blade. Does he even know who or what the Earthbound were?

But eventually he gets tired of talking. "Come, we need to get started. No time like the present."

I lean closer, and place one hand against Blade's cheek. "I'll figure out a way to get us out of here," I whisper, for his ears only. "I promise. I love you." I say the words I needed to say again, and tears start to fall down my cheeks. "Whatever happens, I'm going to get us out of here."

Blade closes his eyes and lies back, like he's too tired to even respond. My tears start falling even faster, and I have to push down the sob that wants to work its way up my throat.

"Enough of that," says Connor impatiently. "Come on."

I reluctantly stand up and follow him back out into the main lab area, wiping at my face. I need to be strong, to show no fear. I can't let them see how upset I am. As we walk back into the lab, I see Dr. Green and Gavan huddled together in one corner, and by the glance they both give me, I'm fairly certain they're discussing how quickly they can get rid of me.

"Are you sure that the other two are okay with me being here?" I say to Connor.

"I'm the team leader, and it's my money," says Connor. "They're happy to be here and working. Aren't you?" he says, raising his voice at the end, to confirm.

"Wouldn't change your mind if we weren't," says Gavan, still surly and not bothering to hide it.

"Of course," says Dr. Green. But her expression is stony, and she has the same expression she used to get at Ravenwood when one of the patients tried to cross her. She had more power to get revenge on them back in the old days. "We'll keep her until she's no longer useful. Then perhaps I can use her for my experiments." Her eyes are glittering with excitement, and I realize for the first time that she actually enjoyed the torture that she inflicted on Poppy, Daphne and me.

"Now, now. Of course I wouldn't do that, Hazel," says Connor through gritted teeth. He's not even looking at me, he's glaring at Dr. Green. It's so clearly what she's been promised by Connor that I have to let out a snort of vaguely hysterical laughter. The three of them are so ego-fueled that they can't even manage to keep their stories straight or work together for the common good.

"You need to work on your stories," I say.

"I'm the one in charge," repeats Connor firmly. "What I say goes. Understand?"

I nod reluctantly. What I understand is that this is an unholy alliance of evil, and if I push the right buttons it could be toppled fairly easily. I just have to bide my time. The thought gives me some hope.

"Excellent," says Connor. "Now that we have the working parameters set, let's get to work."

I glance at Connor, wondering what's really going through his mind. He has a strange light in his eyes and a determined set to his chin. I don't know what he's really working toward with all of this, but I'm fairly certain it's not so he can give the spell web over to the director when it's done.

Connor glances at me, and catches me staring. "But first, I think I'll take your bag," he says. Before I know what he's doing, he's stolen my backpack off my shoulder, and whisked it behind him.

"Give that back," I growl, panicked. "That's mine."

"I'm fairly certain that it's got any number of devices inside it to help bring down this operation, and I don't intend to let you do that, Hazel." He walks over to a tall metal locker near the entrance to the lab, and throws the bag inside. I wince at the thought of the explosives inside the bag being treated so cavalierly. He locks the door with a four digit code, and then turn to smile at me.

"Come. Let's get to work," he says, gesturing to a seat near Gavan.

I head over to where the books are lying on the far countertop, wishing I didn't feel like I was being forced into my doom.

CHAPTER
THIRTY-EIGHT

The notebooks are indecipherable. That's at least one consolation.

I worked on them all yesterday afternoon, until they let me finish for the day, and I was led to a basic room with just a bed and nightstand and a really big lock on the outside to keep me in.

It reminded me so forcibly of Ravenwood, I barely slept a wink. Instead I talked out loud for a long while, for the benefit of the others waiting in the next town over. I mentioned what I'd seen and what the set up was like. Everything I thought might be useful to them if they had to get in stealthily or even attack. I'd have given almost anything for an answer from one of them, something that would have told me that they could hear me, just so I didn't feel so alone.

It was a relief when the light came on in the morning and I was allowed to get up and shower. I wore the jacket with the pin on it again, just like yesterday. It gives me a strange kind of comfort to know they're listening to everything that's happening, and it's not just me experiencing it alone.

I've been working on the same books this morning—ever since I was led back into the lab by a surly guard—and they're just as much a mystery. They let me see Blade, but I wasn't allowed to go close to him. Connor said I'd get to sit next to him for five minutes later if I achieve what I'm supposed to achieve today.

I shake my head. Given the indecipherable mess in the books, I don't think that's going to happen. At least, not unless I do something to force it. I glance over to the locked cabinet that's holding my bag with all my goodies in it. I'm pretty sure if they left me in here alone for a little while, I could get the bag out. But I don't know if I'll ever have that opportunity.

Connor and Dr. Green are sitting nearby, working on another project that seems to involve lots of angry whispering. They clearly have no intention of leaving the room.

Gavan is just down from me on the same bench, ignoring me like it's an Olympic sport—not that I care about whether he talks to me or not. But he definitely doesn't look like he's planning to go anywhere either.

So far my plan is to get as much as I can from these books, which I happen to know are completely authentic. The chalice who created the spell web used these. Except I'm studying the book Gavan was looking through when I arrived yesterday, and it's literally gobbledygook. It may as well have been written by aliens from another planet, for all I'm going to be able to decipher it.

Except... every now and then, I catch a glimmer of something. Like it's a code, and I'm on the cusp of being able to crack it. I glance over at Gavan and wonder if he can sense the same thing. Is it some kind of chalice clue? Something that only another chalice would recognize?

But if he's seen anything or understands the clues, Gavan isn't saying anything.

"If you can't actually read it, how do you know you need lots of demons?" I ask impatiently. I'm not even sure Gavan will answer me.

And he doesn't for a couple of long seconds. "Stands to reason, doesn't it?" The words burst out of Gavan, like he can't help himself. "If you're going to make a spell web, you need to generate the power from somewhere. Demons are the logical choice."

"So you think what? That because I was a researcher at a university that I'm going to be able to understand this?" I gesture at the books. "It makes no more sense to me than it did to any of you." *Thankfully.*

Dr. Green stands up and lets out a scornful noise. "I told you this was useless. She's a scrawny slip of a girl with no real knowledge and a power she doesn't understand. How is that going to help us?" Her expression is a mix of vindictiveness and self-righteous indignation, but she's not even talking to me.

It's like I'm a bug beneath her notice.

Instead she's focused on Connor. She knows very well he's the one in charge, after all. I shiver, but manage to hold my fear inside, and not to let it take over. If she manages to convince him that I'm useless, then that'll be it. My life is hanging in the balance, being pulled in different directions by three very unstable, twisted individuals.

Except I'm not giving Connor enough credit.

"You need to calm down. You're underestimating her," he says. "Isn't she, Hazel? You've learned a few things about your powers now, haven't you?"

"Just because she accidentally figured out how to work with the genie doesn't mean she knows what she's doing now," snarls Gavan.

"What about the helicopters?" asks Connor smoothly. He looks to me again. "Did you make the helicopters, Hazel?"

I widen my eyes and try to look innocent, but it's not fooling Connor.

"Of course you made them. And if you're smart enough to make helicopters into demon-killing machines, then you're smart enough to decipher these books. You have two hours. Then we'll start cutting off pieces from your favorite jaguar."

Dr. Green smiles like this is a triumph for her, and perhaps it is. Maybe Connor will let her be the one to cut Blade's fingers off? For a moment, my vision blurs, and my breath hitches and I struggle with the overwhelming desire to scream.

And then it's gone again. Because it's not unexpected. That's what Blade is here for, after all. Insurance for them, motivation for me. I peer back down at the book. I have two hours to think of a way out. That'll have to be enough.

There's something here... An image that almost makes sense. I focus on the page, and the whole thing flashes into clarity before it disappears again. There's something familiar about the image, like I've seen it somewhere before. The little demon inside me starts buzzing about, and it's like it wakes up the mountain memories, because they start pushing at me as well. There's so much power sloshing around inside me it's a wonder that I'm able to get up.

But there's something about the way the little demon is acting. It starts flashing images at me, and they're too fast, as usual. But I catch colors, impressions. I think it's showing me the images of the chalice when he was trying to create the spell web.

I look down at the scribbles on the page, squinting down at it like I don't really want to see it. And the image emerges again out of the squiggles. It's a diagram of sorts. Two demons, one chalice in between them. A triangle of electricity attaching all three.

Could this mean something? Is this similar to what the original chalice used? I don't know, but it's enough of a clue that I feel compelled to try it out. I sit in silence for a couple of minutes before I make a decision. "I think I need to get a demon out," I say. "To test a theory."

"You can't let her do that," says Dr. Green quickly. "She'll have the power of a demon inside her."

Gavan shrugs. "She's already got three demon energy orbs inside her. If she wanted to use the demon's power, she'd already be doing it."

"Why the hell didn't you tell us that earlier?" she snarls at Gavan. "That's important information."

"Because we still have her jaguar," says Connor, his eyes flashing with amusement. "She's not going to use that power until her jaguar is safe. She's predictable that way."

I glare at Dr. Green. Damn right I could take her down right now if I wanted to. But Connor is also right. I'm biding my time, waiting for the right moment when I can take all three of them out at the same time. It should worry me that Connor is completely aware of what I'm trying to do, but I guess that's part of the game for him. The ability to win, despite the odds. Given the excited expression on his face, I think he enjoys the risk.

"Fine. You're the boss," Dr. Green snaps at Connor.

CHAPTER
THIRTY-NINE

Dr. Green stalks toward the demon area, opening the door with a snap, and letting it close behind her. I glance at Connor, who gestures with his arm for me to follow her. As I open the door into the cavern, I get the same intense wave of demon energy as yesterday. It feels like it does when you're inside in a cool air-conditioned building, and you open the door to go outside into sweltering summer heat. A wall of warmth that's overwhelming and almost pushes me back. I hesitate at the entrance, catching my bearings, then take a breath and stride inside after Dr. Green. I check on Blade down the back of the room. He's still there, breathing shallowly. The other two come in after me and stand near the entrance. I don't know why they don't come in, maybe they understand the dangers in here after all.

Dr. Green certainly doesn't seem to. She appears to be the one in charge of the demon area, which I find interesting, given that my birth father is the one with the demon powers. I wonder why. Is it that they can't trust my drunken birth father with the keys to anything important?

Or is it that she just doesn't understand how close she is to death inside this demon trap?

"Just one demon?" Dr. Green asks me sarcastically, like she thinks I couldn't handle more than one. It surprises me that she doesn't realize how far I've come since she last saw me. Clearly the other two aren't sharing information.

In all, they seem like the worst alliance of evil ever formed. I'm surprised they've managed to make it this far.

They don't like or trust each other, and they're all keeping things from each other. "Actually, I'll need two," I say. I need to figure out how to use their mutual distrust against them.

Dr. Green goes over to the cage, and I watch carefully, trying to figure out what exactly I'm trying to do. The picture I saw briefly on the page seemed to indicate that I should be able to sing to two demons and have them join together to create an even larger demon. I'm not sure why it's a good idea to have two demons together, but it gives me something to do, and hopefully gives me more time to figure out a plan to get out of here.

My little demon is dancing around inside me, somehow pulling pieces of the memories out, and acting like it has all the answers I need. The images are still too fast for me to understand, but I know the demon's trying to tell me something. I just hope it's going to be useful, and that it'll happen before I have to do something to these demons.

Dr. Green glances at Gavan. "Maybe you should stand closer, just in case you need to help with this," she sneers. She clearly knows he's not going to come closer.

Gavan gives her a sullen look. "I'll stand far enough away that maybe *she* gets killed first," he says, gesturing with his head at me.

For a second, I look at him. Really look at him. He's

boorish and mean, with bloodshot eyes and hair so wild that it looks like it's trying to escape. It's stunning to me that this man is related to me. That he is my flesh and blood. I'm so pleased he didn't raise me, that I had my adoptive father and mother with me for most of my life, so I could feel their unconditional love, and understand that this man doesn't represent the way people should be.

Then I let out a breath and turn to watch as Dr. Green opens the cage door.

Two demons immediately zip out through the open cage door. Another one attempts to follow, and Dr. Green uses some kind of wand that she had hidden in her pocket to force it back. She shuts the cage door again with a firm slam.

The two demons have immediately flitted away up to the ceiling of the strange room, hovering high above us. They know something is going on, and they're trying to figure out the best way to escape. It's not going to be long before they decide it's going to be through the two men waiting at the door.

But first I'm going to run a test. I have enough demon energy inside me to try what I saw in the picture, and I'm curious enough to try. My little demon seems to be excited by the idea. Plus it will distract the three amigos for a while.

I open my mouth and let out a note. Long and high, it's more than Connor and Dr. Green will be able to hear. But Gavan might. If he's anything like me, he can hear the sounds that he's singing. I realize in that moment that I've never actually heard him singing to demons. I'm not even sure he can anymore. He said to me once that he'd burned out his powers over the years. Maybe drank them away.

But I'm not worried about him right now. I'm concentrating on making sure the two demons are within my power and doing what I want them to do.

They're dancing high in the ceiling of the cavern, trying to move away from the sound I'm making. But at the same time as running, they're also compelled to come to me. I see them fighting the compulsion, trying with all their might to stay away, to keep floating high above us all.

But there's no way they can resist me. I've learned too much. I'm more powerful now than ever before, and it's simply because I've been given access to knowledge. To the ability to unlock the powers that have lain dormant inside me all this time.

The demons come lower and lower, and Dr. Green steps away from the door of the cage and moves closer to Connor, like she doesn't quite trust that I've got it under control. Personally, I think by the door is the least safe place, because as soon as they realize it's the only exit, the demons are going to want to head in that direction.

But I guess that's only if my idea doesn't work.

The demons come down, lower and lower, until they're both in front of me, twin balls of glowing blue light. Once they're in range, I hold out my hand, as if I'm going to touch one of them. I don't quite know how I'm going to achieve the connection that was in the diagram, and I hesitate. My little demon bounces high inside me, and suddenly an image from when I created the helicopters in Newport News pops into my head. I used the line of blue electricity, the same as the one that zapped Detective Capello.

Can I use the same thing now? I don't know.... *But it's worth a shot.*

I pull on the power of the demon energy orbs inside me, thinking clearly what I want it to do. Then I feel the distinctive fizz of energy and a thin blue line of lightning bursts out from my hand. It hits the first demon, the slightly larger one, directly, and the demon makes a sound like a hiss.

The line passes all the way through the demon and then turns around and hits the second demon right through the middle as well. The line of blue light comes back to me, and I grab it with my other hand. It writhes in my hand, and I struggle with it for a moment, trying to keep the fizzing energy under control.

The demons are struggling too, trying to unlock themselves from the line of blue light that's now binding them together. I tighten my grip on the end, then pull the two ends tight. I change the tone of my singing, making it lower. This time going to a tone that's at the other end of the register, again unable to be heard by most people, humans and supers alike.

The demons both start trembling uncontrollably, their glowing shapes almost painful to look at. It holds like that for an interminable length of time, the two demons straining with everything they have against my power, and me using everything I have to force them to my will.

And then, with the sound of static and an enormous *bang*, the two demons suddenly become one.

I step back, astounded that it worked.

The line of blue light that came from my hands disappears. The single demon standing in front of me is now the same size as the demon that attacked me at the Stanford University Campus, all those months ago. Somehow joining them together has made the two of them more powerful than the sum of them separately.

I take a step back. The blue light that made them has used up all the spare energy inside me. I'm feeling weaker than I have in a while. In fact I feel like I'm about to faint.

My little demon is still bouncing around inside me, but my deep well of energy is lower than usual.

As I look up into the large demon in front of me, I realize that I didn't think this through very well. Creating the demon has taken everything I had. I don't have enough power left to sing and absorb the demon.

Oh shit.

CHAPTER
FORTY

D r. Green makes a strange noise to the right of me, and the demon's eyes immediately latch on to her.

Before I can move, or even think, the enormous demon pounces in her direction, changing into its more human-like shape as it flies through the air and lands heavily in front of her.

Its forearms are larger than my waist, and the things sticking out of it are all kind of... crafty items. Like scissors and knitting needles. Like maybe one of the demons lived behind the house of a nice little grandma who liked to quilt and knit.

Except I don't think this demon is going to use its metal items for anything so innocent as knitting.

The demon is ignoring me and the other two entirely. It's focused on Dr. Green. I'm guessing she did some not-so-nice things to the demons. Maybe taunted them. Tested on them, perhaps. It seems a little like this is a grudge attack.

The demon steps closer and Dr. Green cowers away from it.

No matter that I can't stand her, I can't let her be killed by a demon. I scream as loud as I can, but it's not as strong as usual, and the demon just gives a quick shake of its body, like a dog after a fight, and ignores me. I glance at Gavan, but he's just watching in fascination, and it's clear he's not even going to *try* to stop the demon from attacking Dr. Green. Connor has backed away, and is now standing near the door, like he plans to bolt any second. I guess he has no powers against a demon like this.

Kind of like Dr. Green.

I turn my attention back to the demon, just as it lifts its arm and swings it down and across, knocking Dr. Green into the air like she's a rag doll. She flies across the room and slams into the bars of a cage, falling limply to the ground. The demon stalks toward her, and I scream again. This time I see the shudder goes along the skin of the demon. It hears me, but its compulsion to attack Dr. Green is stronger.

For a millisecond, I wonder why I care. Why am I trying to save a woman who has been so terrible to me over the years? All I know is that I can't stand by and do nothing. Just as the demon sweeps one enormous hand into the air and throws it down toward Dr. Green, I let out another scream, filled with every last ounce of my power, cobbled together from the dark corners of my soul.

This time the demon bursts into nothing, leaving nothing but an explosion of ash in the room around us. I cough a little, trying not to breathe it in. An enormous orb comes out of the middle of the ashes and speeds toward me. I can feel the pulse of power from where I'm standing. I prepare myself for the pain of being hit with an orb that size, clenching my fists, and holding myself as still as I can.

But just before the orb hits, it switches direction. It's being pulled away toward Gavan, where it slams into his stomach and makes him glow blue for a moment.

He sneers at me, an evil light in his eyes. "Can't have you being too powerful, can we?" he says. He looks shaken, despite his expression. He turns and limps back into the lab, as if what just happened is another day at the office for him.

Connor at least looks like he's affected, although he looks more annoyed than anything else. He leaves the room and shuts the door. I collapse to my hands and knees, only just able to hold myself up. I squeeze my eyes shut, feeling weak and scared. Gavan just showed how little empathy he had for someone he was supposed to be working with. He won't even think twice about killing me. Maybe he'd even be inclined to instigate my death.

Once most of the ash has settled on the ground, I cautiously head over to where Dr. Green is lying still on the ground. There's a possibility she could still be alive.

If she is, we need to get her to a hospital or... something. But as I move closer, I can see that she's not moving at all. And when I stand over her, I can see a giant knitting needle sticking out from the other side of her chest. There's blood everywhere. Her eyes are staring lifelessly up at me, and I shudder, backing away.

She's definitely dead.

I thump down onto the ground in a sitting position next to her body. I can't believe she's dead. It happened so quickly. I stare down at her, trying to figure out how I feel about her death. She was my tormentor, my torturer. She performed operations on me, she got into my head, and tried to convince me I was crazy.

Instead of the happiness or even the intense satisfaction I would have expected to feel, I feel numb. Demon energy is pushing at me from the demons in the cages all around me, calling to me like I'm lost and it's my home.

I sit like that for a long time. So long in fact, that Connor comes back in the room.

"It killed her," I whisper to him, staring at her face in death.

"I'll get someone to come in and clear the mess away," says Connor, as if that's what's most concerning about what just happened.

"She must have been tormenting them," I say. "It seemed like it had a grudge against her. The way it latched onto her so quickly."

"Probably. She was a bit like that," says Connor carelessly. Does he know she used to torment me and the other patients at Ravenwood? Maybe he does. I glance back at her body. There's a certain justice to this that I can appreciate. She picked on the wrong creature when she decided to torment demons. For the first time, I feel thankful to them.

"Did you discover what you needed to?" asks Connor, bringing me back to the here and now. He doesn't seem worried that he has a dead researcher in his lab. At least more than that it's an annoyance to have it cleared away.

I nod once, a tiny movement that I almost wish he couldn't see. I did discover what I needed. I know how to merge two demons together to create an even larger one. And that's the basis for making the spell web, I'm certain of it. There's something about this process that just seemed right, like I'd always known how to do it, deep down. The little demon pushed me along, and I think the memories helped the demon. It's some kind of weird symbiotic relationship that I'm going to have to figure out later, when I have more headspace. Right now, all I can be is grateful that I have them helping me.

Especially since I have a feeling that the actual spell web is going to have to be much bigger, and much scarier to produce, and I'm going to need a lot more demons than *two*. I look around the room, trying to count how many are in here. There have to be a hundred demons—maybe more —in various cages. How did they get so many in one place?

And more importantly, will it be enough?

"Come on, then," says Connor, holding out his hand to me. "You've just made more progress on this project than these two idiots have made in months. Clearly I made the right decision by bringing you here."

I take his hands and let him pull me to standing. I don't feel strong enough to have done it by myself. Connor takes advantage and pulls me against his body, laughing as I push him away.

I glance behind me to the back cage, where a pair of amber eyes are watching. A snarl of teeth is on show. Blade saw everything that just happened. I'm sure he knows that Connor is the one who pulled me close just then, but what about the monster demon I just created? What does he think about that? I didn't mean to get Dr. Green killed, and I still feel numb, but I'm definitely not sad she's dead. If I could talk to Blade about it, maybe he'd be able to reassure me that it's okay not to be sad that someone died, especially someone like Dr. Green.

But I can't talk to Blade, and I'm not sure if he's well enough to advise me on anything right now, anyway. I need to get that band off his leg so he can heal. That's going to be my next priority, now that I've shown Connor that I'm making progress.

I stumble back out into the main lab, where Connor's talking to Gavan, and they're looking through the book, trying to figure out where I found the instructions to amalgamate the two demons. I can't even say where exactly it was. There was a diagram, or so it seemed to me at the time.

"Show us where you found it," says Gavan, pointing to the book. He's looking at me angrily, like it's my fault he didn't find the diagram first. His eyes are glowing blue—he's so full of demon energy that it's coming out his damn eye sockets. That's the second time he's stolen demon energy from me. It's not that I'm hugely bothered by it, I don't always enjoy having demons inside me. It's more the principle of the thing. He keeps stealing from me. Not doing the work, and taking all the rewards.

For now, I just have to accept it. What's done is done. The only problem will be when I need the power from the demons to overcome the lot of them and make our escape. Then I might need to let a few of the demons out and grab their energy for myself.

I skim across the pages, looking for the one I found, but I can't see anything that matches. When I look back at the page where it should be, it's not a diagram after all. It's more a bunch of squiggles that make no sense. What does it mean?

Connor looks at me like I'm hiding something, his eyes narrowed. "You better not be trying to trick me," he says. He's lost his smug amusement, and there's an ugly glint of menace in his eyes. He's more concerned about not being able to find the diagram in the book than he was about Dr. Green's death.

"Of course not," I say snappishly. "You're holding all the cards, remember?"

"Good. I'm glad you remember that." He turns to Gavan. "So, do you know how to make the spell web now?"

"I know one more step," says Gavan grudgingly.

"Excellent," says Connor with a smile, switching back to good cop. It's tiring, trying to keep up with the way his moods switch from happy to sad to angry and back again.

"What do you want me to do next?" I ask as I lower myself carefully down into a chair. I feel quite bruised after all that.

"Keep looking through the book for clues. I need to check on Mei, make sure she's still alive. Can't have her dying before we get the spell web in place." He smirks at me.

My heart skips at his mention of Mei. She's here. So close.

Connor sees my reaction. "Gavan, you stay here with her, watch what she does. Don't let her do anything other than go through that book."

Gavan grunts in reply, anger replacing the frustration. I don't know if he's annoyed that I'm here helping, or if it's just a general dislike of me.

I sit down in front of the book and start flipping the pages. I feel floaty, like I'm not entirely with it. Again, there's a sense that I can almost make something out, that there's a code that I'm on the verge of figuring out, but I can't quite catch it. I keep looking, but the harder I look, the more it makes my head hurt. The patterns on the pages are starting to swirl around in front of me, and I cover my eyes, trying to stop the dizzy feeling it gives me.

When I open my eyes again a moment later, the dizziness is gone—and so is the nonsense text.

Suddenly I can read it perfectly, like it was always here, and I just had to look at it a certain way, at a certain angle. I glance up at Gavan, but he's absorbed in the text that he's working on. Has he ever seen the text like this? Or is this new?

"Gavan," I say cautiously, intending to see if I can wrangle the information out of him.

"Shut it," he says without looking up. "You don't get to talk."

"Are you annoyed at me because of something I've done? Or is it just your usual assholeness?"

"I said, *don't talk*. Or I'll make you sorry." He looks up finally, and his eyes are glowing an even stronger blue. It makes him look scary, like he's part demon. He seems to have tipped over, like he's leaning more and more into the dark side of our demon abilities.

Suddenly I don't want to know what he thinks or learn more about what he's been doing. Not if it means I'll end up like him.

I don't say another word, looking down at the text in front of me, wondering how the hell I'm going to get us out of here.

FORTY-ONE

I slam the book shut and rub my eyes.

Shit.

The man who created the original spell web was a chalice. That much is clear.

It takes a large amount of power to do it. That's also clear.

What I'm not clear on, even after reading this stupid book cover to cover, is how to take the demon energy and turn it into a spell web that's connected across the world to every single supernatural out there.

There's a piece missing, and I don't know how to find it.

It's going to drive me nuts before the end of this.

Gavan is still sitting on his side of the room, ignoring me. Connor hasn't arrived back yet. I stand up, letting out a huff of breath. I pick up one of the other books that are sitting on the countertop. Gavan looks up and practically snarls at me.

"Don't touch anything you've not been expressly told to touch," he says.

"I've finished with this book. I need to look at some of

the others," I say, exasperated with his whole pissed off attitude. I should be the one who's pissed off. I'm the one who was forced to come here.

Instead he's acting like... wait.

He's jealous.

He didn't force me here, Connor did. And he's pissed off about it. All that stuff about Gavan knowing he wasn't powerful enough; they were Connor's words, not Gavan's.

That immediately puts a whole new spin on this situation. It gives me something to work with. Something to make their alliance even more unstable.

Maybe I can get rid of another ally of the director's. Cause some disturbance among the ranks, while I'm here.

"If you need any help with that book, just let me know," I say innocently. Like I'm not baiting him or attempting to get him angry. "You know, if it's too hard."

He's closer to the edge than I realized because he leaps to his feet and surges over toward me. I stand up from my stool and back up, my hands raised. "Whoa. I was just trying to help. No need to get angry about it."

"Don't talk to me. I don't need your help. I'm the proper chalice in this family, not you. You're a weakling. Couldn't hold a candle to someone like *me*." He's saying the words in a strangled voice, like he's trying to speak the words past his own objections. He punctuates each sentence with a jabbing finger pointed in my direction.

Surely he knows that's not true. Unless something has drastically changed since last time I saw him, his powers have been substantially weakened by his drinking. Has he been ingesting demons for breakfast? But I don't think that's it. I think he's just annoyed that his knowledge isn't enough. He's just not powerful enough to make this happen without me.

But I'm not stupid enough to say that out loud. "Yes. Absolutely. You're the brains. The powerhouse of the family. I'm the weakest link."

"Now don't talk to me again," he snarls, and stalks back to his seat, grabbing his book and turning his back to me.

Aside from the scary moment when I thought he was going to leap on me and punch my lights out—which he would probably be able to do given the fact that he's twice my size, despite his bloodshot eyes and pot belly—this is actually perfect.

He's angrily not paying attention as I pick up another one of the books from the counter. He's definitely not paying attention as I look down at another book filled with what looks at first like a mess of squiggles and lines.

And when my head starts hurting, and my little demon starts buzzing, and those lines and squiggles merge into something more legible, he's not paying me any attention at all.

This book is filled with smaller spells, ones that aren't as useful for the formation of the spell web. I'm about to put it down and try another one, when I see something about power bands. A way to use demon energy to create a block on someone's power.

That's what they've got on Blade's leg.

I don't quite know how they got it on his leg as a jaguar, other than perhaps they knocked him out somehow.

But as I read the instructions for how to get it off, excitement fills my stomach. This is it. I know how to get the band off him. I can steal the keys to the door of the demon cave—they're just sitting on Connor's desk in lab—and go get that damn power band off Blade.

All I need to do is create a distraction so Gavan doesn't notice when I head into the demon cave. Given all the explosive devices that I've got in the bag that Connor locked in the cabinet, I don't think that will be a problem. I just have to get to my bag. I read the instructions in the book again, and then lean over in my chair as if I'm stretching. I glance over at Gavan, but he's still sitting with his back to me. He's completely ignoring me, but that's okay. It's just what I need. I tip toe over to the cabinet, trying to figure out what the code might be. What would Connor use?

I don't have time to mess around guessing, so I flick a number over, and make it a line of ones. Pulling on the lock, it comes undone. I blink at it for a moment, stunned that Connor would do something so stupid. But I guess he hates to lose, so any number higher than one would feel wrong to him. I turn the cabinet lock, and slowly ease the door open. Pulling out my bag, I set it on the floor and then shut the cabinet door. Gavan hasn't even looked my way. I creep back over to where I was sitting, and lower myself back into the stool as if I've been there the whole time.

I grab the book, putting it in my bag, and bring the explosives onto my desk. Something rattles against the explosives at the bottom of the bag. I peer in. It's the cursed pen, still wrapped up.

I shrug, and pull it out. It can't hurt to try the cursed object. I edge off my chair and walk slowly over to Connor's desk in the corner of the room. Careful not to touch the pen, I let it roll out of the cloth covering it, and onto the desk, leaving it next to another pen, just within reach if he needs it. I'm not sure how often Connor uses this desk, but it's worth a try.

Then I go slowly back to my stool, trying not to bring attention to myself. I sit down and look at the explosives in front of me.

They're not the kind of explosives that need to be lit, they're more of a switch being flipped. I pause for a moment, not sure how to make the best use of them. Do I just throw them at Gavan? What would make him get up? What would distract him?

Something that made him feel like he was under attack. Demons? Maybe. But perhaps from another angle? Maybe I should try to make the explosives go off outside the door? Like we're under attack from outside forces?

I think he'd feel more afraid of guns than demons.

Gavan seems to have given up on me and his guarding duties. He doesn't even notice when I stand up again, trying not to draw his attention. Maybe he assumes that I won't go anywhere without Blade. And he'd be right. Except for the fact that I'm determined to get that power band off Blade's leg so he can heal up. I have three of the tiny explosive devices in my hands. I need to get to the door and throw at least two of them outside. Luckily I set them up to have a small delay in going off once the switch is flipped.

I make it to the door. He doesn't even notice. He's really concentrating on that book he's reading. When I look at him, I think he's seeing what I'm seeing, but perhaps only when he has a higher level of concentration. He seems to be really focused down on the pages, absorbed in whatever he's reading.

All the better for me.

I open the door a crack and throw out both the explosive devices. I make a crouched run for the other side of the room, hoping to get away from the door before he notices.

He looks up, scowling at me where I've stopped, trying to act casual. "What the hell are you doing?"

"Didn't you hear that?" I ask. "There was shooting outside the door." I try to look scared, which isn't that hard, to be honest. Gavan's expression has gone from surly to kind of obsessed and scary. I don't think he cares enough about Connor's authority to actually bother with keeping me alive. He certainly didn't care with Dr. Green was killed.

He looks toward the door, frowning. He didn't hear anything—because there was nothing to hear—but he didn't see me move either. I'm hoping he realizes how little attention he was paying to anything else.

He opens his mouth to say something—probably horrible—when one of my explosions goes off down the hallway. I jerk away from the door at the same time he does. Even though I was expecting it, the explosion is louder than I thought it would be.

"What is that?" he barks.

His eyes look crazy and I flinch away from him.

"I don't know. I heard shooting. And now explosions."

"Wait here." He stands up and storms over to the door. As he puts his hand on the door handle, another explosion goes off, and he jerks back from the handle like it burned his hand.

There's silence outside the door, so he opens it quietly and peers around. There's nothing happening outside the room, so he walks out into the hallway.

I take my chance and race over to the door, locking it behind him. Now he can't get back inside, and I have time to go undo Blade's band around his leg. I get the key to the demon cave from the desk where Connor left it, and then my backpack of devices and the small book that I was reading. I hesitate, but grab a few pieces of fruit from the bowl on Connor's desk as well. Then I use the key to go back into the room filled with demons. The now-familiar energy hits me, and I suck in the air, enjoying the feeling of absorbing the energy without having to have an orb invade my body.

My little demon skitters around inside me, clearly enjoying the moment as much as I am.

I lock this door behind me as well—I'm pretty sure Gavan won't be locked outside the first one for long—and run to the end of the room, down past the rows of demons locked in cages. It's like a wave as I pass by, the demons ruffle their glows, move from one side of their cages to the other as I run.

But I'm not interested in them. There's only one person I want to see.

Blade.

FORTY-TWO

lade's lying on his side on the floor of his cage, his body unmoving. For a second, I'm worried he's dead. That something happened to him since last time I was allowed in here to see him.

And then I see an ear twitch. His eyes open half-way, and he watches me race the last few feet to the edge of his cage. He huffs out a breath, like he's saying hello, and my stomach churns. He doesn't even have enough in him to growl at me anymore. I crouch down on the ground in front of the cage, reaching one hand through the bars to touch his cheek. His usually sleek fur is matted and rough—I wish I could push some of my energy into him somehow to help him heal.

I pull out the ancient book to read through the spell again. Taking a band off seems to be a matter of absorbing the demon energy that's been placed inside it, which I figure can't be any harder than absorbing an orb from a demon I just killed. I don't have long; I can hear Gavan banging on the door outside the lab, and I know they'll find a key and let him in soon enough. I'm going to have to just wing it.

I feel around the cage for the universal key I left there the other day when I first arrived. At first I can't feel it, and my stomach churns. How am I going to be able to do this if I can't get inside the cage? Then my hand hits something made of metal, long and thin. The key. I pull it triumphantly out from under Blade's leg. He barely moves.

I put the key into the lock, hoping against hope that it's going to work, and then I turn. I hold my breath, waiting for something to happen, but the cage is still locked. Rattling the cage makes Blade open his eyes, and he looks up at me with such a weary expression, I want to weep. He doesn't look strong enough to even stand on his own feet.

"You have to keep fighting, Blade," I say fiercely. "You hear me? I won't take no for an answer."

He huffs gently, and then closes his eyes, like it's too much energy to do more.

My fear for Blade sliding through my stomach, I focus on the deep well of power inside me, attempting to connect it to the power I can feel inside the cage. It's a demon cage, that much I know. There must be a way for me to unlock it, I'm sure of it.

The well of power shimmers, but there's no connection. I go deeper, using my despair for Blade to give me the extra edge required to force the power to my will. I drag the energy out, molding it like some kind of strange glowing clay. I've never used it like this before, but I'm desperate. I'm still holding the key inside the lock, so I push the energy out through my hand and into the key, along the metal and into the lock. For a long moment, everything hangs in the balance, and I feel like screaming. And then suddenly, there's a tiny 'snick' and the lock is undone.

I pull open the cage door, and it slams back against the side of the cage as I push my way in, anxious to make sure Blade is okay. Without thinking, I reach out to grab the power band, but as soon as I touch it, I get zapped with electricity.

"Ow," I say, flicking my hand to ease the pain. Does it hurt Blade like that? Is that why he's so exhausted? "I'm getting you out of this band, Blade," I say, partially for Blade, and partially for the benefit of Mr. Fookes, Daphne and the others all listening in via my pin.

I look back to the book, and read the instructions again. It's just like untwisting yarn. You just have to concentrate and do it piece by piece. I focus on the band, and then start humming softly under my breath, using the song to connect to my chalice powers. I start pulling each strand away from Blade, gently, delicately. I don't make the mistake of touching the strands with my hand again. The first strand comes out slowly, untwisting from Blade's leg. I sing a note designed to draw it in to me, and the glowing piece of power sizzles for a second, then disappears inside my skin. Blade shifts restlessly. If he could talk, I'm sure he'd be questioning what the hell I'm doing. Luckily for me he's still in his jaguar shape, and half out of his head.

Still humming, I focus on the next strand, then the next. Each strand takes time to pull away from the others, and as I'm pulling, they crackle with excess energy. I feel like my hair is probably standing all on end, with all the excess static electricity. I don't know if this is hurting Blade, because he's lying still on the floor of the cage next to me. I'm too scared to check to see if it's because he's unconscious.

There's a moment described in the instructions, where it becomes obvious that the only thing you can do is to snap the cord using a high note, to get the final section off the prisoner.

I'm waiting for the moment, scared that I've missed it, and that all this will never work... when it happens. I can see the cord getting thinner, the movement jerkier, and the sparks not as bright. It's now.

Working quickly, I sing a note so high and pure, only the angels would be able to hear it—and maybe a few demons—and I then jerk back on the thin band, using the energy inside me as an anchor.

Almost to my surprise, the band snaps and comes off Blade's leg in one smooth motion. The last line of energy spins in the air, wild and free-flowing for a second, and then it rushes for me, like it's attached by elastic to the other end of the power I was using to destroy it.

It hits me with a force I wasn't expecting, and I let out a grunt of pain. The wild electricity buzzes inside me for a few moments, and I feel like I've been hit by a lightning strike.

Then it's gone, absorbed down into the depths of my power.

I shake my head, trying to get rid of the feeling of being electrocuted. "I don't think I'll volunteer to do that again," I say to Blade, trying for humor. It falls flat, because I don't think he's conscious.

Running one hand over the fur of his neck, I watch his face, waiting and hoping I wasn't too late. "Come on, Blade. Open your eyes. I love you. That has to mean something. You have to survive this. For me." I'm trying not to sound too desperate, but that's all I feel in this moment.

Scared and desperate.

I'm sprawled out beside him, half in and half out of the cage, and I just keep running my hand down the side of his neck. Around me the demons are watching, their dark soul-less eyes taking in the floor show. The only sounds are the swishing noise as the demons move around their cages, and the slow breathing of my jaguar in his cage.

I'm so tired from not sleeping all night, and so relieved that I managed to get the band off Blade's leg, that I just lie there for a few minutes, exhausted and half asleep, waiting for Blade to wake again.

Eventually movement jerks me awake, and I find myself staring into a pair of angry, amber eyes. I let out a relieved breath. If he has the energy to be angry with me, then he's already feeling better.

"You're awake," I whisper, smiling at him through bleary eyes. I reach out and stroke one hand down the side of his cheek.

He growls at me, and his hackles rise along his back, like he's thinking of attacking me, or maybe biting off my arm. I just smile mistily, and let him get it out. I'd much rather have him growl at me in jaguar form than human form. At least this way I don't know what he's actually saying—I'm fairly certain the only words he's got for me right now are bad ones I don't want to hear.

And I know he needs to stay in his jaguar form to heal faster.

Despite his obvious anger, and the snarl that's baring his teeth at me, I can't stop reaching out and touching his muscled flank, stroking a hand down his side. Touching him anywhere I can find that hasn't got a wound, to make sure he really is okay. To make sure he really is here, and safe.

Not dead.

Not gone.

I take a shuddering breath and send thanks to whatever spirit looks after the supernaturals in this world.

"I love you," I say again, just in case he didn't hear it properly when I said it before. "I love you, Nico Blade."

And despite his growls, Blade leans into my caress. He gives a loud jaguar purr, and then licks my hand on his flank. He's just as pleased to see me as I am to see him. He's already looking much better, his wounds healing, his eyes clearer than they were.

"Blade's okay," I say out loud, for the benefit of the others listening, smiling at him as I say it.

Everything feels like it might work out, now that Blade is out of that cage. I take a deep breath, and it seems like the stone that I've been carrying around in my chest has been released. Maybe things will be—

Suddenly, there's a loud banging noise on the other side of the door into the demon area. I turn, and see Connor's angry face in the tiny window on the door, and the real world comes crashing back to me.

I'd almost forgotten where we were.

I turn back to Blade. "There might be another problem we need to solve," I say.

FORTY-THREE

It sounds like Connor is making some kind of threat to me through the door.

"I don't know if there's a way out of here," I whisper to Blade, gazing into his fierce amber eyes. We're still sitting face to face at the entrance to his cage. "I just wanted to get you out of that band and out of your cage."

Blade lets out a jaguar sigh, like he knew that was the case.

"They're going to break down that door, and they're going to be angry. They're going to try and use you to control me."

He growls, a low tone that sends shivers down my spine.

"It's fine. I won't let them do that. I think I'm more powerful than either of them seems to realize. More than I realized really. But..." I hesitate. "I feel like we shouldn't leave until we can save Mei as well. Connor said she's here, but she's dying. We don't have much time to save her. Maybe we should just play the game for a little longer?"

Blade looks up at me, and I can see in his eyes the

understanding of what I'm saying. Maybe I'm imagining it, but I swear he expected me to say that. Maybe he knows me well enough to know I'd never leave anyone behind if I could help it.

"I won't let them put you back in the cage or put the band on you again. But... I might need you to pretend to be more wounded than you are. Maybe more subservient? Perhaps you stay as a jaguar? Pretend you can't change back to human?"

He snarls, showing me his teeth, but it's all for show. He nods his gleaming black head, his bright green eyes shining in stark contrast, even in the dim light of the cavern.

"So we're agreed? We stay. We find Mei. We get her out of here." I say the words out loud for the benefit of everyone listening in to the device via my pin. I'm trembling, because I'd rather try to find a way out of here right now, to maybe let all the demons free and run for our lives. But while that might work to get me and Blade out of here, it won't work for the others. Mei, Damien. Whoever else the director has decided to store in the dungeons. I've made sure Blade can heal, now we need to save the others.

Blade gives me a look that says he agrees, but it's a protest as well. He's not entirely happy. But then, neither am I. I don't want to stay here with Connor and Gavan trying to trick me into doing terrible things. I definitely don't want to meet up with Lakas or the director again.

But before I can second-guess myself, a loud smashing sound at the door makes me jerk around and stand up. I look down the glowing alley way of demons and see the door caving in, almost blown off its hinges by whatever method they used to open it.

Guards pour into the space, their guns up and at the ready, like they think they're about to battle a hundred enemies. They look around at the caged demons, and their faces begin to twitch. They definitely didn't know what was in here before they stormed in.

I hold my ground, standing still and watching carefully, determined not to show fear. Next to me, Blade has come to his feet as well, standing beside me like some kind of sentinel.

Together, we could take on these guards. I'm sure of it. I have the sparking energy from the power band inside me, wanting to get out. Plus cages and cages of demons to use as an additional power source.

But I'd rather not.

I'd rather save Mei. Maybe to make up for the decision I made to wish for Mr. Fookes instead of her. Or maybe just to save her because it's the right thing to do.

Connor appears through the throng of guards and spots me straight away. He smiles, like there's no problem, like he wasn't just screaming like a banshee at me through the door. He murmurs something to the lead guard. The man salutes and barks and order, and the guards turn around and leave again. While all this is happening, Connor walks carefully down the aisle toward us.

I don't say a word, just watch him as he approaches. I like to think I've got a grim expression on my face, something that indicates general bad-assery, but there's a high chance I just look worried.

I honestly don't know quite know how to convince Connor that he's still in charge, without letting him put Blade back in the cage. I'll just have to wing it...

"Well, now, isn't this sweet. You decided to break your kitty cat out of jail," says Connor snidely as he halts a few feet away. "But you seem to have forgotten the second half of your plan?"

"I refuse to sit by and let you continue to torture him," I say. My voice doesn't even break. I'm kinda proud of that. Standing up to the bad guy is growing on me.

"That isn't how this works, Hazel. You don't get to demand the terms." Connor's voice is soft, but there's no mistaking the menace behind what he's saying.

I hesitate, trying to think this through. How can I make this seem like his idea? How can I convince him?

"If you want me to concentrate on creating a demon spell web, you need to leave Blade alone. I can't work if I'm worried he's about to die all the time."

"I don't have to do anything," says Connor. "I'm the one in charge here." His eyes flash blue at me, and I realize that he's only holding onto his anger by a thread.

But I won't let him put Blade back in the cage. Even if it means ruining our plan to get Mei back. "If you want to have a functioning spell web in the least amount of time, you'll agree to my terms," I say, my tone hardening. I have to make this work. "It'll be a much more painful experience for you if you don't. Otherwise I'll be trying to escape every five minutes, or attempting breaking Blade free again. I'm perfectly capable of doing it. Especially since you promised me you'd let Blade go if I handed myself over to you."

Connor's eye gives a tiny tick, another tiny sign that he's about to explode. He's not happy, but the idea of me blowing things up and causing problems every five minutes has him hesitating. I swallow hard, trying to push down my fear.

"How can I be sure that you won't do this again?" He waves behind him to the door, as if I were the one who blew it open. Maybe in his mind, I am.

"If Blade is allowed to stay by my side and help me with the project, then I promise I won't try anything." I don't even bother crossing my fingers behind my back. I don't count a promise to someone like Connor as a real promise.

"You've broken the rules, Hazel," says Connor, his face finally falling into the rage that he's been holding tight to his chest. "You have to pay." He takes a threatening step toward me, and his ice-chip blue eyes don't look rational. Beside me, Blade snarls, showing all his teeth. Connor all but snarls back at him. In a fight between them when Blade is in top form, Blade would win, every time. But he's been lying in a cage for several days, wounded and untreated. There's a chance Connor really could take on Blade. And then what?

I put one hand on the back of Blade's neck, to remind him of his promise. I have to force myself to remain where I am, and to face Connor head on, because I recognize Connor's rage. It's the same kind of rage he had when he met with me in his office tower and blackmailed me into working for him. The way I turned him around then was to offer him something he couldn't refuse. The only thing he was really interested in.

"I'm close," I blurt out. "I know how to create the demon energy we need for a new spell web. I just need to read the other books to give me the final calculations. If you give me what I want, you'll have the spell web up and running within twenty-four hours." As soon as the words leave my mouth, I regret them. Twenty-four hours isn't enough time. How will we find Mei in that time?

But then, from what Connor said earlier, maybe Mei doesn't have that much time either.

It's enough for Connor. A gleam of excitement appears in his eyes, replacing the rage as if by magic. He likes the idea of being able to promise the spell web in twenty-four hours. He's planning to kill us anyway. It doesn't matter to him if he lets me keep Blade by my side. I can practically hear the thoughts churning through his brain.

Connor glares down at Blade. "If he stays in his jaguar form, then we have a deal. As soon as he changes back into his human form, all bets are off."

I let out a breath. "Agreed," I say.

CHAPTER
FORTY-FOUR

"You can't be serious," says Gavan, his expression puckered with annoyance. "You're letting him out of his cage?"

"We've reached an agreement. The kitty-cat stays by her side. Hazel will create the spell web we need. The deal is done."

"You didn't even—"

"Silence." Connor's voice is cold and sharp and laced with steel. He's finished messing around. "The deal is done." With that, Connor turns and stalks out the door of the lab. It's been blown off its hinges, and several guards are attempting to put it back together. Before he disappears around the corner, Connor glances back at me significantly, no doubt intended to be some kind of warning. Of dire consequences? Of doom and gloom? This situation is already pretty bad; I don't need him to make it any worse.

Ignoring Gavan, I turn back to the pile of old books and research journals on top of the counter. I may as well get to work. I just need to read through all these, see what I can find that's useful. While also finding out as much as I can about where Mei might be.

That's all.

The warmth of Blade's fur next to me is soothing. He sits quietly, watching carefully as I pore over the pages. They don't make sense, they're just ridiculous squiggles, but I know the ability to read them is lurking inside me, waiting to come out. I just have to be patient.

A couple of times, my little demon starts buzzing, and then the mountain super memories flash through my head, making me feel woozy. I never quite manage to see the images properly, but I feel the memories inside me, a quiet, solid energy that reminds me of the First Elder. I know the little demon is trying to tell me something, and is trying to use the memories to help me somehow. But it's still too overwhelming, too fast, for my senses to comprehend.

Instead, I keep looking at the books. After a while, my head starts hurting, and my eyes become itchy and sore, and I feel dizzy from staring at the weird squiggles. It makes me feel strange, like I'm floating, and I have to close my eyes, to avoid throwing up.

When I open my eyes again a moment later, the dizziness is gone—and so is the nonsense text. Like the previous time, the words have suddenly become legible. The letters have rearranged into words I can read, and I hungrily devour what it's saying.

This book is directly from the original chalice, the man who made the first spell web. I glance over at Gavan. Why hasn't he taken this book already? He's been reading and rereading that same one since I first came in here, and it makes no sense.

Unless... He really can't read any of it? Is he just pretending to see what's in the books? Would that explain his unreasonable anger? I mean, I did kidnap him, so he has some grounds for being annoyed, but then he tried to kill me, so I would've figured we were even.

Apparently not.

But if it's because he can't read any of it, and he's jealous or annoyed that I can, and that I'm making more progress than he did all the time he was working with Connor... Well, that would make sense too, given what I know about him.

But it doesn't really matter. His anger at me is irrelevant. He was never a real father to me, and I'm not planning to recreate a father-daughter relationship with him any time soon. I stare down at the book in front of me, reading through lines and lines of equations, tests on the best way to merge demons, and how they reacted.

There are so many sections crossed out in this journal too. I touch one of the crossed out experiments, and I think back to the memories Mr. Fookes had on the big screen. Those crossed lines mean more than just a failed experiment. They mean people *died*. My hands shake as I use my finger to read line by line, ensuring I don't miss a thing.

There are strange notations around the edges of the pages, and they help me understand more about this particular chalice, and even chalices in general:

Severed souls = more power. No point looking for lost souls.

He clearly wasn't attempting to help any lost souls get back to the other side, that's for sure. But the fact that he knew about them seems important.

Chalice power relies on demons. Need more demons! How can I get more demons??

I glance toward the cages in the demon cavern. He clearly figured that problem out.

There needs to be a center. Something to hold this together.

What can I use? A mountain super? Or would a dragon be better? I can get them to find me a dragon, I'm sure.

I feel a shivery chill down my spine at the easy way he talks of using someone for his spell web. It's like he didn't see them as real people, just pieces of a puzzle he was obsessed with finishing. I keep reading, desperate to find the answers I need, and at the same time, afraid of what they will be.

I keep reading, wishing I didn't feel so many ghosts through the pages of his research notes. I'm about two thirds into the journal, when I find it.

The final recipe for how to create the spell web.

I can't believe it, even though I'm reading it right here inside the book. My little demon starts jumping about inside my stomach, and I have to put one hand over it, to calm it down.

Apparently the original chalice discovered we all have a latent connection to every other supernatural in the world. Because it's latent, we don't know it exists. Creating a spell web involves merging a large number of demons together so that it creates a giant ball of demon energy—I was on the right track earlier when I joined the two demons together—and then using a supernatural volunteer to hold it all together in the middle. Whoever is at the center of the energy ball becomes an internal conduit to all the other supers, their latent connection amplified by the demon energy. I find it hard to imagine who might have volunteered for a job like that. *Other than Mei, I guess.*

Once the connection has been established, it can be used to access the power of supernaturals from around the world. The chalice also talks about needing to be the one outside the spell web, controlling how it works externally.

I'm squirming with excitement in my chair, and I want

to say something out loud, just to let the others listening via the microphone in the pin know I've found it, but I don't dare. Not with Gavan just sitting over there. I look down at Blade, and give him a scratch. I try to let him know something is up, just using my expression, but it turns out that's harder than it sounds. He just looks up at me with his enigmatic jaguar expression, presumably thinking I'm bonkers.

So I just scratch behind his ear, and turn back to the book, trying to absorb everything on the page, in case it's important. There's a set of scrawled directions, written just below the main instructions on how it all works, for how to connect the supernatural to the giant demon energy ball once it's been created. It mentions that the necessary connection between the supernatural volunteer and the demon orb is only temporary, but that's it.

What's clear is that a chalice is the only person who could possibly have created a spell web that would be powerful enough to survive for more than a few months.

My stomach is churning as I read over the text twice more, just to make sure I'm not misreading some part of it. This really is the instructions for creating another spell web. I glance up at Gavan, and then back down to the text. Why has no one else read this and replicated it before now? Is it because people distrust chalices so much?

It occurs to me that maybe only another chalice could decipher it, so no one else actually *knew* what was in here. Maybe other people just saw old books with squiggly annotations in them and never figured out how to see beneath that? I'm pretty sure even Gavan, who *is* a chalice, can only read parts of it. I don't think he'd have let Connor bring me here if he could read it. If that's the case then it's surprising that these books actually survived this long.

I reread the text yet again, trying to absorb it all so I

don't forget the instructions. Based on what I'm reading, I think the spell web Mei has inside her would never have lasted. That one was made by another man—Vincent, I think Mei said—who was the leader of the Earthbound before he was killed. But he wasn't a chalice and he didn't know how to use demon energy.

The current spell web isn't full strength, and according to the tests run by the original chalice in this book, it would have imploded long before now if Mei hadn't used up so much of her enormous dragon strength holding it together. It's a testament to her power that it lasted this long. The sooner I can find a way to create a new one, and do it according to the methods so meticulously created by the original chalice, the better.

What isn't so clear to me, even now, is what happened to the supernatural who ended up in the middle of the first spell web. The text mentions several attempts at merging the spell web into a supernatural before the successful attempt, but they all have a line slashed through them, as if in angry response to some unmentioned event. There are also day counts below the crossed out lines. *One day. Two days. Half a day.* I'm pretty sure they represent the death of whoever volunteered to help with the testing in each case.

But despite the fact some of them died in the earlier experiments, it must have worked in the end. The proof is the fact that we've had a working spell web for the last three hundred years. It states that the time inside the spell web is only temporary, so how did the original chalice get the volunteer *out* again once the spell web was created?

If I could figure that out, it would help me get Mei out of the spell web. I turn the page, trying to see if there's more information. Perhaps there's something more about the supernatural volunteer later on?

There's another scribbled note that catches my attention, on the top corner of the margin two pages on from the full directions. It's scrawled really messily, but...

Spell to unlock a lost soul's memories = same spell to unlock the spell web

Wait. *What?*

FORTY-FIVE

"Gavan," I say urgently, forgetting his anger at me. "Is there a spell to unlock a lost soul's memories?"

What if it's that easy? If I can get Gavan to tell me the spell, I can use it to free Mei. Excitement fizzes in my stomach. A spell would explain how chalices were able to help lost souls in the past. I'd been thinking that it was going to be an almost impossible ongoing task, if it required investigators like Poppy and Detective Capello every time. My little demon is jumping around inside me like it just won the lottery, so I know I'm onto something.

"Not going to tell you, even if there is," Gavan says in response, without even looking in my direction.

I take it as a yes.

But it's not enough. I need the actual spell. "Have you ever done it? Helped a lost soul?" I ask, trying to get him to talk.

"Stop talking."

I clench my fists in my lap, trying to calm my frustration with him. "It seems like a pretty fundamental part of what we're supposed to do," I continue, ignoring his demand for silence. "To help them get back to the other side, before they turn into a rampaging severed soul. Like that lot." I gesture toward the demons inside the cages. There's too much is riding on this to not try to get it out of him.

Gavan slaps one hand down on the book he's reading, and turns to look at me. "Haven't you been paying any *attention*? The lost souls don't have any *power*. It's only the severed souls that are any use to us. There's no point helping a *lost soul*," he holds up his fingers in quote marks to indicate his derision for that particular term, "back to the other side like some sort of goody-two-shoes guardian angel, because we don't get anything out of it. Killing the severed souls... now that has a huge benefit." He practically snarls the words at me, his eyes glowing a malevolent blue.

I'm stunned. I can't even speak for a moment. Blade leans in next to me, and I feel the comforting presence of his fur against my thigh.

My birth father really is a monster.

I have to swallow down the bile in my throat to reply to him. "So you just let them become severed souls so you can take their *energy*? Despite the danger to everyone else around you?"

"Pfft," he says, waving one hand around. "What have other supers ever done for us? Killed and blamed the chalices for being who we are, that's what. Arabella was right, there *is* a conspiracy against us. I've seen it happen, time and again, chalices being killed off in mysterious ways, just as they start gaining a bit of traction. That's why I decided to stay in Pismo Beach, to hide out."

"Until you met Connor?"

"He promised me safety." Gavan shrugged. "With you

running around, causing problems wherever you went, I was starting to feel unsafe again."

I lean back, my eyes widening in surprise. "Me?" I glance down at Blade to see what he thinks, but he's just glaring at Gavan like he's preparing for an attack.

"Yes, you. Going about, drawing attention to us again, like the idiot you are."

"I didn't do it on purpose," I say indignantly, unable to stop myself. "I didn't know anything about how to be a chalice. I just wanted to find out more, and you refused to tell me."

"And you put *me* in danger by doing it," snarls Gavan. "Always thinking of yourself, never of other people. Typical. *Now get back to work.*" He turns away again, and hunches over the book he's reading, clearly marking the end of our conversation.

I take a breath, my brain whirring, trying to take in everything he's just said. Gavan thinks there really are people trying to kill off the chalices. Who? And why?

But more importantly, there's definitely a spell for finding out the memories of a lost soul, and it's maybe connected to getting someone *out* of the spell web. It might be how I can help Mei to escape from her spell web prison.

I flick through the pages of the book, my brain whirring. I've already read this book several times over. I don't think another read through is going to give me more information. I need to do something more practical. Something that gets me closer to actually creating the spell web, and helping Mei. Something that gets me closer to being able to go home. I give Blade an absent rub along the side of his cheek, and he leans in closer again, giving me his weight. It's comforting to know he's here with me, and not stuck in that cage. He makes me feel like I can do everything I need to: I can save Mei, create a spell web and keep it out of Connor's hands, take on my father and win.

Because right now, even though I have the exact recipe for how to make a spell web, I'm not sure I can actually do it. And even though I have a major clue about how to get Mei out, I don't think I can find the right spell. Nothing feels like it's clicking into place. Perhaps if I could see what the spell web looked like, maybe that would help? Just as I think that, images start flickering through my brain. The memories from the mountain supers. They're too fast to help, but I know the little demon is doing it, trying to help.

I need to see it—

I look up quickly, an idea forming in my head. "Gavan," I say. "I need to see Mei." I want to feel what the spell web feels like inside her, using my chalice senses. Plus, if I can get them to show me where Mei is, that'll help us when it's time to escape. Two birds, one stone.

"Nope. Not happening." Gavan doesn't even look up.

"I'll tell Connor you're causing trouble."

"I don't care," snarls Gavan, like he really does care and hates that it's the case.

"Call Connor and ask if I can visit Mei," I say. "I need to see what's happening inside her body. If I'm going to make a new one, I have to see the old one." I also need to see if I can sense anything more about the spell web, and this possible spell for lost souls/unlocking the spell web. But I'm not going to tell him that.

Gavan narrows his eyes at me for a moment, clearly trying to decide how far to push his bad cop act. Just as he opens his mouth—probably to reject me once more—Connor does me a favor and walks in the door again.

"Connor," I say, probably with more enthusiasm than I've shown him since I've been here.

He looks at me in surprise. "What do you want?" he asks suspiciously.

"That's just what I was thinking," says Gavan, looking at me with a nasty expression.

"I need to see Mei," I say, quickly rushing on when he starts to shake his head. "She has valuable clues as to the makeup of the spell web. I won't talk to her or anything, but I need to see her, to sense the connection to the spell web that she has. It'll help me make the new one." It's also my best shot at finding out exactly where Mei is being kept. I hold my breath, hoping against hope that Connor goes for it.

He's hesitating.

"I'm close," I say persuasively. "I just need to know what a working spell web feels like. I can use my powers to sense it, I learned it from reading the notebooks." I gesture back at the notebook I've been reading. "I just need to sense it on *her*."

"Fine. A couple of minutes with her won't hurt. It's not like she's conscious anyway." He gestures toward the door, and I hurry over, intent on not letting him change his mind. Blade shadows me, and I wait for Connor to make some kind of objection to his presence, but other than a dark glance down at Blade, he says nothing.

Connor takes us up two floors, and down a long hallway. He leads us into a hospital room, and against the far wall, with an oxygen mask over her face and a heart monitor beeping slowly in the background, lies Mei.

I stifle a gasp and my heart shrivels up inside my chest. Mei looks terrible. Her skin is sallow and gaunt and she's pale, thin, and lifeless. I feel like I'm seeing another ghost. If it weren't for the heart monitor's beeps, I would have assumed she was dead already.

315

I'm truly shocked to see her looking so different from the vital and charismatic woman I met not so long ago. A stab of guilt hits me. I should have found her before now. Before it came to this.

"She said she was dying," I whisper. "But I didn't really believe it."

"They don't think she'll last the week," says Connor carelessly.

I slowly walk closer, my hand over my mouth, feeling sick to my stomach. I desperately search for some sign that there's more life in Mei than it seems at first glance. I can barely see her breathing. It's like her body is so heavy she's disappearing into the bed beneath her.

For the first time, I realize we might be too late to save Mei. The thought hits me like a demon orb to the stomach, and I stumble slightly. A lump forms in my throat and I force myself to keep moving. I have to check on her. I have to see if there's anyone still there, or if this is just a shell of Mei. A memory of her, fading quickly.

When I'm standing right next to the bed, I stop. Her gaunt face seems empty of expression. I reach out and place one shaking hand over hers where it lies on the bed. It's still warm, but there's no strength to it. No life.

I close my eyes and concentrate on the spell web. I can feel the energy inside her, the way it's zigzagging around, trying to find purchase. It's a little panicky, like it knows its host is almost gone, and it needs to find another way to keep on going. It feels familiar, and at the same time, completely strange. This spell web wasn't made from demon energy, but there's something in me that understands the spell on a primal level. It's just what I needed to understand the spell web in order to replicate it.

I'm about to let go, to leave her in peace, when something hits me. A tiny spark of energy, something so small that I might not have noticed it if I wasn't watching closely. It's a tiny life force.

Mei.

She's still in there, still alive enough to say hi. To make contact. She's trying to let me know that I should still fight for her, no matter what it looks like on the outside.

I'm going to get you out of there again. I promise her. *This is not the end of your story.*

I don't even know if I can keep that promise, but I feel the need to make it in every fiber of my being. I won't give up on Mei. I'm going to get the spell web out of her body and bring her back to life.

If it's the last damn thing I do.

CHAPTER

FORTY-SIX

I'm still thinking about the waxy sheen to Mei's skin an hour later as I'm sitting in the lab, reading the last of the notebooks. This one has given me useful information on how to keep demons in line and make them do my bidding. It's not going to help me with any of my immediate problems, but it's going to be useful long term.

When I get out of here.

Which is definitely going to happen.

Blade is sitting next to my stool, his eyes never leaving my face. He looks a million times better than he did when he was in the cage—his black coat is sleek and shiny again, and his amber eyes stare out at me like a beacon in the darkness. He seems to have made it his duty to watch my every movement and make sure no further harm comes my way.

It should probably be giving me the creeps, the way he's staring at me, but instead it's calming. I like knowing he's there. It centers me, gives me a place to come back to.

I heave a small sigh. I know how to create a new spell web. But I can't tell Connor until I know how to get Mei out of her spell web. I'm determined to keep my promise to Mei. The spell for unlocking lost soul memories seems like my best shot at saving her, but it's the one piece of this puzzle I don't have.

I just have to hope that I'll find it soon.

I wish I could be more sure about it. Then I think of Mei's lifeless body. Her sunken eyes. I don't have *time* to be sure. I have to take action now. Surely the original spell web chalice would have written such an important piece of information down somewhere?

I'm convinced it must be in one of these books. I flick through the pages of the one I'm looking at, the words leaping out at me, but I know it's not here. I've read through most of these notebooks several times.

There's only one I haven't searched through.

I glance over at Gavan, trying not to show that I'm looking. He's still hunched over his bench top, feverishly copying information down into a second journal. He's barely left the chair he's sitting on the whole time I've been here, and he's been going over the same small book that whole time. I've gone through all the other books, and I'm feeling stuffed with knowledge I didn't have before.

What's in there that he's poring over so diligently? I need to know. He's hogging it for a reason, and I have a feeling that the reason has something to do with the spell I'm looking for. Whenever I glance his way, he snarls in my direction.

I need to look in that book.

I stand up, making a decision. This is too important, I don't have time to play around. Lives are at stake. I walk over to Gavan, my eyes focused on him. Blade pads along beside me.

At first Gavan ignores me, but when I'm standing right

over him, he looks up. His eyes are glowing blue, and he looks like some crazed fae king, about to murder all his subjects. "What do you want?" he asks in an aggrieved tone.

"I'd like to read that notebook," I say. "It's the only one I haven't read."

"No," he snarls. He snatches it behind his back.

"I need to read it," I say again, and this time, I let my demon glow show on my body. Usually I'm trying to hide it whenever the glow appears, but this time, I let it out full force. My little demon dances inside me, and I feel my deep well of power surge up. Even the mountain super memories —which have always seemed more like an extra burden than a power source—seem to awaken and offer their support. I lean over Gavan, letting him feel the full force of my powers. "Connor would want me to read it," I say.

The thought of Mei dying before I can save her urges me on. The memory of her gaunt face makes me growl at Gavan. I don't have *time* to pretend anymore.

I'm way more powerful than my birth father. I know this now. I've been reading notebooks about how to use my chalice powers from a chalice powerful enough to invent the first spell web. It's given me the confidence I didn't have before. And despite everything my birth father has always said about how weak and broken I am, I'm stronger than him.

He's got demon energy from the two demons I merged inside him, and I still know I'm stronger than him. I know how he did that now—a silly parlor trick mentioned in one of the notebooks—and I know how to stop him from doing it again. I'm not putting up with any shit from my father ever again.

My whole body is glowing blue, and beside me Blade is

snarling, his teeth on show. He's a large animal, and it's intimidating at the best of times. Right now, he's damned scary.

"I told him he shouldn't let the jaguar out," growls Gavan. "It's made you cocky." His eyes flash blue, almost like he's testing to see if that scares me.

I just keep staring him down, unwilling to give him an inch. "I'm more powerful than you, and we both know it," I say, my voice harsh. "I could crush you right now if I wanted." He might have years on me, he might have the knowledge from all those years, and he might even have two demon orbs to use against me... but he's wasted his natural power away with years of drinking and bitterness. I'm not scared of him any more.

I reach out with one hand and take the notebook from his hand. Still glaring at him, willing him to fight me on this. If he so much as looks at me funny, I'm going to take him down. I'm itching to do it. Blade's tail swishes beside me and I know he feels the same way. I didn't know how angry I still felt until right this moment. It flares up inside me, a bright burning light. He's my father, my blood, and he's never wanted that. Never wanted *me*. If he doesn't owe me anything, if he doesn't want to care about me, then I don't have to care about him. I don't have to give him the benefit of anything.

I give him one last look and then stalk back to my spot. I'm almost at my stool when Blade growls and leaps around me. He lands lightly but with both eyes trained on where my father is now standing as if he's going to storm at me, his hands clenched, his whole body tense. His eyes are glowing blue with an intensity that almost matches the glow from a real demon.

Blade growls, and Gavan twitches, shaking his head like he's trying to get rid of the voices.

I hope there aren't any voices inside his head.

"Stay away from me while I read it," I say warningly. "Blade is going to sit there and watch you like a hawk for the next hour. You do anything, and you'll regret it. Connor will make you regret it too."

Gavan growls but subsides. I don't know if it's my mention of Connor, or if he's just planning his next move. It doesn't matter, I got what I wanted. I sit down and start turning pages. As with the other notebooks, at first everything seems to be a bunch of nonsense. The words shift around on the pages and my head starts to hurt. And then suddenly it makes sense.

My stomach sinks. This book isn't anything at all about the spell web. The way Gavan was protecting it, I thought perhaps... but no. This one is all about the binding ties they put on Blade. I read through it quickly, wanting to understand how it works and how I could use the same kind of tie. But it doesn't solve my problem. There's no mention of the spell to unlock lost soul memories.

I still don't know the spell I need. I throw the book onto the bench in frustration and stand up, pacing the floor on the other side of the room from Gavan. Where else could I find the spell? I could ask Gavan, but I know what his answer will be. I doubt even Connor could make him tell me. Who else would know? The mountain super memories might hold it, but I can't access them. My little demon, he might know too, but he's equally inaccessible.

I look toward the demons in the cages inside the cavern. Would any of them know it? Maybe. I stand up, as if drawn to them by some kind of magnetic force. Deciding to look at them through the small window in the door, I walk over, still trying to figure out how to fix my problem. The blue glow feels familiar and comforting. The door doesn't lock any more after they broke it in, so without really thinking about it, I open the door and walk through. As always, the demon energy hits me like I've walked into a tropical storm made of electricity. Blade pads along beside me, his enormous jaguar form offering comfort. Behind me I hear Gavan making a growling noise, and then he presses a button on his phone. He's calling for back up. I don't have long.

These demons are all severed souls, their rational thought replaced by the sole focus of gaining more power. I don't think I'll get any kind of a rational answer from any of them... But maybe I could get a sense of something? A hint of what I need to do?

My little demon bounces inside me, and I know what it thinks. I need to try and access the memories somehow. I move over to the closest cage, wondering if there's a way I could do it using demon energy. I hold up my hand to the lock on the cage, and use the well of energy to connect with the chalice energy inside it. It's something I learned in the notebooks, and it feels amazing. I've never felt so connected to my power as I do right now.

As soon as the cage unlocks, the demon hurtles out into the cavern, directly for me. I scream, almost without thought, and the demon bursts into ashes seconds before it would have hit me. Ash floats to the ground, and I try not to breathe it in, my heart pounding from the adrenaline. The demon energy orb floats into the air, hitting my stomach seconds later.

The demon energy settles into my stomach, and I close my eyes. I don't know exactly how I'm going to do this, but it must be possible to use this energy to somehow corral some of the memories.

You need to help me, I think in the general direction of my little demon. *Find the mountain super memory that will tell me how to unlock the lost soul memories.*

I focus on the idea of the images slowing down, of being shown them at a speed I can actually see them at. The demon energy swirls inside me, glowing blue and black sparkles. The little demon is there, messing with something, and for a few long seconds I just stand there, holding my breath, hoping against hope this works.

Memories splutter into life inside me. But they're still too fast. I can't seem to make them slow down.

I need your help. I ask my little demon again. *This is important. We need to make this happen.*

There's a break, where nothing happens, and then suddenly I see it. An image of the original spell web chalice, standing in his workshop, drinking from an old earthenware cup. He looks tired and sad. The only light is from a candle and it creates flickering shadows across his face.

A tiny demon hovers in a small cage on his bench top, locked in a cage no bigger than the size of a toaster. It's just a tiny blue glow, no bigger than a my palm. He picks up the cage, and opens it. The demon emerges, hovering nearby, and he smiles down at it. "You deserve to be set free. I have kept you for too long. You have been my muse throughout this journey. But it is now nearly over."

The little demon rises to hover in front of the chalice, who puts his hands up, surrounding the demon with his hands and closes his eyes. I get a sense that he's digging into the demon somehow, maybe excavating the memories he needs.

He starts murmuring something under his breath, and I can't quite catch it. He repeats the same words, over and over again, and no matter how much I strain to hear them, I can't quite catch them.

And then suddenly the memories disappear. I scream inside my head. *No!* It wasn't enough time. I need to know the words he was saying. *I need the spell.*

I'm slammed back into the real world, standing in front of an empty cage. I stumble slightly, and it's only Blade's solid presence beside me that keeps me upright. It wasn't enough time, I didn't hear the words. It didn't—

But when I lift my head, I feel the echo of the words inside my head.

Invenire memoriam. Proferte memoriam. Memoriae monstra.

I have the spell.

FORTY-SEVEN

I 'm still standing inside the cavern, trying to gather my thoughts, when Connor appears at the door. He's smiling, but it feels like the kind of smile that a crocodile might give you before he devours you. "How's everything going in here? Playing nice?" He glances back into the lab toward Gavan, as if he knows exactly what's been happening and is amused by it.

"Of course. But—"

"And where are you at with the spell web?" says Connor, speaking over the rest of my answer. He's not actually interested in whether I'm playing nice with Gavan. "Mei is steadily declining in all her vitals, and the director wants another spell web in place as soon as she dies."

My heart lurches to hear him talking so bluntly about Mei's death. He truly doesn't care. He doesn't see her as a real person. Does he see *anyone* as a real person? His ice-blue eyes are lit with a terrible gleam, and his handsome face is flushed. This is the culmination of all his plans. He thinks I'm about to give him the power he's been so desperate to have this whole time, and he's excited about it.

What an idiot.

I look at him for a second or two, assessing the situation. I know everything I need to know to do this. I think. And given Mei's condition, I don't have time to waste. "I know how to do it," I say. "I can do the first part here with the demons. But the second part needs to be done with Mei present. The transition from one spell web to the other will go more smoothly if I can do it wherever she is." It's a lie, but one I hope he doesn't think about too closely.

"The director wants you to create the new spell web in the same room where the old spell web lived. I can get them to take Mei down there," says Connor. "When do you want to do it?"

I take a breath. "Sooner the better," I say. "How about right now?" Blade growls beside me, but it's without heat. He's protesting me doing this at all, not the timing. I hope the others are still listening in from wherever they are—hopefully somewhere near to the compound. I don't know quite what I want them to do, but now's the time to do it.

"Now will be perfect," says Connor. "I'll get Gavan."

Without waiting for them to come back, I turn and open myself up to the demon energy in the room. It's pushing at me, attempting to devour me whole. It swirls over me, seductive and powerful.

This is going to be the most dangerous part of this whole process. I'll be letting out multiple demons and attaching them together, creating one enormous demon. I'm going to attach as many demons as I can together, and I'm going to have to be careful about my limitations. I'm fairly sure I can control it, but it's mostly theoretical at this point. I glance behind me to where Connor and Gavan are standing in the doorway, ready to run at the slightest provocation. It's not like daddy dearest is going to lift a finger to save me.

"Anyone want to help with opening the cages?" I ask Gavan and Connor, mostly ironically.

They both shake their heads.

I shrug. Nothing more than I was expecting. I walk up to the closest cage and use my chalice magic to mingle with the magic of the lock. One second the cage is locked, and the next moment, two glowing demons are zipping out into the air in front of me. Their blue light makes all our faces glow with strange shadows and it reminds me of the memory with the chalice.

Before either of them can get any ideas in their heads, I start singing a song that will sooth them and keep them passive. It's just a matter of using the same electrified rope of demon energy that I used last time to create one demon out of two. It's easier than last time, because the demons fight me less as I lasso them with the cord of electricity. Blade keeps an eye out close by, pacing up and down just out of range of my electricity.

In minutes there's an enormous glowing demon standing in front of me, twice the size of any demons I've ever seen before.

I go to the next cage and open it. The next glowing demons escape into the room. These demons are more suspicious, and they sweep up and out, circling the ceiling of the room. They're just little glowing balls of light, zipping around above me. I keep singing and calling them to me, not letting them run.

This time there are three demons. I focus on the deep well of energy inside me and allow the electricity-filled rope to emerge from my hands again. I quickly bind the rope through the chest of two of the demons and pull. They scream and fight, but moments later, they're merging into one bigger demon. The third demon is shifting about nervously, but it doesn't move; my song is holding it in place. I lasso it with my electricity and pull it into the second merged demon. I pull them together again, and the three demons merge, creating a massive demon. Now I have two larger demons. I lasso both of them and pull them together again. This time when they merge, there's a roar that almost splits my ear drums.

So far I've merged five demons, and the demon that's been created is standing above me, looming like all it wants to do is snap my head off. Every speck of my concentration is on not allowing it to do that.

My hands are slippery with sweat, and when I try to open the third cage, I have to try a couple of times before I can get my grip sufficiently attached to open it. Two more demons emerge, this time warily floating around the larger demon, curious but not scared. Maybe they're now considering that joining the larger demon might have some positive repercussions.

I merge them like I did the others, pulling on the well of energy inside me. Somehow it's not draining my energy like other uses of the power would have. It's giving me more energy, like I'm somehow linked to the enormous demon that I'm building. As it gets bigger, so does my power. There's a strange wind all around us, whipping up my hair, making the air around me sizzle with electricity, like the energy is so powerful it's creating its own storm.

The next cage gets emptied into the giant demon, then the next. The power is everywhere, inside me, all around. It's like I'm part of the demon I'm creating, and it feels like the most amazing thing I've ever felt. I'm on a high of energy, buzzing and fizzing with it. I keep going, no longer focused on the end result, I just want more of this delicious, addictive energy that I get every time another demon or three is added into the enlarged demon in the center.

The enormous demon isn't moving, it's just watching me as I gather more and more power into it. Like it knows that I'm helping it, that it will benefit from letting me do what I'm doing.

I've almost forgotten why I started creating this mega demon. The energy is flowing over my body, silky and seductive, drawing me in and making me feel all-powerful. It feels so good, I moan out loud. This is what being a chalice means. This is the kind of power I could've been using all along, if someone had bothered to teach me how to do it. A kernel of resentment grows inside my chest, curling shoots out into my body.

I add another two demons to the mega-demon, their energy sliding into the air, fizzing with excitement. There's so much power in the air it's crackling. It hurts to breathe, the electricity zapping at my throat.

Connor and Gavan are no longer at the door. They've shut it behind them, and probably locked it. What they don't understand is that locking a door isn't going to keep me in here. My power is too great. It's expanded beyond the level of ordinary. Beyond the level of *extraordinary*.

There is nothing equal to the all-encompassing power I feel right in this moment. It's stronger than the most violent volcano eruption. It's bigger than the most tremendous tsunami wave. It's bigger than anything nature can fling at the world. This is demon power, and it's everything.

I keep moving along the rows of cages, freeing the demons, and then merging them into my colossal demon. It's so big that it has to crouch to fit in the space, glowing so brightly it lights up the whole area like some kind of weird blue-coated day. It no longer seems threatening, it's more like an enormous dog, loyal and loving to me, its owner. The metal bits and pieces that were attached to all the individual demons look silly and puny on the arms of the enormous demon. Its fingers are the same size as my entire body, but I'm not afraid. Because I know demon power. I'm intimately entangled with the power that's in this room, and I'm the one controlling it. It feels... beyond anything. It's sweet and tender and harsh and sharp all at the same time, like a bee sting that somehow gives you an orgasm.

I don't quite know how I'm controlling all this power, but I am. I wouldn't have been able to do it before I read the notebooks. They've given me a whole new understanding of my chalice abilities. I'm learning and building on my chalice knowledge right now, even as I stand here, soaking up the energy that's leaking out from my mega demon. I wish I'd known how to control all this energy before now. It would have made my life *a lot* easier. For a moment I imagine if I'd had my mega demon at Ravenwood and it makes me smile to think of Dr. Green running screaming through the hallways.

But that's not what happened, because no one taught me how to use my powers. My resentment grows a little more, the shoots unfurling inside me.

I keep merging more and more demons into the enormous one at the front, focusing on nothing but the energy that I'm creating, and the glorious feeling of power that's running through my veins. Then suddenly, it's done. All the demons in the room are merged together into one that's now crouched uncomfortably within the confines of the cavern. Its eyes are blazing with want, and it's looking around the room, as if searching for another demon to add to its collection. It's the ultimate creature, its sole desire is for more energy, to be bigger, more. And I'm the one who controls it.

I feel dizzy but elated. I take a halting step, then another. My body feels battered, like all the power in the universe has been flowing through me. For a split second sanity returns and I can see clearly that I'm about to collapse. There's a weight covering me that feels insurmountable and there's only so much that one body can handle. I've reached my limit. Except there's one last thing I need to do.

I look up at the demon, and find its eyes fastened on me. It makes me forget everything else, forget what I was supposed to be doing. I'm intimately connected to this demon, I feel the power raging between us, like we're both joined in a way that can't be explained or understood. It's the most amazing power I've ever felt, and the joy of it makes tears form in my eyes. The demon is gazing down at me, and for the first time, I don't see soulless black eyes. I see a whole spectrum of emotions, too complicated and intricate for me to have ever comprehended before now. I see love and fear and a need for power. I see tenderness and hope. The demon reaches out one hand to me, and for a moment, I hesitate.

I know what the next step is supposed to be. Except now that I'm here, the power feels so amazing, so energizing, so all-consuming that I don't want to let it go. And the demon feels like a friend, like my best friend, the one creature who knows me inside and out and accepts me one hundred percent for who I am.

I don't know if I can let it go so easily.

I also have a feeling that if I go ahead with my original plan, it's going to hurt. A lot. The demon sees my hesitation and it gestures as if to say, all this could be yours. All you have to do is decide to go with us, instead of against us. All you have to do is be a true chalice. Someone whose power blends so perfectly with demon power that it's indistinguishable.

My legs are shaking, and I realize I'm weakening. I don't have long. But in this moment, it feels like there are many more reasons for me to choose the demon. Tendrils of power leak out from the colossal creature, calling out to me, offering me comfort and pleasure. The other direction seems only to offer me pain. Do I keep to my original plan? Do I save the others? Suddenly their needs seem so much less important than this beautiful new power seeping into my very bones. I take an electricity filled breath and soak up the energy that's now an integral part of me. I've never felt this glorious in all my life.

And then suddenly there's a sharp pain in my thigh. Agony shoots up through my body as I try to bat away whatever is causing it. My hand come into contact with a soft, sleek jaguar head.

Blade.

I look down at him, shocked. He's biting my leg, his large teeth sunk into my flesh.

"What the hell?" I say to him, but the pain is already working. The demon energy recedes and I remember who I am. What I'm trying to do.

His amber eyes are looking up at me, begging for my forgiveness, but he clings to my leg like I'm his dinner and he hasn't eaten for weeks. His large jaguar body is basically all muscle, and there's no way I could fight him. But it doesn't matter. He's brought me back to reality. Back to saving Mei, back to stopping Connor, Gavan and the director. Back to everything that matters to me. He's watching me intently, like he's waiting for something.

"It's okay," I whisper to him. I reach out, and stroke his head. "Thank you."

Blade opens his mouth and releases my leg. Blood immediately appears on my leg, but it doesn't feel too bad. I think he kept it painful but not deep. At least I hope so, because I don't have time to deal with a full-on jaguar bite. I look back up at the giant demon. It's still there, looking down at me with its mesmerizing black eyes. But I'm out of the spell the demon power was casting over me. I know what I have to do. Blade stands next to me, leaning against my side, trying to give me comfort. I put one hand on his back, using his strength to steady me.

And then I scream. Long and loud. It's the highest pitch scream I've ever done, and I don't think anyone other than me, the demon, and Gavan can hear it. It has to be like that, for a demon this size.

The demon covers its ears, as if that's going to stop what's happening. As if that's going to keep my chalice powers from working. Part of me grieves for what I'm doing to my demon, a creature of my own creation. I looked into its soul, I saw more inside it than I ever knew existed. But it's my responsibility to destroy this demon. Not only to save my friends, or create a new spell web. But also to keep a creature like this away from the world. It would mean destruction and devastation on a scale far greater than anything the dragons of old could ever have managed. So I scream on, delving into the deepest hidden corners of my well of power to create a scream that cannot fail to hold the demon in its thrall.

I scream until it feels like there's nothing left inside me to scream. And then I scream some more. The walls of the cavern are trembling, and I worry that perhaps I might absorb my demon creation, only to have the walls collapse and crush me to death. But I can't think about anything else. I have to focus all my attention on the demon. Because it's close, and it's struggling against me. It's not letting its power go without a fight. It's pushing back on my screams and holding on for longer than any other demon I've ever fought has done.

This is my creation, and I'm proud it has lasted this long. I'm proud that it fought to survive. I'm proud that it didn't give up without a fight.

But I need its power. I need to end this, to make the world a safer place for everyone.

And so I scream. And scream.

And with an enormous rumbling bang, the demon explodes into an enormous cloud of black ash, flying out everywhere like a mushroom cloud from a bomb. I fling my arm up over my eyes, and I'm slammed back against a cage from the pressure of the explosion. Blade is slammed back beside me. He shakes his head to clear it, then looks at me to check if I'm okay, his amber jaguar eyes glowing in the eerie after glow of the cavern.

I'm too busy staring at Blade, feeling thankful that he's here with me. I barely register the enormous orb that flies out of the cloud of ash and is hurtling toward me. It's bigger than I am. It slams into my whole body, and it's like I've been hit by ten bolts of lightning all at once. My entire body hardens to rock, and electricity bounces around inside me uncontrollably.

For a moment, I'm lit up, brighter than anything else in the world.

And then everything goes dark.

CHAPTER
FORTY-EIGHT

P ain wakes me. There's darkness all around, but the pain splits my head, sharp and agonizing.

I moan. I don't remember what happened, or why I'm in such agony. Did I fall? Hurt myself? What could possibly have happened?

And then I remember. The giant demon. The explosion of ash. The orb. Demon energy churns inside me, primal and instinctive, waiting to be used. I'm full to bursting, and it's agonizing, like I've devoured a colony of lightning bugs or maybe chewed on electricity cables.

I open one eye, and then the other, expecting to see the cavern, covered in ash. My body dirty from the explosion, Blade next to me, maybe knocked out as well. I even reach out, expecting to feel the comfort of Blade's sleek fur next to me.

My hand hits a metal rail, instead. I'm lying in a hospital bed, in what appears to be a hospital. My body is clean of ash, and no one else is around. Wait. No, that's not true. On the other side of the room, there's another woman lying in the bed.

Mei.

I'm in the same hospital room that Connor showed me to when I wanted to see Mei.

My brain slowly starts firing. Where's Blade? Where are the others? How much time has passed?

I don't know what's happening, and it's terrifying.

I try to move, and discover one of my wrists is attached by a metal handcuff to the side of the bed. I pull on it uselessly, as if I can just pull it off with my own strength, but I'm weaker than a kitten, so it just rattles around in the silence of the room. Before I can start working on getting it undone using the demon energy that's surging inside me, the door to the hospital wing opens, and Connor strides in, his face smug. Gavan is behind him, skulking along in his usual manner. I scowl at them both.

"Where's Blade?" I say impatiently, my fear driving me. "What happened? Take this handcuff off me before I take it off myself."

"I don't think you're in a position to demand anything anymore, Hazel," says Connor lazily. He's wearing an expensive blue suit, and his icy-blue eyes are shining with unholy delight.

I blink. What happened while I was unconscious? Why is he acting like this? "What are you talking about?"

Connor tips his head to my leg. "I'm talking about this." He pulls up the bedside blanket. Around my ankle is the same band of electricity they put on Blade's leg when he was first kidnapped. I sneer at Connor. With the amount of demon energy I have inside me, I could bat that away with one hand tied behind my back. I glance at my hand in the handcuff. I might literally have to.

"That doesn't work on me," I say, leaning forward to grab it off with my free hand, just like I did for Blade's band.

Except it *does* work. When I touch the band, I get zapped with a stinging electric shock that makes me jerk back, hissing in pain.

"What have you done?" I ask savagely, trying to access my power. I'll show them what it means to cross me.

But I can't.

Even though I can feel the power churning inside me, I can't access it. This band is holding my power in check, keeping me from using it on them.

"We've tamed your power," says Gavan, finally coming out from behind Connor. His face is half-burned, but his bloodshot eyes are filled with the light of triumph. "You thought you were so much better than me, building that demon. But *I'm* the one who's got you captured. *I'm* the one who controls you now." He looks like he had to fight hard to get the band on me. I hope it hurt.

I look from Gavan to Connor, and my throat constricts. I try to get the band off my leg again, but the pain is even worse this time, sending electric shocks over my whole body. I scream, but it's just a normal scream, no power in it at all.

"There's no point in trying to get out of the band," says Gavan. "I studied the text. I know how it works. The words weren't easy to read, but they were there, and eventually I got them all."

It's the first time he's admitted it wasn't as simple for him to read the texts as it was for me. Did he see how easy it was when I was reading them? Did it make him even more jealous? Is that what this is about?

I need to think. I need to get out of here, to figure out what to do next. Except I can't think though any of that because my brain is fixated on one thing. *Where's Blade?*

I know that I won't get any answers asking the question

straight up a second time. "What do you want?" I ask instead, my throat raw. I look around for a glass of water, but there's nothing next to my bed, not even a table.

"You will create the spell web for us," says Connor, his words slow and precise. "And when it's done, we'll get rid of Mei, so her spell web dies with her, and then we'll be in control of the new spell web. If you do all that for us, you might just live to see another day."

"And if I don't?"

"Then neither you nor Mei will live to see another day," says Connor, his eyes flashing with menace. "We intend to have the power of the spell web in our hands, and there's nothing we're not prepared to do to make that happen." He means every word that he's saying, and see it in his eyes.

Next to him, Gavan smiles, like he's anticipating my refusal. Like he's already planning my torture.

"You're double-crossing Director Holden?" I whisper. My hand moves distractedly, and the handcuff rattles against the metal bar. Do they understand what they're doing? He's not someone who forgives easily.

Connor sweeps one hand wide in an overly dramatic gesture. "It's not *double-crossing* him. We've just changed our minds. We're seeking other opportunities."

He's seen the potential for the power of controlling the spell web. And he's not afraid of the director or Lakas. For some reason, Connor isn't afraid of anyone. I think there's some kind of screw loose in his head. Is this what all sirens are like? Or is this a special personality quirk of Connor's? I want to yell at him that he should be afraid. That both Director Holden and Lakas will eat him alive for what he's doing, but that would be helping him. And at this point, I really don't want to do anything that might constitute helping Connor.

"I need help to create the spell web," I say desperately. "I'm not strong enough."

"Gavan can help," says Connor, and Gavan nods eagerly. I wonder if he's already planning to double cross Connor? Thinking that if he's part of the making of it, he'll be able to control it?

"I want *Blade* to help," I say.

"I'm afraid Blade will never be able to help you again," says Connor with another smirk.

For a second, I don't understand. Can't understand. *Won't understand.*

I peer at Connor and then at Gavan, looking for a different understanding of his words. But they're both looking back at me with smug expressions, like they won this round. Like maybe they think they've won all the rounds. I let out a moan. There's only one interpretation of what he's saying.

Blade's dead.

They killed him. Or maybe I killed him when the energy orb entered my body? The reaction was enough to knock me out, it could have killed Blade.

"What happened to him? Where's Blade?" I ask, desperately searching for another answer.

"Your explosion knocked him out. We decided it was time to eliminate the threat. So we did," says Connor with a nonchalant shrug. Except I see the glitter in his eyes. He's glad he killed him.

And maybe that means they *did* win. Because without Blade...

And then the pain hits me.

This pain is worse than the pain from the band. Worse than the pain from absorbing the colossal demon's energy orb. Worse than any pain I've ever felt. I look up at Connor, seeing him through a haze of hurt. His eyes are lit up, and he's still smiling at me, like he just gave me good news. It hits me, then.

He *enjoyed* saying those words to me.

He *enjoyed* seeing the pain that I know is on my face.

And he's enjoying knowing that he was the one who caused me such pain.

And in that moment, I vow that I will be the one who kills Connor McKenzie.

I will kill him, and I will *enjoy* it.

CHAPTER

FORTY-NINE

"You can't force me to do anything," I say dully. "I won't do it. There's nothing you can threaten me with." They lost their leverage when Blade died. Now I don't have to do anything for them. I can just die in peace. Mei will die as well, but I'm not even sure I could have saved her at this point. Maybe this is what was always supposed to happen?

At least I won't be making a spell web so that Connor and Gavan can use it. It doesn't give me any satisfaction to know that. I'd rather be working on the spell web—even if I were doing it for Connor and Gavan—with Blade was still alive, than living in this nightmare reality with his death.

"But I think you will," says Connor silkily.

I look up at him from the hospital bed. Hatred suddenly burns hot inside me. "No. *I won't*."

Gavan lifts his hand, and suddenly the band around my ankle springs to life, burning so bright it's visible even under the blanket. It sends a painful electrical shock up my leg and into my body, burning everything it touches, making me scream. It feels good to scream, to get it out, to let the universe know how I'm feeling. It seems to go on forever, but maybe it's only a few seconds.

"Well?" says Connor softly. "Any change of mind?" He's excited, and I think perhaps he's enjoying watching me in pain.

I sneer at him, reflecting his expression back at him. "Is that the best you've got?"

Connor narrows his eyes and flicks his hand as Gavan lifts his hand again, making the painful electricity burn its way up my leg again. I scream. I let it all out, until my throat feels raw and my body wasted. But it changes nothing. I won't help them, not anymore. They can bring on the pain, it's nothing compared to the pain I feel knowing Blade is dead. I close my eyes and concentrate on making myself at one with the mattress beneath me.

"Go get the others," says Connor.

I crack open my eyes and watch as Gavan moves with unusual speed back to the door of the hospital room. I can't begin to understand what else he's got up his sleeve. But it doesn't matter. Nothing matters now. I fix my stare down at the rough hospital blanket, my eyes roving over the lines and valleys as if my life depended on it. Perhaps it does. Because if I think about anything else... that just might break me.

The door opens again, and against my best intentions, I look up.

Several people shuffle into the room. Guards hold the arms of four people.

I take a tiny gasp of breath. It's Mr. Fookes, Daphne, Zane, and Freddie. My chest hurts. What are they doing here? I was so careful not to say the safe word. To make sure they didn't come in here. Did they hear what happened when I absorbed all the demons?

They look like they've been in a fight. Mr. Fookes has a massive black eye forming on his face. Daphne looks like she's been pulled through a bush backwards. They're all covered in bruises and cuts. Clothes ripped. And each of them has a matching band around their ankles, just like I do.

They look defeated. Like they gave it their best, and it wasn't good enough. I know how they feel. I thought I'd done it. That I was in charge.

And now here I am, broken and defeated. I should have let my colossal demon live and allowed the power to consume me. At least then I'd be free and Blade would still be alive.

"Now will you do what we want?" asks Connor silkily.

"Don't do it," yells Daphne, suddenly starting to struggle against the guard holding her still. He punches her in the stomach, and she folds over in pain.

Mr. Fookes pushes against the guard holding him as well, trying to get to Daphne, to get at the guard who just punched her. His guard slams him in the head with the butt of his gun, and Mr. Fookes slumps to the ground.

"Stop it," I yell. "Stop hurting them."

"It'll only get worse, if you don't help," says Connor. He makes it sound reasonable, as if he's just trying to help me. As if all this is my fault, that I'm being irrational.

I look between Connor—with his dead eyes and his zero compassion—and my friends. I know he's capable of having them all killed. He doesn't care.

I have no choice. I don't care about saving myself. Blade is gone. But I have to save my friends. I have to buy them enough time, to find a way out of this. "Okay," I whisper. "I'll do it for you. But I want them with me while I work on it."

"Again with the demands, Hazel. You keep misinterpreting your position in all this," says Connor.

"I need help. They can be my helpers." I don't care if I'm begging. I've lost everything else. I won't lose them.

Gavan snarls at me, like he's about to say no, but Connor shrugs like he doesn't care. "Fine. If you cause problems or don't do what we ask, it'll be easier to kill one of them in front of you if they're already there."

I suck in a breath. His words are casual, like he's talking about washing the dishes or handing out notes at a meeting. But he literally means everything he's saying. I can see it on his face.

Connor nods to himself, as if my horrified response is enough. "You will create the spell web in the room where it was originally created," he says. "We'll all go there now. No time like the present to recreate history."

My brain ticks over quickly, trying assess the situation. "I'll need the notebooks from the lab. Just to make sure I'm doing it right."

Connor nods and flicks one hand to a spare guard, who immediately turns and leaves the room, presumably in search of the notebooks. Connor turns back to me, eyebrows raised.

I have no more excuses to delay. It's about the last thing I feel capable of doing, but I manage to pull myself up to sitting. I'm still wearing my jeans and T-shirt, and they're mostly covered in ash. Somehow it comforts me. I created that massive demon. I gathered that power together, and then I absorbed it. If I did all that, surely I can figure out a way to get out of this? I've managed to get out of so many situations that have seemed impossible. Surely this isn't the end?

I climb out of bed and lean down to peer more closely at

the electrified band of energy that's sparking on my ankle. It's glowing blue, and there's a reflected glow all along my legs... except maybe that's not a reflection? I hold out my hands, and for the first time, I notice that I'm glowing all over my body. It's not a bright glow, but it's there. The demon energy inside me might not be able to get out, but it's putting on a show. I wouldn't be surprised if my eyes were glowing blue as well.

The enormous pool of demon energy swells inside me, sensing my desire to use it, but it can't get out. It's blocked by that stupid band on my leg. I don't understand how something so small is so powerful. I wish I'd taken more time with that damned book of Gavan's. I scanned it quickly, giving it back when it seemed to be useless in terms of what I needed. I should have known better. I should have known there was a reason Gavan was holding it so close. I underestimated him, and now look where I am.

I'm stuck here with my power inside me, desperate to be used, pushing against its barriers. I feel the pressure of it building in my chest How long can I exist with the enormous power inside me pushing to get out, and the band on the outside keeping it in? It's already aching, and I imagine it won't be long before it's agonizing. My only choice seems to be to use it, preferably to create a spell web that will cover us all instead of the one inside Mei, and maybe then use the lost soul spell to rescue Mei. I don't know how I'm going to do all that without giving the power over to Connor, or him killing me and my friends as soon as it's done. I refuse to let any more of my friends die.

Unlike... I swallow hard against the sob that's working its way up my throat. I can fall apart later. Right now, I have to focus. But I vow to myself, that whatever else I do, I'm going to destroy Connor and Gavan. Preferably into smithereens.

It occurs to me that I'm being a little arrogant. Can I really build a spell web like the original chalice did all those centuries ago? I don't have the same knowledge. I don't have the same years of experience. There's a chance I'll mess all this up and end by killing myself and everyone else around me. I pull back the curtain and look over to Mr. Fookes, Daphne, Zane, and Freddie. They're all looking down at the ground, shoulders hunched. Perhaps I shouldn't have insisted they stay with me? It seemed like the best way to ensure that if I figure a way out, they'd be safe as well. But have I signed their death warrants? Is this the end for our little group? I take a deep breath, trying to find calm. A sense of focus. I *will* get them out. Everyone.

Except... where are the others? Poppy and Iris? Did they escape? Or something worse...? My brain skitters away from that thought. There's only so much I can deal with at the moment. One thing at a time.

Gavan grabs my arm and tries to drag me across the room.

I yank my arm out from his hand. "I can walk by myself," I growl at him. He lifts one arm, as if he's about to slap me around.

"Gavan," says Connor sharply. "That's enough. We have her controlled. There's no need for you to hold her."

"She'll get away—"

"No, I don't believe she will," says Connor thoughtfully. "It's her greatest weakness, you see. She feels responsible for people when they get close to her. She won't leave while we have her friends."

I wish I could tell him he's wrong.

But he's not.

CHAPTER
FIFTY

The room he leads us to is in the basement of the main building.

The walls and floor are made of stone, and the doors are large and made of intricately carved wood. It's dark and damp, and it's hard to know why they think this would be the best room to keep the spell web in. But I'm not in charge, so I keep my mouth shut.

Someone flicks on some lights, and that makes it brighter, but not necessarily better. There is a raised dais at the front of the room and chairs along the edge of the room. At the back of the room there's a large circle carved into the stone, with symbols and words marked out around it. The power inside me is thrumming with excitement, like it knows that it's about to be released. Even my little demon has come to the surface and is playing around in the waves created by the fizzing demon energy.

On the walk down here, Mr. Fookes kept making faces at me, like he was trying to tell me something. But my brain isn't functioning properly and I couldn't understand what he was trying to tell me—and I'm struggling to make myself care. All I can focus on is getting this band off my leg and everyone out of here in one piece.

And killing Connor and my father.

"Right. So get to it," says Connor, sitting down on one of the chairs at the front of the room and gesturing at the stone dias. He leans back and puts one ankle over his other knee in a casual pose. He's clearly expecting to have a front row seat for this experience.

They pull in Mei's bed behind everyone else, and my eyes are drawn to her. She looks so small on the bed. Like the spell web has drained every last piece of her magic and her soul out of her. It's like a parasite, only able to exist by taking from other people. Is that what my spell web will be like? Is that what it's going to do to me? To whoever I put inside it?

Should I really be trying to do this? The risks are so high. What if I fail, and Connor gets control of the spell web? What if I kill everyone, including all my friends?

The questions are whizzing around in my head, making me feel dizzy. For a second, I'm so overwhelmed, I don't think I can do it. It's all too much. The only thing that keeps me going are my memories of what it was like when the humans knew about supers. How they reacted with such fear and suspicion, and how badly they hurt so many supers. The spell web is something that benefits supers as well as humans, that keeps the peace, and enables us all to live in harmony.

"You have to take the band off me. It's the only way I'll be able to do it," I say. I'm not lying. I glare at Gavan. I know he's going to want to keep the band on me the whole time, even if it makes no sense.

Connor smiles up at me, and it's as if we're in some delightful and completely different environment, maybe on a beach watching a romantic sunset or Parisian cafe, and I've said something amusing, just for his benefit. "Of course we'll take the band off, Hazel. But you must remember that the lives of your friends depend on you behaving." He gestures at the back of the room, and I see Daphne and Mr. Fookes on their knees with guns pointed at their heads. "Nothing you could do would be faster than the time it would take for my guards to pull the triggers."

I can't help my tiny whimper at his words. There's something about the juxtaposition of the way he's saying it —in a delightfully amused tone—and what he's saying that makes it seem ten times worse.

Mr. Fookes keeps his lips squeezed shut, as if holding in what he really wants to say, but he gives his head the tiniest of shakes, and glares at me as if to say, "No, don't listen to Connor." But the trouble is they're my friends. I can't just abandon them.

So I move slowly up to the dais and push a few things around so there's space for me to work. There's a big stone podium, which I assume is where the spell web is supposed to rest—at least its physical presence in this room. I look behind me to the stone wall and the carving etched into it. The large circle holds a number of words and symbols inside it. I recognize some of the symbols—the one for chalices, mostly—and there are words I understand —demon, energy and orb. I also see something that steadies my nerves. The lost soul spell: *Invenire memoriam. Proferte memoriam. Memoriae monstra.* If it's here in this room, I must be right about how to use it. It must be the way to get the supernatural volunteer out of the spell web again. I can use it to save Mei, and to pull out whoever is going to go into the web when I create it. I glance over at Connor. I need to avoid putting Gavan inside the web. I look around at the guards. At least one of them would be a more neutral person to work with than my birth father. If I could just—

There's a commotion at the entrance of the room, and the guard who was sent to get the notebooks returns. He talks to one of the officers, and they seem to be having an argument, but eventually the officer glances over at Connor, like he knows his superior won't like delays and gestures to the guard to stand at the side of the room. The guard hands the books to the officer and moves away to stand at the side of the room, his cap pulled down low. There's something about the way he holds his head that triggers a memory, like he reminds me of someone, but I shake my head. I don't know any of the guards here.

The officer takes the notebooks and brings them to me on the dais. He hands them over, looking worried.

"Problem?" I ask quietly.

"No, everything is fine." He glances back at the guard who just came in. "Just an unexpected rotation change," he mutters.

I nod, as if this means something to me, and take the books from him. I don't care about the guards. I'm focused on making the spell web and getting my friends free, and there's no room to concentrate on anything else. The notebook I need is in the middle, and I pull it out, placing the others on a chair nearby.

I look around the room, over to where Mei is lying helpless in the bed, to Mr. Fookes and Daphne who are kneeling on the ground, to Freddie and Zane who are being held by four other guards. They're all watching, as if waiting for the moment when I save them all. Like they think I have some secret plan that will get us all out of this.

And I have nothing. I've got a power that I can't use,

and friends who are being held at gunpoint, who will die whichever way this goes. I even lost the one person—

But I can't go there. My brain skitters away, protecting me from the pain it knows I'll experience.

So I focus back on the book. I read the instructions through one more time.

"I need someone else. A supernatural to be the link between my demon energy and the rest of the supernaturals in our world."

Connor gestures to Gavan. "I thought we already established that Gavan would help?"

"Not Gavan. I... uh... I don't know if this will work. I'm not sure I can guarantee his survival." It's the truth, but not the reason I don't want my father to be part of the spell web.

Connor nods, his eyes scanning the room.

"What about one of your guards?" I say quickly, planting the idea in his head. All the guards suddenly go still, like if they don't move, they'll go unnoticed. I feel guilty about it, but I'll do my best to protect them, whoever they are.

But Connor shakes his head. "No, I prefer not to waste a guard. How about one of your friends?" He looks between Mr. Fookes and Zane. "I prefer to use the most powerful creatures I can, when possible."

"No," I say too loudly. "That's not what I meant." I don't even know if this will work. I can't let them be hurt.

Connor smirks. "I'm sure it's not. But it's your only option. Get the genie," he says, gesturing at Mr. Fookes.

Daphne screams, "No!" And her guard hits her on the back of the head with his gun. She slumps forward. Mr. Fookes, who was standing beside her, attempts to attack the guard who hit her. The guard simply points his gun at

Daphne's head. Mr. Fookes subsides and allows the other guard to pull him away. The band on his leg glows brightly as if he's pushing against the power.

"Bring the dragon over to where the genie was. We need someone to keep her honest," says Connor, watching what's happening with delight. Gavan is standing behind him, scowling.

"Take off the band on my leg, and I'll make your spell web," I say. Energy is swirling around inside me, like it can sense what's happening. The chance to break free is getting closer.

Connor nods and gestures to Gavan.

The original chalice tried to make the spell web so many times. There are pages and pages of crossed out lines. I remember the explosion we saw in the mountain clan memories, what the crossed-out lines mean. Is this all a terrible mistake? Am I about to make some more crossed out lines?

The power in this room will be immense, that much I know. I can protect my friends as best I can from the energy explosion that the creation of the spell web will take, but there's no way I'm going to protect Connor, or Gavan, or even the guards. They can all fend for themselves.

Gavan climbs reluctantly up onto the dais and holds out his hand in the direction of the band on my ankle. He pulls the strand of electricity off my ankle, more roughly than was necessary. It hurts, but nothing more than I'm used to. I want to kick Gavan in the nuts but manage to hold myself back. I don't want to start anything—not yet at least. Gavan steps back away from me quickly.

As soon as the band is fully removed, the power surges through me. I open my arms and let it flow over my body, filling every part of my being with brilliant blue demonic magic, sending sparks of energy along my skin. It feels so big and wild that for a moment I'm lost on the waves of the magic, unable to find my footing. It feels too much, too big, too... everything.

"And from Mr. Fookes," I managed to say as I fight the feeling of being overwhelmed by the demon energy.

Gavan shakes his head. "No, he'll attack," he says to Connor. "We can let them all go free again."

Connor gestures to the guard. He picks up Daphne from the ground—she's only just opening her eyes again after the last hit—and holds her tight against him, the gun pointed at her head. "If he tries anything, she will be the first to be killed."

Mr. Fookes lets out a strangled noise. Gavan smiles, and returns to the dais. The guard pulls Mr. Fookes up next to me.

"I'm sorry," I whisper. "I was hoping he'd use a guard." I'm barely holding onto the power that's now surging inside me.

"Don't worry," Mr. Fookes whispers back. "Everything is under control."

I give him a strange look, but I don't have the capacity to figure out what he's talking about. Everything single nerve ending on my whole body is tingling, overwrought with sensation. The enormous amount of demon energy that's inside me is overwhelming, and it wants to get out. And along with the demon energy there's something else trying to get out from inside a locked cage.

The mountain clan memories.

They've been locked inside me, unable to get out. Until this moment, I wasn't powerful enough to actually see them on my own. But now they're flashing across my conscious, flashes of color and energy. Some of them are familiar. The scenes we saw on Mr. Fookes's projector. But now there are more of them. Flowing on from the settling of the First Village, to more from the time of the dragons when they flew unrestrained through the skies. The mountain clans always had a strong attachment to the dragon shifters, and they tried to help them, to warn them what was happening.

Except I can't concentrate on them right now. There's too much going on, too much energy surging inside me. I push them back down. I can watch them later.

The demon power flows around me, billowing out into the atmosphere, buzzing and biting the very air we're breathing. I can feel it tingling across my skin, and I shiver in anticipation. Despite everything, part of me is excited to be creating something like the spell web, so immense, so powerful.

But there's still one thing I need to do before I can create the new spell web.

I have to rescue Mei.

CHAPTER
FIFTY-ONE

Without opening my eyes, I send out a whisper of demon energy to where Mei is lying on the hospital bed at the back of the room. Her life force is so faint, I can't find it at first. The spell web is lying weakly over her, protecting the last of her life at the same time as it's killing her.

I pulse demon energy in her direction until it's surrounding her, giving Mei some protection from both the spell web and anyone trying to harm her. Without me even directing it, the demon energy enters her body, moving along her skin, through her veins, along her arteries, across her flesh, flowing through her very soul, and giving her sufficient magic to keep her alive for just a little longer.

The spell web inside her body is just as weak as its host. It occurs to me that because it's so weak, it should be easier for me to unlock it using the lost souls spell and free Mei. What happens when there's no longer a host? I don't know, but if it doesn't automatically dissolve into nothing, I'm going to have to somehow destroy what's left of Mei's spell web, at the same time as I create my new one.

There's a possibility I should be more worried about all this, but I'm not. There's too much demon energy surging through my veins. I feel a little like I could take on the world. I give Mr. Fookes another look, and he's watching me intently, like he really thinks he'll need to help me at some point. It's not the perfect solution, having him up here, being the super who helps me create the spell web... but I'm glad it's someone I'm comfortable with. The idea of doing anything like this with Gavan makes the hairs over my whole body rise up in horror.

I glance behind me, to remind me of the words of the spell, and then start murmuring them under my breath. I lift my hands over the podium up the front, to hide what I'm really doing, but my entire focus is on Mei and pulling her out of the spell web. The words get louder and louder, and then I feel it. The tight grip that the dying spell web has on Mei is being loosened, the bindings falling away. I use my demon energy to yank her away from it, hard and fast. On the outside, her body doesn't move, but inside, she's free. Her spell web flares up, then dies. It's like it was only holding on for Mei's sake, not its own.

"What just happened?" snaps Connor.

I open my eyes. "The old spell web just died. I will create the new one now." I don't mention that Mei is still alive. I don't want him to know that she's going to be okay, that my demon energy is even now inside her, protecting her. My little demon buzzes inside me, urging me on.

"Get on with it," he mutters, glancing around the room. Does he think a human is going to leap out and arrest him? They'll be able to see the supers again, at least until I can get this new spell web up and running.

Which won't take me long. My demon energy is growing even larger inside me. It's somehow expanding, becoming more than it was originally. And it wasn't small to start with. Sparks are coming off my body, dripping away from my fingers as I stand on the dais, holding it all in, trying to force myself to move onto the next stage in the process. Despite everything, I feel a moment of fear. And then it passes as I let myself fall into the demon energy surrounding me.

The magic is so big, so all encompassing, I can sense everything in the room, the heartbeats of every person, the pumping of their blood, every little intake of breath. I feel Connor's excitement, Gavan's resentment, Daphne's fear, Mr. Fookes's triumph... Wait. What?

I flick my eyes open.

Everything in the room is tinged with blue. Connor's face is bathed in blue light as he looks up at me. Every part of me is glowing.

"What's wrong, now? What are you waiting for?" snaps Connor.

I turn my gaze on him, and he blinks.

"It will take some time, I think," I say slowly, trying to enunciate all the words correctly. It feels like I'm speaking down a long hollow pipe. I'm so far away from the realm of my physical form, it's hard to concentrate. "This is not a fast process." Hopefully that gives me more time to figure this all out.

I glance at Mr. Fookes. He's watching me, and then his eyes dart to the corner of the room. I manage to hold in my instinct to immediately look in that direction. Instead I use the demon energy that's overflowing all around me to sense what's over where Mr. Fookes is indicating.

The guards at the door are milling about strangely, like they're having trouble figuring out what's happening. I can't see their faces, just sense where they are. Several seem to be walking away down the hall. Connor and Gavan haven't noticed—they're both focused on me—and neither have the guards holding Daphne and the others. I keep my eyes averted, trying not to give anything away. Is this part of some kind of plan Mr. Fookes has in play? For the first time, I think properly about what he whispered to me. *Don't worry, everything is under control.*

He's got a plan, and whatever it is, Mr. Fookes thinks it's good. And therefore so do I. The only thing I can do to help is to keep them distracted by continuing what I'm doing. I have to do it anyway. I have to create a new spell web now that the old one is dead.

So I'll create a new spell web... and then I'll use it to break Connor and Gavan into teeny, tiny pieces. I take a breath, then grasp Mr. Fookes's hands to begin the process of creating the connection through him. I hold the seething demon energy steady inside me, just pulling out a tiny line that snakes its way into his body, searching for his supernatural essence. *His magic.* It feels a little like how I used the electrical thread to join the demons together, except I can't use the same kind of overpowering demon energy on Mr. Fookes. I'm trying very hard to make sure I don't harm him, or do anything to his magic. This is all just theoretical, I'm not even one hundred percent sure I can get him out again once the web has been created. I feel a wave of guilt. I saved him from his toaster, only to run the risk of trapping him inside the spell web. If there were any other way to do this, I'd do it.

As soon as I think that, my little demon leaps out from wherever it was hiding, and suddenly mountain memories are flooding my head again. At first it's too fast for me, but then they slow down, and I watch as the original chalice works methodically through the night barely taking time to eat or sleep. I learn his name—Felix—and I see him moving ever closer to finding a way to make the spell web work. Everything is happening in seconds rather than minutes or days.

I see him realizing that the spell web was too unstable at the beginning, that it needed someone to hold it together at the center while it gathered momentum. I see the mountain supernaturals at his side, a steady influence, keeping him on track. I see the brave supernaturals volunteering to take on the spell web, people who believed in what he was doing, who thought he could find a way to save their children from the dragons with his research. So many people lining up, so many of them dying for the privilege. I see each new attempt, and every time, the supernatural on the inside dies within hours or days. But they always die.

I feel like I'm sinking, drowning, beneath the memories; there were too many people who died to make it happen. My heart is so sore I don't know if I'll ever be able to feel again. I'm about to stop, to let the memories disappear back into my subconscious, when I see it.

The moment when the first spell web came into being.

And in the middle of the spell web isn't just any supernatural. It's Felix, the original chalice.

That's how he made the spell web last. He couldn't find a way to make it stick with another supernatural, so he used himself. It's like everything suddenly makes sense. It's the one niggling thing that didn't quite make sense, even as I was reading the notebooks. As I watch, time speeds up. Months become years, and Felix dissolves into pure energy, becoming one with the spell web.

He sacrificed himself to create the spell web.

And I know, somewhere deep inside me, that he did it because it was the only way to make it work. But he also felt it was the only way to make up for all those people who died because of his research.

I take a deep breath. The demon energy sparks out around the room, lightning crackles. The burning smell of a sizzling piece of wall makes my nose twitch. But I don't react to any of it. I'm letting the realization wash over me.

The only way for the spell web to truly work is for a chalice to be at the center of it. Other supernaturals might last for a while—Mei being a case in point—but for a spell web to truly continue on... it has to be a chalice.

And the mountain elders knew that. When the First Elder gave me the memories, he knew that it would have to be me that created it.

Me who kept it going.

Me who sacrificed myself in the middle of it. That's why he gave me the memories. That's why he sent me on my way. I needed to find this out for myself.

And somehow that feels okay. It feels right.

Blade is gone. I don't want to try and live my old life without him. There's nothing else I need to do in the world, not without him. I don't want to wake up one day and find myself alone and angry, fighting with everyone and everything around me, resentful and lonely. Rejected and terrified, just like my father. Wondering if maybe demon energy is the way to make myself feel whole again. An empty shell of a person, living life moment to moment with no true connections.

More importantly, I don't want any other innocent people to be hurt by my actions.

My friends will be fine; Mr. Fookes will look after them. He has a plan in place and I can make sure Mei is okay before I allow the spell web to consume me.

Everything seems to fit. My life will mean something, and so will my death.

I take a breath. It's time to get this show on the road.

Letting go of his hands, I push Mr. Fookes out of the spell, and let the energy surround me. Mr. Fookes is yelling something at me outside the spell web, but it doesn't matter. I've made my decision. I can't use anyone else, when Felix—the man who devoted his life to creating the spell web and knew it better than anyone else—used himself to create it. It has to be me. I lift my arms up high, allowing the energy around me to sizzle and burn.

I recall the steps from the book, and start following them one by one, firstly by molding the demon energy inside me into an enormous ball of power. It needs to be compacted, held tight so that it can burst in a big enough explosion when the time is right. Then I use the latent supernatural connection that Felix discovered to connect the enormous well of demon energy inside me, to all the other supernaturals the world over, molding it into a spell that keeps us all connected, linked by this one central place.

I start with the supers in the room with me, skimming over them, dipping into their magic and opening up the connection with the spell web I'm creating, and then moving on. I use the enormous demon energy well inside me to push me out further. It spreads out over the whole compound, and then out wider, to the next town and then the entire state. It's like a thin film of energy, coating every-thing. Every time a new person connects to my energetic coating, there's a little click as they fall into place. Then it's across the whole country, tiny little links popping into place, and then it spreads to the entire world. The feeling is unlike anything else I've ever experienced. I'm everywhere at once, connected to every single supernatural the world over. It feels overwhelming and exactly right at the same time.

I'm on the cusp of finishing the spell, and making it all happen, when the mountain clan memories burst into my head yet again. I'm too occupied with controlling the enormous amount of energy that's now circling the entire planet, and can't do anything to stop the memories, so I let them run their course. There's nothing in there that will change what I'm about to do.

This time it's memories of what happened to the spell web once it was created. Images of what happened when a new faction of the Earthbound took over. They used it to destroy the dragons completely, to feed their own agenda. Instead of controlling the dragons, they destroyed them, decimated them.

Annihilated them.

They took the power of the spell web and made it something it was never supposed to be. Even if I'm at the center of the spell web, just like Felix was, the spell web can still be abused by outsiders.

And in that moment, I know I need to stop that from happening again. It would be so easy for someone like Connor or Director Holden to come along and somehow wrest control of it.

I need there to be a gatekeeper, an incorruptible person who will never let the rules be swayed. For that to last, for it to be passed down, from generation to generation, a rock-solid bond. And then suddenly I know who it should be.

The mountain supers.

I think of the guard to who looks after the vault in the second-hand record store. He was a good, yet kind, guardian. He helped me when I needed it but stood firm when the rules required it. He protected his people by not telling me more than I needed to know. I know he would be perfect to guard the spell web. Then there's Carlos, the guard at the SIG Headquarters. He was strong and good and kind to me. And Carrick. Even though he's mad at me, he's a good man. The First Elder. Another strong, yet fair man. I know his people would take care of a power like the spell web. They'd guard it as it should be guarded. Rock solid.

And they'd wield the power as it should be wielded.

Using an instinct that I can't name, I allow my demon magic to seep out into the air around me. It tingles as it moves out from my body, humming with energy. It moves out into the hallways, making the guards shiver as it passes through their bodies, and through the stones that make up this part of the building.

I'm looking for someone. A mountain super. Someone to represent their clan in this changeover of power.

And then I find him. He's larger than most, but powerful. He's locked in a cell not far from where we are, in the dungeons of the compound.

Carrick. *He's here.*

And I'm going to break him out.

CHAPTER
FIFTY-TWO

Turns out, Carrick doesn't need my help to break out.

Something has made the guard walk away from his post, and he's already walking down the dark hallway to investigate. Carrick and Elena—the dragon healer I met in Newport News—are together in a stone cell and Carrick is touching the stone on the walls. My new senses easily feel his magic as he uses it to break free. A stone dungeon probably wasn't the best cell for a mountain super who's connected to the very earth. My main question is why it took Carrick so long to break out. But his escape happens so fast, I think Carrick must have been preparing for it, waiting for the right moment. He's a smart man. I feel even better about my decision to link him to the spell web.

He hesitates for a moment outside his cell. The woman remains inside. I'm trying to figure out why when the guard comes striding back down the alley. He doesn't notice Carrick, who has somehow hidden himself against the rock, blending into the wall. And then Carrick punches the guard in the face, an enormous knockout punch from one of his large fists. The guard goes down and stays down.

Carrick crouches down and gets the keys to the rest of the cells from the belt of the unconscious guard. He gestures for the woman to come with him, and they go down the row of cells, unlocking the doors. There are several people I don't recognize. And then suddenly there's someone I know. Damien. He's conferring with Carrick. They seem to be making a plan. They lock the guard in one of the cells. All of this I can somehow sense through the demon energy that's pulsing inside me.

But I need them to come to me. To the spell web. I use a sliver of the spell web covering to put the idea of coming to the spell web room inside Carrick's head. He resists it. He's planning escape. He wants to get Elena out of the compound. To freedom.

I show him an image of Mei, lying in the hospital bed, weak and helpless. And in the spell web room. I get the sense he's been in the room before, and as soon as I put the idea that Mei is in the room inside his head, he barrels directly for us. Damien and Elena follow.

For a moment, I think I've made a mistake. He's going to come running into the room and create the kind of situation I was trying to avoid. But then he slows down. His tread becomes stealthy, and his movements sparse. Elena and Damien follow him mutely, their footsteps silent.

I leave him to find his way to us and return my attention to the room. Gavan is standing next to Connor, and he's arguing heatedly. That doesn't seem good.

Perhaps he knows more about how long it's supposed to take to create a spell web than I realized?

I take a breath. This is it. I have to make it happen, now or never. Just like I watched Felix do in the memories, I hold out my hands and concentrate on allowing the demon energy—that's now connected to every other supernatural on the planet—to flow out from my body and into an orb shape in front of me.

The moment I let down the barriers, demon energy bursts out from the confines of my body, leaping down my arms, ecstatic to be free from its bonds. I use my chalice powers to form it into a ball in front of me, compacting it down into a glowing sphere of demon energy that sparks and spits. Blazing heat is coming off the ball of energy, but it doesn't burn me. Instead it energizes me.

Connor steps back away from the ball, but my father stays close, just out from the dais. He's got his arms folded across his chest, and he's watching me like a hawk.

Despite everything, they still think they've got me under their control. They still think I'm going to give them the spell web once I've created it.

The next step is the flaming lines of energy, the same as the ones that I used to merge the demons. Chalice energy needs to be wrapped around the demon energy many times, until it holds it tightly in place. I'm aiming for a ball of string look, at least that's how I'm imagining it.

Energy flows out from my hands, and I wrap it carefully around the demon energy ball sizzling on the podium. The whole thing sparks and spits, like a blazing blue fireball of yarn, but I have it tightly controlled, putty in my hands. The chalice fire line goes around and around the ball, tighter and tighter.

Occasional lines of energy spark out from the ball, and one hits my father in the chest. He grunts and takes a step back, but his eyes don't leave my face. He's determined to keep me under control. For a moment, all I can see is his face, all I can remember are the terrible things he's said to

367

me. Broken. Weak. Stupid. Wrong. My magic falters for a second, and I see him sneer.

He's still, even now, waiting for me to fail. I harden my determination, and keep going. Damned if I'm going to let him get to me. I know I'm stronger than he is. The line of spark-filled magic weaves itself around the ball, covering the entire orb in fiery energy.

Eventually, it's done.

The ball in front of me is tight, the center so compacted that the energy is about to burst. And that's what's going to happen soon. It's going to explode in an enormous energy bomb that will join back up and create the final spell web... with me inside it. I'm the one who connected all the supers together, it's my magic that's the basis for this web of power. I'm the center.

I look up. Fix my gaze on Daphne and Zane, and then Mr. Fookes next to me. I wish there was more time to say what I want to say to them. To tell them how much they've meant to me. I look at Freddie. He might have been the guy who sent me on a crazy mission to the SIG headquarters, but it wasn't on purpose. He's been here with me all this time. He didn't have to come into the Compound and try to rescue us.

Us. Me and Blade.

My heart finally breaks. Tears fill my eyes, and then overflow down my cheeks.

Blade is dead. Connor killed him.

Everything I'm doing right now is for Blade. To make his death mean something.

I turn to look at Connor, and for the first time, I let him see it. My rage. My full and powerful anger directed at him. He kidnapped me. He kidnapped Nelson. He's been killing people without thought since I've known him. He killed *Blade*.

So this is it. He doesn't get to do it anymore.

Connor's eyes widen. He stares at me, and his smug expression melts away. He's realized he isn't in control after all. "Kill her!" he yells. But he's left it too late.

The rebellion has already started. Carrick is fighting two guards at the door. Two punches from the big mountain super, and they're out. Just past him, I see Poppy and Iris in the hallway, fighting another guard. My heart leaps. They're here. It must have been part of a plan, for some of them to get in and find me. The others waited.

Then I notice one of the guards inside the room seems to be attacking the other guard at the door. He's on our side as well? How did they turn a guard?

The two guards holding Zane and Daphne hesitate. They don't know what to do—should they help their comrades or do they keep holding the prisoners? I can almost see the indecision on their faces. Beside me, Mr. Fookes leaps down off the dais, and races toward Daphne. He's growing larger as he moves closer, expanding in all directions like he did in the bowling alley. The two guards back off, terrified of this new development. The guards don't seem to be used to this kind of fighting. They're not an elite unit of soldiers. They're used to guarding people that can't get out.

But Connor isn't even thinking about his previous threats to Zane and Daphne. He's shouting to the guards to start shooting at me instead. A couple of guards turn, raising guns in my direction. But the guard fighting on our side is too quick for them. He leaps at the first guard, a snarl visible on his face, his amber eyes flashing fire. Zane and

Carrick follow closely behind, and they're soon dragging the guards out into the hallway.

And that's when I realize.

The guard.

Amber eyes.

Snarling.

The guard is Blade.

He's here. Not dead at all.

I feel like screaming and crying all at one time.

Connor lied to me. Blade isn't dead.

Of *course* Connor lied to me. It's what he does.

I can't breathe with the joy of it. Of having him returned to me. I'm crying but they're happy tears, tears that are flying on the wings of a bubble of happiness. Blade is back from the dead, and the terrible weight I was drowning under is lifted from my chest.

But then it hits me. A crack appears in the bubble of happiness. And out of that happiness crawls the deepest, most intense sorrow. I can barely breathe with the idea of it. Because I can't turn back. I have a mission now. A way to end this safely for everyone. And it doesn't involve a happily ever after for me. It doesn't involve me going back to Blade and living with him. It doesn't even involve me ever speaking to him again. I feel like that crack in my happiness is opening up so wide that it's totally consuming me. I don't know how to control the wave of grief that's crashing down on me. I just know that I need for someone to pay.

I turn back to Connor, the most obvious person to take it out on, but he's not there. I search the room, and I can't see him. I'm just about to use the spell web that's hovering in my senses to find him, when he comes to me. His arm clamps around my neck. So tight I can't breathe. I took my eyes off him for a few seconds too long.

"Stop it!" screams Connor. "Stop fighting, or she dies!"

The fighting comes to a stop, mostly because all the guards seem to be already on the ground, and the only people left are on my side. I sense rather than see Gavan hiding behind Connor.

Everyone is watching the three of us on the dais. I try to smile down at them. My friends. My people. I try to let them know that this is perfect. That this is exactly how it's meant to go.

"No!" yells Blade. He can see what I'm about to do. He knows me well enough to guess.

I let the energy collide on the inside of the ball, and it shrivels down into nothing for the tiniest of milliseconds. Time seems to stand still, to hang in silence for the longest time. I focus on Carrick and find his mountain magic—that I know and can feel intimately because of the memories inside me—and bind him to the spell web as it is created. And then the demon energy ball bursts back out again, throwing bright, hot, burning energy over everyone in the room. It's white hot energy, so powerful that no one should be able to survive it.

I desperately cover the people I love with protective magic, my friends, the people who came here to save me. Mr. Fookes, Daphne, Freddie, and Zane. Carrick, Elena, Poppy and Iris.

Blade.

My heart shatters again at the idea of leaving him behind, but I have no choice. This needs to be done. Memories burst into my mind, but this time they're not from the mountain clans.

They're my memories. Of me and my friends. Of Blade.

Sharing a secret laugh under the covers in my bed. A touch. His smile. His amber eyes filled with anger. Filled with heat. With desire.

My heart breaks into a thousand pieces. And then everything in the room turns and even brighter white, heat burns through everything and the spell web becomes real again.

And just before I lose consciousness, I remember. I reach out with a single powerful line of demon energy and give as much of it to Mei as I can. Her body jerks in response, and she takes her first deep breath since she entered the room on a hospital bed.

And then I'm sucked down into the spell web orb, the center of everything.

Mei's free. Awake and alive. Ready to live the rest of her life.

And I'm not.

CHAPTER
FIFTY-THREE

I come back to consciousness slowly.

It's strange. I still feel like me. I still have a shape that represents me, a body. It's just not the same body I used to have. But I'm in the middle of a blue, glowing, electricity-filled orb. I can see things happening around me, but I don't think they can see me. Not if the way they're reacting is any guide. My little demon is here with me, whirring around next to me, rather than inside my stomach. I can understand a little more of what it's saying, and it seems to be excited that it's inside the spell web. Maybe it's an upgrade from being inside *me*.

I don't know how long it's been since I was last conscious, but it doesn't seem to be long. The grief is still raw on their faces, the tears still visible on Poppy and Daphne's cheeks. I look away, unable to deal with the hurt I've caused them.

There are bodies on the ground next to me. Connor and my father. Dead. All I feel is a fierce sense of satisfaction that they're both gone now. That they won't continue causing trouble in the world. And if it takes my own slow death to do it, then so be it.

They both died in the explosion, at the birth of the spell web. I wonder why they never realized that was what it would be like? It seems obvious to me now that anything so powerful would be created in an enormous blast of energy. But to be fair, I didn't realize until it was almost time for it to happen. As I carried all that demon energy around inside me, it dawned on me that what we were doing was... enormous. And that the fallout was likely to be extreme.

Luckily everyone else seems to have survived with only a few mild scrapes, cuts and burns. I was able to protect them from the worst of it. I feel proud of that. We survived, even when it seemed like we couldn't possibly survive. It occurs to me that my mother's premonition was right. She saw me, her as-yet-unborn daughter saving the world, and that's what I just did. Not that anyone will know about it, or celebrate what I did with songs or anything. But I'll know, and so will my friends.

The little demon whirrs next to me. *My little demon knows as well.*

It makes me feel more connected to my mother, like maybe she saw more of me than should have been possible, because she saw me in her visions. I got to see her in the mountain memories, to watch back scenes from her life. We were each lucky to see more of each other than is usually possible.

I watch from inside the spell web as they start moving about in the room. It's like they're in slow motion. Mr. Fookes is organizing the guards. A few of them were caught in the spell web's fallout, but most were in the hallway and have survived. They seem to be showing a remarkable willingness to switch sides and help Mr. Fookes, now that

Connor and Gavan are both dead. At a guess, I'd say that Connor was using his siren abilities on them to keep them loyal. Now that he's dead... all bets are off.

Daphne is sitting near Mr. Fookes, a blanket around her shoulders, and her hair standing out in every direction. Someone has found an ice pack and she's holding it to the back of her head where the guard hit her. Every minute or so Mr. Fookes looks over to make sure she's okay. She's watching him right back, soaking him in like she thought she might never see him again. Maybe she *did* think that, when she watched him up on the dais, about to be consumed by the spell web.

Iris is standing beside Mei, who's still lying prone in the hospital bed. Iris is using the heirloom to help Mei recover her strength—although with the amount of demon energy I pumped into Mei, I think she'll be fine in no time without Iris's help. Damien is standing next to Iris, watching what she's doing like a hawk. He looks much older than last time I saw him. He's been through a lot since then. I'm glad he has Mei back. It makes what I'm doing easier, seeing Mei recovering with her father there to take care of her. I wonder where Seth is, and if anyone has called him?

In another corner, Freddie is talking to Poppy and Zane, all three looking tired and drawn. They keep glancing up toward me in the orb, although I don't think they see me. All they see is the glowing orb dancing over the podium. They seem to be plotting something, although I can't for the life of me figure out what it might be.

Everyone seems to be recovering, albeit slowly. They'll all be fine, it'll just take time. That's what I really hoped would happen. For Mei to come back to her family, to Seth and Damien. For Mr. Fookes to have Daphne, and for everyone else to be able to live their lives again.

The one person I haven't been able to look at so far is Blade, but I force myself to do it now.

He's been at the edge of my awareness this whole time, but it hurts too much to look at him directly. When I turn my full focus onto him, I gasp as pain slides across my mind, slicing through me like a surgical knife, sharp and brutal. He's sitting on the edge of the raised dais, his elbows on his knees, his head in his hands. He's shaking and distraught. I never doubted what he felt for me, that he loved me. But now I know it for sure. That's the hardest thing to watch; his complete and utter devastation. I want to tell him it's okay, that I'm... satisfied... with what I did.

I wish I didn't have to do it, but I still think it was the only decision I could make.

But watching him sob into his hands, I don't think that would be enough for him right now. I think he might question why I left him, why I couldn't find another way to save everyone. He'd probably tell me that it was all too risky, that I shouldn't have gone running into danger like I did. And I don't have an answer for that. Not yet. Not one that would make complete sense. Because hurting him is the last thing I ever wanted to do.

The only thing I can say in my defense is that I thought he was dead. I thought my life didn't matter any more, because I'd be living it without him. I made decisions based on that, not on him being alive. That's what I wish I could tell him. That's what I want him to know. That I didn't leave him on purpose.

I thought he'd already left me.

I feel movement next to me, and it's a relief to turn away from Blade. I discover Carrick standing next to me on the dais, staring into the spell web. At first, I think he's just struggling to come to terms with his new connection to the magic spell that covers the entire world. I wonder if it amps up his magic at all?

But then he speaks to me.

"I never got to say I'm sorry to you, Hazel," he says softly. "And now it's too late. I need to say I'm sorry for being angry with you. I was upset. Mei was missing. We weren't thinking..." He glances over at Mei and Damien, who are talking quietly in the back of the room. "We were all upset."

At first, his words don't make sense to me. It's like Carrick is speaking another language. He's saying sorry? Saying that maybe I wasn't to blame for not finding Mei when I had the chance?

I blink. The spell web around me buzzes with energy.

But what about all the people who were hurt? All the lives lost?

"She blamed herself for not finding Mei earlier, you know," says Mr. Fookes softly, coming up behind Carrick. "She did what she thought was right at the time. She couldn't break her promise to me. And then she thought that it was her fault every time Director Holden did something to hurt more people using Mei and the spell web."

Carrick's face goes pale. "It wasn't her fault. It was Director Holden. I know that." He glances behind him to where Damien is standing at the back of the room with Mei. "Damien knows that."

At first, I just stare at Carrick like he's suddenly sprouted alien wings. All this time, I thought they were angry. That everyone thought I'd made the wrong decision. And now, in a couple of sentences, Carrick has put all that to rest.

But when I stop to think about it, it doesn't really make any difference. I mean, I'm glad to know they don't hate me. That maybe I didn't make the wrong decision when I saved Mr. Fookes over Mei. That maybe my decisions were just decisions, and not the worst decisions ever.

But it doesn't change the fact that I've ended up inside the spell web. There's no other way for this to end and it doesn't matter who forgives me. I have to accept that. The original chalice searched, he let hundreds of people die testing out his theories, and even he couldn't find a way. I want to shout at them, to tell them they need to move on with their lives. That this is the way it's supposed to be. That I'm doing this for their sake. But they can't hear a thing.

And that's when I decide to do it anyway. I need to do something to make myself feel better. So I yell at Carrick. *"You're forgiven. Now just leave it be! Move on with your life!"*

The little demon whirrs around me, excited by all the noise, and it makes me laugh. At least I'm not completely alone in here.

But then Carrick mutters something under his breath. "She's in there," he says softly.

I lean in closer, wondering if I heard him properly.

Then he says it again, louder. "She's still in there."

Mr. Fookes looks at him, puzzled.

"Hazel's still inside the spell web. I can feel her. She's talking to us. *She's in there.* And that means we can get her out."

I shake my head. No. That's not what I meant. He's going to undo everything I've just achieved. All the good I tried to do.

Blade looks up, his face ravaged. "Don't say things like that if you don't mean them." His voice is so raw and ragged, it's cutting my heart open again.

No. *No.*

Don't give him false hope.

"I can hear her. I know I can," says Carrick, his voice thick with emotion. "She's in there. There's a chance."

I shake my head. There's no chance. I can't leave the spell web. If the original chalice couldn't find a way out, there's no way I can do it.

They need to accept it, like I have.

CHAPTER
FIFTY-FOUR

"We have to try," says Carrick again.

He looks at Mr. Fookes, who's standing next to him, peering into the spell web. "Do you think it's possible? What do you know about the spell web?"

Mr. Fookes slowly walks around the podium, peering inside like he thinks he can see me in here. Up close, his face looks haggard as well, dark shadows under his eyes and lines out from his mouth. He stops and stares away into the distance, like he's trying to remember everything he's ever been told. "We both had the mountain clan memories placed inside us," he says eventually. "I haven't been able to see all of them, but I do know the spell web was made by a chalice. And I'm pretty sure he had to sacrifice himself when the time came to create it. It wouldn't work other-wise, no matter what he tried. I think Hazel did the same thing, based on the memories. The original chalice was convinced it was the only way to create a spell web that would last."

"Do you think we can get her out?"

"I don't think it's ever been done before."

"Doesn't mean we can't do it," says Freddie urgently, striding over to join the other two. His face is set. "She's done so much for us. She was prepared to die for us. We should do everything we can to try to save her." Freddie is glaring at Carrick, like he's waiting for the mountain super to disagree.

But don't they get it? I did it for them. I don't need them to pay me back. I just need them to make it worthwhile. For them all to live good lives.

"I know how much she's done for us," says Carrick. "She fought the demons in Newport News like it was her own backyard. She never once questioned why she should be helping."

"*No*," I yell at Carrick. "*Stop. This isn't what I want. You're going to ruin everything. I can't leave yet. The spell web will fail without me in here.*" He doesn't seem to be listening. I'm desperate to be part of this conversation, but there's no way to join in.

"That's what she's always been like, even when she was trying to keep to herself," says Mr. Fookes. "She used to fix all the appliances for everyone in our apartment building. Could never turn me down. Always willing to help people."

Daphne comes over, arm in arm with Poppy. "She got us out of Ravenwood. She let herself get captured when our escape went wrong, just so we could get out of there," says Daphne, tears rolling down her cheeks.

There's a noise from the back of the room, and everyone turns to see Mei climbing slowly out of her hospital bed. Damien is by her side, trying to get her to take it easy. They all watch silently as Mei walks slowly over to the podium, helped by Damien. She's still gaunt and pale, but she's more alive than I ever thought she'd be again when I first saw her in the compound hospital.

She clears her throat. "Hazel saved my life. Today. Right here. She brought me back from the dead. She's actually saved my life more than once, and for that I'll always owe her." She pauses to take a few ragged breaths, and my heart lurches. I can't bear to see her so fragile, not when she was always so strong. I instinctively reach out through the spell web, wanting to give her more strength. I don't know quite how to do it, but Mei's body seems to know how to accept the energy that I'm trying to give her. She's got some kind of connection to the spell web, more than any of the others in the room, except maybe Carrick.

She looks up in surprise, directly at the spell web. "She's in there," she whispers. "She really is. I can feel her." She stands a little taller, and gives herself a shake. Already she looks better. She steps closer to the spell web, to me, and holds up her hand, like she wants to touch me, but there's too much electrical current on the outside of the orb. Staring straight at me, she starts speaking. "I never expected you to break your promise to Mr. Fookes, and I'm mad at my father, Carrick and Seth for ever asking it of you. You're the bravest, strongest person I know, and if there's any way to get you out of the spell web, then I'm going to do it."

"No," I cry out, distraught. *"You can't get me out. It's not going to work."*

Damien clears his throat. "She's definitely still in there?" he says, looking uncomfortable.

"Yes. And we need to get her out," says Mei sternly. "After everything she's done for us, you included. We can't give up without a fight."

Damien lets out a sigh. "You know you're in trouble

when your daughter is smarter than you are," he says softly to Mei. He turns to me. "I'm sorry Hazel. I'm sorry I ever asked you to find Mei. I'm sorry I was angry at you. I was just upset. We all were."

I sit back inside the spell web, stunned at his apology. Confusion, pleasure and sadness are all intermingled inside me, and all I can do is stare at Mei and Damien.

"Then let's make this happen. Let's get her out of there," says Freddie, rubbing his hands together like he's anticipating success already.

At his words, I remember what they're talking about, what they're trying to do. Surely Freddie should understand better than anyone that I have to stay inside the spell web? He's the *voodoo king*. He understands spells. I feel like screaming. Do they not realize that this is it? This is where they need to leave me? If anything, the things they've been saying, the apologies they've given, it's all just made me *more* determined to stay inside the spell web, to keep it in place, and keep them all safe.

Do none of them understand?

Apparently not. There's a general agreement from everyone else in the room to what Freddie is saying. Everyone except Blade, who's sitting apart from the rest of them, staring into space. I don't know where to put my attention. Do I try to console Blade, or convince the others that they need to stop?

"How do we do it?" asks Mr. Fookes.

Carrick hesitates. "She's given me a connection to the spell web. Like a guardianship, I think."

"Instead of the Earthbound?" Freddie raises his eyebrows like he thinks that's going to cause problems. Perhaps it might, but I don't care. The Earthbound let it get into the wrong hands. Maybe the Earthbound *were* the wrong hands.

"Yes," says Carrick slowly.

Freddie looks from Mr. Fookes to Carrick. "What about the power of three?"

Mr. Fookes looks unsure. "I'm not sure I can do it that way again," he says. "And Hazel is inside the spell web. I don't think she can do it from in there."

"Definitely not," says Daphne in a stern voice. "It almost killed you last time."

"What about the heirloom?" asks Poppy.

Freddie shakes his head. "It won't help for something like this."

"I think we should call a few people, ask for help," says Poppy.

There are murmurs of agreement around the room.

"I think I can connect to her, tell her what we're doing. And then we do it," says Carrick.

I know what you're trying to do, you idiots! I yell the words. But it doesn't work. Carrick doesn't seem to hear this time.

Instead Carrick stands in front of me, and I feel a deep rumbling inside the spell web, then a feeling of warmth and goodness spreads out inside the space, and despite myself, I'm comforted. I'm glad I chose Carrick to connect to the spell web. I hope he's okay with it as well.

"Let's do this," says Carrick.

And suddenly they're all working together. Discussing what needs to happen. Carrick gets on the phone with the First Elder, Mr. Fookes sits with Daphne, trying to go through the memories, to find anything relevant. Damien is talking to Zane, and then they're on the phone talking to God knows who. Freddie and Iris are conferring next to Mei, who's back in her bed, but already looks much better. I can feel her along my spell web senses, and I can tell she'll get back to normal. Already she's stronger. It makes me wonder again where Seth is? He should be here, too.

The only person who's not doing anything is Blade. He's sitting in a chair on the side of the room staring at the spell web. I wish I could think it was me he was staring at. But I know for a fact that he can't see me.

I'm not visible on the outside. I'm not even sure my body is visible on the inside of the spell web. It's like I'm in another dimension, inside the energy, part of the magic. I don't even know what I would be if they managed to somehow pull me back out of here.

Would I be a person? Or perhaps just an amalgamation of lots of tiny pieces of magic?

Blade stands up. He walks over to the spell web. And he stands there staring at it. *At me.*

And this time it wrings out my heart, makes my chest feel like it's being squeezed tight by some kind of clamp, until I can hardly breathe. He's looking straight at me, and I see the heartbreak that's ravaging his face. I see the wildness in his amber gaze and I feel the jaguar so close to the surface, he's on the verge of changing. It's only his willpower that's keeping him in this human form. I want to close my eyes, to not see him like this. But I can't. My eyes hungrily devour him, tracing every line of his face, trying to remember him, so that when they've all gone and left me here alone, I'll still have his face to keep me company.

Because that's how all this is going to end.

Me, alone.

If the super-smart chalice who created the first spell web couldn't find way out, then neither will they.

FIFTY-FIVE

There's no way for me to tell them that it's pointless, so they keep going. They keep trying.

Connor and Gavan's bodies were removed by impassive guards, under the stern gaze of Carrick. I watched it carefully, wondering what I should be feeling. But I didn't meet my birth father until a few months ago. He was horrible to me the whole time, and now he's dead. I've decided that it's okay I'm not sad that he's dead. Just because he was related to me by blood doesn't mean he was my family.

I mourned my real father, the man who raised me and taught me to be the person I am today. And as I sit inside the spell web and watch these people moving heaven and earth, trying to find a way to pull me out of the spell web, I realize they're my family now, too.

They're the people I care about, the ones I've lived alongside and who have helped me through everything I've been through.

And that means the world to me. I love them all, and that love fills my heart and makes it feel so big and so full, that if I were outside in the real world, I'd probably be crying.

And if staying inside the spell web for the rest of my life keeps them all safe, it's worth it to me.

So I watch them all. I take them all in and try to memorize their features, to make sure I never forget anything about them... for as long as I live. I watch them endlessly, because inside the spell web there's no time, no sleeping, no anything. Just the little demon, who buzzes around beside me, keeping me company.

Blade doesn't sleep either. Whenever he has down time, he comes back into this room, and sits and stares the spell web.

The others are in and out of the room, and I can see they're building up some kind of plan. Something is coming together and I have no idea what it is. They never plan near me.

I've been learning more about the spell web since I've been in here and I've realized that I'm not entirely stuck inside this one room. I can reach out along the spell web. It stretches in all directions, and is mapped out like a series of glowing red grid lines over everything in the world. I can use it to find people. See things. I begin by searching through the compound, finding Blade when he's not in the room with me. Then I start thinking about Seth and why he still isn't here.

Did they not know how to reach him? Has he given up on Mei?

I can't understand how either of those things could be true, and I can't bear the thought of Mei and Seth not being together after everything they've been through... so I search for him along the web.

Instinct tells me where to go and it's not long before I

find him, his fiery essence shining like a beacon along the gridlines. He's in his phoenix form, inside a bare cave, hidden far up in the mountains. There's nothing else in the cave with him other than a few meagre supplies and the bones of animals he's presumably eaten.

He's curled up, sleeping, almost hibernating. His phoenix body looks worn and ravaged, like he's been living a hard life since Mei was kidnapped. I wake him with a push from the spell web.

He snorts awake, and a burst of flame comes out his mouth. I didn't even know he could do that. I send calming thoughts, trying to comfort him.

"Mei is alive. She needs you. You need to come to Carrick's compound," I whisper the words into his mind. I don't know how much he can hear. Carrick and the others at the Compound don't seem to be able to hear me when I talk.

Seth's head raises and he looks around like he's trying to figure out if someone is in the cave with him. He snarls, and thinks it's a trick.

"She's safe, she's alive, she needs you," I repeat. I think he can hear me. Is it something to do with me being in the spell web's grid? Or his phoenix abilities?

Or is it just because I really want him to understand me, and I'm putting everything into making him listen?

But Seth shakes his head, resisting the words. Almost as if he couldn't bear it if they're not true.

"You need to go to her at Carrick's Compound. This is real. Go!"

He stands up, but he's still hesitating, like he can't quite believe it.

I'm impatient with him now. *"Go!"* I yell along the spell web.

He shudders and then turns his body to the entrance of

the cave. He stands there for a full minute, staring at the light beyond the darkened cave, as if he's having to psych himself up to leave. His phoenix body is just a dim reflection of the burning flames I saw over him when I first met him at the prison. What's happened to him? Then he takes a running leap, and he's in the air, his powerful wings soaring on the wind currents, heading in our direction.

Inside the spell web, I let out a sigh of relief.

The little demon buzzes next to me, and I smile. It feels good to help.

I look down at the little demon again, thinking hard. "I want to help you, too," I say. "While I still can."

The demon goes still. Not buzzing. Not fizzing. Not moving.

Still.

I look up at the wall behind the spell web. The words of the spell for lost soul memories is on the wall.

Invenire memoriam. Proferte memoriam. Memoriae monstra.

I whisper the words, over and over. At first, there's nothing, and I wonder if being inside the spell web is affecting my ability to do spells. But I keep going, and after a while, images start to appear, blurry at first. I keep whispering the words, and as I whisper them, the little demon's story is unraveled and laid bare.

His name was Tobias and he was a powerful supernatural. He had one sister, and his parents died when he was young. His death in a car accident in Pismo Beach was premature, he was too young, he had so much he was planning to do, to achieve. And it was all because of a cursed object he had been given by a jealous friend.

My brain slowly chugs through the information, preoccupied by the idea that he was cursed. Does he want me to find the friend? What kind of justice am I expected to achieve?

But then I start to think about his history more closely.

He was a powerful supernatural. He lived in Pismo Beach. He died in a car crash with his sister, Arabella.

He's my Uncle Tobias. The car accident he died in was the accident that killed my mother. He was a chalice, too.

Suddenly I can't breathe. I'm seeing stars. All of which feels weird, because I'm not entirely sure I actually *need* to breathe any more.

He's my Uncle Tobias.

Did you know? I ask the little demon.

The little demon buzzes around erratically. I think that's a no. Not until the memory spell. He just knew he needed to make something right, whatever happened.

He was given a cursed object, maybe on purpose. I see the object traced back, from the man who gave it to him, to going to buy it... at Larry's Pawn shop.

"So what do we need to do, to make it right? I can't bring you back to life," I say. "I don't want to hurt your friend."

The pawn shop. Stop them from hurting other people. Ruining other lives.

I hear the words clearly inside my head. It's the first time the little demon has been able to talk to me, to say the words. They're the words that describe the desire that was strong enough to bring him back.

"Okay," I say. "Let's destroy the cursed object business."

I remember the cursed pen that Walter gave me. I left it on Connor's desk in the lab, but I forgot about it after that. "Let's start with the cursed pen in the lab," I say. I don't know if you could say that Connor's death was because of the object or not, but it's a good time to destroy it in case it gets into innocent hands.

I reach out along the spell web, until I find myself in the lab. There's a supernatural guard in here, although there are no more demons, and no more researchers. We're all dead or... trapped. The books have been tidied away into a shelf, and Connor's desk is empty, like he was never there.

But the pen is still there, in the little pen holder on the desk.

I'm not sure how I'm going to do it, but in the end, it's easy. I whisper to the guard at the edges of his subconscious that he needs to get rid of the pens. Burn them all. So he leaves his post, picks up the entire pen holder full of pens, and takes it down a few flights of stairs to another section of the basement. There's a massive boiler room, and a furnace for rubbish. He throws the pens in the rubbish, and within seconds, they're all gone.

Then the guard blinks, looks around, and walks quickly back up to his post.

"I think I can make people do stuff," I say to Tobias. "This changes things."

He buzzes around distractedly.

When Carrick comes into the room a few minutes later, I try it out. I move out onto the spell web, and whisper in his ear. *You need to stop this. There's no way to save me.*

He looks up, and smiles. "She's talking to me," he says to Mr. Fookes, who's in the room with him.

"What's she saying?"

"That we need to stop what we're doing."

"You think we should listen to her?"

Carrick shakes his head. "No. We're making good progress."

I try to push him into giving up, to sway his mind, but it

turns out it's not that easy. He's as strong as a mountain, and as solid as a rock.

"Then let's get to it," says Mr. Fookes and they walk back out again.

If I can't just get them all to do my will—maybe just some people?—then I need to find my head investigator, Poppy. She's the one who's been searching for my little demon's real life. I head out along the spell web, and I'm in luck. I find her and Daphne sitting outside, making a list of things they need Zane to get for them.

"I need your help," I whisper in her ear. *"I need you to come to the spell web room. Come help me."*

Poppy stands up. "I think Hazel needs our help," she says. "It sounds urgent. We need to get to the spell web room, right away." She starts running toward the entrance of the building, going through a decorative arch and then running along a tiled hallway. Daphne is following her not far behind.

I feel bad. I didn't mean for her to run.

A couple minutes later, Poppy runs into the spell web room, looking around for some kind of threat. There's no one here but me.

Poppy deflates. "I was imagining it," she says raggedly. "It wasn't real."

I reach out along the grid, this time sending her comforting thoughts.

She backs up a step. "Hazel?"

"Yes. It's me," I say carefully, using the spell web grid. I'm careful to use the connection between her and the spell web to talk. I've figured out that's the trick to getting them to hear me.

"You do need my help? What do you need?"

Carefully and slowly, using my tenuous connection via

the spell web, I outline what I've learned. Who it is that I have inside the spell web with me. And what needs to happen to set him free.

Poppy sits down heavily on the nearest seat. Daphne comes in moments later, puffing a little. Mr. Fookes comes in right after. "I thought we might need more help," she says.

"Hazel's definitely inside the spell web," says Poppy, looking slightly stunned. "She's in there, and she's still trying to help people. She wants to help the little demon that possessed her. She wants to set him free, and she needs our help."

CHAPTER
FIFTY-SIX

A few hours later, Mei is sitting with me in the spell web room, doing stretches on the floor. I think they've decided to keep me company, because ever since I talked to Poppy, there's been someone in here with me. Sometimes they talk, sometimes they just get on with what they're doing.

Mei's still weak, but I can see the fierce determination on her face. She's going to get better, and it's going to happen sooner rather than later. And knowing Mei, it'll happen. It's not just about her physical strength. There are emotional wounds that will have to heal. I see it in the hunted expression that appears on her face when she thinks no one else is watching. The fear that makes her jump a little more quickly at strange noises than before.

Which is why she jumps half out of her skin when someone appears at the door in a grand rush, stumbling into the room like he's only just learned how to walk.

Seth.

She turns, and her expression seems to crumble. It's like she's been holding herself together for this moment.

"*Seth,*" she whispers.

He's standing there, staring at her like he doesn't believe it's really her. "Mei," he whispers. "You're alive."

She nods. She's still sitting on the ground, her legs out in front of her. I'm not sure she knows how to react. And then suddenly she's moving, faster than I would have thought possible, scrambling to her feet, and throwing herself at Seth. He opens his arms and then tightens them around her, like he never wants to let go. Both of them are crying, and it's breaking my heart. They're back together now, and that's all that matters.

They move apart, Seth holding Mei's head in his palms, whispering to her, kissing her cheeks like he can't believe she's real. Mei smiles through her tears, letting him talk. After a while, Mei glances back over her shoulder at me. "Sorry, Hazel. I'm going to have to leave you for now," she whispers. Then she leads Seth out of the room, hands tightly clasped, to find somewhere more private.

I let out a sigh. Another piece of the puzzle fixed.

After Seth's return, life goes on around the compound, and I watch everything that's happening inside it and outside. Poppy leaves on her mission to right Tobias's wrong. The others are working on whatever they're working on to try and get me out of here.

My little demon—Tobias—sits inside and observes everything with me. Sometimes we speed through the memories, watching them at twice the normal speed. Except now I can understand it. The spell web gives me the power to see so much more. I've watched them so many times, I've memorized some of the scenes. I could tell you word for word what my birth mother says to the First Elder about her daughter—me—saving the world. I find other small scenes with Arabella and the First Elder and I watch them all greedily, trying to get a sense for who she was.

It's not been long—maybe a day or two, I'm not entirely sure—when the First Elder arrives in person. I wasn't expecting him, so when he walks through the door, I take a step backward—or at least the version of it that I can do inside the spell web.

He comes up to the glowing orb and stares into it, like he's looking for something. I feel a ping of magic inside the web, and I know it's him. He's somehow able to connect to me inside here.

He calls Carrick over. "She's definitely in there. Wide awake. Watching everything," he says.

"Will it work?" asks Carrick.

"No clue. Only way to find out is to try."

It's less than an hour later when more people arrive.

Seth comes in, holding Mei's hand as if he's never letting go. Some of the ravens arrive. Mike, Seth's brother, and his wife Tracey are the only ones I recognize.

Blade's sister Suzanne arrives and has Blade's grandmother Anna in tow. Fleet follows closely behind them. They give Blade a big hug that seems to take forever, and I wish I was out there so badly, it almost tears me in two.

My mouth falls open like I'm trying to catch flies when I see the guard from the secondhand record store arrive in the room. He comes over to the spell web, looks around sheepishly, and then whispers to me, "My name is Adric."

What are you doing? I whisper to the room, trying to figure out what's happening.

Not long after, Detective Capello—Marco—arrives with Walter and Poppy. Poppy comes straight over and gives me the thumbs up. She's done it. Marco follows her over.

"She's in there?" he says to Poppy, his voice awed.

"Yeah. You can talk to her, we're pretty sure she can hear you."

"Hazel, uh, hi," he says, his expression serious. "I just want you to know, we arrested Larry. Got him on stolen goods charges. Then searched his place and discovered his stash of cursed objects, which the human officers who were there saw as illegal weapons through the spell web. Some of them could have killed hundreds of people in one hit."

Tobias is buzzing around inside the spell web beside me, excited by what they've just said. I smile and wish I could cry in here, because this feels too important not to express emotion.

"We released the curses on all the objects, with help from Walter, and some advice from Mr. Fookes," says Poppy.

"And Larry has enough evidence against him to put him away for a good long time," adds Marco.

I look at Walter, trying to see if he's feeling any resentment at the idea that his job has just been taken away from him, but he's smiling. "I've got a new job," he says to me. "I'm working with Poppy now. We're gonna investigate for people. Find things. Help them out."

I desperately wish I could be out there with them. This feels like a momentous occasion. I'd be hugging Walter, and jumping up and down with Poppy over how well they fixed my first lost soul 'wrong'.

"What happens now?" I ask Tobias, realizing that he should be disappearing off into the ether. "Aren't you supposed to go back to the other side or something?" Is it because he's in the spell web with me?

Tobias buzzes and spins as his answer, but I immediately understand. He's a severed soul, not a lost soul.

"Possessing me counts against you?" I say, upset on his

behalf. I was expecting him to move on to where he was supposed to go. Some of my elation at our solution to the puzzle fades away, but Tobias doesn't seem to mind. I guess as far as he's concerned we've got it pretty good in here.

And as far as I'm concerned, it feels good to have used the chalice spell, even if it was only the ones, and to have helped Tobias with the wrong that he came back to fix. It's kind of like I've achieved what chalices are supposed to in their time on this earth. I wish I could have been more involved—perhaps the one to break down Larry's door?—but I did my best with what I had.

Marco nods his head, and Poppy smiles up at me. "We've got to go, they're roping us into helping with the plan," she says. They're gone before I can ask what the plan is.

More people keep arriving as the day goes on. A large figure arrives through the door, another mountain super. It takes me a moment to realize it's Carlos, the guard from SIG headquarters. On his arm is a small crooked woman, with a crooked smile that's looking right at me. *Hattie.*

Behind them is Alvera, plus the other members of the Council.

Then Nelson arrives with his mother holding his hand tightly as she looks around the room. He goes to Blade and sits with him, not saying a word.

One of the strangest arrivals of the day is a tall, thin man, about my adoptive father's age. He's got shaggy hair and is wearing black jeans and a black T-shirt, and has a feather earring in one ear.

Randy-freaking-Crowe from *Sunday Lies.*

He's here.

What the hell is he doing here?

Randy comes over to the spell web and peers at it. He turns to Carrick. "You sure she's in there?" he asks.

"Positive."

Randy clears his throat. "Hey... uh... Hazel. You don't know me, but I knew your dad. Your adoptive dad, that is. And your birth mother. We grew up together. Your dad, he was one of my best friends."

If I could've sat down, I would've. He's my father's best friend? Randy *freaking* Crowe?

"Anyway, when they said there was something I could do to help his daughter, I came right away." He clears his throat. "There's more I'd like to say, but I'll wait until you're out of this electricity ball."

I don't know what to say to him, but that's okay because I don't think he expects an answer. He slopes off to the side of the room to consult with Damien.

This gathering of people is the hardest thing I've ever had to witness. I want to stay inside the spell web, so I know they'll be safe, that they'll be protected, and the humans will continue to live their oblivious lives and not come hunting our kind.

But I so desperately want to be out there with them all as well.

CHAPTER
FIFTY-SEVEN

When they start bringing in large chunks of stone and placing it around the spell web in a circular shape, I'm curious. They're building a wall around the spell web. Blade comes to stand next to me, watching the glowing ball of light, as if he can't bear to not have me in his sight. Everyone leaves him alone, which is unsurprising given the wild and vicious look he has about him right now.

His beard is growing in, his hair is standing on end and his beautiful eyes are bloodshot. He's trying not to hope, but I can see it there on his face. I wish I could reach out and touch him. Tell him that I can't leave. Tell him that as much as I want to be out there with him, I can't. Tell him that I love him, and I wish it didn't have to be this way.

Tell him not to hope.

And then the wall is too high, and I can't see him anymore.

At least not with my eyes. The senses of the spell web are everywhere, and I've learned enough so that I can use them like they're my own. I can still feel the people crowding into the room, all of them busy with different aspects of this plan, whatever it is.

And then suddenly it seems they're ready. Movement stops. Everyone is standing in little groups. The mountain supers are together at the front, surrounding the stone wall they built.

And as soon as their power begins to inhabit the stone, I understand why. It's like a conduit, a bridge for them to use between them and the spell web. The mountain clans have a powerful connection to the earth and stone. Carrick has a powerful connection to the spell web.

So they wind their way around me, inside the stone. And behind them, I feel all the other supers who are here today. Each of them loaning their magic to the mountain supers at the front—Carrick, the First Elder, Adric, Carlos. The rest of the Council Elders, even the nephew who disapproved of me. They're all standing around the wall they built, using it to encircle the spell web, and bring it under their control.

The fact that I gave Carrick a connection to the spell web is helping them. I watch what they're doing, and I don't know what to do. I have to resist; I know I do. But how? I don't want to hurt them, and everyone else connected to them.

That feels like the wrong thing to do.

Tobias, my little demon, watches with me, buzzing around me in circles. I don't get any answers from him either.

So I wait. I see how far they get, how much of an intrusion they can make into the spell web, into my little cave inside.

Bit by bit, piece by piece, they push their way in. They're using the power of the other supers behind them as well;

they're connecting somehow through the central force of the mountain clan, maybe even the spell web. I can feel Mei's energy close by, and through her, Seth, Damien, and others. They're all working together, inching forward, pushing through the boundaries.

And then suddenly Carrick is there.

He's there with me inside the spell web, his large form towering over me, his expression as solid and comforting as ever. I could reach out and touch him he's so real. I don't know how he did it, but he's here.

"What are you doing?" I say indignantly. I guess I never thought they'd actually manage to make this work.

"I'm rescuing you," he rumbles, his voice low, like he thinks talking louder might wake the neighbors. "Come on, we don't have much time. This is a one-shot kind of deal. We're using up power that we can't get access to again." He holds out his hand, and I want to take it. With everything inside me, I want to take his hand and go back out there.

"I can't," I whisper. "I have to stay here, to keep the spell web stable."

"You can't do it from the outside?" Carrick's expression falls.

I shake my head, misery in every molecule of my being. "This is the only way."

"Hazel, come on, come back with me now. We'll figure something out. Blade needs you. We all need you."

My eyes fill with tears—that I thought I couldn't shed in here—and I blink them back. "It has to be this way. It's the way the other chalice, Felix did it."

"There must be another way," says Carrick. "We'll figure it out. But we need to hurry."

I start to shake my head—

And then suddenly a tiny buzzing light is whizzing

around between me and Carrick. Tobias. My little demon. My uncle.

And I get a very clear message from him. He's a chalice, too, even if he's been in a demon form for so long. He's happy inside the spell web. And he wants to take over for me.

I frown. *What?*

I can do it, he says, speaking directly to me for only the second time.

"What's happening?" says Carrick. "Come on Hazel, we have to hurry."

I look up at Carrick then down at the glowing ball of light that is Tobias. My heart skips a beat.

Could it be possible?

Is a demon strong enough to look after the spell web?

Tobias says, *Yes. Of course I am.*

Why didn't the original chalice do it this way? Why didn't he test a demon?

Because he didn't trust demons. He didn't think we would do anything like this to help anyone else. Maybe other demons wouldn't do it. But I will. For you, Hazel, I will. I know you will help others of my kind, just like you've helped me.

"Come, Hazel. You have to come now." Carrick grabs my hand and pulls, and for a second longer, I resist... and then I let him drag me out of there, falling through fizzing and sparking energy.

"Thank you," I yell, as I fall.

I land heavily on stone, my thoughts mixed-up and muddled. I don't know who I am, or where I've been, and when I look up and see amber eyes, at first I wonder if I know him. But I feel safe, despite the wildness in his eyes, and I reach out and touch his chin. Whoever he is, he's handsome.

"Hazel," he says in an anguished voice.

And then I remember who I am, and what I'm doing, and who he is.

Everything rushes back into my head, and the words gush out of me. "Blade. Oh Blade, I'm sorry. I love you so much. I love you more than anything."

And when he crushes me to his chest and says my name over and over again, I can't help smiling so hard it feels like my face is going to break, despite the tears.

I'm home. Where I'm supposed to be.

FIFTY-EIGHT

I hold onto Blade's hand, unable to let go, even now, a week later. It feels solid, the callouses rubbing against my soft skin, his coiled strength evident even through his hand.

It still feels strange to be out in the real world after spending more than two days inside the spell web. It wasn't long, but it felt like forever.

We're loitering on the veranda of Freddie's house, Blade standing quietly next to me, giving me the time I need to ease into this meeting with Damien. He asked us to visit today, and it's harder than I thought it would be. I haven't really talked to anyone since Blade carried me out of the spell web room at the compound.

Anyone but Blade that is. He's been protecting me like a mother bear, growling any time anyone suggests even a phone call. We've been at another of Blade's secret hide-outs, giving me time to rest up, and find my equilibrium again. I'm not sure I've found it quite yet.

I guess that's why Blade is being so overprotective.

That, and the fact that he thought he'd lost me. I know how it feels, because for a few hours, I thought I'd lost him too.

Everything out here feels bright and sharp. Sometimes I have to take a step back, to close my eyes and let the world pass me by for a few moments, trying to get myself back in the flow. Blade understands. He stops and stands with me. Lets me breathe.

Other times, I miss the little demon that was inside me. Tobias. We spoke in emotion and images and magic, but he was a part of me for all that time. It seems empty without the demon inside me.

Everything feels strange and new, not least of which is the idea that I had so many people coming together to help free me from the spell web. People who believed in me and loved me and wanted to help.

It makes me feel fuzzy on the inside, and at the same time sends a shiver along my skin. There was a time not so long ago that I was all alone. I'd become someone who was too scared to engage with people. I thought that having people close to me meant pain and hurt and suffering. I believed that was the way my life would always be.

Look at me now. I'm part of a family, based out of a magical apartment building, with a hot boyfriend who likes to fight demons.

My life is pretty awesome.

I swallow over a lump in my throat and stare at the wooden door to Freddie's house. I haven't talked to Damien since he helped get me out of the spell web, but I'm looking forward to seeing both him and Mei.

Damien and Mei are staying with Freddie, at his house on the cliffs in California. Carrick is back at the Compound, and this time he's really in charge. He has the spell web at his back, his connection to it is strong, and so far Director

Holden hasn't said a word about any of it. I'm pretty sure he's fuming.

But that doesn't matter right now. I'm too excited about seeing Mei again. She's free of the spell web, no longer dying.

"You ready?" asks Blade, looking down at me, his eyes a bright forest green.

I smile up at him, and for a moment, get lost staring at his familiar face. He smiles back down at me, and leans in for a chaste kiss on the lips. "I'll take that as a yes," he says.

Blade knocks on Freddie's front door. It's a strange old house with multiple layers and weird balconies poking out from different directions. I'm pretty sure it must have magic in it, maybe even some magic like Mr. Fookes's apartment building. But it also has heaps of room inside and plenty of places for Mei and Damien to stay and recuperate.

The door swings open in a mad rush, and suddenly Freddie's standing there, his expression breaking into a genuine smile of welcome. He hugs Blade, giving him a slap on the back, and then gathers me up too, swinging me around like a lunatic. It makes me laugh, even as I tell him to put me down. At one time, something like this would have set Blade off, but he's forgiven Freddie now, and we're good.

"They're in the front room playing chess," says Freddie, rolling his eyes. He leads the way along the hallway, past all the cabinets with their intriguing objects. I slow to a dawdle, and peer inside at some of the strange trinkets. There's nothing with the ugly greenish-brown glow that indicates a cursed object. *Thankfully*.

Freddie stops outside the double doors that lead into the space where I first met him. There's a sliver of light leaking around the edge of the door, and I still remember the amazing vista that's visible from the room on the other side.

"Do you remember?" I ask Blade and Freddie as we pause at the threshold. "The first time we came here?"

"Yes. Freddie tried to proposition you," says Blade in a mock-growling voice.

"I *helped* you, if you remember," says Freddie, feigning hurt.

"I saw my father again for the first time in years," I say, trying to keep it serious. "Even if it was just on a recording. And I started my journey to where I am now. To knowing about my chalice abilities."

Blade puts one arm over my shoulder. "Even then, I knew you were special," he says.

I look at Blade and then Freddie. "Thank you both. I mean it. I'd never have done this without you both helping me in the beginning."

Freddie smiles, and there's something wicked in his expression. "I'm glad you said that," he says. Then, with a flourish, he opens the double doors into the front room.

I gasp.

Crowded inside the light-filled room is everyone who was at the compound with me a week ago, plus some who weren't. They're all grinning at me and holding up full champagne flutes.

"Surprise!" The word is a cacophony of noise, shouted by a variety of voices, and I look around the room, suddenly tearing up, overwhelmed by the emotions that are swamping me all at the same time. Happiness and joy are the predominant ones, but there's relief and pride and love as well.

Blade moves in closer to my side, concerned. "I said

you'd be okay to have a small party," he whispers in my ear. "Is it okay? We can leave again if it's too much."

I grin up at him. He'd do it too; drag me off, even though everyone is here to see me. "Thank you," I whisper back to him. "But I'm good. So far at least."

And then I'm being pulled into a massive three-way hug with Poppy and Daphne, and that's the last time I get to talk to Blade for a little while. Everyone is crowding around me, wanting to hug and talk.

"Blade said you needed space. But we're hoping you've had enough space now," says Daphne.

"It's good to see you," I say, feeling like the Cheshire Cat, I'm smiling so wide.

Mr. Fookes comes forward and gives me a big hug, and then Nelson and his mother. One by one, everyone comes up to me, and hugs me, telling me how glad they are that I'm back. My heart feels like it's full to bursting with all the love in the room. The whole time, Blade is there at my back, making sure I'm okay, that I'm not tired, and that everyone remembers to give me enough space.

We're nearing the middle of the room when a tall, lanky man comes up to me. His hair is tidier than last time I saw him, and he's wearing a shirt and suit pants, but I'd recognize Randy Crowe anywhere.

"I love your music," I blurt out, feeling a little star struck. I've listened to this guy's music since I was just a kid.

"Thanks. Your dad was a big influence on me. He helped me through a rough patch when we were kids, and he always supported me. I was sorry to hear that he'd been killed." He ducks his head, and looks away.

"Thank you," I say, still not quite believing this conversation is real. "My dad had all your records, but he never said he actually knew you."

"Yeah, well, that would be typical Elias, he didn't like to blow his own trumpet."

"I think he had to give up a lot when he went into hiding with me, but he never gave up listening to music, especially your music," I say. Beside me, Blade grabs hold of my hand and gives it a gentle squeeze.

Randy gives a quick, if sad, smile, pleased at my words. "Thanks, I appreciate you saying that. He was a good guy, your dad. He was a good friend, too." He hesitates. "On that note, I have something important to talk to you about, to do with your dad."

I nod, wondering where this is going. I can't even begin to guess.

Randy takes a breath, like this is a big deal. "Before the band got famous, your dad and I, we went in on a business venture together, fifty-fifty. I think you've been there? Every Day is Sunday Records?"

"I've been to the store, and I saw all the old pictures of my father. I figured he was one of the managers of the store, years ago."

"We scraped together the cash, and created our own record store, just the way we wanted it. We bought the building and everything. That's why the mountain supers have their hidden lockup down there. Elias knew a guy and they made an arrangement."

"Wow, I didn't realize." I'm genuinely stunned. "What happened to it?"

"Yeah, well, nothing happened. We never got around to selling it," says Randy, looking sheepish. He rubs his hand over the back of his neck. "The mountain supers kept paying us to use it as a front for their secure lockup under the store, and we just kept on selling records. It makes a decent income, so when your dad disappeared..."

"You just kept it?" I can't keep the surprise out of my voice.

Randy shrugs. "I didn't know what to do with the place, so I just kept it open. You're Elias's only daughter, so his half ownership of the store goes to you."

CHAPTER
FIFTY-NINE

I stare at Randy like he's mad. "Are you kidding?"

"You're a half owner, along with me," says Randy again. "Elias hasn't been getting his share of the profits for a long while, so there's a bit of back pay for you."

"Back pay?"

"Dividends, really. Twenty years' worth."

"What?" I squeak the word at him.

"It'll buy you a nice little house somewhere, or maybe a boat to sail the world. Whatever you like really," says Randy, like it's nothing much.

"I don't— I can't—" I glance helplessly at Blade but he just shrugs back.

"Let's get together next week and talk it over."

"But—"

"No buts, Hazel. It's yours. It's just a matter of working out the details." Randy leans in and gives me a quick hug. "Your dad would be proud," he says, then determinedly walks away.

"Did that just happen?" I ask Blade, still feeling stunned. "Or am I hallucinating?"

"That just happened. You're practically related to Randy Crowe." Blade grins.

"How much money could there be? I can't take twenty years' worth."

"It belonged to your dad. That means it's your inheritance. I'm sure he would have wanted you to have it."

I nod uncertainly. I'm so used to the idea of just getting by that the idea of being given a lump sum of money is disconcerting.

"Do you want to sit down somewhere?" asks Blade.

"I still haven't see the two people I came here to see," I say. "Where are Damien and Mei?"

"Down the back of the room," says Blade. "Let's go sit with them."

We push our way through the crowds, until I see them in a cushioned window seat at the back, with the magnificent view of the ocean behind them, and an old chess set between them. Hovering behind Mei's shoulder is Seth. He's the first to notice me, and gives me a welcoming nod, moving forward to grasp my hand in his. He looks much better than last time I saw him, although there's still a hint of wildness in his eyes.

"Hi Hazel," he says. "Blade."

Blade stiffens slightly behind me, ready to react to anything that Seth might say to me that he deems inappropriate. He gives Seth a curt nod.

"Hi Seth," I say cautiously. I'm not entirely sure how Seth feels about me. Does he still think I should have rescued Mei instead of Mr. Fookes?

I'm at ease with that decision now. I made the choice that was right for me at the time, and it was nothing to do with being somehow influenced by my chalice powers. But is Seth okay with it?

This close, I can feel the heat coming off him, and a tiny part of me wonders if he's about to shift into his phoenix form, and this is all some kind of trick. Seth hesitates for a moment longer, and then he leans down and hugs me tight. I try not to feel shocked.

"I owe you," he whispers. "I owe you for Mei's life, and for mine."

I look over at Blade with wide eyes, but he's equally surprised.

Seth pulls back from the hug, but keeps his hands on my arms, looking solemnly down at me. He's very tall, so I have to look way up to look in his eyes. "I know it was you who found me in that cave, and called me back," he says. "I was almost too far gone into my phoenix form to ever come back. I can't ever thank you enough for saving me. For bringing me home."

"I... uh... I just wanted to see you and Mei back together. That's all I ever wanted," I say, stumbling over my words. I never expected this kind of an apology from Seth.

"I know. And I'm sorry I was angry at you for not using your wish to find Mei. I was distraught and looking for someone to blame. When you saved Mr. Fookes instead, I went a little crazy. I wasn't thinking properly. It's not a good excuse, but it's the truth."

"It's okay. It was a scary time. I'm just glad we're all back together again," I say, glancing at Blade. He's holding tight to my hand again, and standing closer to me than is strictly necessary. It feels good to have him at my back.

Mei and Damien are watching silently from their comfortable spot. Once Seth moves back, having said everything he wanted to say, Mei stands up and walks over —limping slightly and her body still thin—to wrap me in a huge hug. "Thank you," she whispers in my ear. *"Thank you."*

Damien is waiting just behind her, smiling at me like I'm a long-lost family member. He gives me a huge hug and a kiss on the cheek, which from him feels like he's giving me some kind of award. He looks older now; his hair has gone silver at the sides, and I think he'd be more visible in a crowd. His days of being an undercover agent are probably over. But I think maybe he's too well-known around the world for that now anyway.

Damien motions with his hand. "Come, sit with us. I have something I want to talk to you about." Seth pulls up a couple of high-backed chairs to the window seat and gestures for us to sit.

So I take a seat and keep breathing and watching as Mei sits and laughs and tells us how she's going with her recovery.

"Hazel, we invited you here for more than just to say hi," Damien says eventually.

I nod and wait. I'd been pretty sure that was the case.

"I have something for you. The mountain clan went to clear out Gavan's things."

I can't help the twitch that flits across my face, and Damien—always observant—sees it.

"Don't worry, I'm not trying to give you a memento from your birth father. But he had some things from your birth mother. I thought you might want to have them?"

Eyes wide, I nod slowly. I've heard her through her voice on a CD and through the songs she sang, and then through the mountain memories the First Elder gave me. She's almost as dear to me now as my adoptive mother is, despite the fact we never met.

Damien holds out an envelope. It's faded and worn

with brown stains on the outside that look suspiciously like coffee stains.

I hesitate, but eventually reach out and grab the envelope. The lure of something that belonged to my mother is too great. It's heavier than I was expecting. Glancing at Blade, I can't read his expression. What does he think?

My real parents are my adoptive parents. They looked after me, cleaned up my scraped knees, read me bedtime stories, and helped me grow. But my birth mother, she didn't *want* to die in that car accident. She didn't leave me by choice. I open the envelope and peer in. The silence in the room around me is almost palpable.

It's a picture I see first. I pull it out. An old photo, faded with time. It's of Arabella, my mother, sitting in a hospital bed, holding a tiny swaddled baby. Next to her are my father Elias and Randy Crowe. They're all grinning broadly down at the baby.

I turn the photo over. The words '*Hazel meeting the gang for the first time*' are written in scrawling handwriting.

I flip it back. My mother looks young and fresh-faced. Happy. My chest feels heavy with emotion, and I have to take a couple of breaths to steady myself.

Handing the photo to Blade, I pull out the other objects in the envelope. There's a ring with a flat blue stone and a jagged gold line going through it, and a small journal. I flick open the journal, and there's more of her scrawly writing. It's my mother's writing. Her words. And when I look closer, I see that she's writing about me. About what it's like to have a baby, to have someone she loves so much that it hurts her heart.

I don't notice that I'm crying until drops of water fall onto the journal. I frantically wipe away the tears, blotting at the handwritten text, trying not to let it smear.

"It's my mother's writing," I whisper.

"It's her journal from around the time you were born. Gavan must have kept it. Read it." Damien hesitates. "It's not an excuse, but there's a passage where she says that you're the most important thing in her world, more than anything or anyone else. The First Elder said that despite everything, Gavan was always extremely possessive of your mother. I think perhaps he read that and became jealous of you. That's why he could never look at you without being resentful."

"I was just a baby," I say.

"It's a good thing he let you go, Hazel," says Blade. "You had a great childhood. That's the best thing he could have given you."

"I had an awesome childhood," I say softly.

"The ring is made of demon stone and gold. It's a traditional ring of the Chalice line, similar to your pin. It was your mother's ring. She wanted you to have it, but Gavan had it hidden among his things."

I look up at Damien. "Thank you. For getting these to me."

"They're yours. It's only right."

I slip the ring onto my finger, and it fits perfectly. The demon stone hums gently against my skin. I reach out and grasp Blade's hand again. He looks down at the photo of my mother, and he smiles.

"She looks just like you," he says.

I can't say anything, just grin back at him, my heart full.

~

THANK YOU!

Thank you for reading *Spells and Demons*, the final book in the Demon Hunter in Hiding series.

I've loved spending time with Hazel and Blade, and I hope you have too...

If you'd like to read more about Mei Walker and Seth Barnes, plus Mei's father Damien, Carrick the Mountain King, Zane the moody dragon, and many others, try my other series set in the same world - **The Dragon Rising Series.**

The first book is called **Hidden Dragon**, and I've given you a sneak peek into the book on the pages that follow.

Excerpt from Hidden Dragon

Si's muscles flex as he swings his long fighting stick at me.

He looks like an avenging angel; his short black hair is slicked back off his face, and his dark eyes give nothing away. Mostly those same eyes are wreathed in smiles, lines crinkling around the edges, but in a fight, he's hard and unforgiving.

To him there is nothing more than to win or lose, to live or die.

Perhaps he's right.

I know he's only trying to save me from my enemies.

I block his next attack with my own fighting stick then leap back out of range, taking a quick swipe to his side as I go.

Si's expression doesn't change.

I'm sure it hurt like hell—there wasn't enough time to pull up his supernatural defenses—but he's a pro at hiding his emotions.

Sweat's dripping off me, and my legs and arms feel like jelly.

We've been at this for a couple hours now.

Fight and retreat.

Smash and return.

I'm tempted to call time, but I know I have to fight on. If I give up, Si will make it ten times worse. He's big on lessons that will make me stronger.

Life doesn't just stop because you want it to. If this was a real fight, do you think your enemies would let you take a break?

Si shifts his fighting stick to the other side, his loose cotton trousers swishing as he moves gracefully into a different fighting stance and attacks again—this time slamming his stick toward my midsection.

I block, then attack, kicking one leg high toward his face.

He evades and steps back. "You're not concentrating, Mei. You're going to get yourself killed," he says, frowning.

His voice is rough—some long-ago fight messed with his vocal chords.

Probably defending me, for all I know.

But with his smooth olive skin and thick dark hair he could pass for any age between twenty-five and forty.

It's his chameleon genes, I guess. He could be two hundred, for all I know.

A shiver runs along the spell web clinging to my skin, alerting me to another presence nearby; Jeff has stepped into the training ring alongside Si. The older man might have slowed down with age, but he's a dangerous opponent, and uses whatever tricks he can.

Like surprise, for example.

Luckily I have a secret weapon—my link to the spell web makes it impossible for anyone to sneak up on me at close quarters.

I turn, pushing out a back kick, attempting to put Jeff off and give myself a few seconds to prepare for fighting the two of them at once.

Jeff avoids my kick and I feel the movement behind me as Si attacks again.

Sidestepping, I manage to avoid a stick to the head.

I strike out at Si with my stick, landing it against his side, even as I avoid another attack from him.

I twist in midair, landing with a thump, and roll into a low fighting position.

Jeff can't quite keep up with my movements, and I turn fast behind Si to land a kick on Jeff's stomach.

He grunts and moves backward.

I take no satisfaction from scoring a point over Jeff. It's like hurting an old faithful dog—a Rottweiler with big teeth, and a nasty streak—but an old dog nonetheless.

Even worse, today he's wearing a lurid Hawaiian shirt instead of his usual dark shirt and tie. He's even got a bit of salt-and-pepper stubble on his face.

He looks like a damn tourist instead of a wily SIG agent.

"You're scared of the new agent," says Jeff, his breath puffing as he tries to recover from my kick. "Maybe he'll be a stickler for the rules. Won't let you go off on your own like I do."

He smirks at me, his bright blue eyes perceptive.

That's how Jeff wins his fights these days—through mind-fucking his opponent. He's not fast or particularly fit anymore, he's just tough and smart.

And it works.

Despite the fact I *know* it's an attempt to make my emotions take over and put me off, I feel anger and resentment rising up.

Who the hell does he think he is?

He doesn't know what I'm feeling.

I take a deep breath and let it out, trying to release my animosity. I narrowly sidestep a punch from Jeff, only to have Si land a solid hit to my leg.

My resistance crumbles along with my leg.

I stagger to one side, barely escaping another slam from Si's stick.

Who am I kidding?

I don't want Jeff to go.

He's the one who figured out how to keep me safe. He's

been around a long time; he watched me grow up, which is more than my own father did. And maybe he's a little on target. What if the new guy *is* a total jerk? I try to imagine the replacement SIG agent. All I can picture is some starched-up dude in a suit.

And just like that, Jeff lands a punch to my side and I spin backward. I only just manage to stay on my feet.

"I heard he goes by the rules," Jeff taunts. "Talked to an old friend at the cadet academy. He's fresh out of training and won't want to ruin his chances of promotion."

The words make my hands clench tighter around my fighting stick. Another ripple goes through the spell web and I finally use it in my defense. I reach out along the glowing grid and push a pulse of energy toward Si. He blinks and shakes his head, stepping back out of my range. I can't do the same to Jeff, because he's human, but I hit out at him with my stick—I'm too distracted to even get close.

Desperately, I try to find my focus. I know I won't get any points for taking on the two of them at once. Si barely counts Jeff as an opponent these days. The spell web ripples in warning, and Si's weapon slams into my side, knocking the breath out of my lungs with his precise positioning. Where Jeff is all brute strength and trickery, Si is precision and accuracy. I stumble backward.

Jeff takes the opportunity offered and kicks my legs out from under me. I land on my back; stars fill my vision, and for a millisecond, I wonder what I'm supposed to do. They've got me on the ground, two against one. Si and Jeff loom over me, both waiting for my next move. They're not stupid enough to think I'll stay down.

There's really no question what I'll do next.
Magic.

I seldom use it. Si says it's a crutch and has banned it in the ring. But desperate times...

And Jeff started it.

Water from the nearby fishpond slams into the two men towering over me before either of them knows what's happening. It knocks them both down, pushing them away so I can scramble to my feet. Seconds later, I use my stick to strike three precise hits to both Si and Jeff.

This time Si knows it's coming and has already pulled his protective chameleon scales over his skin, and probably doesn't feel it. Jeff rolls away with a grin, and I can see he's enjoying my response.

I strike again with my stick, directly at his smug expression.

But Jeff's been doing this too long to be caught by a cheeky sideswipe to the head and he ducks back out of range.

"I'm thinking I might not come back, like I planned. I might take a long cruise. Maybe meet someone," he says.

Even though I know it's a lie designed to knock me off balance, I still let his words affect me. I stumble and glance toward Jeff. He knows I'm strung out by his impending retirement, and he's using it against me.

Jeff just raises his eyebrows at me. "You better keep an eye on both opponents, Mei. You never know when the other will strike."

Again, a ripple along the spell web alerts me seconds before Si slams his stick into my left thigh. I crumble to the ground, but manage to turn it into a roll at the last minute, and come back to my feet, a little bit away from Si. I turn toward him, ready to take him down once and for all.

Behind me, Jeff speaks again. "I came out to let you

know your father's coming tomorrow. He's going to do the debrief himself."

I drop my guard in surprise. My *father*? I haven't seen him since I was four years old. An emotion I can't name grabs hold of my heart. I turn to Jeff again. "What?"

An arm snakes around my neck from behind and pulls me into a lock position, slamming me into the ground and holding my face to the floor. I struggle, but can't break the hold. My concentration is shot; I can't access my magic. Even the spell web feels like it's smothering me. It tingles along my skin, making my magic short circuit.

I'm done.

"Enough," I mutter. "You win." They're cheating, not letting me fight Si properly. They've been doing more and more dirty fighting in the last year. I don't know why I'm surprised every time it happens.

"You can't give up like that," Si says. His voice is inches from my ear. He speaks softly, with only the barest trace of an accent. "You'll die."

"It's not a fair fight. Jeff knows all the buttons to press. I won't be fighting someone who knows that much about me."

"You don't know that. You have to train for all eventualities. It's the only way to survive," Si replies, before letting me go.

"Is he really coming?" I uncurl from my prone position on the ground, but remain seated, my legs crossed.

Jeff hesitates, then nods. "He is. Said he wants to meet this new agent personally."

"He didn't do that when *you* started." I don't remember much about it, but I'm certain my father didn't come out twelve years ago when Jeff first came on the job.

"Maybe he didn't think you'd make it to twenty at that

point," Si says. "There's less than two months to go now. There's more at stake."

I try not to let the words hurt. Si isn't trying to sting me, not like Jeff would have in the ring. He's just stating a fact. What I am means more to my father than who I am. He's not coming to visit with his daughter; he's coming to protect an asset. This new agent probably means more to him than I do.

I'm not even entirely sure why my father feels so strongly about protecting me. I know I have enemies, people who believe I'm dangerous. They've been trying to kill me since I was born. My father thinks I'm important too —not because I'm his daughter, but because of something inside me, something they think I can do.

The irony is, they're all wrong. I don't have anything different or special inside me. At least, no more than every other supernatural out there.

Si extends his hand out to me, and I take it, letting him pull me to my feet. I sigh. "I'm going for a swim."

"Don't be too long. He'll be here soon," Jeff says. There's nothing but concern in his voice now.

I nod, but don't look back as I head along the path between the trees that goes to the river. It might have been part of my training, but Jeff's words are like a thorn under my skin. I need time to lick my wounds and regain my equilibrium.

My steps get faster the closer I am to the water. Soon I'm all but sprinting toward the roar of the waterfall. I emerge out of the forest next to the pool where the river has widened beneath the surging waterfall; the spray hits my body and I let out the breath I didn't know I was holding. As I gaze up at thirty feet of water gushing over the rocks, I can literally feel the power leaking into the air around me. This place has been my savior more times than I can count. It's not just because I have water magic; it's that it soothes me, it envelops me. It shaves off the hard edges of my life and gives me peace again.

I strip down to my bra and panties and start the climb to the top. My body falls into a familiar rhythm, and I let the energy soak into my body, consciously allowing my fears and worries to slip away.

By the time I reach the top, I've almost recovered; I'm clear headed and ready to face anything. I hold my arms out to the side, take a deep breath, close my eyes, and dive over the edge into the water.

End of Excerpt...

If you'd like to read more about Mei, head to your favorite retailer to purchase Hidden Dragon.

Hi, my name's Trudi Jaye and I've got a secret.

A secret society, that is.

Especially designed for people like you who love reading my books, the Trudi Jaye Secret Society is a place filled with magic and laughter, and most of all… free stories.

Everyone who joins the society is given access to an ancient tome full of the stories, novellas, bonus epilogues, and deleted scenes from all the different Trudi Jaye series.

Called **The Shadow Archives,** you can access it by clicking the link below, and joining the secret society…

Join Trudi Jaye's Secret Society… if you dare!

www.trudijayewrites.com/shadow-archives

Other Books by Trudi Jaye

Dragon Rising Series
Lost Dragon (Prequel Novella available via the Trudi Jaye Secret Society)
Hidden Dragon
Searching Dragon
Fighting Dragon
Cursed Dragon
Warrior Dragon (coming soon)

Demon Hunter in Hiding Series
Dreams & Demons (Prequel Novella available via the Trudi Jaye Secret Society)
Secrets & Demons
Agents & Demons
Magic & Demons
Dragons & Demons
Spells & Demons

Elemental Witch Series (With Tania Hutley)
The Trouble with Magic
The Problem with Witches
The Danger with Demons

Firecaller Series
Salt (Prequel Novella available via the Trudi Jaye Secret Society)
Subtle Knife (Prequel Novella available via the Trudi Jaye Secret Society)
Fire Mage
Royal Mage (coming soon)

Dark Carnival Series
The First Wish (Prequel Novella available via the Trudi Jaye
Secret Society)
If Magic Were Wishes
The Gift
Magic for Lost Souls (available via the Trudi Jaye Secret
Society)
High Flyer
Hidden Magic
The Shadow Prophecy

Hi! I'm Trudi Jaye and I'm the author of this book.

I live in New Zealand on a beautiful rural property surrounded by horses and cows (not mine!) with my lovely husband and my cheeky tween daughter.

I've been writing since I was a kid, and for many years I worked as a magazine writer and editor, on topics ranging from hardware and electronics to holidays, recipes and university-level research projects.

Now I write novels full time.

I enjoy yoga, although I'm not very bendy, and karate, although I don't like the idea of hitting anyone.

Visit me on my website: www.trudijayewrites.com